OMEGA 1 - THE CREATION

A Jack Davidson and Shay Lynn Adventure

David J. Story

OMEGA BOOK SERIES

To contact David J. Story:

Omegabookseries@Hotmail.com or visit www.Omegabookseries.com or @OmegaBookSeries

1st Edition 2023

ISBN: 979-8-9880085-1-4

Edited by Gregg Stephenson

Cover Designed by Getcovers

CONTENTS

Sharon Lynn Martin and Me.

Most of all, I would like to mention my late wife, soulmate, and best friend, Sharon "Shay" Lynn Martin (10/24/62 – 7/17/22).

She is the inspiration for the creation of the character Shay Lynn. I will love you forever. Her memory will live on forever through the spirit of Shay Lynn, and this book series is in memory of her.

This book series is also dedicated to the thousands of missing children and adults who are forced into the Human Trafficking system each and every year. Forced to live in slavery every day in the world of Human Trafficking. Most never to be seen again buy their loved ones.

PREFACE

The story you are about to read is Fiction. Many of the situations depicted in this book are true. However, the names, some details, and locations have been changed to protect the identity of the victims.

Have you ever been disappointed by the actions, or lack of, of the legal system? For instance, how about when someone is set free of a horrific crime because of a minor technicality? Did you say to yourself, "That is wrong? Something should have been done?"

What if your son, daughter, brother, or sister was kidnapped and sold into slavery, but the people responsible got away with it due to an error in the paperwork? Suppose some high-dollar lawyer could "game the system" and get their guilty client off.

What if.... ***YOU*** had the means and resources to do something about it?

What if a group of these disappointed and fed-up citizens banded together to do something about it?

This story is about such a group of everyday people just like you. People who have suffered from injustice. People who know someone who was, or is, the victim of a broken legal system. People who are tired of the failures of the legal system.

Now, put yourself in the shoes of the children who have suffered or are still suffering from being used as sex slaves. What if someone had done something about it before ***you*** were forced into slavery?

Join Jack Davidson and Shay Lynn, along with the others of The Omega Group. As they come together and bring justice to those who have beaten the system. Some may call it vigilante Justice, Street Justice, or simply wrong, but it is the only justice many victims will receive.

Enter the dark world of sex trafficking and slavery. Once a person has been forced into this world, they may escape physically, but emotionally, they will forever be prisoners.

Child sex crimes have been an issue for much of recorded history. As a society, we have failed to keep our children safe from sexual predators.

Families have been shattered and destroyed when a family member, a friend, or a total stranger robs them of their children, using them for their own perverted needs. Sometimes they are found and returned to their families. Sadly, however, the vast majority are never to be seen again. They are either so broken they cannot find their way back, or they are simply removed from the world through no fault of their own.

Children, and sometimes adults, are taken for many sick and horrendous reasons. These include the prostitution of others, sexual exploitation, forced labor, slavery, or similar practices, and the removal of their organs.

Law enforcement agencies and the courts have tried and failed to reign in this evil. Sometimes it's up to the streets to hunt down and bring these perverts to justice.

This is a story about a small group of individuals that have had enough. They have found themselves taking up the fight for the innocent when the establishment has failed.

They are not superheroes, nor or they specially trained former military. They are like you and me, people who've had enough and have taken it upon themselves to do something about it. They slowly grow from a band of misfits into a crack team working together to save as many children from the horrors of sex and slave trafficking as they can.

As they work their way through this dark and evil world, they find that the world of sex trafficking is bigger and more sinister than they could have ever imagined.

Maybe you'll find a part of you within one of them. How would you react if you or a loved one were taken and thrown into the dark world of sex trafficking? How far are you willing to go to protect a loved one from being another figure in the growing world of sex trafficking?

Maybe someday soon, you'll be part of the Omega team.

"Vigilante"

vig·i·lan·te

/ˌvijəˈlan(t)ē/

noun

a member of a self-appointed group of citizens who undertake law enforcement in their community without legal authority, typically because the legal agencies are considered inadequate.

The International signal for help.

The signal is performed by holding one hand up with the thumb tucked into the palm, then folding the four other fingers down, symbolically trapping the thumb by the rest of the fingers.

Please call 911 or your local law enforcement authorities if someone performs this hand gesture.

Make sure you note each person's clothing, age, sex, and race, as well as the location, direction of travel, and vehicle if used.

Your actions could save someone's life.

Chapter One

The Macon Trial

The word ***Predator*** refers to any animal that lives by preying on other animals. A Lion in the jungles of Africa stalking its prey to provide food for itself and others in the pride for survival, or a shark, in the Atlantic searching the deep dark sea for food are prime examples.

Predators often use an ambush to capture or kill their prey. They are often opportunistic, hiding in burrows, using camouflage, or setting traps. The predator then uses a combination of senses to detect and assess their prey and chooses the opportune time to strike. Many predators actively attract their prey towards them before ambushing them.

No other species has developed this skill to the degree that some humans have. We even have special words for these human predators, the worst of these... pedophiles.

In a small southern town, about eighty-five miles south of Atlanta, on Interstate 75 is Macon, Georgia. The town is famous for music lore, outdoor adventure, Civil Rights history, and southern cuisine and culture. Macon is a growing middle Georgia town with around 200,000 people living in the city. Located near the state's geographic center, it has earned the nickname, "The Heart of Georgia."

It was just another day for most people in Macon, Georgia, but for a hand full, it will be a day that would change their lives forever. It was a warm and humid day, not much different than any other midsummer day. There was a 75% chance of rain that afternoon, and the wind was starting to pick up. People were going about their business, shopping, preparing for summer vacation, going to the movies. The normal stuff that most mid-size towns go through every day. Around the city's courthouse, things were starting to stir with the trial that shocked this Georgia town to the bone.

Charles Darwood was on trial for the kidnapping and sexual of assault of Crystal Lockman some eight months prior.

Inside the courtroom, the jury was seated, expectantly waiting for that day's trial to start. It was day two of the trial, and the jury had heard the opening statements of both the prosecution and defense attorneys in the case. The low voices of the spectators and jurors were heard throughout the courtroom. Suddenly, the voice of the court bailiff was heard.

"All rise, the court of General Session of the State of Georgia, County of Bibb, is now in session. The Honorable June Mayweather presiding."

As the judge entered the courtroom, all talking stopped, and everyone stood and looked as Judge Mayweather entered. June Mayweather was a tall, slim built woman that looked to be in her mid-forties. She had light brown hair that was tied back in a low ponytail. As she approached the bench, she looked over to the jurors and smiled. She stepped up onto her bench and took a seat in her chair.

Judge Mayweather shuffled some papers around on her desk and, without looking up, said, "Everyone please be seated. The trial of the State of Georgia vs Charles Darwood is now in session."

Judge Mayweather finally looked up from her papers on her desk and said, "Prosecution, you may call your first witness." She turned her head to look over at the District Attorney's table, where Attorney MaryBeth Dommer sat.

Ms. Dommer is in her late fifties with short black and graying hair. She is slightly on the heavy side but was nonetheless very attractive. She had served as a prosecuting attorney right out of law school as well as serving for 15 years as an Assistant District Attorney in the prosecutor's office in Atlanta before moving to Macon. For the past 6 years, she has served as the District Attorney of Bibb County.

Sitting next to Ms. Dommer was her legal aid, Kenneth King. Mr. King was only 2 years out of law school and had become one of Ms. Dommer's most trusted assistants. Mr. King was only 26 years old and stood about five foot six inches tall. He was very self-conscious about his short stature but made up for it with his wit and confidence. He had the gift of being able to read Ms. Dommer's mind and having briefs and information in her hands before she asked for them.

The defense and prosecution had completed their opening statements the day before. It was very uneventful and ended without a hitch.

As Ms. Dommer was rising from her seat, she said. "With the permission of the court, the prosecution calls..."

Suddenly, a loud voice came from the defense table, "Your Honor, may we approach the bench?"

Everyone in the courtroom turned and looked at attorney Douglas Rayford, the defense attorney for Charles Darwood. Judge Mayweather motioned both Ms. Dommer and Mr. Rayford up to her bench. As the two attorneys approached, Judge Mayweather turned off her bench microphone, so the jurors and spectators could not hear the conversation.

"Ok, Mr. Rayford, what have you got?" asked Judge Mayweather.

"Your Honor, I think it would be better if we discuss this in your chambers." replied Mr. Rayford.

Judge Mayweather looked back and forth at the two attorneys and said, "Very well, let's see what you've got, Mr. Rayford."

The two opposing counsels and their teams followed the judge out the door. They proceeded down the short hallway, flanked on both sides with pictures of past judges that had served and worked in service to the community. They entered one by one into the judge's chambers.

The parade of suits behind Judge Mayweather would remind someone of a mother duck leading her ducklings to water.

The jury and spectators started looking at one another and talking among themselves. Many had questions written all over their faces, wondering what was happening behind closed doors.

In front of the window in the Judge's chambers was a neatly kept dark oak desk. Behind the desk was a table with pictures proudly displaying her husband and children. The far side wall was lined with bookshelves holding volumes of legal books, all neatly filed. Directly in front of the bookcases, facing each other, were two modern but simple brown leather couches.

As the last person entered the judge's chambers and closed the door. Judge Mayweather turned and asked, "Mr. Rayford, do we need to sit, or is this going to be brief?"

"No. Your Honor, this shouldn't take long, but MaryBeth might want to grab a seat." Came the reply from Douglas Rayford, with a little smile.

Judge Mayweather cocked her head slightly and looked over at MaryBeth while leaning back on her desk. "Well, Mr. Rayford, let us hear what you've got to say."

"Yes, Douglas, let us hear what you've got. This is an open and shut case. We are not looking at any deals for your client." MaryBeth replied with a smug look on her face.

"Judge Mayweather, we are asking that any evidence taken from the search of the laptop computer be inadmissible. Furthermore, we are also asking that the search of the barn and anything removed from that search be inadmissible too." Douglas, now looking over at Marybeth, sporting a look of victory on his face.

"YOUR HONOR! This is crazy! On what grounds?" cried out MaryBeth, as she turned toward Douglas.

Judge Mayweather dropped her head down and closed her eyes. She reached up with her right hand and, with her fingers, started rubbing her forehead.

"Your Honor..." Marybeth started, but Judge Mayweather raised her left hand and motioned for her to stop talking.

Still leaning on her desk, Judge Mayweather folded her arms in front of her. Looking at Douglas Rayford, she softly asked, "So Douglas, you want the key evidence against your client excluded? On what grounds?"

"Fruit of the poisonous tree." Douglas stated while looking at MaryBeth.

"WHAT IN THE HELL ARE YOU TALKING ABOUT?" MaryBeth yelled as she took a couple of steps toward Douglas.

Mayweather stood erect and took a step toward the two attorneys, thinking they would come to blows.

"What poisonous tree?" exclaimed Mayweather, "This tree better be the tree of death if you expect the evidence to be excluded!"

"The decision in Mapp v. Ohio established that the exclusionary rule applies to evidence gained from an unreasonable search or seizure violating the Fourth Amendment." Douglas stated.

"You are full of crap, Douglas!" MaryBeth said, now with a calmer tone.

"Please explain." The judge said as she proceeded to walk behind her desk to sit down. "I'm all ears, and it better be good."

MaryBeth turned to look at her assistant Kenneth King and mouthed the words, "What the fuck?"

King returned the look at MaryBeth and slowly shook his head in pure shock. He walked over to stand next to her, leaned over, and whispered, "I don't have a clue what he's talking about."

"Well, you're no damn help." MaryBeth replied.

"Your Honor." Douglas started, "It has come to my attention that the search warrant for the barn was not valid."

"WAIT a second!" MaryBeth said, "There was nothing wrong with that search warrant for the barn!"

Judge Mayweather raised her left hand to motion for MaryBeth to stop talking. "Let's all hear what you've got, Douglas." She added.

"Well, your Honor, the search warrant was for a barn located on 492 Lisa Dr., the property of my client Mr. Darwood." Douglas said as he paused for effect.

"Continue, Mr. Rayford." The judge said.

"Yes, please continue, Douglas." Said MaryBeth as she looked over at Kenneth.

Kenneth sat back down in the chair nearest to him and opened his laptop to start looking through files trying to find a copy of the warrant and who served it.

"What is the problem then?" the judge asked.

"Well, it appears that the barn in question belongs to Mr. Kevin Teal, that resides on the property to the rear of my client's property. As stated on the warrant, his address is 6840 Lisa Ct., not 492 Lisa Dr.." Douglas said as he looked up from his notes to look at the judge.

"What are you saying then, Douglas?" The judge asked.

"Fruit of the poisonous tree, Your Honor." He replied. "Anything taken or removed from said barn can't be used as evidence against my client."

"Your Honor, the items found in that barn along with the plaintiff and key witness were found in that barn." Came MaryBeth's reply.

Judge Mayweather placed her hands together as if praying, with the tips of her fingers on her mouth. "I see." She said to Douglas as she looked over at MaryBeth.

Total silence in the judge's chamber seemed to forever. The only sound that could be heard was the grandfather clock in the corner ticking away time.

Finally, Judge Mayweather leaned back in her chair and placed her arms on the armrests of her chair. Looking over at Douglas, she said, "What else do you have? You mentioned something else."

"Yes, Your Honor, the chain of custody of the items taken from the residence of my client's residence with an air of victory.

"What are you saying caused this additional screw-up to Ms. Dommer's case?" said the judge in a most irate tone.

"It appears that the detectives who secured the evidence at my client's residence did not report straight back to the evidence room after leaving with the items taken." Said Douglas.

"How in the hell do you know that, Douglas?" MaryBeth said.

"I've got the same question. How do you know this?" The judge joined in, asking Douglas to explain.

"Well, Your Honor, from the time that the detectives radioed dispatch that they were leaving my client's residences, it was just over 2 hours till they signed the evidence into the logbook." Douglas said, leaning forward with his hands on the judge's desk. "It is only a 30-minute drive from there to the evidence room, forty-five at most. It appears that the detectives took a detour on the way to check in the evidence." He added.

"First off, Mr. Rayford, get your hands off my desk. It is not a prop for you to use. Second, I want the so-called detectives, you, Ms. Dommer, and you, Mr. Rayford, in my chamber within the hour and whoever else is involved in this FUBAR!" said Judge Mayweather as she stood up with a dismayed look on her face. "We need to let these fine members of the jury go for the day. We've, I mean you have wasted enough of their time today, Ms. Dommer."

The four of them exited the judge's chambers and proceeded back into the courtroom. As the judge entered, the bailiff said, "All rise, the court is now in session."

The two legal teams took their places behind their respective tables as the judge sat behind her desk.

"Be seated." The judge said. "New evidence has been presented to me, and I will need to take some time to review this evidence. The court is adjourned until 9 a.m. tomorrow morning." The Judge slammed her gavel down, stood, and walked toward the door.

MaryBeth walked toward the judge as she exited the courtroom. "Your Honor, I need a word with you."

The judge stopped just inside the hallway leading to her chambers and turned to see MaryBeth, who was right behind her, followed by Douglas. As the door closed behind the three of them, Judge Mayweather asked, "What's wrong, Ms. Dommer? You screwed something else up?"

"Uh, well, no." Replied MaryBeth. "Kenneth just contacted one of the detectives involved in the case, and he's off today with a doctor's appointment."

"I don't give a fuck if he's attending his own funeral. I want him in my chambers in one hour. Do I make myself clear? Or do I need to be a little clearer?" Judge Mayweather said, looking sharply at MaryBeth.

"No, Your Honor, I'll let him know." She replied, looking down as the judge turned toward her chambers.

MaryBeth turned, looked at Douglas, and said. "I guess you're happy. You're going to let a pervert walk."

"It wasn't me. I'm just trying to get justice for my client and a fair trial." Douglas responded.

"And what about justice and a fair trial for the 12-year-old little girl that he took and molested?" MaryBeth shot back.

"That's your problem, not mine. Your side screwed this one up." Douglas responded with a smile.

Sitting out in the lobby of the city of Macon's courtroom C was 12-year-old Crystal Lockman. She was nervously waiting with her mother and father, Sue and Bill Lockman.

Crystal was seated between her mother and father. She was wearing her favorite white dress that came down to halfway between her knees and ankles. She was staring off into space, thinking about what was to come, when she must answer questions about that day when she was taken and molested by that monster. That monster that she has not seen in over 8 months will be sitting there looking at her.

This was something she had feared for weeks. There were many sleepless nights since that mid-summer afternoon, walking home from the neighborhood swimming pool. After all, it was just five houses down from where she lived, and felt safe walking that short distance alone.

But on this sunny Tuesday mid-afternoon, her life would change forever. Both her parents were at work, and they had given her permission to walk to the pool alone. It had been about 2 weeks after school had let out for the summer, and she had met some of her friends at the pool.

After several hours of swimming and talking with her friends, she said goodbye to them. Crystal started the short walk home from the pool. She noticed a blue van parked on the side of the road with its engine hood up. A man was outside of the van as if he were finishing working on something under the hood. She didn't think much about it because she had seen the van several times driving in the neighborhood.

As she approached, she saw the man close the hood of the van and start putting something into the open side door of the van. As she got closer, she smiled at the man as he turned toward her. The man said something, but she could not quite understand what he was saying. She slowed up her pace as she approached him.

"I'm sorry, sir, I couldn't understand what you were saying."

"I said, it's a beautiful day out today." He replied.

Crystal smiled and said, "Yes, it is. Don't you live around here?"

The man nodded and pointed back over Crystal's head. "Yes, back in that direction."

As Crystal turned her head in the direction the man was pointing, an arm grabbed her around the midsection, and a hand went over her mouth. She tried to scream, but with the much stronger man picking her up off her feet, squeezing the air out of her smaller body, and with his large hand placed over her mouth, there was nothing she could do. She tried several times to scream, but she was unsuccessful. She heard him close the door of the van. Now what seemed like a harmless friendly man just seconds ago turned into a nightmare. She was looking into the eyes of a totally different-looking face. The man's eyes were wide open, and he had a blank expression now on his face.

Terror started to overcome her small frail body. And then everything went dark.

Out in the courtroom's hallway, Crystal was suddenly startled as she heard a noise over to her left. The doors of courtroom C opened suddenly, breaking her out of her trance and nightmare. Something she had relived over and over in her mind daily.

Her father, Bill, stood as a man approached dressed in a dark blue suit with a white shirt and red tie. Crystal was still trying to come out of her brain fog when she finally recognized the man approaching them. It was Mr. King, her attorney's legal assistant.

Bill Lockman saw a concerned look on Kenneth King's face as he approached and knew something was wrong.

Bill turned and looked at Sue and spoke. "Sue, take Crystal down the hall and get her a snack please."

Sue, looking up at Bill and then over at Kenneth, knew something was wrong. She touched Crystal's arm and said, "Come with me, darling. Let's get ourselves a snack. I could use one." The two of them stood up and proceeded down the hall toward some vending machines.

Bill looked back at Kenneth and asked. "What is wrong? I can tell on your face that something is wrong!"

Kenneth looked side to side, not making eye contact with Bill, and spoke softly in order that others around them couldn't overhear him.

"There seems to be a slight problem." Kenneth said.

"What do you mean a slight problem? You told us this was going to be an open and shut case." Bill spoke angrily and loud enough to attract the attention of several people standing near them in the hallway. Kenneth gestured with his right hand for Bill to keep his voice down. This, however, only added to the anger that Bill felt.

"DON'T TELL ME TO KEEP MY VOICE DOWN!" Bill shouted.

Now Sue and Crystal could hear Bill, and both knew something was up. Others in the hallway stopped their conversations and turned their attention toward the two of them.

Kenneth touched Bill's arm and said, "Follow me. MaryBeth is waiting in a conference room to discuss what is going on."

Kenneth proceeded down the hallway, and Bill turned to follow. As Bill turned, he saw Sue and Crystal approaching, both with concerned looks on their faces. Before they could speak, Bill motioned for them to wait in the hallway.

The two entered the conference room through the hallway door. Inside, and standing to one side of the room, was MaryBeth. She was making some last-second adjustments to her shirt and hair. In the middle of the room was a large table with eight chairs pushed neatly up to the table. On the far end of the table was a stack of file folders, a notepad, and a pen.

MaryBeth turned and, while motioning toward the table, said, "Mr. Lockman, please come in and take a seat."

Bill looked at her with an angry look on his face and said, "No, thank you, I'll stand." As he walked to the end of the table.

They stood there looking at each other without saying a word, which seemed like forever. Finally, MaryBeth broke the tension in the room.

"Mr. Lockman..." She started.

Bill cut her off before she finished, "Just cut to the chase. What the hell is going on?"

MaryBeth paused a second and then continued, "There is an issue with the search and evidence recovered by the detectives in the case."

Bill, who was now showing more concern on his face, "What kind of issue are we talking about?"

"Well," MaryBeth began, "The warrant issued for the barn where Crystal was kept was issued for the wrong address."

"It was a typo." Bill replied.

"It's more than that. The barn wasn't even located on Darwood's property." She added.

"And what does that mean?" Bill asked.

"It means that anything removed from that barn can't be used as evidence in the trial." She replied.

"But what happens to Crystal and the nude pictures and clothes that were taken from the barn?" Bill replied now with more anxiety in his voice.

›rry, Bill, but none of it can be used. Sorry." She said as she looked down at her papers on the desk.

"And Crystal's testimony?" Bill asked.

"Inadmissible." She said.

"Fruit of the poisonous tree." Added Kenneth.

Bill gave Kenneth a sharp look as if to say, shut the fuck up. "What about the things taken from the house? Is there a problem with that too?" He exclaimed loudly to MaryBeth.

"Sorry to say yes." MaryBeth said sheepishly, looking up from her papers. "The detectives involved in the search may have taken a detour while the items were in their custody."

"So?" Bill said.

"Chain of custody. The detectives didn't report directly to the station to check the items into the evidence room after they left Darwood's place." MaryBeth replied.

MaryBeth said, "The judge has ordered the two detectives involved in the case to report to her chambers immediately. She's going to try and get this all sorted out and see if we can salvage any of this material for trial."

Bill looked more concerned, and tears started to form in his eyes, "And what if you can't use any of the material?"

"Let's try not to think about it right now. We're going to do our best to keep everything listed as evidence in the trial." She replied, looking down at her file.

"The judge is going to hear both sides and find out what, if anything is inadmissible in court. She'll more than likely take what she hears and sleep on it and let us know in the morning."

"That's it? We wait?" Bill asked.

"Yes. Sorry, I wish I could say more." She said, "But that's all we can do right now. Kenneth and I will be in the judge's chamber fighting to keep all the evidence in." MaryBeth tried to reassure him.

Kenneth took two steps toward Bill and said, "Mr. Lockman, take your family home and try and get some rest. I know it's going to be hard and next to impossible, but please try."

MaryBeth added, "That's all you can do right now, try and get some rest and be back here by 9 a.m. tomorrow, and we'll see where this goes."

Bill nodded, then turned and walked out the door. MaryBeth looked at Kenneth and shook her head. "This is one screwed-up mess, I don't see how it's going to end well."

The next morning just before 9 a.m., courtroom C of the Macon, Georgia, courthouse was packed. Word had gotten out about the trial, and rumors of a possible mistrial were flowing through the city.

Reporters were standing against the wall in the back of the courtroom, and local news trucks lined the streets surrounding the courthouse. There was electricity in the air as concerned friends and townspeople packed the courtroom. As the jury entered the room, all eyes turned towards them, and the conversations of those in attendance started to slow and soon stopped. Sitting behind MaryBeth and Kenneth in the very front roll was Bill Lockman, and noticeably Sue and Crystal were not with him.

The voice of the court bailiff was heard. "All rise, the court of General Session of the State of Georgia, County of Bibb, is now in session. The Honorable June Mayweather presiding."

Judge Mayweather walked straight to her bench and took a seat without looking up at the jury or spectators. You could hear cameras clicking from the back of the room as reporters took pictures in hopes of catching something or someone that would give them front-page news headlines.

Judge Mayweather opened a folder on her desk and took some time to review it. She looked up and noticed that everyone was still standing. She looked at both MaryBeth and Douglas with a blank and tired look on her face. "Everyone, please be seated."

The judge, while looking at MaryBeth, started speaking, "In my years as a judge, I've witnessed many screw-ups and mistakes by both the defense and prosecution. Some were overcome and didn't affect the outcome of the trial, and others did. And there were those, like this one, which were open and shut cases."

The judge paused for a second and then continued, "Ms. Dommer and Mr. Rayford, would you both stand up."

MaryBeth looked over at Kenneth and whispered to him, "This doesn't look good for us."

"Please, both of you approach the bench." The judge said. Both MaryBeth and Douglas slowly walked up to the bench.

"Ms. Dommer, outside of the items that we talked about yesterday in my chambers, do you have any other evidence that you'll be using in the case against Mr. Darwood?" The judge asked sharply, and MaryBeth knew that her case was toast.

"No, your Honor, outside of the items discussed yesterday, all we have is circumstantial evidence." She replied regretfully.

"Mr. Rayford, do you have anything that you would like to add while the three of us are here?"

"No, Your Honor."

"Very well, return to your seats." The Judge said, motioning with her right hand as if swatting a fly away.

The judge then turned her attention to Charles Darwood. "Mr. Darwood, would you please stand?"

Darwood and Douglas slowly stood and faced the judge.

"Mr. Darwood, there is a lot I would like to say to you right now, but being a judge and being respectful to the court, I'll keep it to myself." She paused, looked down at her papers, and looked back up at both of them.

"There have been some problems with the handling of this case, and it saddens me that I'm going to have to side with the defense in my ruling." again, she paused.

Voices were beginning to be heard in the courtroom, and the sounds from the back of the room of cameras clicking sounded like automatic gunfire.

"QUIET! ORDER IN THE COURT!" the judge rapidly banged her gavel on her desk.

The courtroom slowly started to quiet down as the order returned.

"It saddens me at this time to declare a mistrial with prejudice, Mr. Darwood. You are free to go."

The courtroom erupted in screams and outbursts of, "NO! Fry, the Son of a Bitch!" while others screamed, "Guilty!"

The judge dismissed the jury and court. As she stands and heads to her chambers. You couldn't hear the bailiff shouting, "All rise." as the judge stood and exited the courtroom. The screams of the courtroom continued for several minutes.

MaryBeth turned to Bill Lockman and said, "I'm sorry."

Bill asked, "What next?"

"Nothing, it's over, the state and my office failed, and the city failed Crystal and your family." MaryBeth replied, now with tears rolling down her face.

Bill then looked over at Charles Darwood to see him smiling and throwing his hands up in the air in a sign of victory. Darwood was then surrounded by several law enforcement officers and ushered out a side door to safety.

Outside, as Bill, MaryBeth, and Kenneth exited the courthouse, they were swarmed with reporters trying to get a statement from them.

But no statement was given. All three jumped into a car and drove off while reporters snapped pictures of them leaving.

Back in the judge's chamber, Judge Mayweather, noticeably upset over the result of the trial, removed her robe and hung it on a hook next to her door. She slowly walked over to her desk, sat down in her chair, and turned to look out her window. She saw what looked like a hundred people outside the courthouse screaming, "No justice for Crystal. No justice for Crystal."

She knew her hands were tied, and she also knew that Charles Darwood was guilty as hell. But she had to follow the law, and the law had failed this little girl, who had to live with this nightmare for the rest of her life. Knowing that the monster who took her that day also took her innocence. Mayweather was now sitting behind her desk, crying with her hands over her face. She will forever know that he will be out there, looking for other little girls, to take and do horrible things to them.

She took a deep breath, dried her eyes with a Kleenex, and tried to compose herself. After gaining her composure, she took a deep breath, leaned forward, and picked up the phone. She dialed a number that she wished she never had to dial. When a voice on the other end answered, the judge said. "Vic, I've got something for you to look at."

Chapter Two

PAPA DOWN

The hunter was lying in the tall grass on the edge of the woods, looking up as clouds started moving in from the west, with a slight breeze blowing directly on his face. This was making an early frosty winter evening a little more unbearable. In the distance, he heard an old owl calling out and the sounds of crickets that seemed to be in the hundreds all around. His hunting partner was lying close by.

It is deer season, and they were out there stalking their prey. He caught a slight movement over to his right, about two hundred yards away. Out of the corner of his eye, he spotted two deer grazing at the edge of some bushes. After a few minutes, the two deer, one buck about 8 points and a smaller doe, moved slowly towards the left. Still grazing, the two deer moved further into view directly in front of them. So far, they had not noticed them or picked up their scent.

The two deer were standing next to one another, and he could see them clearly now in his scope. He watched them slowly moving, still to their left, the buck looking up every now and then. Perhaps he was looking for threats, or maybe he had picked up their scent and was trying to find them.

The hunter's heart started beating faster. He knew time was running out as they began to lose daylight. The sun dipped behind the trees in the back of them, throwing a dark shadow over them and about seventy-five feet ahead. Another 15 minutes or so, the target would be in the dark and harder to see. The light was getting darker and then brighter as the clouds moved across the sky, temporarily blocking the setting sun.

He took a deep breath, breathing in slowly for 4 seconds, holding it for 4 seconds, slowly letting it out for 4 seconds, and then holding his exhale for 4 seconds. He repeated this three or four more times until he could feel his heart slow down and his breathing leveling off.

He heard a whisper just above the sounds of the crickets around them.

Shay Lynn, his partner in crime, was lying next to him about five feet away. As he slowly turned his head to the right, he could see that she was lying there looking through a pair of binoculars.

He whispered back to her, “What did you say?”

She replied, “I said, how much longer are we going to lie here?”

Looking at her with a slight grin on his face, “Why, you’ve got somewhere better to be?”

“NO.” Came the reply from Shay. “I’m just getting eaten up by these damn bugs!”

“I told you to put some spray on before we got out of the car.” He replied with a slight smile on his face, not wanting her to see.

“Well, I forgot.” Came a sharp but irritated whisper. “Besides, I’ve got to go pee.”

“You should have done that before we left.” He said. Without looking, he could feel the daggers coming from her eyes that he knew she was throwing at him.

“I want to wait another couple of minutes.” He whispered.

“It’s going to be too dark in a couple more minutes.” She replied.

“Let’s get on with this and get out of here.” She whispered now in a calmer voice.

“Give me the range again.” He asked.

“It’s the same as it was last time, 245 yards.” She replied, “He hasn’t moved.”

“The wind is still the same, from right to left, about 5 miles per hour.” Shay added.

Taking a check on the wind again, he wanted to make sure it had not changed. He lowered his head, looked through his scope, and slightly adjusted. “Got it.”

Shay replied in a more monotone voice, “Send it.”

Within a second after she said that, he slowly squeezed the trigger on his H&K MR762A1. With a jerk that buried the stock into his shoulder, the .308 round left the suppressed barrel with a muffled but audible report.

Within what seemed like forever, he heard the voice of Shay, still in a whisper but more excited, “HIT! PaPa down.”

PaPa is the military phonetic alphabet code word to represent the letter ‘P’ of the alphabet. Shay liked referring to the sexual perverts and pedophiles as PaPa’s when referring to or talking about them.

He was still looking through his Leupold 3-9 VX-R Patrol Scope and saw a spray of blood on the wall behind the target. Slowly looking down, he saw the motionless and crumbled body of Charles Darwood, lying on the ground with blood flowing out of the center of his chest and pooling in a dark crimson puddle next to his body.

They had been stalking and watching the movements of Charles Darwood for the past couple of weeks. They were looking for the best time to remove this scumbag from this world, so he could never harm another child again.

Charles Darwood was a known sex offender and pedophile. He had gotten off several months ago during a trial on a minor technicality. The prosecution had failed to protect vital evidence that linked Charles to the kidnapping and sexual assault of a 12-year-old girl named Crystal Lockman.

Charles had previously served two three-year sentences in the local jail. He was released early on both occasions due to good behavior. He had also been accused of several other sexual assaults, but there was never enough evidence to convict him.

"JACK! Let's get the hell out of here!" Shay said in a more hurried and concerned voice.

He started breaking his H&K down and slid it into its bag. He looked over to Shay, where she was stuffing her binoculars into her bag and grabbing the blanket they were lying on.

"Did you get everything?" he asked.

"Yes." She replied.

"How about my spent brass?" he asked, as he was looking around for it, making sure they didn't leave anything behind.

"Yes, I got it. Let's go." Shay said as she headed into the woods, back toward their car, parked on a dirt road about one hundred yards away.

He grabbed his bag containing the H&K, another small bag they had used to carry water, and some small miscellaneous items they might have needed on their trip.

After about 5 minutes of slowly creeping through the woods, they reached the car. They looked at each other as they stuffed all the gear into the trunk. Jack looked around to ensure he didn't see anyone else in the area.

"Dinner?" he asked as he turned his attention back to the car.

"What?" came her reply. "My ears are still ringing a little from the shot. All I can hear is my heart beating."

"I said dinner. Where do you want to go for dinner?"

"Oh, sorry, I saw a small diner down the road towards town. We passed it on the way here." She replied. "And you're buying too."

"Why am I buying?" he asked.

"For making me stay out there longer than we needed and getting eaten alive by those giant bugs." She replied sharply.

"Good job, guys." Came a raspy voice over each of their earpieces, "Now head back, Keven..."

They both reached up and turned their earpieces off in mid-transmissions.

"I told you. You should have put on some spray."

"Dammit, I said I forgot!" she snapped as she got into the car.

"Well, you should have asked." He looked over at her as he was starting the car.

"Asked what?" she replied.

"Asked to borrow my bug spray. I had some in my bag." He turned slightly to look into the rear-view mirror, smiling at her.

Giving him a look that would send shivers up the spine of most men, all she said was, "Asshole. Let's go, I'm starving!"

The ride to the diner was quiet. The sun had set entirely, and it was now dark. Just before pulling into the parking lot, Shay looked over at him and said." Jack, I know this isn't your first."

She was looking for the right words, "Your first kill, I mean."

"No, this was my third. The second one was in Florida, just before we met." He said calmly.

"How does it feel, taking another person's life?" she asked.

Pulling into the parking lot and putting the car into park, he turned to her and said, "How does it feel?"

"Yes." She replied.

"A lot of recoil. That .308 has a nice kick to it."

He looked at her, and she rolled her eyes, saying, "You know what I was asking, and that is a corny saying."

"Well, I think it was funny, and I've been waiting a lifetime to say it."

"Honestly, I don't feel much at all." Came his reply.

"Why not?" she asked with a puzzled look.

"I think they all deserve it for what they did." He said in a low tone, looking away.

"You're probably right." She said, "But taking another person's life has got to bother you somehow."

"Nope, not really. I don't consider those that I've shot as being human." He said in a matter-of-fact tone.

"Well, I don't know if I could pull the trigger and kill someone, as you did, and not let it bother me."

Jack turned toward her and softly took her hand, "What about the guy who raped you?"

He could see tears pooling up in her eyes and her lips quivering, "I don't know, that was several years ago."

"But it still haunts you, doesn't it?"

She turned her head away and said, "Yes. I've had nightmares ever since." After a slight pause, she continued. "I don't know if I will ever get over it."

"I understand." He replied.

She turned her head quickly and looked at him, "How could you ever understand? You're a guy! Have you ever been raped?" she exclaimed in a not-so-calm voice.

Jack sat there looking at her without saying a word for what seemed like forever. She had a drop-dead expression on her face as if he could never know.

He turned and looked out the front windshield. "Yes, I have." He replied softly.

"What?" she replied. "What have you?"

"When I was 10, my stepdad would take me into my bedroom whenever my mother was not at home and force me to have sex with him."

"You never told me that." She looked at him with a surprised look on her face.

"Well, it's never come up." He said as he looked away again. "I found out later that he had repeatedly raped my older sister too. He continued raping me until I turned thirteen."

"Well, whatever made him stop?"

"My mother found out and kicked his perverted ass out."

"Whatever happened to your sister?" Shay asked with a surprised but concerned look on her face now.

"She went into therapy until she was 19." As he lowered his head.

"How is she doing now?" Shay asked.

"She....... She." Now tears were flowing from Jack's eyes. "She killed herself."

"MY GOD!" Shay replied. Now she had more tears running down her face than before.

"It all but destroyed my mother. She was never the same after that."

"What about you?" she asked. "Did you have any therapy?"

"Yes and No." He said calmly.

"What do you mean, yes and no?"

"I went to therapy." He said, looking out the driver's side window. "It didn't seem to help. So, after a few sessions, I stopped going."

"What about your stepdad? Did he ever go to jail?" she asked.

"No, he didn't."

Turning her head away, "What happened?" she asked.

He looked at her and said, "When I was 20, I tracked him down to a small town in North Carolina."

"And then what? Did you confront him?" she asked.

"Sort of." He replied.

"What do you mean, sort of?"

"He was my first kill." Jack said, looking down at the floorboard of the car.

"How did you find him?" Shay asked.

"G-Man tracked him down for me."

"You're talking about Tony. Right?" she asked.

"Yes, Uncle Tony. He found out what had happened to us soon after my mother kicked my stepdad out."

"Did Tony help you kill him?" Shay asked, now getting extremely interested in the story.

"No, he didn't. And he didn't know that when I found him, I was going to kill him for what he did to me and my sister."

"When did he find out?" she asked.

"Shortly after, it happened. He knew something was up after he had heard that my stepdad was gunned down on the street."

"Did he ask you about it?" Shay asked as they sat in the car, still outside the diner.

"When I showed up at his house a day after it happened, he knew I had something to do with it."

"Wow! And he didn't turn you in? I mean, he does work for the FBI, you know."

Jack looked at her, "No, he took me in and helped me. He said that he would take care of things and not worry."

"Why didn't he have your stepdad arrested after he found out?"

"Well, as you can see from Darwood, the law and court system don't always work out for the victim." He turned back and looked out the window. "Sometimes you have to cut out the middleman and take the law into your own hands."

"Street justice or vigilante justice, some call it." Shay said.

"Call it what you want. Sometimes it needs to be done. If the justice system doesn't do it, it leaves it up to others." Jack said as he leaned back in the seat.

"Are you still hungry?" he asked Shay.

"I could eat. Besides, we have a long drive ahead of us. I want to put as many miles between us and this town as possible."

As they both got out of the car, she came around the front of the car and froze. Off in the distance, they heard the sounds of sirens as several police cars came rushing in their direction.

"What are we going to do?" she asked.

"Nothing, just act natural." Jack replied.

As the sound of the police cars approached, Shay was visibly shaken. She took Jack's hand, and they slowly walked into the diner.

Just then, three police cars went screaming by, with their blue lights flashing and sirens screaming for people to get out of their way.

Shay squeezed Jack's hand out of relief when she realized they were not coming to arrest them for murder, at least for now.

They took a booth near the back of the diner and tried to look as normal as possible. There were about fifteen or so people already sitting in the diner. It was a good thing that the police cars went screaming past as both Jack and Shay entered the diner. It took the attention away from them as they entered. No one seemed to notice the couple enter and slowly walked to the back of the diner, passing a couple of empty tables as they went.

"Can I help you or get you a menu?" asked an older woman who worked there.

This startled Shay, who looked up at her and said, "I just want a cheeseburger, fries, and ice tea to drink, please."

"And for you, sir?" the waitress asked Jack.

"I'll have the same." He replied.

Before Jack had finished giving his order, Shay was up and headed to the restroom.

Shortly after sunset, a call to 911 came into the Macon dispatch center. The caller reported that a body had been discovered outside a local resident's home. The caller didn't want to identify himself, so the 911 operator took down the information and immediately dispatched the Macon County sheriff to the address that the caller gave.

Within 10 mins of receiving the dispatch, three Macon County Sheriffs' cars pulled up to Charles Darwoods home. Getting out of their vehicles, they started a slow and cautious approach toward the front of the house. Upon reaching the front door, they knocked and identified themselves.

After three attempts at knocking and receiving no response from inside the house, two officers proceeded around to the back of the house, guns drawn. The lead officer looked around the corner as the two officers reached the back of the house.

He saw what looked to be a body lying on a small deck, unable to identify the body or condition. The two officers slowly approached, calling out, "Macon County Sheriff's office, let me see your hands!"

The body on the deck remained motionless as the two officers slowly climbed up the three steps leading to the deck. The first officer approached the body lying on the deck and checked to see if he had a pulse. Looking up at the other officer, he shook his head, letting the other officer know that he was dead.

He radioed the other officer that was waiting in front of the house and informed him about what they had found and said they were going to make entry into the house. After about 5 minutes, the two officers had completed their search of the house's interior. While they were inside, the officer guarding the front of the house radioed dispatch, requesting detectives and a crime scene unit.

Within 20 minutes, detectives Sergeant Michael Conley and Sergeant Lance Stafford arrived on the scene. They both walked around to the back of the house, where the body was found.

Conley knelt next to the body and looked over the bloodied body for a few seconds. Without looking up, he told Stafford, "It's Darwood for sure. From the looks of it, he was shot with a high-powered rifle."

Conley pointed at the wall to the blood splatter, "Looks like a through and through. I can see where the bullet entered the wall." Conley and Stafford both looked at the blood splatter on the wall.

"Here's where the bullet entered." Conley said while pointing at the small hole in the wall behind where Darwood would have been standing.

Stafford turned and looked out into the now dark woods, panning back and forth as if looking for something.

"It appears that the shot came from up the hill in the woods." Stafford said.

Conley looked around at Stafford, "Could be a stray shot, it is deer season, and there are a lot of people out there shooting." Stafford said.

"If that's the case, we'll never find out who shot Darwood." Conley replied.

"I agree. We'll have the crime scene investigators wrap things up here and call it a night." Stafford said while nodding in agreement. "I'll call it in." he added.

"While you do that, I need to make a call." Conley walked off the deck and around the corner of the house, where he took out his phone and dialed a number.

When the person on the other end picked up, Conley said, "Just found Charles Darwood's body. Someone put a bullet right through the middle of his chest."

"Is he dead?" asked the person on the other end.

"Yes, he was dead before he hit the ground." Conley replied.

"Any witnesses?" asked the person.

"None that we have found. Looks to be just a stray shot from one of the hunters around here." Conley said.

"Very well. Thanks for letting me know."

Conley placed his phone back into his pocket and joined Stafford in front of their car. They both got in and drove off, leaving the crime scene unit to wrap things up.

Judge Mayweather slowly disconnected the phone and placed it next to her on her desk. She picked up the paper she was reviewing before the call as if nothing had happened.

Jack and Shay had finished their meal and were back on the road, putting as much distance between them and Macon as possible.

Shay took over the driving after they finished eating. And after they had been driving north on Interstate 75 for a while. Shay looked over at Jack. Jack was leaning back in the passenger's seat, looking as if he were about to nod off to sleep.

"Jack, how do we know the person we kill deserves it?"

"They are checked out very thoroughly. The group ensures it's a good kill before they send us out." He replied.

"I just want to make sure that the people we." Shay struggles with saying, "We kill, truly deserve it."

"They do, don't worry." Jack said as he tried to get comfortable in his seat.

Things were quiet for the next several miles as Jack drifted off to sleep. He was thinking back to where this all began. His childhood, meeting Hunter and Vicky, Shay, and where they all were now. A lot has changed in his life in the past several years. And he was sure, as he slowly dozed off, that it was only the start.

Chapter Three

THE CREATION

It was the first day of summer break for the local school kids in Anderson, South Carolina. Most 10-year-olds looked forward to when school let out for the summer. A time of fun and games, going fishing, going to movies, swimming and staying up late, and everything else most 10-year-olds loved to do.

You would think that a young boy growing up just outside of Anderson, South Carolina, would be looking forward to summer break. But Jack had a different outlook on summer break than most kids.

Jack's father, Curtis Davidson, would take him camping, hunting, and fishing every chance he got. He always looked forward to those times with his dad.

When Jack was eight years old, his father died from a heart attack one afternoon while at work. Jack was devastated when he lost his father. He missed his trips to the lake and overnight camping and hunting trips that he and his father would go on.

Jack's dad had left him an old S&W model forty-nine revolver and a Marlin 30-30 deer rifle. His mother, Linda, wouldn't let Jack have the guns until he turned ten, and only if Tony was with him.

Many times, Uncle Tony, Linda's brother, would tag along on the trips whenever his schedule permitted. Tony James was a deputy sheriff for the Anderson Sheriff's office. Due to his job as sheriff, Tony never married as he felt it would be unfair to a spouse to live with that kind of stress. He grew close to Jack and treated him much like his own child.

When Curtis couldn't make a trip due to work, Tony and Jack would often find a way to go. Jack saw Tony more as a big brother and loved having him around.

Even after Jack's father died, Tony and Jack continued their fishing, camping, and hunting trips. They would talk about the times when Jack's father was with them, all the fun and games they would play.

As Jack got older, Tony taught Jack how to shoot. When Tony was in the army, he was an Army marksman and was very good with guns. These trips would continue until Jack was in his late teens.

Jack was a natural with a gun. And soon, Jack was out shooting Tony in long-distance shooting. Tony introduced Jack to CMP, Civilian Marksman's Program. He would sometimes take Jack to Talladega, Alabama, to compete in competitions there and others around the local area.

Jack always placed in the top ten at all the competitions he entered. He was a dead shot out to 300- yards and wasn't too shabby out to the 600-yard mark. Tony soon got Jack an H&K .308 rifle from the police department's stolen weapons department, which had been there for years and never claimed.

Linda had met Bobby Edwards shortly after Jack's father Curtis passed away when Jack was almost nine years old. Soon after Linda and Bobby met, Bobby moved in with Linda, Jack, and Jack's older sister Judy, and they married a couple of years later.

Jack and his sister Judy never did like Bobby from the day they met him. It wasn't that they felt that he was trying to take their father's place. It was more in the way he acted and treated them when Linda wasn't around.

Bobby never did like to do the things that Tony and Jack did. He never wanted to go with Tony or Jack on their trips. He preferred to stay home with Linda and Judy.

Tony had an opportunity to apply for a position in the FBI. This was something that Tony had worked towards and dreamed of for years. He was successful and was assigned to the FBI's field office in Columbia, South Carolina.

This was only about a 2-hour drive from Anderson, and Tony would visit Jack, Judy, and Linda as often every month as he could. During the summer, Jack would spend long weekends and every chance he could at Tony's home in Columbia.

They continued their hunting and fishing whenever Tony's schedule would allow. This continued until one day. Tony got word that he was being transferred to the field office in Houston, Texas. Jack was fifteen at the time and didn't take the news very well. The loss of his surrogate big brother, Uncle Tony, caused Jack's anger towards his stepfather to grow in intensity.

From day one, when Bobby moved in, Jack and his sister's life changed. Bobby was a very controlling and angry man who took it out on him and his sister. Bobby was a building contractor and often worked from home. He would use Jack and Judy as his personal servants and demanded they keep the house spotless. They would wait on him hand and foot whenever Linda wasn't around.

When he was ten, Jack didn't know that Bobby was demanding much more from his older sister. Whenever Linda wasn't around, Bobby would molest and demand sex from Judy. He would tell Judy that he would kill her younger brother Jack if she said anything.

Soon after Jack turned eleven, Bobby started the same thing with him. He would also threaten to kill his older sister to keep him quiet.

Neither Jack nor Judy knew that each other was being used as sexual playthings by their stepfather Bobby.

Jack knew when his mother, Linda, left for work. His world would turn upside down. He would start shaking each morning when he heard his mother leave for work.

The words, "I'm leaving, love you all." Those were the words that started his nightmare each day. A nightmare that would go on for years and only get worse.

Did Linda suspect or know what Bobby was doing to Jack and Judy when she wasn't around? That is something no one would ever know.

Jack never let on to Tony what was going on behind closed doors at his house. Tony had noticed that Jack became a little more withdrawn, but he wrote it off as Jack missing his dad and Jack getting older.

Tony also assumed the moods and anger he saw in Judy were just a phase she was going through as a teenage girl. Tony didn't have any children of his own, so he was clueless when it came to how kids acted. Linda never let on like anything unusual was going on with her or the kids, so he thought everything was normal. Or as normal as a household with two teenage children could be.

Jack continued to visit Tony in Houston as often as he could, and they kept up their ritual of hunting and fishing.

At age 16, Jack was almost six foot tall and about 140 pounds. Bobby had backed off on his sexual advances toward Jack as he was getting nearly the same size as him. However, Bobby kept the threat of harm to his sister if Jack said anything about his past sexual assaults on him. Bobby continued to make Jack do most of the work around the house and took most of the credit when Linda came home.

Bobby had sent Jack to pick up some things at the local hardware store. Bobby was planning on spending time with Judy, taking advantage of Linda and Jack being gone for several hours. However, on the way to the hardware store, he discovered that he had forgotten Bobby's list.

As Jack returned home, he heard crying coming from Judy's room. He opened her door and saw Bobby on top of her. She was crying and trying to resist Bobby's advancements. Jack saw red! He grabbed Bobby by his hair and drug him off his sister. He yelled at his sister to run, and she grabbed a sheet and ran out the door.

Jack did the best that he could to fight off Bobby, but he was much stronger than the 16-year-old. Both ended up with bloody faces and bruises on their face and hands.

Bobby warned them both that if they told anyone about what had happened, he would kill Linda. He then stormed out of the house, got in his car, and drove off.

When Linda came home, she saw Judy crying on Jack's shoulder and the dried blood on Jack's face and hands. She demanded to know what had happened, but Jack told her that he and Bobby got into a fight over chores. Linda went into Judy's bedroom and saw that it looked like a tornado had hit the room.

Bobby returned home a couple of hours later, only to find all his belongings thrown out on the front porch. He tried to open the front door, but Linda met him at the door. She had Jack's father's Smith and Wesson .38 revolver in her hand. She told Bobby she wasn't sure what happened, but he was to leave and never return. And if he did, she would kill him. Bobby turned and gathered his belongings and left, never to return.

Linda contacted her brother Tony and told him what had happened. Tony dropped everything and took the first flight to Anderson he could get. On his arrival at Linda's house, she told him what the kids had said happened and what she thought really happened. Tony talked to Jack and Judy in separate rooms, but the two stuck to their stories.

Tony said he would investigate it, but if the kids were not going to say what Linda and him both suspected, then there was little he could do.

Judy and Jack both enter therapy. However, Jack only went to a few sessions. Judy did continue her sessions for another year.

The scars and trauma were too much for Judy to carry, and she took her own life with an overdose of pills.

It was too much for Linda, and she started drinking and taking drugs. She would never be the same again.

Jack was determined to get justice for his sister and for what it did to his mother.

After a couple of years, Jack was able to track Bobby down to a town in North Carolina. Jack got in his car and drove all night to find the person that destroyed his family. He was out for blood.

Jack was driving down one of the streets close to where Bobby was living when he saw him walking down the street. Jack parked his car a few yards away and exited the vehicle. He walked fast to catch up with Bobby. As Jack got closer to within eight feet, he looked around to see if he saw anyone around. It was getting late, and most people were home sitting down for dinner.

Jack said, "Bobby!"

Bobby stopped and slowly turned around to see who had called him. When he turned, he saw Jack standing there with his dad's Smith and Wesson 38, model 45 revolver pointing at his head.

Bobby froze and said, "What are you planning on doing with that gun, BOY?"

Jack just smiled and said, "This is for what you did to my sister, my mother, and me."

Jack fired a fatal shot right into the forehead of Bobby. His body dropped to the ground. Jack just turned and walked back to his car, and drove off.

A couple of days later, Tony heard a knock on his door. When he opened it, he saw Jack standing there, with a blank look on his face. Jack looked at Tony and said, "I did it." And walked inside. Tony slowly closed the door behind him and didn't say a word.

Sharon (Shay) Lynn grew up in a small Nebraska town. She went to school and did the things a typical 8-year-old would do at that age.

One day while at school, an aide interrupted her class. She informed the teacher that Shay had to report to the school counselor's office. When Shay entered the counselor's office, she saw a police officer standing there with her school counselor. They asked Shay to come in and take a seat. Then they proceeded to tell her that her mother and father, Nancy, and Wayne Lynn, had been killed in a car accident earlier that morning.

Shay was devastated and started to cry. She didn't know what to do and was totally confused. Being told that both your mother and father were suddenly killed is a lot for anyone to handle, much less an 8-year-old child.

The officer and counselor did everything they could to calm Shay. But all Shay could think of was her mother and father and that she would never see them again.

The counselor told Shay that they had contacted her aunt Vicky and that she was on her way.

A few hours before telling Shay, the school counselor had called Vicky Vickers and told her of her sister and brother-in-law's death.

Vicky picked up the phone and called Kevin Steal. Kevin was the company's Jet pilot and her personal driver. After a couple of rings, Kevin picked up the phone. "Yes, ma'am, what do you need?"

She explained what had happened and instructed him to call and have the jet ready and for him to get the car and pick her up.

Kevin worked and stayed in one of the guest houses located on the Vickers ranch. Within minutes she was aboard Vickers Internationals private jet, a Cessna Citation Sovereign, and heading to Nebraska to see her niece Shay. Cruising at 425 knots, it would take no time for her to get there.

She had called ahead to arrange a car to be waiting for them at the airport. She and Kevin would drive straight to Shay's school and pick her up.

On the way to Nebraska, Vicky made several phone calls back to her office, located north of College Station, Texas. She spoke to her assistant at Vickers International and told her to call and make all the necessary arrangements for Nancy and Wayne.

Vicky knew that she wanted her sister and brother-in-law brought to Texas. She would like them to be buried next to her mother and father.

She had been asked soon after Shay was born if she would be Shay's Godmother. She agreed without any hesitation, knowing that there were no other family members to take Shay if anything happened to the two of them.

After picking Shay up from school, she took her back to her house to pick up some things. Shay was still in shock and couldn't help with the things she might need and was still too young to know. She grabbed one of the only things she cherished, a stuffed black and white horse from Vicky for her 6th birthday.

Vicky had also contacted her attorney on her way to pick Shay up. She had asked him to take care of all the legal and financial arrangements regarding Nancy and Wayne.

Once they arrived back at Vicky's ranch in Texas, they began getting things out of the car when Midnight came running from around the side of the house.

Midnight was a solid black Labrador Retriever that had been in the Vickers family for eight years. He was born almost the same day as Shay was born. They both loved each other and every time Shay would come to visit, the two of them were inseparable.

Midnight sensing that something was wrong with her best friend Shay slowed his approach, lowered his head, and slowly wagged his tail. Upon seeing Midnight, Shay seemed to perk up and gave Midnight a big hug. They both walked into the house, followed by Vicky.

Vicky wanted to get Shay into a normal routine and enrolled her in horseback riding lessons and karate classes. Shay took to both as she was a natural athlete.

After school and after her homework was done, Shay would help tend to the horses, and several times a week, she had her private martial arts class there at the house. Vicky had asked her friend and long-time friend of her father, Hunter Stockton, to teach Shay some additional self-defense classes in addition to the more formal ones she was getting.

Hunter was a former Army Ranger and director of the Vickers Private Investigation Agency that Robert Vickers had founded shortly before his death.

Hunter really didn't have much formal martial arts training. He was mostly a good old street fighter. He also co-owned a gun range located just a few miles away.

On Shay's 11th birthday, Vicky came into her room early that morning to surprise her.

"Shay." Vicky said, "I need you to go out to the barn and feed the horses."

"But Aunt Vicky, it's my birthday. Why do I have to do it today?" Shay said as she wiped the sleep out of her eyes.

"Horses still have to eat, even on your birthday. So, get up." Vicky said with a slight grin on her face.

Shay slowly got out of bed and got dressed. She put on her red cowgirl boots and cowgirl hat and prepared for another day. She headed out to the barn just as she had done for the past several years. Shay loved the horses and loved being around them. But having to get up early on her 11th birthday was just not right. Besides, Aunt Vicky had several other people, from time to time, come and help around the ranch. Why couldn't they do it just this one time?

She slowly walked to the barn, with both arms and shoulders drooped down as if she had been walking 100 miles in 110-degree heat.

Shay reached the door of the barn and opened it with a grunt. She grabbed a feeding bucket just inside the door and headed to the horse feed.

As she rounded the corner, she came to a dead stop. Standing there was her Aunt Vicky holding the reins of a beautiful black and white Appaloosa horse. The horse had a big red bow around its neck and stood there motionless.

Shay dropped the bucket as her aunt said, "Happy Birthday, Shay!"

Shay let out a scream, as only an 11-year-old girl could, and ran to her Aunt Vicky and gave her a big hug.

Vicky smiled and said, "Now, if you don't like him, I can take him back." Vicky was now laughing.

"No way!" Shay said, and with that, Vicky handed the reins over to her.

Shay took the reins from Vicky and started rubbing the side of the horse's neck.

"What are you going to name him?" Vicky asked.

Shay took a step back and slowly circled the horse as she took in every inch of her new present.

She stopped in front of the horse and started rubbing its nose, and said, "Patches." She kissed the horse on its nose and said, "Your name is Patches."

Shay rode Patches every chance she could. She would be gone for hours, riding all over her Aunt Vicky's 300-acre ranch. Midnight was always with her running alongside her and Patches. In the last hundred yards, they would race to see who could get back to the barn first. Most of the time, Shay and Patches would win, but she would let Midnight win every now and then.

One late autumn afternoon, Shay didn't come back.

Her aunt Vicky contacted the local sheriff's office, and a search soon followed.

Helicopters, people on horseback, and four-wheelers covered every square foot of the ranch as well as several miles in all directions.

Patches was found tied up in a cluster of thick trees and brush later that afternoon. Tire tracks were found leading away from where they had discovered Patches. Right next to where the vehicle was parked was the body of Midnight. You could see in the dirt surrounding the area that a struggle had occurred and that Midnight had fought to his death, trying to save his best friend, Shay. But a single gunshot had kept this K-9 protector and lifelong friend from success.

A note was pinned to the saddle with the words handwritten, '*2 million dollars or you'll never see the little girl again.*'

The FBI and Texas Bureau of Investigation were contacted, and they set up a command center the following day at the Vickers ranch.

Around noon the next day, a call was received at the ranch. The person on the other end of the phone gave Vicky instructions describing how and where to deliver the money.

The FBI and TBI were tracing the phone as the kidnappers were giving the instructions to Vicky. Unfortunately, the phone that the kidnappers used was a burner phone, but they were able to trace it to an area outside of Atlanta, Georgia.

A massive manhunt was underway for Shay Lynn in and around the metro Atlanta area, with little luck.

Radio and TV networks were broadcasting her description over and over several times a day.

About eight days after the reported kidnapping of Shay Lynn, a young couple was having a picnic in a local Atlanta Park when a young girl walked up to the two of them. They stopped what they were doing and looked at the young girl. She was covered from head to toe in dirt, and her clothes were torn and filthy. The couple asked where her parents were, but the little girl didn't answer.

While the young lady held the now crying little girl in her arms, her boyfriend called the local police. Within a few minutes, a patrol car pulled up, and a Fulton County police officer exited the vehicle. He approached the three standing there as the young girl stood beside her newfound friends. He asked her her name and the young girl said, "Sharon Lynn."

Now recognizing her, the officer reached for his radio and contacted his supervisor. Word of Shay being found alive soon reached Vicky. She flew as fast as she could to Atlanta, where Shay was being checked out and attended to at St. Joseph Children's Hospital in Downtown Atlanta.

The people responsible for taking Shay were not found and got away with the ransom. Shay had escaped her captives during the night while they were asleep. She had been walking through the woods all night before finding the couple in the park.

Weeks after returning to Texas, Shay dove back into her martial arts. She would work through her anger of losing again what was near and dear to her heart, her best friend Midnight, on her opponents.

Hunter introduced Shay to an IDF (Israeli Defense Force) trainer he had met while stationed in Israel. Stan Rosberg was a master in Krav Maga and owned a gym in the area. Shay studied under Stan Rosberg until she turned 18 and earned several black belts in different forms of martial arts.

Shay joined the Marines at age 18 and soon became one of the self-defense instructors for the Marines. Even being only five feet one inch tall, she could hold her own against most of the other Marines she helped train. After serving four years in the Marine Corp. and after winning several self-defense awards in the Marines, she left the Marines and started working for her Aunt Vicky.

She continued her Self-defense training after leaving the Marines with family friend Hunter Stockton.

Little did Jack and Shay know at the time their pasts would soon bring the two of them together. Their pasts would be a foundation that would shape their future and the future of many others like them.

People are a creation of their past.

Chapter Four

BIRTH OF MEGA

For years after Shay's return home from the eight long days in captivity, Vicky kept feeling a huge weight on her shoulders. She was still reliving the nightmare and the thoughts that she knew Shay was also having.

How could she ever stop that from happening again to Shay or another little girl? What could she do to see that it didn't happen again?

The courts and law enforcement have failed regarding sex trafficking and child kidnappings. So, what could she do? She's just one person? If the courts and law enforcement can't stop it, how could she?

She remembered a conversation she had, in private, with one of the FBI agents that was working on Shay's abduction. She couldn't recall his name, but she did remember him saying how helpless he felt and wished he could do more.

She remembered them talking about how the Justice System was so bogged down and too understaffed to handle these kidnapping and sex trafficking cases and that there had to be something done to stop this from happening.

She looked through her records and soon found his name and number. She picked up her phone and dialed.

After about three rings, a male voice answered, "SSA James, how may I help you?" she remembered that SSA stood for Supervisory Special Agent, his title at the FBI.

"Mr. James, or should I call you SSA James? This is Vicky Vickers. Do you remember me?"

"Sure, I do, Ms. Vickers. How are you doing? And how is Ms. Shay doing?" he asked. "And please call me Tony."

"We are doing as well as to be expected, all things considered. Shay jumped back headlong into her martial arts training, swearing that this would never happen to her again. She's in the Marines now and teaching self-defense."

"Good thing she has you and something to occupy her mind." Tony said.

"Do you remember our conversation inside the barn the day Shay was taken?"

"Yes, I do. It has been weighing on my mind ever since." He said, "But let's not talk about it over the phone."

"I agree." She said, "How about I come down to Houston, and we have lunch, say, next Friday?"

"Next Friday would be great. I've taken off that day because I have a doctor's appointment that morning. I should be free after, say, around 11:00 that morning." He replied.

"Here's my cell phone number. Text me where you want to meet and what time, and I'll be there." Vicky said.

"Will do, Ms. Vickers. I'll see you then." And they both hung up.

She dialed another number, and a voice answered on the other end, "Evening, Vicky. What's going on?"

"Hunter, can you come by the house tomorrow? I've got something I want to talk to you about." she said.

"Sure thing. I can do that. It sounds serious, is everything ok?" Hunter asked.

"Yes, everything is fine. I just have had several things on my mind and wanted to run them by you." She said.

"Ok: is ten tomorrow morning good?" he asked.

"At the house." Vicky said.

"Sure. 10 o'clock at the ranch, I'll be there. Do I need to bring anything?"

"No, just an open mind." She replied.

Vicky walked out of her office and onto the deck. Her home office was located on the 2nd floor of her house and overlooked the pool and tennis court.

She saw Kevin reading next to the pool. She leaned over the rail and called out, "Kevin, can you sweep my office and recheck the phone for bugs?" she asked.

"Sure thing Ms. Vickers, I'll get right to it." Kevin put down his Pilot Weekly magazine on the table next to him and started to get up.

"Oh, check the car too for bugs and trackers. And while you're at it, give the jet a once over too." She added as Kevin was getting up.

"Planning for guests, Ms. Vickers?"

"Just Hunter tomorrow morning, but I'll need you to drive me down to Houston next Friday, so the car can wait till later."

"Yes, ma'am. Is there anything else you'll need me to do before Hunter gets here?"

"No, that should do it." She said as she turned and walked back into her office.

Hunter arrived at Vicky's house at 10 a.m. sharp the next day. Hunter stood five foot ten inches tall. He had a stocky build and short hair and spoke in a hard, raspy voice. He had been a long-time friend of the family and never needed to knock on the door to come in. He had his own set of keys and was welcome anytime he wanted. He was more like an older brother to Vicky than an old friend.

Hunter walked into Vicky's office and said, "I figured I'd find you in here. So, what's up?"

Sitting behind her desk, Vicky looked up from her computer, "Morning, Hunter, close the door. Let's sit over here on the couch." Vicky pointed over in the direction of the couch as she stood up.

"You sound serious." Hunter said, "We've never met behind closed doors before unless it was something important."

"Yes, it is. I want to talk to you about something that I feel strongly about but could get us in serious trouble."

"Do I need a drink before we get started?" he asked.

"Sure, get me one too." She said with a chuckle.

"Ok, where do I start?" she said while looking out the window.

"Just start talking. The suspense is killing me. I've never seen you so keyed up over something. Talk, I'm all ears."

"Well, you know when Shay got taken and how it affected her." She started.

"Yes, it affected everyone. I've never seen you so upset and at your wits end." He replied.

"Well, I feel I need to do something about it, Hunter."

"You and me both, but what can we do? The cops never did find out who took her, and you can't hire a bodyguard to watch after her 24 hours a day, seven days a week." Hunter said.

"You can't blame yourself either. This happens every day all over the world. We were lucky that we got Shay back. Millions of kids go missing every year, never to be seen again." Hunter said, taking a sip of his beer and leaning back on the couch.

"Besides, when and if the people are caught, many times, they get off or spend very little time behind bars." He said in an angry voice.

"If it was up to me, they would be castrated, tortured, and killed." He said as he got up and walked over to the window.

Vicky got up, walked over, and stood next to him at the window. "That's what I'm proposing. What if it was up to you?" She said in a near whisper.

Hunter turned toward Vicky and said, "You're proposing that I do this?"

"I'm proposing that we do this, you and me." She said, with tears in her eyes. "Someone has to make those sick bastards pay for what they have done. And maybe stop them before they have the chance to do it to some other poor little child!" Vicky said with a tone full of anger.

"What you're proposing is that You and I track these people down and kill them?" Hunter points back and forth between the two of them.

"Not you and me personally, per se, but yes, that is what I'm saying. Can I get you another drink?" she asked as she turned and walked over to the bar.

"Yes, make mine a double. Hell, make it a triple. I think I'm going to need it before this day is over." He said as he turned back and looked out the window.

"Ok, fill me in on this great plan to rid the world of evil you've got all cooked up." He said as Vicky approached him with his drink.

"We need to build a team. People that we can trust 100%. We can train them to do what is necessary to stop these people from ever hurting a child again." Vicky began.

"What's this WE shit? I've not agreed to anything yet." Hunter interjected! "What you're talking about is highly illegal and is nothing more than vigilante killing."

"Vigilante is a member of a self-appointed group of citizens who undertake law enforcement in their community without legal authority, typically because the legal agencies are considered inadequate. I know what a vigilante is." She replied.

She went on to say, "Law enforcement has tried and failed. The courts have tried and failed. Sometimes it may be up to others to hunt down and bring these perverts to justice."

"You're not talking justice with a trial and courts. You're talking street justice." He said solemnly.

"DAMN RIGHT, I AM. That's more than Shay got! Did she get justice? Did she get a chance to argue her case as to why she shouldn't be kidnapped? NO! Where are the people that kidnapped her today? They are still out there, and God knows what they have done to other children." Vicky was now yelling, not at Hunter but at the world in general.

"Vicky, I never said I wasn't with you. I'm with you 100%. I just want you to know that we could spend the rest of our lives in jail, or worse, if we're caught. And we'll have to live with our actions the rest of our lives."

"Don't you think I know that?" She replied.

"What do we do next?" he asked.

"Start putting together a team. I'm meeting with Tony James next Friday, and I'm going to feel him out to see if he'll help."

"Tony James, where have I heard that name before?" he asked.

"He's one of the FBI agents that worked on Shay's abduction."

"WHAT?" Hunter asked. "You're going to talk to an FBI agent about your plan to track down and kill people? I'm sure that's going to go over really well. Do I need to go ahead and get your bail money ready? Or should I make arrangements for your stay at a mental hospital for the next 20 years?" Hunter said as he began raising his voice out of anger and shock.

"What in the hell gave you this brilliant idea to run off and tell the FBI of your plans to track down and kill people?"

"He and I had a conversation that night after Shay was abducted. He said some things that made me think that he would buy into something like this."

Hunter stood there for a few seconds staring at her without saying a word.

"We both talked about how child sex crimes have been increasing. As a society, we have failed in our efforts to keep our children safe from this danger. How families have been shattered and destroyed by either family members, friends, or total strangers taking their children and using them for their own perverted purposes. Sometimes they are found and returned to their families, as in Shay's case. However, they will never see the world or feel the same again. Tony admitted that Law enforcement has tried and failed. The courts have tried and failed, also. Sometimes it just may be up to the streets to hunt down and bring these perverts to justice."

"Do you think he will buy into it and help?" he asked.

"There's only one way to find out when I meet him next Friday."

"Do you want me to come with you when you meet this FBI man?"

"No, as you said, I may need bail money, and I don't want to implicate you in this plan."

"God help us." He said as he raised his drink as if to toast their new venture.

Vicky arrived in Houston around 10:30 a.m. and got word from Tony for them to meet at a local park just north of Houston at 11:15.

Vicky had arrived about 20 minutes before Tony and was reviewing some notes when he drove up.

Tony got out of his car, a red Toyota Camry, and walked over to where Vicky was parked. As he approached, she rolled down her window.

"You wanted to talk?" Tony asked.

"Yes, but not here." She said, "Lock your car and get in. We'll talk somewhere else."

"You don't like this park that I picked?" he asked.

"It's not that I don't like it. I just will feel more comfortable talking somewhere else." She added, "But before you get in, I want Kevin to check you for any microphones or tracking devices you might be wearing."

"What's with all the cloak and dagger shit?" Tony asked.

"Just a precaution. I like to play it safe."

Kevin checked Tony and nodded to Vicky that he was clean. Kevin opened the door for Tony to get into the back seat. Kevin got into the driver's seat, and the three drove off.

After a few minutes of silence, Tony finally broke the awkward silence, "So where are we going?"

Vicky sitting in the front passenger's seat turned and said, "Just up the road a bit, not too far."

"Ok, but you're not trying to kidnap a federal agent, are you?" Tony asked with a smile.

"No, you're free to get out anytime you want."

After a couple more minutes, they pulled into the George Bush International Airport and drove around into an empty hanger. Once they stopped, Kevin turned off the car's engine.

"Kevin, would you take a walk and let us talk."

After Kevin left the car, Vicky turned and said, "Sorry for all the spy stuff, but because of what I want to talk about, I want to make sure it stays between you and me."

"You've really got me curious about what you want, so let's hear it."

"Well." She paused, "Hypothetically speaking..." She then began explaining her idea to Tony.

Tony sat in the back seat, taking in every word that Vicky said without showing any signs of agreeing or disagreeing. Vicky laid out her idea for almost 20 minutes before she said. "Well?"

Tony looked out the side window for a few seconds before he turned back to look at Vicky. She had a look that was between sheer terror, what have I just done and are you in or out, on her face.

"Well, hypothetically speaking, someone just confessed to plotting to kill someone to an FBI agent. And hypothetically speaking, that agent is bound by law to arrest that person and bring them in for questioning, hypothetically speaking, that is."

"Well?" she asked nervously.

"If hypothetically speaking, if said FBI agent were to agree with this hypothetical idea, he and anyone involved, if caught, would spend the rest of their lives in prison." He added, looking right into her eyes.

"How could I, I mean," she stuttered a little, "how could someone trust that this hypothetical FBI agent wouldn't turn them in? What guarantee would a person have?"

"Ok, Vicky, about what you have just said with all the finesse of a bull in a China shop, I will assure you that I have thought of the same thing over the years. Maybe if I tell you something that you can use against me, that will ease your mind some."

Vicky looking more assured now, said, "Ok, please tell."

Tony began, "Well, many years ago, my sister's husband was molesting my nephew and niece over and over. I didn't find out about it till years later. I couldn't do anything about it because they wouldn't admit to it. Years later, after he was kicked out of the house, my niece killed herself because of what he did to her. A year or so after that, with my help, so to speak, my nephew hunted down and killed his stepfather. He showed up at my door the next day. I knew what he had done without him saying a word. But I never said anything, and I covered it up. So, in reality, I was a party of a murder, and I was just as guilty as my nephew Jack, who pulled the trigger. Jack and I would spend the rest of our lives in jail if anyone were to find out."

"Now, where do we go from here?" she asked.

"How many people know about this plan of yours?"

"Just you and one other, Hunter Stockton. He's a lifelong friend, more of an older brother."

"And what does he think about this plan of yours?" Tony asked.

"He's behind it. He thinks I am crazy coming down here and talking to an FBI agent about it. But after our conversation in the barn, I just had the feeling it was ok."

"Let me put some things together, and I'll contact you in a couple of days. We can talk some more about it then." Tony said.

Vicky honked the car horn, and Kevin returned to the car. The three rode in silence back to where Tony's car was parked. As Tony was getting out, Vicky said, "I look forward to hearing from you soon."

Upon returning home, Hunter was there to meet Vicky. He wanted to know every detail of what was said and what took place during her meeting with the FBI man.

They both sat, talked, and planned their new venture. They played the "what if" game each day they talked. They would add or take away ideas from the previous day's meeting.

Vicky received a call from Tony saying that he would be free for a few days and would like to come up and continue their conversation. Vicky gave Tony the directions and said that he could stay in one of the spare rooms at her house.

Tony said that he was going to be bringing someone else with him if it was ok with her. She agreed if that person could be trusted. She said that she would also have someone join them.

A few days later, Tony and the other person arrived at Vicky's house. Kevin opened the door when they knocked, and the two walked in.

"Nice seeing you again, Kevin." Tony said.

"Please, follow me." Kevin shook both of their hands, then turned and walked towards Vicky's office.

When they entered the office, Vicky and Hunter were already there. Vicky was sitting behind her desk, and Hunter was sitting on the couch reading the local sports section of the newspaper.

They stood up and walked over to greet the two guests.

"Kevin, please check these two gentlemen for bugs." She said.

As Kevin was doing this, Hunter approached the two of them.

"Hi, I'm Hunter Stockton." He said as he stuck out his hand to shake their hands.

"I'm Tony James, and this is my nephew, Jack Davidson."

"Good to see you again, Tony. Nice to meet you, Jack. And you've both met Kevin." Vicky said as Kevin was finishing up with Tony and checking Jack out for bugs.

Jack looked at Kevin as he began scanning. "Is he your butler?"

Kevin looked up at Jack as Vicky said, "No, however, Kevin does work for me, but he's not my butler. He's my 'go-to' man and personal pilot. He makes sure I get to where I need to be on time and safe."

"He's like your personal bodyguard or something?" Jack asked.

"Something like that." She replied.

Jack walked over to the window, "Nice place you have here. I see that you have an airplane too. You must be someone important or something."

"Important? No." Vicky said, "All thanks to the hard work of my father. He left me with a lot of money and responsibility."

"My father only left me with two guns and some good childhood memories. Which my stepfather took away from me." Jack said in a bitter tone.

"Ms. Vickers, if you don't need me anymore, I'll leave you and the two gentlemen and Hunter alone," Kevin said.

Hunter looked over at Kevin, "What? I'm not a gentleman, you fart."

Kevin just smiled and closed the door behind him.

"Jack, if you're nice to Kevin, maybe he'll give you a ride in the company's jet." She said.

"Cool, what kind is it?" he asked.

"It's an 8-passenger Cessna Citation Sovereign with a top speed of over 425 knots per hour." She said, "Maybe he'll even let you fly it too."

"Well, let's get down to business." Hunter said, "I don't mind telling you that when Vicky told me she was going to go to the FBI with her idea, I thought she was crazy."

"Did she explain to you, when she returned, what I had told her about myself and the issue with Jack and his stepfather?"

"Yes, she did." Hunter said, "So this is the kid who capped the old stepfather."

"Yes, I am." Jack replied with a smile.

"Glad to meet you, kid." Hunter came back with his raspy voice and a smile.

Vicky told the two of them of her plans and the ideas she and Hunter came up with over the past week after meeting with Tony. She said she could fund the startup operations through a shell corporation she could set up.

"The way I see it, we're going to need a lot of money to kick this venture off." Tony said.

"Also, it will take a lot of money to keep it going in the future too." Hunter added.

"Agreed." Vickey said, "But we can't really charge for the services rendered. It's not like them having a bounty on their heads that we can collect, and the local authorities are not going to give us a reward."

"I have an idea about someone that owes me, and I think he would be open to it." Tony said as he went on. "He's a Black Hat Hacker I busted a few years back. We caught him hacking into college computers and changing students' grades for a small fee."

"And he was moving money from some criminal organizations into his own account that he had set up and using that money to fund some of his own activities." Tony added.

Hunter said, "That's interesting. Where was he when I was in school?"

"They didn't have computers back then." Jack said with a smile.

Hunter looked over at Jack and bobbed his head up and down slightly while he bit down on his lower lip.

Tony pointed over to Jack with his hand up in a stop motion and a look that said, shut up.

Hunter said, "No, that's fine, let him speak. If he's going to be part of this team, he's got a voice. No matter how stupid it sounds or childish it may be." Hunter looked over to Vicky and smiled as she shook her head.

Hunter smiled at Jack and said, "Kid, I like you. You say what's on your mind."

"Getting back to the topic at hand. Ok, we have the finances taken care of. Also, a computer guy that can help with the future financial needs." Vicky said.

"Hunter can help with the training. He was an Army Ranger 1st sergeant. He can also help with the weapons and any other areas we will run into."

"I can do some of the leg work on the people we are going to target using the FBI's resources." Tony said.

"What about me?" Jack asked as he walked over from the window. "What is my role in this group of thugs?"

"You're the executioner." Hunter replied.

"You want me to be this group's John Wick or that old James Bond dude?" Jack asked.

Tony looked at Hunter, saying, "I don't know about that."

"Don't I have a say so in this, besides I'm probably the only one in this group who has killed someone." Jack said with a tone of excitement.

"G-Man, you've said you have never killed anyone while in the FBI or as sheriff." Jack said as he was looking at his Uncle Tony.

Jack looked over at Vicky and then at Hunter. "How about you two? Any kills in your pasts?"

Hunter said, "None I'd like to talk about. And Vicky has none that I know of unless she would like to confess something right now."

Vicky shook her head.

"It's settled. I'm the hitman in this group." Jack said with a bit of satisfaction in his voice.

"Fine." Tony said, "You're a good shot with a rifle at about 400 yards. I have to admit."

"We'll have him reaching out much further when we finish with him." Hunter said, "I'm part owner in an outdoor gun range. With the right equipment and training, we'll have you shooting way past that. There's a guy that shoots there. He's a former Olympic Gold medal shooter, and I can get him to help."

"I also own a private investigation company," Vicky said, "however, I don't want anyone there to know anything about what we are doing. The fewer people that know about this venture, the better."

"Vicky," Hunter said, "you know I'm the director of that company, so I can have them do some of the work for our group without them knowing directly who it's for. I can tell them it's for a client."

"Well, it looks like we have a start. But we still have a lot of work ahead of the group." She said.

"This could be the beginning of the end for all of us if we get caught." Tony said.

"What are we going to call our group?" Jack asked, "We can't just keep calling it The Group."

"Well, as Tony said, this could be the end of us." Vicky said, "God said He's the beginning of the end. And God help us. This may be the end of us all. So, let's call ourselves, The Omega Group."

Chapter Five

The Recruitment

Upon returning to Houston, Tony got fast to work on planning how he would help his new cohorts in crime. He sat in his office, thinking about what had happened over the last few days.

Tony tried several times throughout the day to get his work done. He had case files stacked up on his desk over eight inches tall.

Tony leaned back in his chair and wondered if a person he had in mind would be willing to work for the Omega Group and how he could approach this person with the idea and not have it blow back on him.

An idea came to Tony, and he got up from his desk and headed for the elevator. While waiting, he reached into his coat pocket to see if his new phone was there.

He had stopped by a truck stop after he and Jack left Vicky's and had picked up two new burner phones for himself and Jack. He paid cash for both so that no one could track the purchase. He told Jack only to use the telephone to contact Vicky, Hunter, or him about anything dealing with the Omega Group.

Once outside, Tony walked a couple of blocks down the street to a small park and sat on one of the benches, where he called Vicky.

"Hello." Vicky answered.

"This is Tony. On the way back, I picked up a few burner phones and gave one to Jack."

"That's a good idea." She said, "So, what's up?"

"I pulled the file of the guy I told you about. His name is Raymond Ray." Tony said with excitement in his voice.

Tony told Vicky what he knew of Raymond and how he thought he could help the group.

She agreed that he could be of some use to their endeavors. She told Tony she would have Kevin drive down and pick up the file tomorrow. And that Kevin would meet him at the same park where they had met before, at around one tomorrow afternoon.

It was only about an hour and forty-five minutes from her place to the park. Kevin could be there and back by dinner time. She could have Hunter over for dinner, and the two could look over the file on Raymond Ray.

Upon Kevin's return, she told him she didn't need him for the rest of the day. Hunter was coming over to talk business, and she would order Chinese for them.

Kevin told her that if she needed him, she could call him on his cell phone and that he would take one of the horses and get some riding in.

Hunter showed up around a half hour later. Vicky told him that she had decided to order some Chinese for them. Shortly after the food was delivered, they sat on the couch in her office and began looking over the file Tony sent on this Raymond guy.

"Vicky, what do you think about this computer nerd Tony likes?" he asked.

"I think he may be instrumental. But we need to check him out first and see what else we can dig up on him."

"I'll make copies of the file and redact anything that will tie it back to the FBI or Tony. Then I'll have our two guys at VPI investigate him a little more." Hunter said.

VPI was short for Vickers Private Investigation Company, one of the subsidiaries of Vickers International. It was a company that Vicky's father founded shortly before his death.

The company only had two full-time employees, Jim Appleton and Robert Green, who worked as investigators. Hunter was the acting Director of VPI, and he was going to use VPI's resources to help the Omega Group without Jim and Robert knowing it. VPI used informants and subcontractors as their needs dictated.

Any business that the Omega Group would give them would be disguised to be for another client.

About a week later, the report came in from VPI. They hadn't found much more information than in the FBI's file on Raymond.

Hunter sat down again with Vicky, and the two reviewed all the information they had on Raymond.

"Well," Hunter said, "what do you think about Raymond?" he said, "You want to bring him onboard?"

"Do you have an angle we can use to ensure he doesn't flip on us and blow everything out of the water?" she asked.

Hunter went over how he was going to approach Raymond. She told him to go ahead and meet with him. Hunter said that the investigators found out he liked to eat lunch at the same restaurant every day, and that's where he'll meet him.

Hunter had picked a table outside of the restaurant that was located just outside College Station. He could see who was coming and going and would be able to see when Raymond approached.

When Raymond walked up, Hunter said, "Hey kid come over here. Let's talk."

Raymond stopped next to the table, looking at Hunter, and said, "Do I know you?"

"No, but I know you." Hunter responded, "Take a seat."

"Dude, I don't know you. I'm here to eat, not talk to some stranger." Raymond said as he looked around to see if anyone was looking.

"Kid, sit down. Your food will be here in a second." Hunter said a little more firmly in his raspy voice.

Raymond started to walk off when a waiter walked up and said, "Here's your usual Raymond. I put some extra mayo on it as you like it."

Raymond looked at the waiter and then at Hunter, sitting together with both hands on the table. Hunter then motioned with his right hand for Raymond to take a seat.

"Oh, and waiter, could you bring some extra sugar? My friend Raymond likes five bags of sugar in his tea and only three here on the table."

Raymond looked intently at this man he'd never met before but seemed to know a lot about him.

Raymond took a slow look around, thinking that if this guy tried anything here in public, he'd have plenty of witnesses.

Raymond slowly took a seat without taking his eyes off Hunter. With caution in his voice., "Have we ever met? I don't recall ever meeting you, and how do you know so much about me?" Raymond asked.

"Eat your burger before it gets cold. I'll fill you in while you eat." Hunter said as he leaned back in the chair.

Raymond poured the five bags of sugar into his tea and started eating his burger, still not taking his eyes off the strange person across from him.

Hunter leaned forward and placed his arms on the table with his hands clasped. He looked around slightly while chewing a little on his lower lip while bobbing his head up and down a little as if he was approving of how things were going.

"Raymond, may I call you Raymond?" he asked.

"Call me anything you want." Raymond answered with a mouth full of half-chewed food.

"I hear you got all jammed up by the feds on some grade tampering and some transferring of some money that didn't belong to you." Hunter said as he was looking for some reaction from Raymond.

Raymond stopped chewing and said, "Who the hell are you, and where did you get this information?" He was starting to get angry.

"Where I got it is not important right now. What's important is where we go with this information." Hunter pointed at Raymond and himself several times slowly with his right hand.

Raymond placed his hamburger down on his plate and picked up a napkin. As he started wiping his mouth off, he said, "Tell me what it is you want."

"I want you to continue what you're doing but doing it for me and my associates." Hunter said, waiting to judge the reaction from Raymond.

"If you know so much about me, then you know I'm not allowed to touch a computer. And I've got to wear this fucking ankle bracelet, so the FBI and whoever can keep track of me. Was that not in your little file you have on me?" Raymond said as he threw down his napkin on his hamburger.

Hunter looked down at Raymond's plate and then back up at him.

"The Carlos drug cartel and the Russian mob don't know who you are and where you live." Hunter said, looking Raymond directly in the eyes. "I'm sure they would like their money back along with some interest, if you know what I mean."

"You're blackmailing me, right? And if I don't come to work for you and your gang, you will turn me over to the mob!" Raymond said, now showing a bit of anger and fear in his face and voice.

"No, just the opposite. If you don't want to work with us, we both get up and walk away, and you'll never see me again. You'll walk away with a free half-eaten burger and fries and back where you were before we met." Hunter said as he leaned back in his chair and crossed his legs.

"The ball is totally in your court. You walk away; keep your ankle bracelet and lifetime restriction from ever using a computer again." Hunter added.

"Exactly what will I get in return for agreeing to work for you?" he asked.

"You'll lose your ankle bracelet and regain your computer access with unlimited access and resources. And most of all, you'll get the FBI off your back, and the goons from the cartel and mob won't find you." Hunter said, leaning forward again on the table.

Raymond looked up from Hunter's gaze and leaned back in his chair to ponder his options.

"This group you're talking about sounds like it's not totally legal since you've been very vague about what you do." Raymond said, looking over to his right at the passing cars. "What if, whatever your organization does, I go to the cops? What then?"

"Well, you'll become the property of good old Uncle Sam again, and you take your chances with the other organizations that you screwed over." Hunter said, "They'll have a copy of your file to help them locate you."

"You'll turn me in if I blow the whistle on your group, so to speak?" Raymond asked.

"So, to speak, yes." Hunter added.

"Look, kid, we are not here to jam you up or blackmail you into doing something. And as long as you don't cause any trouble, you can come and go as you please." Hunter said as he was pointing his finger at Raymond.

"When will you tell me what you and your group do?"

"Let's take a walk. I'm parked down the street. We can talk better in my car." Hunter said. They both got up and walked down the street to where Hunter's car was parked.

Once in Hunter's car, he explained the group's plans to Raymond. Raymond was very interested and asked several questions about his role and what was expected of him within the group. After about an hour of questions and answers, they shook hands, and Raymond exited the car.

As Raymond started to walk back to the restaurant, Hunter rolled down the driver's side window.

"Hey, kid," Hunter said, "there will be someone here tomorrow at 11:30 a.m. to pick you up. You're going to be introduced to another member of the group."

"I can't tomorrow. I've got a class and test tomorrow at 10. I don't want to fail the test." Raymond replied.

"Skip the class." Hunter said, "Just hack into the computer and change your test score from zero to 100. You've done it before. So be in front of the restaurant at 11:30 a.m. sharp. Oh, and don't tell anyone about our meeting today."

"Heaven forbid, no one would believe me anyway." Raymond turned toward the restaurant, threw his hands up as a sign of surrender, and started walking.

The following day at 11:30 a.m., Raymond stood outside the restaurant as instructed. A black SUV with tinted windows all around pulled up to the curb in front of him. The passenger side window rolled down, and he heard an unfamiliar voice coming from within.

"Get in, Raymond." Came the voice of Kevin Steal, sitting in the driver's seat.

Raymond leaning over and looking in the window, "Do I get in the front or back?"

"I don't care if you sit on the roof, pick a seat and get in." Kevin said in an irritated voice.

"Man, you people need to relax and chill." Raymond said under his breath.

He opened the back door, threw his backpack on the seat, and jumped into the front passenger seat.

They headed north towards the Vickers ranch for about 10 minutes before Raymond spoke.

"Are you part of this Group?" Raymond asked as he used his hands to make air quotes.

"I don't know what group you're talking about." Kevin replied without taking his eyes off the road.

"The group the Hunter dude told me about yesterday. Man, he was wound up tight."

"Guess you'll have to ask him when you see him. I was told to pick you up and take you to the ranch."

They drove up state highway 190 the rest of the way in silence. Just past Kurten, they turned onto a paved driveway. Raymond could see a large two-story house about 100 yards ahead. A large building to the right appeared to be a barn, along with three other smaller buildings standing off to the other side of the house. On each side of the driveway grew large, shade trees. Behind the trees on each side was a split rail fence. Raymond could see 4 or 5 horses grazing in the grass as they pulled up to the front of the house.

Raymond grabbed his backpack from the back seat as the two exited the car.

"Nice place." Raymond exclaimed as he looked around at the horses and house.

"That's what hard work will do for you. Follow me." Kevin replied.

They both entered the house, and Kevin said, "Drop your bag here on the floor."

Kevin then reached over to a table and picked up an electronic hand wand.

"Stand still and hold your arms out." Kevin ran the wand up and down Raymond's body, checking for any electronic recording device.

"Somehow, I'm not surprised you were going to do this." Raymond said with a smile.

Raymond looked around at his new surroundings. The inside went well with the outside of the house. The house was a rustic Texas-style ranch. Hardwood floors went throughout the rooms, and pictures of horses and artifacts hung on the walls.

Just past the entry was a large den area with a fireplace to the right. A full-size picture of a man was displayed over the fireplace. Raymond assumed it was some relative of the person who owned the ranch.

In front of the fireplace were three large couches in a U shape design facing the fireplace. On the mantel over the fireplace stood several pictures of various people.

The den extended up into the 2nd floor of the house. There was a railing that overlooked the den on the floor above, with doors lining the walls behind.

"Raymond, good to see you again. Welcome." Came the voice of Hunter as he came down the steps from the 2nd floor. He extended his hand to shake Raymond's.

Raymond was taken aback, not expecting such a cheerful voice from the man he had just met the day before.

"Nice house you got here."

"Oh, it's not mine. I'm just a close friend of the owner. Come on in."

The two guys shook hands and greeted one another. Raymond noted that this meeting was different from the one just over 24 hours ago.

"Welcome, Raymond." A voice was heard from the 2nd-floor balcony.

Raymond looked up in surprise. A woman with dark red hair down to the middle of her back. She stood about 5 foot 8 and had light olive skin. She had a very calming smile as she looked down at him. She looked to be, maybe, in her mid to late forties.

"Come on up to the office." Hunter said as he turned and started walking up the steps.

Raymond started following Hunter up to the second floor.

"I'll be out by the pool." Kevin said, startling Raymond as he had forgotten that Kevin was standing behind him.

They walked into Vicky's office and over to the couches. "Please sit down." She said, motioning to the sofa.

"You've met Kevin and Hunter, and my name is Vicky Vickers. I guess you're wondering why you're here. I'm sure you have a ton of questions."

"Well, actually, I do. Hunter filled me in on some of the things yesterday. And Kevin, your chauffeur, didn't tell me anything when I asked about this group."

"Kevin is not my chauffeur." She said with a slight chuckle.

She looked at Hunter and said, "You know he hates it when people call him that. We need to figure out a way to change that."

"No." Hunter said, "I think it's funny as hell. I enjoy messing with him about it."

"Well, he's not my chauffeur, butler, servant, or anything like that." She said with a smile. "Let's get down to business and why you're here."

"First, I'm guessing you've accepted Hunter's offer to work with us."

"Well, he sort of made it out like I didn't really have a choice." Raymond said.

"We always have a choice, just sometimes we don't always make the right one or the one that works out the best." She replied.

"Here's the deal, Raymond. You'll be given a job for cover at Vickers International as our IT dude, but your primary job will be to do stuff for the Omega group." She said.

"Vickers International was founded by my father when he was just about your age, and he built it into a multi-billion-dollar business. Its function is dealing in precious metals and petroleum trading. There are only six people that work in that group. Then we have Vickers Private Investigations, VPI. That group only has two investigators, and Hunter here is the director. VPI knows nothing about the Omega Group or even of its existence."

"You'll have an office here at the ranch. And as Hunter has told you, you'll say nothing or talk to anyone about the Omega Group outside of the group itself. Are we clear on that?" she added.

"Questions?" Hunter asked.

"You're hiring me to do your IT stuff, right?"

"Yes." Vicky replied.

"Where, when, and what resources do I have?" Raymond asked.

"To answer your where VPI and Vickers International have offices together in the Bryan area. There are only ten computers, printers, and a server. As for your office here, you can set it up any way you like."

"What about the computers for the Omega Group?" Raymond asked.

"We just purchased a large jet hanger at the airport down the road. We will house our jet in one end, and the other section will be the Omega Group headquarters." She said. "It's being retrofitted as we speak. You will have your main computer equipment located there. Your office at VPI will be your cover story. You'll be on the VPI payroll."

"Regarding the money, your file said you have been known to acquire funds from other sources." She said with a smile.

Raymond scooted forward to the edge of the couch, "Yes, I have done that in the past, and that's one reason I'm sitting here." He said as he was rolling his eyes.

"Thought so. We've set up a couple of offshore accounts that you'll use to transfer money into and use to fund whatever you need."

"In short, kid," Hunter piped in, "you'll have unlimited resources to build and operate whatever system you need."

"Great! But you said a couple of accounts? What are the other accounts used for?" he asked.

"Omega operating money." Hunter added.

"Ok, so when do I start?"

"We have an office already set up for you a couple of doors down. Whenever you can get things rolling, the sooner the better. We've also acquired some account numbers from some questionable companies, and you can do your magic with the money." Vicky said.

"You can stay here in one of the empty bunk houses or add a cot at the hanger, whatever you want."

"You'll be meeting the other team members Saturday at the hangar." Hunter said. "You can stay here tonight, or I'll have the chauffeur drive you back to your apartment. It's up to you." Hunter said with a chuckle.

"I'll hang out here then."

"Good, I'll have Hunter show you around." Vicky said with a smile, "Welcome aboard."

"Can't you get the chauffeur to do it?" Hunter said with a big smile on his face.

"Shut up Hunter." She replied.

Later that afternoon, Vicky and Hunter were working late in her office when they heard a knock at her door. They looked up and saw Kevin standing just outside the door.

"Come on in, Kevin. What's up?" she asked.

Hunter glanced up at Kevin, saying, "I'll be right back. I need to get something out of my office. You two go ahead and talk."

"Ms. Vickers, I've been observing that you, Hunter, that Jack kid, the FBI guy, and now Raymond have been meeting, and I think I've put two and two together, and I want in."

"Oh really, and what do you want in on?" she asked.

"And let's not forget the purchase of the large hanger down at the airport. Three times the size we need to park the jet." He added.

"I know it has something to do with Ms. Shay's abduction. That part, I know. And from the meetings and training that's going on. It might have something to do with going after the people who took Ms. Shay."

"Kevin, don't you think that the police would do a better job in doing that?" she asked.

"Well, we all know they failed in finding Ms. Shay's abductors, and I know how it has affected you."

"Now let me get this straight, Kevin, you are accusing me and the others of plotting revenge for what had happened to Shay?" she asked, "Isn't that breaking the law?"

"I'm sorry, Ms. Vickers, if I spoke out of line."

"Well, you're making some serious claims there, Kevin. Claims that could put me and others in jail." She said now in a loud and firm voice.

About that time, Hunter walked in. "What in the hell are you two talking about? I can hear you downstairs in the living room." Hunter said as he entered the room and walked over to the side of Kevin.

"Kevin here thinks we are planning on tracking down and killing the people who abducted Shay." Vicky said.

"With all due respect Ms. Vickers, I never said kill!" Kevin said in his defense.

"What do you think, Hunter? Those are some serious accusations?" she said with a slight smile.

Kevin stood there, looking down at the floor, sweating bullets, afraid he was about to get fired. Or worse.

"Vicky, what do you want to do with him? He knows too much." Hunter said, looking Kevin straight in the eyes.

"I don't know, Hunter. What do you think we need to do?"

Hunter looked at Kevin as he pulled his shirt back, exposing his Smith and Wesson 9mm on his side.

"Go over and sit down over there on the couch." He said, still looking at Kevin.

Vicky got up from her desk and followed the two over to the couch. She stood behind Kevin, who was now sitting and started strumming her fingers on the back of the sofa.

Hunter stood about 6 feet away from Kevin with his head down and rubbed his forehead with his fingers.

"Kevin, my friend, you are partly right." Hunter said, "But we weren't prepared for you to find out this way."

"What do you mean, partly right?" Kevin asked.

Kevin was now looking behind at Vicky and back at Hunter. "What are you saying?" he said in a concerned voice.

Vicky walked around the couch and took a seat next to Kevin. "Hunter and I have been discussing and including you in our little group." She said as she took his right hand in hers.

"But there is more to it. We will not only track those who abducted Shay but as many others as possible. And stop them before they do it to someone else." She said, looking Kevin in the eyes.

Hunter had walked to the bar and got three beers out of the cooler. He walked up to Kevin and handed one to him and the other the Vicky.

"Let us fill you in on more of what we have planned." Hunter said.

The three sat there for well over an hour, talking about the Omega Group, their plans, and each person's roles in the group.

Chapter Six

COMING TOGETHER

At about 10:30 Saturday morning, a black SUV with four people pulled up outside a hangar at Coulter Airfield. The airfield was just a few miles between the Vickers Ranch and College Station.

When the SUV stopped, the four passengers, Vicky, Hunter, Kevin, and Raymond, got out and proceeded into the building.

A few feet inside the building, they found Tony looking out through the hanger door.

"Where is Jack?" Vicky asked.

"He's walking around inside the building somewhere, checking it out." replied Tony, motioning toward the back with his head.

"Here I am." Came a voice from inside one of the rooms. "I was just checking things out. You have a lot of work to do to make this place livable." Jack said.

"Well, that's one of the reasons we are all here today. I wanted everyone to meet and get to know one another." She added, "Since we are all in this together."

"Let's all walk over to the table here and start introducing ourselves, and we'll go over some blueprints of what we have in mind for this place." Hunter said as he started walking over to the table, which consisted of a four by 8-foot sheet of plywood sitting on top of two sawhorses. Each of them took a position around the edge of the table.

Hunter started, "I think everyone has met me and knows a little about me. You'll learn more about me and the others as time goes on. Right now, this is just a short introduction."

"You've all met me and figured out I'm the one who thought this up. But with everyone's input, it will be even better than I had hoped. This is not all of it, and we will keep adding resources to the group as the need arises. Some will be brought in as permanent members of the group, and others will be used as needed as outside resources." Vicky said.

"You've all met Kevin." Vicky started when Jack stepped in.

"Yes, the butler dude." Jack said with a smile.

When Hunter heard this, he broke out into a hoarse, raspy laugh that caused him to double over. He held up his hand as if to say. I'm OK. Just give me a second. "I prefer chauffeur." He said, finally recovering from his laugh as he wiped the tears from his eyes.

Hunter looked over at Kevin, whose face had turned red with anger. Kevin looked over at Hunter and then over at Jack. Jack had already turned away from the group in an attempt to hide his laughter. Raymond looked down at the ground, not wanting to make eye contact with anyone.

"OK! Let's put this to rest. Kevin will be our pilot, and he's also my right-hand man and unofficial bodyguard. He gets me where I need to be safely and on time, and unless you guys want to walk or take a bus to your assignment, you'll start giving Kevin a lot more respect." Vicky said in a stern voice.

"We are all in this together. Each of us will play an equal but different role in this group. Without each other, we will not succeed. One person is no more important than the others. Do I make myself clear?" She said, showing a little anger.

She looked at each person one by one, as each one nodded in agreement. When she looked at Hunter, he still had a big grin on his face.

"HUNTER! Did I make myself clear?"

"Yes, ma'am. Sorry." Hunter said.

"With your permission, Hunter, we'll continue." She said.

"OK, everyone has met me, Kevin, and unfortunately, this asshole standing here," she said, referring to Hunter.

"Raymond, introduce yourself."

"I'm Raymond Ray, the IT guy. You can call me Ray, or some people call me RayRay."

"Hi, I'm Jack Davidson. I guess I'm the John Wick of the group. I guess you can call me Jack."

Everyone looked over to Tony. He was standing there with his sunglasses on, and hat pulled down low on his face. "My name is Tony James, Jack is my nephew, and I currently work for the FBI in their sex trafficking unit. I guess you can call me Tony."

Ray looked closely at Tony, "Wait a second, I didn't recognize you with the hat and glasses on. You're the fed that arrested me!" Ray said, now pointing his finger at Tony.

"That'll be me, kid, and you're welcome. But I wasn't working in sex trafficking then." Tony replied as he pulled his sunglasses down lower on his nose and looked over the top of them.

"OK." Vicky said, "Let's keep moving on to our next topic. We'll have time to get to know each other back at the ranch. I'm having dinner catered for us, so we'll get to know each other better. OK?"

Everyone agreed and put their issues aside for the time being as Vicky unrolled a large blueprint of the building they were standing in.

"Hunter will take you through the layout. Later we'll all walk the building and see everything in person."

"OK, guys, this is it." Hunter started as everyone looked at the blueprint. "We are standing where the Sovereign jet will be parked, and it is two floors high. Right here in the corner is where Kevin will keep his pilot's gear."

"Moving over to the room on the right and through the double doors, there is a storage area, which takes up the first and second floors above. It has access to the stairs leading up to the second-floor storage."

"Leading out the other side is a door that opens into the hallway and to a larger open area in the back."

"On the other side of the hallway is our meeting and planning area where we'll meet, plan and talk about our missions."

"Behind the meeting room is the armory and safe room. It's lined with bulletproof material, and entry is through a heavily reinforced door. Passing through the armory to the back side, you will notice a long room running about 300 feet, roughly the length of the building. This is the practice range, with a lower and upper floor platform to shoot from. Any long-range shooting will take place at my outdoor firing range further north past the ranch."

"The communications area and some workspaces are on the second floor. Ray, you'll build the Omega computer and tracking systems here. You'll have an area for you to build and maintain our electronic equipment, and as you see, across from there, you'll have access to the second-floor storage room."

"Any questions?" Hunter ended, looking at each person standing around the table.

"I want you to walk around and see what we have completed to this point and what other things you might see and think of." Vicky added.

She went on to say, "Oh, and just to let you guys know, if for some reason things go south on us, Ray will be setting up a retirement account for each member of the group. It's not for our normal operating expenses. That's in another account. These individual offshore accounts should keep you happy for many years."

"By the way," Hunter piped in, "this money is not your play money to use right now. And if you decide to leave the group without letting Vicky know or if you go AWOL, you don't get the money."

"You'll have any expenses you incur while with the group covered. That doesn't mean that you can go out and buy a brand-new Corvette or anything like that. We still must maintain a low-key lifestyle. We can't draw attention to ourselves." She added to what Hunter said.

"Vicky has given me a list of account numbers. We'll say, from questionable businesses. These funds will be used to help fund the Omega Group and your retirement plans." Ray said.

"Can any of this money be traced back to us?" Tony asked.

"Why, mister FBI man, you didn't have a problem with it when it was me, and you put those handcuffs on me. Are you afraid some mob or cartel guy will show up at your door and want their money back?" Ray said, looking at Tony.

"Sorry, Ray, I was just doing my job." Tony replied.

Vicky stepped in, saying, "No one will find out. Let's put the past in the past and move on. We have a lot of work to do."

"OK, let's spend some time looking the place over, and we'll meet back at the ranch in about an hour. We can eat and hang out around the pool and get to know more about each other." Hunter said.

About an hour later, all six arrived at the Vickers ranch. Once they got out of their cars, Vicky told them to head to the pool and that the food and drinks were waiting on them. Everyone but Vicky went around the side of the house to the pool. She went inside to put her notes and blueprints away in her office.

As she entered, she came to a dead stop. She dropped her notes and blueprints on the floor, with the papers going everywhere. Out of the darkness stepped a figure. Seeing the person, Vicky let out a scream. Then all of a sudden, the person started charging toward Vicky and grabbed her around the waist.

"AUNT VICKY!" Came a cry, "I thought I was going to miss you."

Vicky squeezed her niece hard in a bear hug. "Shay, what in the hell are you doing here? Why didn't you tell me you were coming?"

"It was a last-minute thing. I've only got a 24-hour leave and wanted to tell you something in person."

After stepping back, Vicky saw Shay standing there in her Marine uniform. "Well, what is it, and how long will you be here?"

"Well, I was about to leave. I was so afraid I had missed you. I got here about 3 hours ago."

"My four years are up with the Marines in a couple of weeks, and I'm not going to re-up." Shay said excitedly. "I wanted to tell you in person and to let you know to get my old room ready. I'M COMING HOME!"

They both screamed and hugged each other again.

Shay walks over to the window, "I've got a flight out of Houston in 3 hours, so I've got to leave. Who are the guys out at the pool? I recognize Kevin and Hunter, but who are the others?"

"Just some friends, no one really important." Vicky said. "You want to meet them?"

"No." Shay said, "Some other time, maybe. I've got to go."

They both hugged each other for a long time. "Tell Hunter and Kevin I'll be home in a month and ready to jump back into my training." Shay said as she opened the door.

She turned and smiled, "Love you, Aunt Vicky. See you in a month."

"Love you more." Vicky said as Shay closed the door behind her.

Vicky was crying and trying to pick up the papers that were all over the floor.

"What is going on? Why are you crying, and why are all the papers all over the floor?" Hunter asked as he entered the room through the kitchen.

"Shay!" she said to Hunter, who was now holding Vicky's shoulders in both hands.

"What about Shay? Is she alright?" Hunter said, now starting to panic.

"Yes, she's fine. She just left." She said as Hunter walked over to the window to see a car pulling out onto the street.

"Why didn't she come and say hello?" he asked, now all confused.

"She had been here all morning and had to get to the airport for her flight."

"Well, what did she say?" he asked.

"She told me that she was coming home in a couple of weeks and that she was getting out of the Marines." Vicky said as she wiped the tears rolling down her face. "She told me to tell you to get her room ready and that she's ready to jump back into her training."

"Well, I'll warn Stan in a couple of days that Shay's coming back."

"You get yourself together and cleaned up. I'll pick this mess up and let Kevin know. I guess I should tell Tony too. I know it's been a while, but he needs to know. They'll meet sooner or later. Did Shay see Tony?"

"Yes, she saw Tony, but I don't think she recognized him." She said, "But we'll cross that bridge when we come to it. I just hope seeing Tony doesn't bring up bad memories from when she was abducted."

"Shay's a strong woman. She'll handle it. Besides, she'll work out any stress at the gym. I feel sorry for whoever is on the receiving end." Hunter said with a smile.

Hunter walked over and put his arm around Vicky as she stared out the window.

"You know Vicky," Hunter said slowly, "the group could use her."

Vicky pushed Hunter away and raised her hand towards him, trying to get him to stop talking.

"STOP! Hunter, I don't want to talk about it right now. Just let me enjoy the moment. I don't want to think about throwing her into the middle of this!"

"I know Vicky, but you're not going to be able to keep it from her. She's a very smart woman, and it will not take her long to figure it out."

"I know, Hunter. I'll deal with that when the time comes. But for now, let's get out with the team, relax, and enjoy ourselves too."

Hunter and Vicky soon joined the party. The team was starting to come together. Everyone was laughing, joking around, eating and drinking. Everyone was having a great time.

Even Ray and Tony seemed to have put things behind them.

Jack and Kevin were sitting by the pool, drinking and having fun. Everything seemed to be coming together.

After another hour or so, Vicky's phone rang. She stepped away from the group and walked over toward the barn.

"Hello, Ms. Vickers. This is Jim Appleton. How are you doing this afternoon? I hope I didn't disturb you."

Jim was one of the private investigators working at VPI. Hunter had asked him to look into something for her.

"We've looked into the subject and have confirmed everything. You want me to email you the file?"

"No. Hunter will pick it up Monday. No rush, thank you, enjoy the rest of your weekend."

She put away her phone and rejoined the others by the pool.

Hunter walked up and said, "Is everything OK? I saw you over near the barn talking on the phone."

"Yes, it was Jim Appleton. He called to tell me that they've finished the verification on the guy you asked them to look into the week before last."

"What did Jim say?" he asked.

"Well, it looks like Omega has their first target." She said with a blank look on her face.

Looking into his face, she said, "Here we go. There's no turning back after this."

"You ready for this?" he asked.

"It'll be a good test run for the team. If we can't handle this two-bit pimp and pusher, we may as well close up shop now." She replied.

"When do we tell the others?" Hunter said with a hint of excitement in his voice.

"Go ahead and tell them to come into the den. We'll tell them about it and see if anyone has cold feet. I'll go up and get my file on the guy and meet you in the den."

Hunter took a deep breath and said, "Let's do it."

Vicky went into the house and headed up to her office.

"Hey guys, let's head inside to the den. We're going to have a short meeting. Vicky and I have something to run by the team." Hunter said as he turned towards the house and entered the side door into the den.

The team slowly moved into the den, continuing their conversations from outside.

After about 5 minutes, Vicky came down the stairs from her second-floor office. Turning to Hunter, she asked, "Do we have everyone?"

He looked around briefly and nodded his head.

"OK, guys," She started, "we have our first job at Omega Group."

"But we haven't even gotten anything finished, and our computer system isn't close to being up to speed." Ray said as he looked around at the others.

"What kind of job are you talking about?" Tony asked.

"One that we have been put together for." Hunter replied.

"OK, guys, here it is. Several weeks ago, I heard that a two-bit pimp and drug dealer was trying to take over a small town in south Florida." She began as everyone started to settle into their seats.

"The local town can't handle the problem. And it's too small for the state authorities to worry about." Vicky said with a touch of anger in her voice.

"I had Hunter send the Vickers PI team down to check things out. The residents think they are there to help find a missing girl from the local area that this guy may have taken."

"Why can't the locals or the FBI do anything about him? Taking the girl, isn't that kidnapping?" Kevin said as he looked over towards Tony.

"The girl is eighteen, so the local police and FBI really can't move on anything at this point. Besides, she would soon fall through the cracks of the legal system and be totally forgotten." Vicky said as she passed a file out with pictures of the target and the missing girl, along with notes from Vickers PI.

"I saw the parents on the national news a few weeks back, pleading for her safe return. The authorities there say that because she's considered an adult, there's not much they can do." She said now with some emotion in her voice.

"I, we," Vicky started pointing at each person sitting there, "can't let this slip by and happen."

"This will be a good test run for our new group." Hunter said, "Small enough target as to not attract much attention and something to allow us to see if we have the guts to pull it off."

"We'll also be able to see what direction we need to go and what resources we'll need in the future." She added to what Hunter was saying.

"If you open your file, you'll see a picture of Sara Ingram. She's the missing 18-year-old that VPI has confirmed is in the target's custody. And the next picture is the target, Derick. We have no last name. He goes by the street name of Banger." Hunter read.

"I see he has an associate by the name of Jimmy Brown, but not much on him." Tony inquired.

"None at this time. Our guys at VPI are still set up down the street from their hangout. They haven't been able to get any information on Jimmy yet." Hunter said.

"The way I see it, Jack and Hunter will take down the target. Kevin, you'll fly them into an airport about 200 miles away. The three of you will drive down to the target area. Kevin, you'll be the eyes on the ground and will keep an eye out on the comings and goings of the target. You'll also monitor the local police frequency for any calls or reports in the area." Vicky said, now in a more serious tone.

"Any questions so far?" Hunter asked.

"Yes, when you say, take down. Exactly what are you saying?" asked Jack.

Everyone looked over at Jack and then at Hunter.

"Well, kid, you wanted to be the John Wick of the group, so there you have it. Do you still have the balls, or do you want to back out? Now's the time if any of you are getting cold feet." Hunter said.

"To make sure we are all on the same page." Ray said, "You want Jack to kill this Derick guy?"

Hunter took a couple of steps in Ray's direction. "Yes, kill, execute, terminate, call it whatever you want." Hunter cocked his head slightly and nodded. "You have a problem? If so, you know our deal."

"NO! I'm good. Things are moving faster than I expected. What will be my role in the execution?" Ray asked with a nervous tone in his voice.

"You'll handle any communications between the strike team and here. Ray, Tony, and I will monitor everything at the ranch." Vicky said, looking at each team member to see any reaction they might have.

"Tony, do you have any questions?" Hunter asked.

"No. I can stay here and help with the planning and anything the local authorities may throw our way."

"Yes, we don't want an FBI agent to be seen in the area during our little outing." Vicky commented.

"Any more questions?" Hunter looked at each of them. "If not, we have two weeks to get up to speed and train for this, so let's put our heads together as a team and work out all the details."

"Ray, you get whatever you think we'll need regarding communications to keep in contact with Jack, Kevin, and myself."

"Tony, I want you to work with Kevin on a plan for surveillance between now and when we leave. You won't be going with us. You'll be staying here at the ranch, helping Ray."

"Jack and I will spend all our time at the range getting ready. Tony, I'll need your input also at the range, helping get Jack ready."

"If you guys don't have any other questions, let's meet back here in four days with what you got so far." With that said, Hunter ended the meeting.

As everyone started to leave, Vicky said, "If you have any questions or needs, call as soon as you can. Don't wait."

Jack was looking out the window deep in thought, not noticing, as Hunter approached him.

"You up to this kid?" Hunter said, now standing next to Jack at the window.

"I think so."

"There is no 'I think so,' you're either ready or you're not. If you don't think you can pull the trigger, I need to know right now." Hunter said in his raspy voice. "Look, I know you shot and killed your stepfather, but this is different."

"How's that?" Jack said, turning and looking at Hunter.

"You had built up anger and revenge in your mind when you killed your stepfather." Hunter said, "This scum bag is different. You've never met him, and he's never done anything to you. This is going to be a cold kill. That's where it's different."

"I can't."

"Good. I'm going to run over to the range and pick up the rifle you'll be using. I will bring it back here this afternoon for you to get accustomed to it. Hell, take it out back and run some rounds through it. Starting tomorrow, you'll be spending several hours a day at the range, getting ready."

The following day, Tony, Ray, and Kevin started planning their part of the mission while Vicky was up in her office on the phone getting more updates from her two private investigators on the ground in Florida.

Jack showed up at the range early the following day, carrying the H&K MR762A1 chambered in .308 that Hunter had given him the day before. This rifle was identical to the military's long-range system designated for its marksmen.

"Nice rifle." Jack said, "I was messing with it last night for several hours after you dropped it off."

Hunter held out a box for Jack to take, "Here's a suppressor for it. I want you to practice with it on." Hunter said, "This is the setup you'll have for the target. You need to be 100% dead on that day, and you only have two weeks to get ready."

Jack put his gun bag containing the H&K on the shooting table and looked up at Hunter, "I'll be ready. When I competed, I've taken several shots past 600 and 800 yards."

"But those were paper targets. This is going to be a live, flesh and blood person you're going to be shooting, not paper. Believe me, it's different." Hunter said as he pointed at two targets out in the distance.

"There are your targets, the first at 100 yards and the other at 200 yards. Here's a case of 300 rounds of .308 ammo." He said as he placed the box next to Jack.

"300 is all I got to practice with for the next two weeks?" Jack asked.

"No, kid, this is your ammo for today. You'll get another 300 tomorrow and another 300 the next day and so forth until we leave."

"You know it's supposed to be raining all day tomorrow, right?" Jack said as Hunter was walking away.

Hunter stopped and turned halfway, facing Jack. He looked up at the sky and back at Jack. "Guess you'll be getting wet. Just keep the gun and scope dry, and make sure you clean it after you are finished."

"Oh, and tomorrow I want all the shots cold bore shots. Take three shots maximum, and then wait five mins before you shoot the next three."

The term "cold bore" shot is usually associated with a sniper rifle, and in simple terms, it means the first shot to come out of a clean barrel of a rifle. After the first shot, the barrel has residue in it, and the heat from the round has caused the inside of the barrel to heat up and expand a little. This can affect the trajectory of the next shot at long distance.

Each day Jack and Hunter were out there just after daylight, and each day Hunter would throw Jack a new curve. One day the targets would be set at one location, and the next day Hunter had moved them somewhere else during the night.

During the second week, Hunter had Jack shooting from on top of a hill overlooking the targets.

After a couple of days, Hunter joined Jack next to him as his spotter. He would look through the spotting scope and have Jack adjust his aim based on a different target that he had picked out.

Vicky was handling the coordination of communications and transportation, leaving the shooting training to Hunter and Tony.

It was three days before they launched their first operation. Vicky had called them all together back at the ranch to go over the plan and update the group on the latest reconnaissance from Vickers Private Investigators.

Vicky told Ray to turn one of the rooms down the hallway from her office into a temporary command center. Ray had set up a couple of whiteboards, large TV monitors on the wall, and three computer workstations. He had also had a station set up to monitor the local EMS and police in the Florida area where Jack, Hunter, and Kevin were going.

Kevin made the travel arrangements for the three of them. He had planned on flying them down to the airport in Orlando, and from there, they would drive for about three hours to the target location.

Tony was helping Kevin with the surveillance details and giving him some quick pointers on how to keep a low profile in the area.

They were finally coming together as a tight team. Surprisingly, Tony and Ray, with their past history together, started becoming close friends.

Vicky was somewhat shocked and pleased at how this small group of people from totally different backgrounds and histories were coming together so well.

Most of the group was sitting around the table, looking over their notes, waiting for Hunter and Jack to arrive.

After a few minutes, Hunter came walking in, followed by Jack about 10 feet behind.

"Sorry, we're late. I had to make a stop on the way over here." Hunter said as he entered the makeshift command center.

"Well, if it isn't the Skipper and Gilligan, did you two get lost again?" Kevin said with a smile.

Hunter didn't even acknowledge the comment and took a seat next to Tony.

As Jack entered, he nodded at everyone and took a seat next to Ray. Hearing Kevin's comment, as he looked around at all the new stuff, he said, "No, we weren't lost. We had to make a stop by the store and pick up some extra batteries for our equipment."

Hunter turned toward Kevin with his head down slightly, smiled, and shook his head. Kevin was doing all he could to keep from laughing out loud. Tony just leaned back in his chair. He sat there and closed his eyes, and smiled.

Vicky said, "OK, guys, let's get down to business. We've got a lot to go over, Kevin. You start."

As Kevin started talking about his plans to get down to Orlando, Ray put up on the three monitors mounted on the wall a picture of the Skipper and Gilligan from the old TV series Gilligan's Island.

The room all broke down into laughter, and Jack looked around as if he didn't know who they were and why everyone was laughing.

Hunter made an open hand gesture toward one of the large screens on the wall, "I am not that fat." referring to the character who played the Skipper on the TV show.

Jack finally caught on to what was taking place and, in protest, exclaimed, "NO Way, nope, nada, I'm out of here, screw that."

"Well, you wanted a code name, kid." Tony said as he pointed up at the screen, "There you have it ...Gilligan."

Jack continued his protest as Vicky tried to get the team back on topic. Each person went over the role they were to have in the mission while Jack sat there slowly, shaking his head in protest.

The day finally arrived. Kevin, Jack, and Hunter were on the ground in Orlando and heading to their target. The others were all busy at Omega Command, taking care of any last-minute details. Vicky was running from her office to the command post and back again. Tony and Ray were in front of their computers, monitoring the local action and the team, which was just minutes out.

Vicky had asked her VPI investigators to return home the day before. They had been sent there to find a made-up client's" missing daughter, who they believed was being held by the Banger, in the building that they were sent to observe. She informed them that the client had received their information.

Hunter and Jack would set up in the same room that the two investigators had occupied the previous several weeks.

Kevin would be set up in an old white painter's panel van that they had bought off the internet the week before. The van had splatters of paint on the sides and several ladders strapped down on the top. Kevin would sit in the back of the van and monitor the radios and hidden cameras that were set on top of the van.

Kevin was parked about 100 feet down the street from the building where the pimp kept his girls and drugs.

Derick's street name was Banger. He got his nickname from banging his girls around if they didn't do as he said. He used some of the local teens to run his drugs and his other side jobs.

He was only about 5 foot 6 inches tall but made up for his short stature with his anger and brutality. If one of his followers or girls got out of line, they would end up with their throats slashed or be found dead from a drug overdose.

Derick had an associate named Jimmy Brown. His role was to babysit the merchandise when Derick wasn't around mostly and to be his errand boy. Jimmy was tall and very slender and seemed to be terrified of Derick.

The VPI investigators noted several customers coming in and out of the building at all hours of the day and night. They had also observed 6 different girls and two boys, all looking to be under the age of 18, each taking turns standing outside the building at some point in time.

Whenever a potential customer would walk up, the one standing outside would escort that person inside, and another one of the young sex slaves would take their place outside.

The VPI team also reported that another person had come to the building a few times. He was identified as Craig, but no last name was ever found on him. His relationship was not totally known to the group.

The street ran north and south in front of the building where Derick had set up his sex slave ring. The street dead-ended into two other streets, both running east and west.

Kevin set up down the street with the van on the north side looking south while Hunter and Jack were up in a room on the eighth floor of a building about 200 yards in the other direction looking north.

Ray had provided the three men with earbuds that were connected to a transmitter linked to the internet. This provided constant communication between the three of them and with the team back at the command center. Vicky and the others could also watch through the cameras mounted on top of the van that Kevin was in.

The building that Jack and Hunter positioned themselves in sat right across from the intersection. This gave them a direct view of the building that Derick was in on the right side, and they could also see the van where Kevin was sitting.

Kevin had a clear view of the front of Derick's building and could see the window that Jack and Hunter were looking out of.

Jack and Hunter kept the lights out in the room, and the curtains pulled slightly. They had hung a black sheer curtain so that no one looking up could see them inside. Jack had his rifle set up on top of a table, and he sat in a chair behind it. This gave him a clear shot covering several yards on either side of the entrance to Derick's building.

Now it was a waiting game, with time on Derick's side. In a few hours, darkness would start falling across the buildings as night approached. There were very few streetlights along the street, making a nighttime shot even more difficult.

"Hold on." Kevin said, "I've got someone standing in the doorway. It's Derick. He's talking to someone on the phone."

"Are you sure?" Hunter said.

"Ray, can you zoom in on him?" Vicky asked.

"Sure thing." Ray replied as he took control of the camera mounted on top of the van.

"That's him." Vicky said with some excitement in her voice.

Hunter had been standing behind Jack, looking through a spotter's scope, "Jack, you got a clear shot?" he asked.

"Negative." Jack said. Jack had already flipped off the safety of his H&K MR762A1. Jack was using a Leupold 3-9 VX-R Patrol Scope on top of the rifle and had it already sighted in for the correct distance. The weapon also had a suppressor attached to cut down on as much of the sound from the rifle shot as possible.

Jack's heart was beating fast, and he was about to hyperventilate. "Try and calm down kid." Said Hunter, "Slow, deep breaths. You'll be fine."

"He stepped back inside." Kevin said in a very disappointed tone.

"OK, that was a good dry run, so next time Jack, you will be ready." Tony said over the communications set.

About 30 minutes later, a car pulled up just past the entry of the building.

"OK, guys, we just had that Craig dude pull up in a red Ford pickup, and it looks like he's got someone in the truck with him. I don't have a good view to tell who it is." Kevin said. "Hold on a second. He's on the phone talking to someone."

"Everyone hold until we have identified all the players." Vicky said.

"Copy." Jack replied.

"OK, he's getting out of the truck and walking over to the passenger's side door." Kevin said.

When the truck door opened, a young girl of about thirteen slid out onto the sidewalk. The guy took his hand and grabbed her around the neck from behind. He started leading her from the truck towards the door of the building.

Suddenly, the two stopped, and out walked Derick onto the sidewalk. The man and little girl stood there about 15 feet from the door. Derick walked up to the two and looked down at the little girl. He took her face with his hand and moved it side to side as if he was inspecting some animal for quality before he purchased it.

"I've got a clear shot." Jack said.

"Negative." Hunter replied, "The girl is too close."

The two men talked for a few minutes while Derick held onto the young girl's arm. He motioned and called out to someone standing in the doorway.

A young girl that looked to be about 15, dressed in old torn clothes, came out and took the new girl by the arm, and led her inside.

The two men walked slowly down towards Craig's truck, talking as they walked.

"Take the shot." Kevin said.

"Here's your shot." Tony shouted out.

Jack aimed squarely at Derick's back as the two stopped next to Craig's truck.

Vicky now joins in with the encouragement, "Take your time, Jack. Breathe in slowly."

Jack was getting more and more stressed with all the talking going on from the others. "Will you guys get out of my head!" He said as he jerked the earpiece out of his ear.

"Guys, everyone, shut up. You're getting on Jack's nerves. Let me talk to him. Everyone else, keep quiet." Hunter said as he gently patted Jack on the shoulder.

"Take your time, Jack. Remember what we talked about, slow your breathing down. Close your eyes for a second and clear your head." Hunter said quietly.

The two men had just finished their conversation when Derick turned and slowly started back to the building.

"I've got a clear body shot." Jack said.

Hunter stood there looking through the spotting scope. "Jack, don't shoot at the body."

This caused Jack to relax a little, and he looked slightly up at Hunter but couldn't see him standing behind him.

"You see the second button-down from the top of his shirt?" Hunter asked.

Jack turned his attention back to the scope on the rifle, "Yes." He replied softly.

"Shoot the button." Hunter said, "Remember, aim small, miss small."

Jack looked through his scope and zeroed in on the button on the shirt and not on the entire chest of the man.

Jack softly squeezed the trigger, and the gun kicked. There was a pop and a flash out of the end of the barrel as the .308 caliber projectile came screaming out of the end of the barrel at over 2,500 feet per second.

Everyone back at the command center was holding their breath. They could hear the muffled shot over their speaker but didn't hear anything else.

Finally, after what seemed like an eternity, they heard the voice of Hunter, "Target down." He said in a somber voice.

"Confirm, Target down." Came Kevin's reply, "We've also got a rabbit."

As soon as Craig saw Derick hit the ground, he knew what had happened. Even though he didn't hear the shot, he saw the blood pooling around Derick's body as he lay there on the sidewalk. His legs were still twitching as the blood and life drained out of him.

Craig opened the door to his truck and drove off, heading right for the building Jack and Hunter were in.

"I've got him sighted. You want me to take the shot." Jack asked hurriedly.

"NO!" screamed Vicky, but she didn't know that Jack had taken his earpiece out.

Hunter realized this and grabbed Jack by the shoulder, saying, "Stand down. Hold!"

"We don't know his involvement in this, so don't shoot!" Vicky was still screaming over the radio, still not knowing that Jack couldn't hear her.

"I've got his tag number." Kevin said.

"We can track him down later. Let's vet him first." Vicky replied, "You guys pack it up and head home. We'll meet tomorrow and debrief everyone."

Jack and Hunter started packing up their equipment and heading out the door to meet Kevin on the street below.

As Kevin started to pull off to meet Jack and Hunter, he saw Jimmy Brown slowly walk out the door. He glanced down at the body of his boss lying in a pool of blood and turned, and started walking away.

Kevin called out, "Guys. Jimmy just exited the building and saw his boss laid out on the sidewalk. He's now walking in your direction."

Hunter and Jack hurried down the stairs trying to get to the street and meet Kevin.

"Copy that. Keep us posted on his location." Hunter said as they hit the bottom level.

"He's crossing the intersection now and will be in front of your location in about 15 seconds." Kevin said, "I'm in the van, about 15 feet behind him. He hasn't noticed me following him."

Jack and Hunter exited the building into an alleyway and headed towards the main street.

"We're in the alley next to the building." Hunter said as he and Jack stood there in the shadows.

"He's walking towards you about 10 feet away." Kevin said as he pulled onto the main street behind Jimmy, heading towards the alley.

"Kevin, pull up in front of the alley. We'll grab Jimmy when he gets to us and throw him inside."

As the Van pulled up, Hunter grabbed Jimmy as Jack opened the van's side door. Once all three were safely inside, the white van slowly drove off.

There were only a couple of other people on the street, and no one paid any attention to what had just happened. It was just another day in that part of town.

"Vicky, we've got Jimmy in the van. What do you want us to do with him?" Hunter asked, now out of breath.

"Well, this wasn't in the plans." Vicky hesitated before continuing, "Bring him back with you."

"Guess we can add kidnapping to our resume now." Tony said.

"Ray, make the call to the local authorities and inform them about the kids inside the basement of the building. I'm sure by now they've received calls about a body on the sidewalk outside." Vicky said as she looked over at Ray.

"I'm not so sure." Tony said, "In that area, people would just step over their bodies and keep going. I'm sure some of the locals have already gone through his pockets and taken anything of value."

Jimmy never spoke a word in the van as they drove back to the airport.

As they arrived back at the ranch, Vicky met the three and their new captive.

"Keep him tied up and gagged and put him in one of the spare ranch houses. The airport location will be finished in two days. We can keep him here until then." Vicky said in a somber voice.

"What are we going to do with him? We've not talked about having a prisoner yet." Hunter replied.

Vicky looked over at Hunter, "No, but we have one now."

Chapter Seven

Jack Meets Shay

They had moved Jimmy Brown from the ranch to one of the rooms at the new Omega Headquarters.

It only took a few days of talking to him before he started spilling his guts. Jimmy's loyalty was to himself and his survival.

He told them about Craig, the Weasel, as he called him. He talked about how Derick was a small-time operator and that he could help them find bigger fish.

He talked about a much larger operation located in New Orleans. He explained how Craig was the middleman of the sex trade between Derick and the operation in New Orleans and how it was run by two guys named Rick and a big guy named Mad Dog.

This operation had more guards and more sex slaves and was yet just another stepping stone to an even bigger operation.

After getting all the information they could from Jimmy, the question was, what now?

Hunter went into Vicky's office and sat down on the couch. Vicky was working on some issues at Vickers International that she had neglected for the past several weeks.

After sitting there for a couple of minutes, Hunter said, "We've got all the information we're going to get out of Jimmy. What are we going to do with him now?"

"I don't know, that's a good question." Vicky said, looking up from her computer. "We can't just turn him loose, and we don't need to kill him."

"I was thinking. He's been blindfolded ever since we took him. He can't identify anyone or tell anyone where he's been held, for that matter." Hunter said.

"And what do you propose?" she asked.

"What if we fly him up north somewhere and dump him at some fleabag hotel?" Hunter replied.

"Sounds better than killing him. Why don't you get Kevin, and you two do that? Oh, and take Jack along too."

"Ok, I'll work out the details with Kevin, and we'll do it tomorrow."

Vicky smiled, "Good, that'll be one less problem we have to worry about. And let's plan this prisoner thing out a little more before we do this again."

"Yes, ma'am."

Jimmy was flown up to Nevada the next day and dropped off at a local motel. The three were back at the ranch later that evening.

Earlier that morning, while the three were dropping their prisoner off, Shay walked into Vicky's office.

Shay had returned from serving in the Marines for a few weeks and jumped right back into her training routine down at Stan Rosberg's Gym.

"Aunt Vicky, can we talk?" Shay asked as she entered the room.

"Sure, what do you need, Shay?"

"Since you've taken me in after my parents' death, we have been totally upfront and honest with each other."

Vicky closed her computer so that she could give Shay her undivided attention.

"Let's sit over on the couch." Vicky said, and the two of them proceeded over and sat down next to each other.

"What's on your mind?" Vicky was afraid to ask.

"I feel like you and Hunter have been keeping something from me." Shay started.

"Like what?"

"Well, like Tony, who has been hanging around here every now and then. I know who he is."

"Who is he?" Vicky asked, fearing the answer.

"You know good and well who he is! He's one of the FBI agents who worked on my adduction!" Shay said with irritation.

"And the other two. Ray and Jack, they are in and out all the time. And everyone stops talking whenever I walk into the room."

"I was up late a few days ago, and I saw Kevin, Hunter, and Jack taking this other person that was blindfolded somewhere. WHAT IN THE HELL IS GOING ON, Aunt Vicky!"

Vicky closed her eyes and sat back on the couch, not wanting to look at Shay.

"Hunter said this was going to happen, but I was hoping that it would be much longer before I had to tell you."

"Tell me what?" Shay said, with tears running down her face.

Vicky turned and took both of Shay's hands in hers, "Ok, let me tell you what's going on..."

The two sat for the next few hours, discussing what happened and the Omega Group. Shay took it all in, and every now and then, she would get up and pace the room and sit back down next to Vicky. Vicky told her everything and answered all her questions.

Shay stood and walked over to the window, "When were you going to include me in this Omega Group that you've hidden from me?"

"I wanted to several times, but I was afraid that you would get hurt, and I could never forgive myself." Vicky said as she walked over next to Shay, looking out the window and putting her arm around her.

"I wanted to, but I also wanted to keep you safe." Vicky said as she squeezed Shay's shoulder.

"Aunt Vicky, you know I'm an adult and can take care of myself." Shay said as she looked up at Vicky. They both were now crying.

"I know, I know." Vicky said, "I'll get the team together, and you can meet them tomorrow."

"I'm supposed to be at the gym tomorrow."

"Ok, I'll have them come by the gym, and you can meet them there. I'll have Hunter make up some excuse to tell Stan." Vicky said.

"So, Stan doesn't know about the group?"

Vicky took a long breath and said, "No, not yet."

When Hunter and the others returned, Vicky told Hunter about her and Shay's conversation. Hunter reminded her that he had told her they would have to tell Shay sooner or later.

"Well, this will give us a good opportunity to see how Jack can handle himself, one on one, all close up and personal." Hunter said with a sly smile on his face.

"And this will give me an excuse to tell Stan why we're all meeting at the gym. We can tell Stan that Jack's going to be Shay's new sparring partner."

"She'll kill him. You know she'll take it out on him, don't you?" Vicky said as she turned and looked at him.

"I'll talk to her before then." He replied.

Hunter called everyone and told them to meet at Stan's Gym the following day. He had told Jack that he wanted him to spar with Shay and start taking defensive training at Stan's place.

Jack had met Shay several times at the ranch but never anything formal. For the most part, she had kept to herself since returning from the Marines.

Kevin, Hunter, and Jack had been back from Florida only a few days when Hunter told Jack about the meeting at the gym. Hunter would meet him and Tony there at 8 a.m. sharp the following day.

Hunter and Stan were standing next to one of the boxing rings located inside Stan's training school.

"What's bothering Shay this morning?" Stan asked.

"She and Vicky sort of got into it yesterday." Hunter replied.

Stan looked over at Shay, "I can tell something is eating at her."

"She'll be fine." Hunter said.

They both turned as they heard Tony enter through the front door.

Hunter asked, "Where's your boy Jack? Did he get cold feet?" he said with a smile and looked over at Stan.

"No, he stopped next door to get himself a Slurpee before he came in." Tony said as he approached the other two men and shook their hands.

Shay was already in the ring doing some stretching before having the match with Jack. She was still fuming about the conversation from the day before with her aunt Vicky.

Stan had closed the school that morning so that they could meet in private.

A few minutes later, Jack walked in with his Slurpee in one hand, sucking on a straw. "Sorry guys, I wanted to get me a drink. I love these things." Jack reached out and shook both guys' hands, and dropped his bag on the ground.

Shay didn't even look over at him as he took a few stretches, still holding his Slurpee in one hand before getting into the ring.

Jack climbed into the ring next to where the three guys were standing. "So, what are the rules?" Jack asked.

Hunter looked at Jack and said, "Rules? Let's just play it by ear, kid. We're here to see how the two of you are together. We'll see if there are any areas that we need to work on."

"How we work together. Sort of like a date." Jack said with a smile.

"Don't know what kind of dates you've been on in the past, but we'll see." Stan added.

Tony looked at Jack and said, "Don't hurt her, Jack. You don't want to start off on the wrong foot with her." Jack walked toward Shay with his Slurpee still in his hand.

Tony looked at the other two guys and said, "I was a Golden Glove boxer in high school, and I was on the FBI boxing team. I taught Jack everything I know."

"Thanks for the heads up." Stan replied.

Shay stood in the middle of the ring with both hands on her hips as Jack walked up to her, still sipping on his Slurpee.

Stan called over to the two of them, "Are you guys just going to stand there and make eyes at each other? I've got things to do today."

Jack started walking around Shay while she stood there, not moving, "Don't be scared. I'm going to take it easy on you." He said, sounding cocky.

Hunter looked at Shay and noticed her jaw stiffening and jutting out slightly.

"Oh, shit." Hunter said, "She just went into kill mode."

Stan looked over at her and said, "Balls are off limits, Shay. Keep it clean."

As Jack slowly circled around behind her, he stopped directly behind. She never moved a muscle. Jack suddenly leaned in towards Shay's back and, spreading his arms out wide, said, "BOO!"

Shay spun around to her right and caught Jack on the right side of his face with an open backhand. This backhanded strike spun Jack around to his left, staggering him slightly. With a wide-eyed look, he looked over at Tony.

Seeing what had happened, Hunter almost drew up into a ball, laughing. "Did you teach him that, Tony?" he said, wiping the tears running down his face.

"They teach you that in the FBI defensive training school?" Stan added as he looked out towards Shay.

Jack walked over to Tony with his Slurpee drink pressed up to the side of his face. Seeing Stan and Hunter laughing only made Jack mad. Jack handed his drink to Tony, saying, "So she wants to get serious, does she."

Shay stood where she was and looked over at Stan. "Dial it down a little, Viper, don't hurt him too much." Shay replied with a subtle nod of her head.

Jack walked up to her and, without saying a word, took a swing with his right fist at her head.

Shay moved slightly to her left, and as his punch whistled past her head, she grabbed his arm with her right hand. She then turned towards him, placing her left hand just below his chin. Taking her left leg, she threw a cross kick to the inside of Jack's right leg, taking him down hard to the mat.

Shay dropped one knee onto Jack's sternum knocking the wind out of him. Grabbing his throat with her right hand, she pinned his right arm to the mat with her left. Shay looked down at Jack and said, "Say, uncle, and I'll let you up."

"Ok, fine, uncle." He said and started to get up. She pushed him back down on the mat.

"Now say, I'm Shay's bitch." She put more pressure on Jack's neck.

"VIPER!" Stan calls out, "Let him up. He's had enough."

She pushed off Jack's body, causing him to wrench in pain. "Fine." She said, getting up and walking over to Hunter and Stan.

Stan tossed a towel to Shay as she approached.

Shay tossed the towel at Jack, who was still lying on the mat. "I don't need it. I didn't break a sweat." she replied as she climbed out of the ring.

Tony looked at Jack, then at Stan and Hunter, "Where did that come from?"

"You know she's Vicky's niece." Hunter said, "She's got some anger issues."

"You called her Viper. Where did she get that name?" Tony asked.

"She's quick and deadly." Stan replied.

"You're telling me." Jack said, still on his back in the middle of the ring. "I wish someone had warned me."

"What and spoil the fun." Stan said as he turned and walked off.

Jack slowly got up off the mat and exited the ring.

Jack followed Stan, pleading with him, "Will you train me too?"

"Why?" Stan asked, looking over his shoulder towards Hunter.

"Because I need you to, please." Jack pleaded with Stan.

"The gym opens at nine a.m.." Stan said as he turned away again and started walking towards his office.

"Great! Thank you, you won't regret it. I'll be here at nine a.m. sharp!" Jack said with excitement.

Stan stopped and looked back at Jack, "I said the gym opens at nine, you be here at five, and you'll be the one that will regret it, not me."

"Will Shay be here too?" Jack asked.

"Why, you want a daily ass whipping like you just got?" Hunter chimed in.

"I want to be as good as Shay." Jack said with a bit of cockiness, starting to come back.

"Son, you'll never be close to where Shay is. I've known her since before she was able to walk. She started martial arts before she started the first grade. After she was abducted, she got obsessed with it and would practice 24 hours nonstop sometimes. When Stan started training her, she was unbeatable. She's had grown men twice her size for lunch. When she joined the Marines, she got even stronger and unbeatable. Stan has molded Shay into a fighter that I've never seen an equal to." Hunter told Jack this as more of a warning than anything else.

"I will tell you a little secret about Shay." Stan said.

Jack and Tony both chimed in simultaneously, "Please do."

"When she's about to strike, she will tighten her jaw, and it will jut out a little. If you ever see her do that, you need to move out of the way. If it's you that set her off, don't run, she's a fast runner too. She'll only run you down, and you'll just be tired when she beats the shit out of you." Stan said without smiling.

Tony and Jack gathered their things and headed for the door.

"I'm glad Ray and Vicky weren't here to see this." Jack said as they walked out the door.

"Vicky wanted Ray to work on the communications center at the office, and I guess she didn't want to see Shay clean the floor with you."

"She didn't clean the floor with me, Uncle Tony."

"I know, Jack. You had her right where you wanted her." Tony said with a smile.

Back at the Gym, Hunter walked over to Stan and stood next to him. "Stan, we go way back, don't we?"

"Yes, we do, my friend." Stan said with a smile.

"I need to ask you a favor, off the books, so to speak." Hunter said.

"One of those favors like the ones we did for each other many years ago? What does my old friend need of me?" Stan said in a low voice.

"You still have your contacts in Mossad from when you worked for the IDF?" Hunter asked.

"Oh. It's one of those kinds of favors, my friend." Stan said as he took a deep breath, looked up, and closed his eyes.

"Afraid so."

"And what services do you need from this organization?" Stan asked.

"I just need a name, a person, that I can get to." Hunter paused.

After a few seconds of silence, Stan said, "A name of a person to assassinate someone? Hunter, you know Mossad doesn't do that."

"Bull shit, NO, nothing like that. I need someone who is good at questioning people and can deal with hard-core types."

"Yes, I see. You need an interrogator. I have just the person. But before I give you his name, I must warn you. He no longer works for Mossad. Shall we say he used methods of getting information that the government didn't agree with. Is this the type of person you're looking for?"

"Yes, I think so." Hunter replied.

"His name is Dr. Wilson. He's known for getting information from people by any means possible. He's not very ethical. And you're in luck. He's local too. He goes by the name of The Surgeon."

"I think he'll be just what we're looking for, but I'll need to run it by Vicky first."

"I'll get you his contact information and let him know you're interested in his services." Replied Stan.

"Hunter," Stan said, just as Hunter was turning to leave, "this endeavor you seem to be recruiting for, does it involve Tony and Jack?"

Hunter stopped and turned back towards Stan.

"And I'm assuming Vicky too. Since you'll have to get her approval." Stan commented.

"Please, Stan, we go way back, and you know how these things work. The less you know, the better."

"Fair enough then. And our little angel Shay. Does she fit into this equation?"

"Yes, it was unavoidable. She started asking Vicky questions, and you know their relationship. No secrets between the two of them."

"Yes, I've known the family now for a number of years. And Shay is very special to me."

"I know. Shay is like a daughter to me." Hunter said softly. "But once Shay found out, there was really no way to stop her. You know how headstrong she is."

Stan looked up at Hunter and laughed, "Yes, I do. Too headstrong for her own good."

"And how do Jack and Tony fit into the picture, if I may ask?"

"Well, Tony's more of an advisor, and Shay will be working with Jack."

"You know Shay is a loner and doesn't play well with others." Stan said with a smile. "This Jack kid, what do you want me to do with him?"

"Sharpen his fighting skills."

"But you've brought me a very dull knife. I don't know how much time and how sharp I can get him."

"Well, do the best you can with what you've got." Hunter said as he started to turn and walk away. "And see if you can do something with that cockiness he's got. It's going to get him killed." Hunter said as the door closed behind him.

A few days later, Jack was eating breakfast at the ranch next to the pool when he looked up and saw Shay heading into the barn. He was still sore and licking his wounds from the beating from a couple of days before.

After he finished eating, he noticed she hadn't come out yet. His curiosity got the better of him, so he got up and painfully walked over to the barn.

He entered through the side door, where he saw Shay entering. Once in, he heard something that sounded like banging coming from a room about 20 feet away.

Jack walked up to the door and knocked. There was no reply. He definitely had heard the noise coming from inside that room. He knocked again.

"What?" came the reply.

"Shay, is that you? It's Jack."

"What do you want?"

"To talk." He replied.

"About what?" came another reply from inside the room.

"About the other day."

The pounding had stopped, "What about the other day?"

"Can I just come in?"

"The door is open. Come on in."

Jack slowly opened the door and saw Shay standing beside a workout bag. She had black sweats on that matched her short black hair. She picked up a towel and wiped the sweat from her face.

"You have something to say?"

"Well, I wanted to say I'm sorry." He said as he was looking around the room.

He was about 10 feet away from where she was standing in what looked to be a 30 by 20-foot workout area. She was standing next to a bag, larger than she was, that hung from one of the rafters in the ceiling. On one of the walls behind her was a full-length mirror. And mounted on the other wall were different sizes and types of training knives and equipment.

"Nice setup you have here." Jack said.

"You said you had something to say?" she replied.

"Yes, I'm sorry about how I acted the other day at the Gym, you know, not taking you seriously." Jack said sheepishly.

She walked over to the wall and retrieved two rubber training knives. She then started working out with them as Jack stood there watching.

"Stan said you're very good, and I believe him. He told me that I have potential." Jack added, trying to get through the wall that she had up.

"He says that to everyone." She said as she stopped briefly.

"Hunter said that we're going to be working together in the group." He said with a slight smile across his face.

"That's what I hear."

"Maybe we can start working out some together at the gym." Jack said, hoping she would agree.

"Maybe sometime soon. Spend some more time with Stan, and once you get up to speed, I'll work out with you." She said, nodding her head with a grin on her face.

"So! You can smile."

He quickly stepped out the door and closed it when he saw her draw back one of the knives as if she were going to throw it at him.

"Hunter, I just got a call from an old friend of mine, Judge June Mayweather, from Macon, Georgia. She wants Vickers Private Investigations to investigate an individual. They had to release him due to a screw-up by the detectives on the case. He had kidnapped and molested this little girl and got off. She knows in her heart that he's guilty."

"Sounds like something right up our alley. I'll have them go down to Macon and start checking this guy out."

"Let's let Jack and Shay handle this one after we get all the information." Vicky said, "May as well jump into this with both feet."

"We can listen to them over the Coms. And you and Kevin can hang back at the airport. You'll be close enough if they need any help."

"I'll get Jack and Shay working together on a plan. Shay will have to be Jack's spotter." Hunter said. "I should have them ready to go in a few weeks while Jim and Robert head to Macon and check this guy out."

"I'll call and let June know that they will be there the day after tomorrow." She said as she reached for the phone.

"We'll have to make this job look like an accident. We don't need a judge or others putting two and two together and coming up with us." Hunter said, giving Vicky a serious look.

"This judge lady friend of yours calls you about the pervert. Then you send two of your investigators down there, and a few weeks later, this guy shows up with the side of his face blown off. That's going to look very suspicious."

"I know. We'll have to play this one very carefully."

"Let me think about this one. As soon as you can get something on this guy, pass it on to me." Hunter said as he started to turn and walk out the door. "You know, Vicky, we don't have to take this if it looks like we'll catch any blowback from it."

"I know, Hunter, but this is a perfect job for what I had envisioned the group for. For now, let's get Kevin to fly Jim and Robert over to Macon. We'll see what they dig up, and the group can meet and see if we want to take the job any further."

"Sounds good." Hunter said as he left the room.

"Dear God, what have I started?" she said to herself as the phone on the other end was ringing.

"June Mayweather." Came the voice on the other end.

"June, this is Vicky. I'm sending two of my investigators down..."

Chapter Eight

The Doctor Is In

Vicky sent the team down to New Orleans after they had checked out the information they received from Jimmy.

They had found out where two of the leading traffickers of this ring hung out, and they sent Jack and Shay into the club.

Hunter and Kevin saw the two men, Rick, and Mad Dog, enter the club. They watched through the window as the two approached the bar and sat a few feet away from Jack and Shay.

After a few minutes and a couple of drinks each, the two moved over next to Shay.

Shay and Jack, sitting next to each other, could see the reflection of the two men in the mirror.

Mad Dog stood facing Jack slightly at an angle between him and Shay. And Rick stood leaning with his right elbow resting on the bar, just inches to the right of Shay.

Rick leaned in closer to Shay. She could smell his foul breath on the side of her face. "Whaz up sweet thang?" Rick asked with a smile.

Still looking straight ahead, Shay replied, "Nothing. My friend and I just want to sit here and enjoy our drinks."

"Well, how bout you, me, and my friend Mad Dog here, step out back and have us some fun." Rick said as he shifted his stance with his back against the bar and both elbows resting on the bar top.

"Look, guys, we just want to sit here and enjoy our drinks. Could you go and bother someone else?" Jack said.

Mad Dog, who stood about 6 foot 3 inches and about 275 lbs., placed his left hand on Jack's right shoulder, squeezed it, and said, "Look, college boy, why don't you just shut the hell up before you get hurt."

Jack raised both hands as if to surrender, "Man, it's cool, and there is no need for violence." Jack told the mountain size man, as he squeezed a little bit harder on Jack's shoulder.

Rick looked at Jack and said, "We're not talking to you. Why don't you run along? We'll have your little girlfriend back after we finish with her."

Still not looking at the two men, Shay said in a calm and monotone voice, "He's not my boyfriend."

Rick moved around behind Shay, putting his left hand on her left shoulder to lean over and kiss her on the right side of her neck.

Jack was watching what was happening and noticed that as Rick leaned over and kissed her, Shay's jaw tightened and jutted out a little.

At that moment, Jack went to stand up, and Mad Dog said, "What do you think you're going to do, college boy?"

With his hands still up, Jack slid slowly to his left and said, "I'm moving."

Smiling, Mad Dog said, "Good, you just run along. We promise to have her home before morning." And then he laughed.

"I'm not going anywhere, just moving a few seats down here." Jack said while slowly moving to his left to sit about 4 feet away.

He looked at the bartender and said, "Sir, can I have a refill on my drink?" The bartender had been watching what was going on from a safe distance.

"Give it to him to go." Rick replied as he took Shay by the shoulders and pulled her away from the bar. "Let's go, baby, and have us a good old time."

Jack lifted his drink as if to give Rick a toast and smiled.

Shay then crossed her right hand over to her left shoulder, grabbing Rick's hand. Her fingers were placed between his left palm and her shoulder. Squeezing to get a good grip, She dropped down a few inches as she lifted his hand off her shoulder. She lifted his arm over her head and stepped to the side.

Now, having the man's wrist in a painful wrist lock, She took her left hand and, with a brutal backhand, struck him with a stunning blow to the back of the neck. Taking the stunned man's head, she drove it hard into the top of the bar. Blood gushed from his nose and mouth. Grabbing his hair now with both hands: she slammed his face again down hard on the bar. This time sending blood in all directions. Shay let go and watched Rick crumble to the floor, out cold.

Hearing the noise, Mad Dog turned, facing his friend as he fell to the ground. He looked at Shay as she slowly turned to face the 6-foot 3-inch man towering above her.

"What the FUCK! I'm going to mess you up, little girl." The mountain-sized man said, taking a step towards her.

Again, without saying a word, she took her right foot and, with lightning speed, planted it right between the guy's legs. He bent over in pain, grabbing his family jewels, and was now looking eye to eye with Shay.

As he was bent over with his knees starting to buckle, she lifted his head with her left hand and, with a sharp blow, drove the palm of her right hand into the chin of the man. This sent him backward and down to the floor, landing about 8 feet away from his friend, who still lay unconscious.

The remaining club patrons, watching the entire episode play out before them, erupted in cheers and applause. All of which had lasted less than one minute.

Shay looked at both men lying on the floor in their blood, slowly walked over, and sat next to Jack.

"Asshole." She said, looking now at him.

"What? This is a new jacket, and I didn't want to get it all dirty the first time I wore it."

Jack looked over at the bartender, who stood with his mouth wide open. And said, "She'll have another of the same."

The bartender, now moving fast, got Shay her drink. "Sure, whatever she wants." He said nervously.

Shay took a sip of the drink and, looking straight ahead, said, "I'll never know why God put men's on and off switch dangling out there in front."

They both quickly finished their drinks and slowly walked past the two men, still out cold on the floor. They walked out the back door and into the alleyway.

A few minutes later, the two thugs woke up and asked which way the two went. The club owner told them they had gone out the back door just a few minutes ago.

The two men staggered out the back door and into the alleyway. As they stopped, Jack and Shay stood beside a black van. The four looked at each other as Jack was about to open the passenger side door for Shay.

The two men slowly walked up to them, still a little unstable from the previous beating, and said, "We've got some unfinished business to take care of."

They were only about four feet away when Mad Dog said, "We are going to beat the shit out of both of you now."

"You mean the four of us?" Jack said as he pointed to two figures standing behind the two men.

"You're not going to make us fall for that old trick. We're too smart for that one." Rick said.

"Oh, but it's not a trick." Came a voice from behind the two men.

Mad Dog and Rick both turned their head to look behind them. Hunter and Kevin stood about three feet behind them, each with a taser in their hands.

"Gentlemen, have you ever rode the lightning bolt?" asked Kevin.

Rick looked at them both, not noticing the tasers in Hunter's and Kevin's hands, "What the fuck are you talking about?"

Two Pops sounded as the two tasers discharged, sending the two thugs to the ground. When they had stopped twitching, they were both loaded into the rear cargo area of the van. Kevin and Hunter bound, blindfolded, and gagged them with duct tape as they lay unconscious.

Hunter and Kevin sat in the back with their new prisoners as Jack drove with Shay in the passenger's seat. Whenever one of the men tried to move, they would get zapped again by the taser still connected to them. They drove for about 20 minutes to an old, abandoned building. When they arrived, Jack pulled the van around back and into the building through a large shipping door. Once inside, Kevin got out and closed the door behind them.

They dragged the two still unconscious men out of the van, strapped them each in a chair, and removed their blindfolds and gags.

A few minutes later, the two men began waking up. As they started to look around, they noticed an older man sitting in a chair about eight feet in front of them.

"Good afternoon, gentlemen. Allow me to introduce myself. My name is Dr. Wilson." He said as he smiled and slowly nodded at each of the two men.

Dr. Wilson was around 62, a former E.R. doctor who also served as an interrogator for MOSSAD, the Israeli intelligence.

He lost his license to practice due to Tardive dyskinesia (T.D.). T.D. is a side effect caused by neuroleptic drugs. T.D. causes uncontrolled or involuntary movements, like twitching, grimacing, and thrusting. Neuroleptic drugs include antipsychotic medications, often prescribed for psychiatric and neurological disorders.

He was known for getting information from people by any means necessary, which didn't sit too well with some of the more liberal members of the Israeli government. He moved to the United States shortly after his work was terminated.

He was what many would characterize as a true Psychopath. A psychopath doesn't have a conscience. If he lies to you so he can steal your money, he won't feel any moral qualms, though he may pretend to. He may observe others and then act as they do so he's not 'found out.' It's not easy to spot a psychopath. They can be intelligent, charming, and good at mimicking emotions. They're skilled actors whose sole mission is to manipulate people for personal gain.

They don't fear the consequences of their actions, and Dr. Wilson was one of the best.

"May I call you Rick?" Wilson said as he looked at Rick with a smile. Rick was still trying to comprehend what was going on.

"And you're Mr. Mad Dog? Is that your God-given name?" he asked.

"My name is. I'm going to fuck you up, old man!" Mad Dog said as he struggled to get out of the chair that he was secured to.

Dr. Wilson leaned back into his chair and crossed his legs, "Now, Now, Mr. fuck you up, there is no need to get upset." He said with a smile.

"What do you want?" Rick shouted.

"I just want to ask you a few questions." Wilson said, still leaning back in his chair.

"We're not going to tell you anything, you bastard. Let us go!" Rick screamed out.

Mad Dog was still trying to undo the tape that had him secured to the chair.

Dr. Wilson uncrossed his legs and leaned forward in his chair with his elbows on his knees and hands grasped together.

"Ooooh, but you will," Dr. Wilson said with a smile, "you will, my friend."

Rick now noticed an I.V. stuck in his arm that led up to an I.V. pole and a bag of clear liquid hanging from the pole.

"What is that?" Rick said as he looked at the I.V. attached to him and noticed that Mad Dog also had the same thing hooked to him.

Wilson got up and walked slowly to a table between them. A cloth covered the top of the table, but you could tell some items were hidden beneath the cloth.

He uncovered a corner of the table, and two syringes sat there. He picked one up, turned, and took several steps over to Rick's I.V.

"What are you doing?" Rick asked.

"This is only to make you relax, my good friend." Wilson said as he stuck the syringe into the I.V. port on the line connected to Rick's I.V. Within 3 seconds, Rick was out cold. His head dropped down to where his chin was touching his chest.

Wilson patted Rick on the top of his head. "There, there, my friend, rest. I will get to you soon."

Wilson then turned toward Mad Dog and walked toward him, picking up the other syringe.

"You get away from me, you son of a bitch!" Mad Dog said as he watched Wilson approach.

He grabbed the I.V. port and stuck the syringe in. Just before he injected the drug into Mad Dogs port, he leaned over and whispered, "I'm going to enjoy this, Mr. fuck you up." Then proceeded to inject the drug into his I.V. slowly.

Mad Dog struggled but quickly succumbed to the drug, going limp, just like his friend.

Rick slowly woke up to find himself strapped down to a steel table. His arms strapped straight out to the side, his legs strapped down and spread apart. He couldn't move either, and he suddenly noticed that his head and body were strapped down to the cold steel table too.

"What is going on?" he was darting his eyes from left to right, but all he could see beyond six feet was total darkness.

He saw Dr. Wilson walking up from out of the darkness. He picked up a small box with what looked to be a cord running out of it. And then he noticed he was naked but couldn't look down past his chest.

"Mr. Rick, do you know what this is?" Wilson said slowly, admiring the box in his hand.

"Well, I'll tell you, it's called a Tens-unit, and if used properly, will feel so good on your tired, sore muscles as it sends little shock waves through them."

"You should get one. I highly recommend it. I use mine all the time."

"However," He said slowly, taking a short breath, "if you attach the pads to someone's testicles, which can be quite painfully shocking." He said with a smirk.

Wilson removed a rubber mouthpiece from the table and placed it into Rick's mouth, "Here, this will give you something to bite down on to help with the pain."

Wilson presses the button, and a shock enters Rick's body through his testicles. This caused him to stiffen up and arch his back as high as the straps would allow.

Wilson allowed the shock only to last for 3 seconds before he turned it off.

"So, Mr. Rick, how did that feel?" Wilson asked.

"I'm not telling you anything." Rick said as he spit out the rubber mouthpiece.

"But, Mr. Rick, we've only just started. I only had it on level one. We have nine more levels to go."

Wilson placed the control box on the table next to Rick's head. He reached over, pulled a chair over, and sat down about 3 feet away from the table.

"Ok, Mr. Rick, here's your first question. Tell us about your sex trafficking ring." Wilson asked as he leaned back in his chair.

"I don't know what you are talking about!" Rick replied in a defiant voice.

"I'll have my assistant apply the next level of shock if that's ok with you?"

From behind the doctor and out of the darkness stepped Shay. Without saying a word, she walked over and picked up the unit's control box. She went over and stood directly above Rick's head.

She held the control box out, turned the power up to level four, and pressed the button.

This time Rick screamed out. His screams echoed all through the building, and then he fell silent. Rick had passed out from the three-second jolt of electricity through his body. Once his body stopped shaking and went limp, he lost all bodily functions and lay there in his waste.

Jack, Kevin, and Hunter were sitting down the hallway in another room. They also had Mad Dog, still strapped down on the table but awake in the room.

"Shit!" Jack cried out, "That sounded like it hurt."

"What are you doing to him?" Mad Dog said as he tried to loosen his straps.

"You'll find out soon enough." Hunter said, walking over to where Mad Dog lay and slapping him lightly on the side of the face.

"This is nothing compared to what you've done to those girls." Kevin replied in a sarcastic voice.

After about 5 minutes, Rick regained consciousness and opened his eyes. Still in pain, he tried to look around and saw Shay still standing over him.

Shay leaned beside Rick's right ear and whispered, "Still want to step out back and have us some fun?"

"Ok, Ok, what do you want to know? Just get this crazy bitch away from me." Rick said as he was trying to look over at Wilson.

Wilson looked at Shay and said, "Darling, will you ask Mr. H to come in? I think Rick here has something to say now."

A few minutes later, Hunter entered the room. He walked up and stood beside Rick, still lying on the table.

He looked up and down Rick's body lying there as he shook his head.

"Ok, tell me about this sex operation you've got going." Hunter began.

"What do you want to know?"

"Where do you get the girls from?"

"Take these straps off, and I'll tell you."

"You don't tell me. I'll have her come back in and light your balls up again. It's up to you, dude. Either way, you'll talk. The question is, will you leave here with your balls intact or fried?" Hunter said as he leaned over and looked Rick in the eyes.

"This guy sets it up." Rick started, "I make a call and place an order, and he delivers them to me."

"These are not your street corner hookers. People pay a lot of money for this merchandise." Rick said.

"Does this guy have a name?"

"Craig, that's all I know."

"Does this Craig have a last name?"

"I don't know it. I just place a call. I tell him what I want, and he brings them to me. I pay him, and he leaves."

"Sort of like pizza delivery, except you get young, innocent girls instead of pizza?" Hunter said, now with anger in his voice, as he slowly walked to Rick's head.

"Yes, something like that."

"When is this Craig guy supposed to show up here again?" Hunter asked as he leaned on the table next to Rick's head.

"Day after tomorrow. He's delivering to me a couple of new girls."

Hunter placed his right hand around Rick's neck, squeezing to cut off his air.

"So, you like raping and abusing young little girls, do you? I should just snap your fucking neck right here and now and leave your fucking body for the rats to eat!"

Hunter released his grip from around Rick's neck. Leaning over with his face inches away from Rick's, "But we're not finished with you yet, you piece of shit. I've got a few more questions to ask you."

"Ok, Ok, Ok! I'll answer your questions, man. Just stop with the shocking and brutality, man."

Hunter reached over, grabbed his face with his hand, and squeezed, "BRUTALITY? COMPARED TO WHAT YOU'VE PUT THESE CHILDREN THROUGH, YOU'VE NOT SEEN BRUTALITY YET."

"How many kids do you have back at that place?" Hunter asked, still holding on and squeezing his face.

"Ten! Eight girls and two boys." He replied.

"Where are they at?"

"I told you, they are in the house!" Rick said, now starting to cry.

Hunter looked over at Wilson, who was holding the switch to the Tens-unit, and with a look of pure anger, said, "Shock this son of a bitch again."

Wilson pressed the button, and a tremendous shock went through his body again. Rick screamed out in pain, and again he lost consciousness.

Hunter looked over at Wilson, "Sorry." Wilson said, "It was still set on four, where Shay had left it."

After a few minutes, Rick regained consciousness, "Man, I answered your question."

"Give me the house layout and where the kids are being held. Or next time, we'll set the thing on the max and leave it on until your balls fall off! Am I clear?"

"Yes, Yes, very. They are held up on the second floor. There are two to a room. We lock them in their rooms only at night. We keep the door up to the second floor locked."

"You said we? How many of you are there?" Hunter asked as he walked around to the side of the table.

"Four. Me, Mad Dog, and two others. We take two-day shifts watching the girls." Rick said, still overwhelmed by the pain from the shock.

"Weapons?"

"Yes, we have a few, one handgun each, two MP5's and a shotgun. That's it." Rick replied.

"Alarm and cameras?" Hunter inquired.

"Alarms on all the windows and outside doors, and the door leading up to the second floor. Cameras on all sides of the building on outside and in the second-floor areas." Rick said.

"Anything else we need to know?" Hunter asked.

"No, so can I go now?" Rick looked at Hunter and then over at Wilson, the best he could with his head strapped down.

"I'm going to leave that up to the good doctor." Hunter said, looking over at him, and the two of them walked out of the room.

They both walked down the hallway and into the room where Mad Dog was being held. Jack and Kevin sat against the wall, looking at their cell phones. Shay had also found a chair and had fallen almost asleep.

"How about you guys leave me, the good Doctor, and Mad Dog alone for a few minutes? I've got some questions to ask him."

The three got up to exit the room. As Shay walked by the table where Mad Dog was strapped down, she took two fingers of her right hand and lightly drug them up the right side of his body as she passed.

"Let me off this table Bitch! I'm going to make you wish you were never born." Mad Dog shouted out as she walked by.

Hunter looked at Shay as she walked past him to the door, "You are ruthless, girl. Now get on out of here. I've got some questions to ask Mr. Dog."

Hunter and Dr. Wilson moved over to the table where Mad Dog was strapped.

"I don't think I can use the same method of persuasion on this gentleman as I did with Rick. His balls are more than two times the normal size. Shay really did a number on them. I don't think he will feel much pain there for a while." Wilson said, looking over to Hunter.

"I'm not telling you anything."

"Oh, how I do love a challenge." Wilson said as he leaned his head back slightly, closed his eyes, and took a deep breath.

Wilson looked at Mad Dog's hands, "I see you have a nervous habit of biting your fingernails. Too bad, I was so wanting to remove them."

Wilson reached into his bag that he had brought from the other room. He pulled out a flambe' burner and lit it.

"Mr. Mad Dog, or do I call you Mr. fuck you up still?" Wilson asked as he walked to the end of the table. "Do you like crème brulee?" Wilson asked, "I so love it. You should really try it sometime."

Wilson took the lit burner and passed it across the bottom of Mad Dog's bare feet.

"You know, Wilson. I can see why the Israeli government got rid of you. You're one sick puppy." Hunter said, shaking his head.

"Ahhhh, but one man's sickness is another man's joy." Wilson said with a smile.

"If I tell you anything, they'll kill me!" Mad Dog said.

"That's the least of your worries. I think you should worry more about the next 10 minutes and what I will do." Wilson said, looking up at Hunter. "You may begin your questions."

Hunter began asking him the same questions that he had asked Rick. A couple of times in the beginning, he refused to answer. So, Wilson put the burner to the bottom of his feet.

After getting all the information they could from him, they wheeled him back into the room with Rick.

"Well, guys, let's get together and return to the van. The good doctor will finish things up here and head back home. I don't think we'll need him anymore on this trip." Hunter said to the others.

The four left Dr. Wilson to finish up with Rick and Mad Dog.

Placing them head to toe next to each other, Wilson then walked over to their I.V. poles.

"Here, this will help you sleep and when you wake up. It will be all over." Wilson said as he started each one of their I.Vs. The I.V. was filled with a sleep-inducing drug called Propofol. It would cause them to be unconscious for about three hours.

"Oh, by the way, are either of you two gentlemen allergic to peanut butter?" Wilson asked just before the two drifted off to sleep.

Dr. Wilson began spreading the peanut butter all over the two guys' bodies. Paying extra attention to their nose, fingers, down their bodies, toes, and testicles.

A few hours later, Mad Dog started to wake up. He was still in pain, but all his senses had not returned to him yet. He looked over to his left and could see about ten or more large rats on something that he couldn't quite make out. As he could focus more, he noticed the rats were on top of Rick and eating him alive.

He felt something nudge the right side of his face and shifted his eyes in that direction. And about one inch from his face, he saw a giant rat looking right at him. Mad Dog let out a scream that echoed all through the building.

"What did Dr. Wilson want with those two large jars of peanut butter?" Jack asked.

"Rats love the taste of peanut Butter. And it gives off an intriguing odor that attracts them." Hunter said.

Once they got back to their hotel rooms, Hunter called Vicky and Ray. He filled them in on the new information they had received on the house where the kids were being held.

After exchanging information and ideas, Vicky instructed Ray to gather whatever he needed and head down to New Orleans.

Ray told Hunter that he could be there in about 6 hours, and he had some ideas on how to get past the alarm and cameras.

Hunter instructed Ray to stop by his gun range and pick up a bag they'll have ready for him. He had already called ahead and had them put some things together that they might need.

Chapter Nine

The New Orleans Raid

The following day, Ray arrived with the bag Hunter asked him to pick up, along with some new electronic equipment. They had found an Airbnb just a few blocks from the house holding the children.

Their first task was to get control of the cameras and alarm system. This was going to be up to Ray and Kevin. They planned to use the van Ray had driven down as a pizza delivery van.

While Kevin and Ray were doing their thing, Jack, Shay, and Hunter were looking over the weapons that would be utilized to make entry into the house.

Hunter would stay in the van with Kevin as a backup if needed. Ray would stay at the Airbnb and run the electronics and communications from there.

They would carry the same weapons to minimize the type of ammo and the amount they need to take. With both carrying the same equipment, switching out the damaged items would be easy if something happened.

They each carried a suppressed CZ Scorpion EVO 9mm short barreled rifle with night vision optics, a suppressed CZ P-10c 9mm handgun with laser sights, and another CZ P-10c without a suppressor for backup. Using the same gun as a backup is necessary, so they will use the same magazines. Both the EVOs and pistols were equipped with attached lights. Each gun was loaded with subsonic rounds, and each carried four spare magazines for their primary weapons.

Each one carried an Ari B'Lilah knife used by the Israeli Defense Force YAMAM, the counter-terrorism unit, which was a gift from Stan. They wore a level III light body armor vest and an IFAK, Individual First Aid Kit.

They all had ear protection with communications and video cameras mounted on their helmets.

This allowed Vicky and Tony to hear and see what was going on back at the Omega headquarters.

Kevin and Ray pulled up in front of the house and stopped. Kevin stayed in the van as Ray got out.

Ray, dressed up as a pizza delivery person, approached the front door of the house. Before knocking on the door, he made sure the hidden camera on his shirt was set and not blocked.

Kevin was set up in the van, monitoring the entire event. Ray was counting on the Wi-Fi electronic security system to be armed when he knocked on the door. With the small cell phone size device in his pocket, he could retrieve the passcode of the alarm system when the person inside the house turned off the system to open the door.

Another device that Ray had brought down with him was in the van with Kevin. It was able to intercept the video camera's signal. They wanted several minutes of recording so that they could override the signal. They would then be able to play a video of the door showing no one there while Shay and Jack were entering.

Ray knocked on the door, with no answer. He knocked a second time, and this time he could hear someone moving around inside the house. They still didn't open the door. Ray tried a third time, and this time he heard a voice from the other side of the door.

"What you want?" came a voice with a slight Cajun accent.

"Pizza." Ray replied in a low voice.

He was hopeful that if he talked in a low voice, the person inside would have to open the door to hear him.

"What?" came the voice from inside.

"Pizza." Ray repeated.

"Putain *(fuck)*!" He heard someone swearing in French behind the door as it slowly opened.

"What fuck you want?" said a man dressed in old jeans and a white wife-beater shirt.

"Pizza delivery." Ray said as he viewed the man now just three feet away.

"Va te faire foutre *(go fuck yourself)*!" came the reply from the man.

"What?" Ray said.

"We do not order pizza, Salaud *(bastard)*."

"Is this 415 Conifer Street?" Ray asked.

"NO! fils de pute *(son of a bitch)*, get fuck out of here." And the man slammed the door in Ray's face.

Ray heard the beeping of the passcode as it was entered into the security system. Once he heard the long beep, he knew the system was armed again. He turned and walked off the porch of the house and down the street towards the van.

Ray opened the door to the van, "Did you order pizza?"

"Funny. Did you get the code to the security system?" Kevin asked.

As Ray was getting in, he grabbed the magnetic pizza delivery sign that was attached to the roof of the van.

"Yes, got it. How about you? Were you able to get the camera feed and frequency code?"

"Got it." Kevin replied, "But we're going to have to come back tonight and get some nighttime footage of the outside so we can loop it."

"No, I'm putting a repeater in the bushes between this house and the Airbnb we're staying in. I'll be able to control the cameras from there.

"I think I just got cussed out in French or Cajun or something." Ray said as he took a bite of pizza.

"I'm sure you did. Let's head back to the others and see what's next." Kevin said as he started the van.

Jack and Shay had been training together with the weapons chosen for the mission, along with several other weapons, daily for the past several weeks. They both felt like they were ready to go in together on this mission.

Ray and Kevin arrived back at the Airbnb and reported to the team what they had seen.

After a short meeting, Ray went into the dining room, where he had his equipment set up.

About 15 minutes later, Ray called out, "Hey guys, I've got the cameras up inside and outside of the house now."

The others all came into the dining room and looked over Ray's shoulder at the monitors.

Ray had set up two monitors. One monitor had the cameras on the outside of the house and second floor where the children were being held. The other one had inside the first-floor cameras and garage.

On the second floor, there was a camera in each of the children's bedrooms. Two kids occupied each room. A camera monitored the hallway and a common area for the children. There was only one bathroom on the second floor, and it also had a camera.

On the first floor, there were two cameras in a den area off the main entry. One of the bedrooms had two cameras and appeared to be set up like a kid's playroom. This was assumed to be a room in which a child could be brought and sexually abused.

The kitchen was visible by a camera, and the dining room was what looked to be a main control location. Several monitors were visible in that room, and one of the guards was sitting behind a desk. He appeared to be watching a movie on a TV mounted on a wall across the room while keeping an eye on the camera monitors.

There was a two-car garage connected to the side of the house with an outside entry and an entry into the kitchen. Only one side of the garage was occupied by a vehicle, and the other side was empty.

In the hallway, they could see three other doors. Two of which were opened, while the third was closed. They assumed that the closed door was the door leading up to the second floor. The other two doors were a bathroom and bedroom for the two guards. Neither of those two rooms had a camera view inside.

Each one of the cameras also had audio, so they could hear what was going on inside, but they couldn't see where one of the guards was at that time.

The one that they could see had a gun in a holster on his side and what looked to be a shotgun leaning next to the door into the room.

"Ok, Ray," Hunter said, “get about 20 minutes of dead feed from the inside cameras. We can loop that feed when Shay and Jack go in. That should give them enough time."

"Guys, I want each of you to study the layout of the inside of the house. We need to work on the best way to enter and sweep the house. Jack and Shay, you two need to know every square inch of the inside of the house and where each door and every piece of furniture is." Hunter said while looking at both Jack and Shay.

"Vicky, are you receiving this feed?" Ray asked over his mic.

"Yes, Tony and I can see everything and hear everything clearly."

"Great." Hunter said. "Tony, we need your input also on this planning."

"I'm on it." Tony replied.

"Can you ask Rick or Mad Dog what's in the two rooms that we can't see in?" Vicky asked.

"I don't think they are up to any more questions right now." Hunter said.

"Was Dr. Wilson able to get the information you needed from those two?" She asked.

"Yes. He has a very stimulating way of getting people to open up." Kevin said.

"Do I want to know?" she asked.

"No." Hunter said.

"Would it be safe to say that we will not have to worry about those two in the future?" she asked.

"Not in this lifetime." Hunter said.

Vicky took a deep breath and slowly let it out. "Understood."

"When is this Craig guy supposed to come by?" Tony asked.

"He could be arriving anytime, so we've got to be ready." Hunter replied.

"Ray." Tony asked, "Can you trip the alarm from your location?"

"Yes, why?"

"I think I see where you're going with this Tony." Hunter added.

"If we set the alarm off, we'll be able to see what their reaction is. Also, if we do it several times in a row, they'll think it was a malfunction and possibly leave the alarm off."

Ray looked over at Hunter, who then gave Ray a nod.

Ray took the mouse and clicked on an alarm button on the screen. As soon as he did that, they could hear the alarm going off and the two guards jumping up. The one at the desk turned his attention to the monitors, and the other went around to the front door.

The guard at the door entered a code on the alarm keypad, and the alarm shut off.

He was looking out the window and asked the other guard, who was checking the monitors if he could see anyone.

Nothing, he replied. He told the man at the door to go outside and look around.

They watched the man exit the house. He slowly walked around the house, checking the windows, rear door, and garage doors as he went.

"Now turn the alarm back on." Hunter instructed Ray. Hunter then asked Kevin to go outside and walk down the street toward the house.

Once the guy outside finished his patrol, he went to open the door to come back inside. As soon as he opened the door, the alarm sounded again, startling both men.

The man at the door entered the code again, and the alarm shut off. The man sitting behind the monitors jumped up and ran to the front door. He ran up to the other man with both arms out as if to say, what the hell are you doing?

You could tell by the tone of their voices that they were arguing with each other about the alarm.

"Ok, Ray, set the alarm off again."

This time when the alarm went off, the man that had been sitting at the monitors pushed the other man out of the way and entered the code to shut off the alarm again. Pointing up to the second floor, he told the other man to go up and check things out.

The team watched as the man unlocked the door to the second floor and walked up the steps. They could see that each one of the children was in their room and sitting up in their beds. He checked each room and took a head count to make sure none of the kids were missing. After he checked out the second floor, he came back down and reported to the other guy.

About this time, Kevin came back in from his walk down the street. "I thought you were going to set off the alarm again?" Kevin asked.

"We did, several times." Jack said, looking over at him.

"Well, I didn't hear anything, and I was about a hundred feet from the house."

"That makes sense." Tony said. "They must not have any alarms outside. You wouldn't want the neighbors to call the cops if you're running a sex trafficking ring out of your house."

"Vicky, Jack, and Shay are going to walk down the street and attach a tracker on Craig's vehicle when he's inside." Hunter continued to update Vicky and Tony on the plan that they had so far.

Shay looked over at Hunter, "You know, there's like a 100% chance that he'll be pulling into the garage when he arrives. We're going to have to get in there to put the tracker on."

"Ray, did you bring that lock pick auto extractor?" Hunter asked.

"Yes, I did. It's in the bag with the other stuff."

"You two remember how to work that thing?" Hunter asked, looking at both Jack and Shay.

"I sure do, boss." Jack replied.

Hunter looked over at Shay and Jack. "The two of you will have to break into the garage and put the tracking device on the van after he goes in." He then turned towards Ray, "You'll have to loop the camera that's out in the garage while they are in there."

With an electronic sketchpad connected to one of the computers, they drew out a rough floorplan of the house. Vicky and Tony could also see this and were able to help with planning the take-down of the house.

A couple of hours had passed, and it had gotten dark outside. They were expecting Craig to arrive at any minute. Jack and Shay were ready to proceed with the plan.

If Craig parked the vehicle out on the street, they would walk down the street as if they were a couple. They would place the tracking device underneath the vehicle and keep walking.

It was dark, and if they approached from the opposite side of the road, it should block the view from the house. They were also hoping that when Craig arrived, he would preoccupy both guards and no one would be watching the cameras.

However, if he pulled into the garage, they would have to break in and place the tracking device on the vehicle while it was in there.

Shortly after 10 p.m., the guard watching the cameras received a five-second phone call on his cell phone. Within two minutes, a van pulled up to the house and into the garage.

Four figures got out of the van, and one of the guards met them at the door leading into the house.

Ray and Hunter had been watching the monitors keeping an eye on what was going on in the house. The other three were chilling in the kitchen and munching on some leftover pizza.

"Hey guy's, it's show time. Dipshit just arrived with two young girls in tow, and he's got another adult male with him." Hunter called out.

The two young girls, one looking to be around 12 years old and the other around 15 or 16, both had a dog leash attached to a harness on their backs.

The guard led the four visitors into what looked to be the sex playroom. Craig pulled the girls along, and once in the room, he unhooked them and pushed them onto the bed.

"Ok. Before Craig and this other character leave, we need to get a tracker on his vehicle." Hunter said.

"You and Shay get going. We don't know how long he's going to be there." Hunter said to Jack in a hurried voice.

Jack and Shay jogged down the side of the road and slowed to a walk just before they arrived in front of the house. Kevin had taken the van, driven around the block, and entered the street from the other direction. He would pick the two up just past the house when they came out.

Jack and Shay slowly walked down the side of the house, trying their best to stay in the shadows. Once at the door, Jack used the lock pick auto extractor and opened the door slowly. Shay slipped in and went to the back of the van, placing the tracking device on the back side of the rear bumper.

Once it was secured by the magnets attached to the tracker, she slipped back out the door where Jack was kneeling in the darkness.

When they both exited the garage, Jack left the door unlocked so they could enter through it later.

They both walked back the same way that they came and met Kevin at the van.

As soon as Kevin had picked them up, they checked with Ray to make sure he was able to connect with the tracking device and that everything was working.

Once back at the Airbnb, the three went back into the dining room and began watching the cameras with the others.

"What if he drives to the airport and leaves the car there?" Jack asked.

"That's the chance we'll have to take. The way I see it, he drove the girls from a main location to here. It's not like he can jump on Delta with two or three captives and fly. There's too much of a risk that he'd get caught." Hunter said.

"If we can get the tag number of the car, Ray can run it and find out who it's registered to." Kevin added.

"True, and if it's a rental, I'll be able to track it back to where it was rented from and hack the computer for the renter's information."

"Ray, you're going to focus on the first-floor cameras. You'll be Jack and Shay's eyes and ears once they are inside the house. Tony, I need you to keep an eye on the second floor and outside of the house for anything that may pop up." Hunter instructed.

"Ok. When they start to go in, I will need everyone to stay off the comms. I need to be the only one that Jack and Shay are listing to." Hunter added.

"Jack, I want you to takeout the guy at the desk. That's Tango One. Shay, you'll cover Jack, and once he takes out his target, you move down the hallway and take out Tango Two. Jack, you cover Shay." Hunter instructed.

"Ray will still be able to hear anything you and Tony say, and he can relay the information to the team. Everyone clear?" Hunter asked.

"Once they are down, Jack, you, and Shay exit the house and head back to the van. Any questions? Now is the time to ask." Hunter said.

Each person replied back with all clear.

Craig, his companion, and the other two men inside the house sat in the kitchen for well over 30 minutes talking about the sex trade and sports.

After a while, Craig and his companion got up and headed to the garage door, followed by the other two men. They shook hands, and the two got into the van and started to back out as soon as the garage door was open.

Once he was clear, one of the men closed the garage door and went back into the house. The same guard who was sitting behind the monitors headed back to his desk.

As the other man went to arm the alarm system again, the man sitting behind the desk yelled out for him to leave the alarm system off. He explained that Rick and Mad Dog were due back tomorrow and they could check it out when they arrived.

He agreed and went to check on the two new guests in the playroom.

After seeing that they were still sitting on the bed, he told the other man that he was going to shower and go to bed.

The man at the desk yelled back and told him that he was going to stay up a little longer and finish the movie that he was watching.

Kevin, Hunter, Jack, and Shay were already in the van and parked across the street from the house. They had been monitoring the conversation inside the house from the van.

Jack and Shay took up positions outside the side garage door and waited for Hunter's signal to go in.

After what seemed like hours, Hunter gave the signal when he heard that tango two was going to take a shower.

"Breach, Breach, Breach!" Hunter said over the com.

Jack and Shay looked at each other, and both took a deep breath. Jack opened the outside door of the garage, and they both entered and closed the door behind.

"We're in and approaching the door into the house." Shay said.

"Tango one is still at the desk, and Tango two is in the bathroom." Came Hunter's reply.

Jack slowly opened the door, and Shay slipped inside and took up a position just outside of the kitchen door. She stood there looking down the hallway toward the bend in the hall, which led to the bathroom and bedroom.

She couldn't see the two rooms but was ready if Tango Two happened to come around the corner.

Jack slipped into the kitchen and stood next to the door leading into the dining room where his target sat.

Jack's target, Tango One, was watching his movie and occasionally looking over at the security monitors.

Ray had put the security camera system into a loop, so all the man saw was previously recorded video of an empty hallway and kitchen.

Hunter, watching the monitors from inside the van, saw that Shay and Jack were set and in position.

"Jack, key your mic if you are ready." Hunter said. But there was no reply.

"Jack." Hunter said again, "Are you clear and ready?"

Jack closed his eyes, took a slow deep breath, and keyed his mic once.

"Shay, key your mic if you are set and ready." Hunter asked.

A short single crackle came over the audio monitor as Shay keyed her mic.

"Ok, Jack, it's on you. We don't have all day." Hunter said calmly over the mic.

Jack stepped around and into the doorway of the dining room. And his eyes met the eyes of his target. They both looked at each other for what seemed like an eternity.

The man behind the desk reached for his gun as Jack aimed his suppressed CZ Scorpion at the man's head. With a thump, thump sound from his suppressed weapon, Jack placed two shots just above the man's left eye.

This knocked the man's head back, and blood splattered the wall behind him.

"Tango One down." Jack said softly, and he lowered his weapon.

Jack turned and headed out to where Shay was standing and took a position behind her. He tapped her on her shoulder, letting her know he was ready.

Shay walked slowly down the side of the wall, dressed in all black and wearing a balaclava over her face, showing only her blue eyes through a narrow slit.

She stopped at the corner of the hallway with her back pressed up against the wall.

She heard the movement of another person just inches around the corner from where she stood.

"Shay, the other man is standing around the corner." Hunter said in the com unit.

Shay slowly moved her suppressed CZ Scorpion around to the right and back behind her, freeing both hands. She then slowly pulled the Ari B'Lilah knife out of its scabbard with her left hand.

She slid around the corner, surprising the other person, as they came face to face.

With his right hand, he knocked the knife out of her hand. He then reached down, pulled his weapon, and attempted to point it at Shay's head.

With her now empty left hand, she struck his hand, pinning it against the wall. This trapped his right hand and gun against the wall causing him to loosen his grip on the gun, which made it temporarily useless against her. In the same motion, and with all the strength that she could muster, she came across with her right forearm striking the five-foot-nine-inch man on the left side of his neck just below his ear, temporarily stunning him. With his right hand still pinned against the wall, Shay reached down to her leg holster and pulled out her suppressed CZ P-10c 9mm pistol.

Shay pumped two rounds into the man's chest and then one round underneath his chin, blowing the top of his head off.

The man never made a sound as she lowered his limp body down to the ground.

Shay leaned against the wall and slowly slid down to one knee. Her face was covered in the man's blood. She closed her eyes, took a deep breath, and lowered her head. She was relieved that it was over.

Jack slid up behind her, looking down at the dead body at her feet, "Tango Two down." Jack said quietly over the com unit.

"Copy that." Came the reply.

"Remind me never to piss Viper off." Jack said back into the com unit.

With the takedown of the house completed, it was time to pack up and head to the airport. Hunter got on the radio and gave instructions to Shay and Jack.

He also gave the final cleanup instructions to Kevin and Ray.

With luck, they would be at the airport on the way back to Houston before they got caught.

"OK, leave the children in their rooms until someone comes and gets them." Hunter told Shay.

"Ray, make sure any video of the takedown is erased. Let's keep a live feed going so we can keep track of things as they unfold there at the house."

"Jack, make sure you didn't leave anything behind. You two get the hell out of there ASAP and head back here to the van. Ray, have the garage door open when we get there."

The van pulled into the Airbnb's garage, and Ray closed the door behind.

"Kevin, call the local police, Family and Children Services, and the Media. Inform them that you heard gunfire and there are children inside the house. Make sure you use one of the burner phones when you call." Hunter instructed.

Vicky and Tony had been monitoring the entire operation from the Omega Headquarters.

"Great job, guys." She said, "Let me know when you're wheels up and on the way back. Tony and I will continue monitoring things back here and keep you guys updated. We'll see you in a couple of hours back at Omega Headquarters."

A few hours later, the Vickers Jet had landed and was tucked away into the new hanger. They joined Vicky and Tony in the planning room.

"So, what's up?" Hunter said, "Any news yet?"

"We've been watching the video feed from the house. It looks like they got all the kids out. The place is crawling with cops and crime investigators." Vicky answered. She had been watching the video feed from the house ever since the team had left.

"The cameras outside of the house don't show much of the street. All we can see are some blue and red flashing lights on the side of the house."

"Nothing on the news yet, but in about 15 minutes, the local news will be on. There should be something then." Tony said as he leaned back in his chair.

Jack and Shay took their equipment into the armory and stored it away. Ray headed upstairs to the communication room to hook up and recharge all the earpieces and radio equipment.

Jack and Shay had picked up a couple of laptop computers and cell phones before they left the house in hopes that there was some valuable information that could be used. Ray had also had them hooked up and charging. He was going to check them out after he rested and had something to eat. He knew he had a long night ahead of him.

Kevin was still out in the hangar, bedding down the jet and checking to make sure it was all secure.

Ray entered the room, and Hunter turned to him and asked, "You still tracking this Craig guy?"

"Yes, they stopped over in Baton Rouge for an hour to eat, it looks like. Now they're headed north up Highway 49 just south of Shreveport."

"Did you ever get any information on who owns the car?" Vicky asked.

"It's registered to an LLC located in Vegas called Young Import and Export. It looks to be a shell corporation." Ray replied as he took a seat at the conference table.

"Any chance this Craig guy's last name is Young?" Tony asked.

"Nope, nothing yet on his last name." Ray said.

"How about checking into this Import company and seeing what else it owns? Maybe it will lead us to something." Hunter said.

"I'll check tomorrow when I go into the office and see if I can find anything on it." Tony added.

Kevin entered the conference room and took a seat next to Shay. Shay had been quietly sitting there reading a Black Belt magazine after she had put her equipment away.

Jack was rummaging through the refrigerator, over in the storage room, looking for something to snack on. He came in the room and saw Kevin sitting there.

"Kevin, you need to start serving food on those flights."

"Sorry, Jack, we don't have a flight attendant to wait on you."

"We could have Shay be the flight attendant." Jack said with a smile as he took a seat across from Vicky and Shay.

Without looking up from her magazine, Shay slowly flipped a bird at Jack.

"She can serve you nuts." Kevin said, laughing.

"No thanks, I've seen what she does with nuts." Jack said, looking over in Shay's direction.

The big screen TV on the wall was tuned into WVUE Fox News with the sound muted. Vicky reached for the remote and unmuted the sound.

"This is Spencer Santiago with breaking news." The picture went into split screen, and you could see a reporter standing outside of a house. In the background, you could see police cars and ambulances along with several emergency personnel in the picture.

"We'll switch over to Sarah Leopold, on the scene with a developing story."

"Thank you, Spencer. I'm standing here outside of what appears to be a sex trafficking house. No one knew what was going on behind these closed doors in this once quiet neighborhood."

"What do you know so far, Sarah?" Spencer asked.

"From an inside source, I've been told that there were about ten children from the ages of ten to fourteen being held as prisoners on the second floor of this house behind me."

"Were there any injuries?" Spencer asked as the screen went from split screen to only seeing Sarah.

"From my understanding, there were two fatalities inside the house." Sarah said, turning towards the house.

"Any identities of the two fatalities?" Spencer asked.

"I've been told that none of the children were injured during what appeared to be a gun battle." Sarah replied.

Off camera, a large SUV with government license plates pulled up to the scene. Four people exited the SUV, each wearing a jacket with big yellow FBI letters on the back. The four proceeded from the SUV towards the front door of the house.

Sarah started walking over to try and stop one of the FBI agents heading to the house.

"Excuse me sir, I'm Sarah Leopold with WVUE news, I'd like to ask you some questions."

Three of the agents continued walking toward the house as the one leading them stopped.

"What is your name? Could you shed any light on what has happened here?" Sarah asked.

"My name is SSA Roger Basiliano, and right now, we are still in the investigation stage. Currently, I have no information to share." SSA Basiliano said.

"Is it gang related?" Sarah asked.

"As I said, Ms. Leopold, I have nothing to share at this time. Thank you." And SSA Basiliano turned and walked away.

The screen went back to showing both Spencer and Sarah.

"There you have it, Spencer. This little quiet community has been turned upside down in what looks like a major child sex trafficking ring. Back to you, Spencer." Sarah ended as the screen went to showing only Spencer.

"Thank you, Sarah. We'll break in with any more information on this story as we receive it. And in other news today..."

Vicky muted the sound again.

"Tony, do you know this Basiliano guy?" Hunter asked.

"No. Never heard of him."

Ray lowered the screen on his laptop so he could see everyone, "I've pulled him up, and it says that he's been with the New Orleans FBI for eight years. The last two have been investigating sex trafficking."

"We need to get out in front of this. We don't need this guy knocking on our door one day in the near future." Hunter said.

"Ray, can you get into the FBI's computer and put some kind of tracking thing in there?" Kevin asked.

"I can do what I did for Tony."

"Wait a second, what are you talking about? You did what for me?" Tony asked in a serious tone.

"I put a back door into your system at the Houston FBI office." Ray replied with a smile.

"Ray, you can get in a lot of trouble for doing that." Tony said, still concerned that it happened.

"Trouble? Like being an accessory to multiple murders, wiretapping, theft, and kidnapping. That kind of trouble? Or are you talking about some other kind of trouble?" Ray responded with a laugh.

"You going to turn him in, Uncle G-Man?"

Tony looked over to Jack and then back at Ray. He smiled and said, "I guess in the scheme of things, it's not that bad."

"Do whatever you need to do, Ray. Just keep tabs on this investigation." Vicky commented, cutting off any additional discussion on the matter.

"Let's start getting whatever information we can on this Craig and the other character and see where that leads us." Hunter jumped in.

"I'll take care of it, and I've also got a lot of stuff to hack through that Shay and Jack brought me too." Ray said. "If anyone needs me, I'll be upstairs working for the next week or so." And he got up and left.

Chapter Ten

IMPORT EXPORT

The next couple of months went to training and development of information that was taken from the Florida and New Orleans operations.

Hunter had hired Nicholas Bryant, a local shooter, to help Jack and Shay with their long-distance shooting. Nicholas was a former Gold Medal Olympic shooter and was a regular member of Hunters gun club.

Nicholas also assisted in the Ranger and SEAL's sniper training whenever needed. The Ranger called him Shadow because out from the shadows, he could take you out. Although Nicholas had never been in the military or had the opportunity to use his sharpshooting skills on a live human target, he was, however, a deadly shot against the local wild boar and nuisance animals.

Jack, with Nicholas's training, was able to take out his targets from over 1,000 yards. He trained Jack on various long-range guns based on need.

Shay concentrated on spotting for Jack in the long-distance shooting. She didn't have the patience to sit and wait on her prey. She was more of a "take action" and not a "lay in wait" type of person.

Shay never improved as well as Jack did in long-distance shooting. Her strengths were in close combat and fighting. Jack was more suited for long-distance fighting. Together they were a great team. Where one was weak, the other more than made up for it.

Nicholas introduced a friend of his to Hunter. Christopher Adams was a scrappy guy from Scotland. He loved to mix it up with just about anyone and would often go looking for a good fight. He never met a man or animal, for that matter, he would back down from.

Nicholas was just over six foot tall, bald, very polite, and easygoing. Christopher, however, was just the opposite. He was loud, five foot ten inches tall, and drank every chance he got. He had the nickname of Red due to his long red beard and hair.

Christopher was a master stalker, knife fighter, tracker, and hunter. He was most comfortable in the wilderness and wasn't very sociable.

The two of them were best friends but were like oil and water. To see them together, you would think that they hated each other. They would argue and disagree with each other on almost everything. However, you never would want to come between the two of them. They were best of friends to the end.

Shay and Red worked hard on knife skills, bow and arrow, including crossbows, and tracking. They never went one on one inside the rink with a match. However, Jack, Hunter, and Kevin would talk for hours about who would win in a one-on-one match.

It was agreed that the only loser would be anyone that got close to them and any furniture within the area. Either way, it never came to pass. Don't know if they just respected each other's skills or what.

During this time, Ray, Tony, and Kevin were trying to break the codes on the laptops and data that were retrieved from Florida and New Orleans.

They were able to link the operation in Florida and New Orleans to Craig, and they finally found out his last name to be Sutton. There was, however, a mystery person that they couldn't identify or pinpoint their whereabouts.

They were also able to tie Craig as some sort of a middleman to a much larger operation. They knew that they were on to something much bigger than they expected. Just how big, they would soon find out.

Right after they had completed the New Orleans operation. Vicky assigned Ray to act as the computer guru for Vickers Private Investigations. They would then be able to use the two investigators, Robert Green and Jim Appleton, to assist in their investigation.

Robert and Jim remained in the dark about the existence of the Omega Group. This was getting harder and harder with each joint assignment.

Ray and Tony were keeping track of the investigation of the New Orleans operation conducted by FBI Special Agent Roger Basiliano.

After the bodies of Rick and Mad Dog were discovered a few days after the New Orleans house incident, Roger linked the four murders together as being committed by the same person or group.

He had also investigated other sex trafficking murders, including the one in Florida but didn't link any of them together. The local police had ruled the Florida shooting of Derick as a drive-by shooting of a rival gang.

Special Agent Basiliano looking into the Florida shooting caused some concern to Vicky and the others. What red flag on that operation even caused Roger Basiliano to even look at it?

Ray had placed a bug into the FBI's computer that would alert him if anything was entered about the Florida or New Orleans operations or any of their names.

Ray had sent a made-up inter-office memo to Agent Basiliano that included a virus. Once Basiliano opened the memo, it would track wherever he went in the system and log any passwords and data he accessed. He had done the same thing with Tony, without him knowing it a couple of months before.

Ray and Tony both were looking into why that murder had popped up on Roger's radar. Was it something they had done? Or was it Craig? Ray couldn't find anything combing through the FBI's files that had linked the two incidents together.

Thanks to the tracker that Shay had placed on Craig's van and the sheer luck that he drove it back to his home, they were able to track him down to a town north of Texarkana, Arkansas. He lived in a large house next to Grassy Lake, off state 355, near Saratoga.

Hunter sent Jim and Robert, from VPI, up to get whatever information they could on Craig Sutton. Hunter had told Jim and Robert that Craig was running a porn ring. A client had hired VPI to see if he was using their runaway daughter. Their daughter was to be 19 years old, so the police wouldn't be involved.

It had been several weeks since the Omega team had all been together. Vicky wanted to meet with everyone and fill them all in on what was going on with the Craig investigation.

Kevin and Vicky entered the Omega conference room where the others had been waiting.

"It's about time, Aunt Vicky. Glad you could make your own meeting." Shay said kiddingly.

"Sorry guys, I was getting some last-minute updates from Jim and Robert." She replied.

"What have they discovered?" Jack asked.

"He's got a very nice lake house on this Grassy Lake. It sits on three point five acres and is owned by the Young Import Export LLC, according to courthouse records."

"Jim told me that there's an eight-foot-tall wall around three sides of the property. Boat dock on the lake and a swimming pool in the back of the house." She added, "Ray, you got anything else to add?"

"Anything else off those computers and cell phones we got?" Hunter asked before Ray was able to answer.

"I've identified three of the numbers by cross-referencing all the phone records. The one number belonging to Craig called the phone we got from the house in New Orleans. And I was able to, based on date and times, identify the phone used by Derick down in Florida."

"There were several other numbers that Craig had on his phone that I've not been able to identify yet. They are all using burner phones with VPN blocking, but he has called these numbers several times." He added.

"What's this VPN blocking crap you mentioned?" Hunter asked.

"They are able to mask or block the location from where they were calling from and the IP address of the phone being used, " Ray said. "A VPN will assign you a new IP address and run your data through different servers that make tracking you very, very difficult. Even if someone were somehow able to get to your IP address, it wouldn't be yours, but one that's hidden behind the VPN's server." Ray finished up by saying.

Hunter looked at Ray and then at Vicky and the others. "I don't know what in the hell you just said." Hunter said in an irritated voice. "Can you track them or not?"

"No." Ray replied.

"Well, why the hell didn't you just say that to begin with?" Hunter replied, motioning with his hand at Ray.

Ray just shrugged his shoulders and went about telling the group of his findings.

"Jim reported that they've seen two or three adult males and a female coming and going out of his place." Vicky added.

"Do they know if they are Johns or if they work for Craig?" Kevin asked.

"Not sure." Vicky replied.

"We need to get eyes inside there somehow." Tony said, looking over at Ray.

"That sounds easier said than done." Kevin replied.

Ray raised his hand as if he was still in school.

"I've got something that I've been working on." Ray said as everyone turned their attention back to him.

Ray lifted his laptop screen and made a few keystrokes on the laptop. After a couple of minutes, he switched the screen on his laptop and projected it on the monitor on the wall. An image of the Omega Group's hanger and the Vickers jet from high up was now on the screen.

"So, what are we looking at?" Hunter asked as he reclined back into his chair.

"Cool." Jack said. "Why is it so green?"

"It's currently dark in the hanger, and what you are seeing is a drone flying with night vision." Ray boasted with a smile.

The image was still overlooking the front of the jet and about fifteen feet above. It slowly moved and circled the aircraft. It moved through the open storage room door and through the other side. It stopped just outside of the conference room door and hovered.

"Kevin, can you open the door?" Ray asked.

Kevin walked over and opened the door leading out to the hallway. Kevin stood face to face with the drone that they had been watching on the wall monitor.

Kevin's face filled the screen, and he stepped aside, and the drone slowly flew into the room. It circled the room and hovered over the center of the table. Slowly it lowered down to the table and powered off.

"What do you think?" Ray asked as he looked at each person in the room.

"Are you thinking about using this thing up at Craig's place?" Tony asked.

"Yes, Jim and Robert had trouble getting close to the house. We can use this to map out the entire property at night, and they wouldn't even know." Ray said as he closed his laptop.

"Ray, how about heading up to the area to meet up with Jim and Robert? Take whatever you need. I'll let them know." Vicky said, looking over at Ray.

"Cool, Tony and I've been working on the surveillance van. It will be a good test run for it." Ray said excitedly.

"Let's talk about future operations and expanding our manpower." Hunter said, addressing the group.

"We're going to need more firepower and resources. It seems the deeper we get into this, the bigger it gets." Kevin replied while he was sitting there at the table looking over the drone.

"The higher we go, the greater chance we'll be running into the Russian Mafia or some other international group." Tony said. "And they are not going to like us messing with their operations."

"We'll have to take that into consideration as we move forward. And when and if we do, we'll have to consider the risk at that time." Hunter added.

"I don't think it's a matter of if. I think it's more of when we do. We keep climbing up the ladder, and eventually, we're going to climb into the snake's den." Tony said, looking at Hunter.

"I see your point, Tony, but what are we going to do? Are we going to stop and close-up shop?" Hunter asked, looking at Tony and then at Vicky.

"Look, guys, I know what we are doing is the right thing. And things are moving fast. Faster than I expected. But I'm all in." Vicky said, looking at each person as she spoke.

"If we need more people and resources, then so be it. But I have no intention of stopping at this point." She added.

"We're going to have to pick our fights. If we run into an operation that we don't think we can handle, then we'll back off." Hunter said.

"We'll never go into any situation unless we are 100% all in agreement." Vicky said, "So let's see where this Craig Sutton leads us."

"Look guys." Vicky said with a serious tone, "I know you are the ones who are putting yourselves in danger while I sit back and watch. I am relying on you to tell me if things get too dangerous or if we're getting in too deep."

"I know so far, it's been easy and with little risk. I think I can speak for the others in the group in saying that we are all behind you." Jack said as he looked over to Vicky.

"I agree with Jack." Kevin said, "But we will have to grow our manpower and resources as we go. I've been working some with Ray, and he's got some great ideas on how we can achieve this."

"This drone will help with gathering data and assistance to the team when they go in." Ray said, "I've also been working on something else."

"Like what?" Shay asked as she leaned forward in her chair.

"Well, we used the night vision down in New Orleans." Ray said.

"Yes, and they came in handy." Jack replied, giving Ray a thumbs up.

"I've found a thermal camera that some of the fire departments are using." Ray started.

"Thermal camera?" Vicky asked, looking at Ray with a puzzled look on her face.

"Yes, it can see the heat from a source." Ray said, looking at Vicky.

"How is this different from the night vision that we already have?" she asked.

"Night vision requires some tiny bit of light to work. They are useless in total darkness. But the thermal ones pick up the heat emitted from a source." Hunter jumped in with the explanation.

"That's right, Hunter, the two working together would be very valuable." Ray said, looking over to Hunter.

"So, we'll be able to see through walls and shit." Jack said, with a smile from ear to ear.

"No. You've been watching too many movies, Jack." Ray replied. "I've taken the thermal and the night vision and mounted both on a helmet. I've added a heads-up mini screen to the helmet, so you don't need the bulky cameras out front like you see in the movies."

"So, we'll be able to see both or one at a time?" Tony asked.

"Oh, that's not the best part." Ray said. You could see the excitement on his face and hear it in his voice.

"Tell us the rest." Shay said.

"I've also added a regular camera on the helmet too. Like the one on your cellphone. And here's the best part. I've got them Wi-Fi connected to a cellphone." He said, now showing real excitement.

"You're saying that you have attached a cellphone camera, a night vision, and a thermal camera on a helmet and married them together?" Kevin asked as he cocked his head to one side and leaned back.

"Yes, and with it connected to the person's cellphone, we'll be able to see what the person wearing the helmet sees back here at Omega." Ray said as he stood up from his chair.

"When is this thing going to be ready for us to use?" Jack asked.

"In a few weeks. I've still got some issues to work out."

"This sounds great. This will really give us an advantage over these sleazy bastards we are dealing with." Hunter added.

"I've already equipped The Hawk with the three cameras."

"The Hawk?" Hunter asked.

"Yes, I named the drone, The Hawk."

"You and The Hawk get up to Saratoga and see what that thing can get us." Vicky said.

"Back to what I said about 30 minutes ago, what about human power? You think Jim and Robert suspect anything?" Hunter asked.

"If they do, neither one has said anything about it." Vicky replied.

"They are detectives, and you would think they would be smart enough to be at least suspicious of something." Tony said, getting up from the table.

"What do you think about Red? Do you think he can be trusted?" Vicky asked.

"What do you think, Shay? You've worked with him more than anyone else." Hunter asked.

"I trust him." Shay replied, "He's become sort of a big brother to me, and I think he sees me as a little sister too."

"That doesn't really answer her question." Hunter said.

"Yes, I think we can. Besides, all you need to do is tell him that he can break things and beat-up people, and he'll be good to go." She said, looking at Hunter and then at Vicky.

"What about Nicholas?" Hunter asked, looking over at Jack, "You've been working very close with him now for a good while."

"I trust him. He's talked a little about how corrupt things have gotten and how law enforcement can't seem to get things done now. Besides Red and Nicholas, they are a package deal, I think. They've known each other for many years. You wouldn't even know it by the way they both act around each other, but they are very close friends."

"If you ask one, you've got to ask the other." Tony added.

"What worries me is that the more people we bring in, the greater chance that we will be discovered." Vicky said as she leaned forward, putting her elbows on the table, and placed her face in her hands.

"I hear you, Vicky, but this is getting bigger than we first planned." Jack said, "We either play ball, or we hit the dugout and go home."

"I know." She said, with her head still braced with her hands.

She leaned back in her chair and looked over at Kevin, "Well, Kevin, do we bring them in?"

"Are we talking about all four of them?" he asked.

"Let's just talk to Jim and Robert right now." She replied.

"I vote yes." Kevin replied.

"Ray, what about you?" she asked.

Vicky went one by one, asking if they should include Jim and Robert in the Omega group. Each replied yes without hesitation.

"Ok then. Hunter, will you approach them and make them the offer?" Vicky said.

"I'll ride up with Ray and have a talk with them. Besides, I want to get a firsthand look at this Craig's place."

"What about Red and Nicholas?" Shay asked.

"Let's see how this thing with Sutton goes." Vicky responded, "I have a feeling that this doesn't end with Sutton."

"I think we should also ask Stan." Shay said in a matter-of-fact voice.

"Stan doesn't want to know any details about the group. He wants plausible deniability." Hunter said, looking at Shay.

"So, he knows?" Vicky asked, looking at Hunter.

"Yes and No." Hunter said as he stuck his hand out and rocked it slowly from right to left, in a maybe, maybe not motion.

"Stan is a man that has a lot of contacts in many different fields. He prefers to stay in the background and not directly get his hands dirty. He'll help when he can." Hunter said.

"He hooked us up with Dr. Wilson and some of the weapons that we have." Vicky commented.

"And none of you go asking him anything about his past. You may not like his answer." Hunter ended as he looked directly at Jack.

"What? Why is everyone looking at me?" Jack said, throwing both hands up in the air.

"I've checked him out through the FBI database to see what I can find. He's like a ghost. There's nothing really on the man." Tony said, "Everyone here has a history that can be traced. But this Stan dude has none. It's like he just appeared one day."

"Look, all I can say is Stan is a great resource for us. But we must use him wisely." Hunter replied.

Vicky pushed herself back from the table, "Ok, we've all got our work cut out for us. Ray and Hunter, you two head up tomorrow and meet with Jim and Robert. Send me what you can get with this drone thing." She said, pointing at Ray's drone.

"Jack and Shay, tomorrow, why don't you two just hang out at the ranch and chill out."

"I've got to head into the office tomorrow. I do have another job, you know." Tony said as he took a sip of his coffee.

Kevin was leaning against the wall and looked over at Vicky, "Vicky, if it's ok with you, I want to do some checks on the jet. It's been a while?"

She nodded, and they all started to leave the conference room.

"I'll catch up with you tomorrow back here if you don't mind. I've got some final adjustments to do on The Hawk before we go." Ray directed his comment toward Hunter.

Hunter and Ray met up with Jim and Robert in their motel room in Saratoga. After they got settled, the four of them took a ride out to see Craig's place.

As they drove, Jim and Robert filled Hunter and Ray in on everything they knew about the compound and surrounding area.

In the almost two weeks of observation, they had noticed a slight pattern in what went on. They went on to explain that Craig had three other guys working for him and that there were always two people at the compound.

They had seen food deliveries several times a week from different delivery companies. They didn't see much as far as cameras on the property, but they couldn't get close enough to the house to really be able to tell.

There were two pit bulls that roamed the property. At least once a day, one of the guys would walk the property wall. He would always have one of the dogs with him and be armed with a sidearm and a SIG MPX short-barreled submachine gun.

The house backed up to the lake. It had a dock, a jet ski, and a small ski boat. The lake was lined with private residences and wasn't open to the public. This stopped them from getting much information from the back of the house. There was only one ramp into the lake, and that was in a fenced area that wasn't accessible to the public.

The house was two stories, with a stone front, and it was just over 4,000 square feet. It had a full basement that was unfinished. It also had a three-car garage that was attached to the right side of the house. The house sat on three and a half acres of land, mostly landscaped open area with a patch of trees here and there. This was all that the courthouse records showed.

They kept the outside of the house well-lit at night, and at the entrance onto the property stood a ten-foot iron gate with a keypad and a security camera. The gate, along with the surrounding area, was exceptionally well-lit.

There are three vehicles registered to Young Import and Export. One was the van that was used down in New Orleans. It hasn't moved since its return and has been parked inside the garage. The two other vehicles were black Escalades with tinted windows. Both had been used during the time that Jim and Robert were watching.

The only occupants of the house that Jim and Robert could see were Craig, a young woman, and the other three men. They did follow one of the vehicles as it left the house and drove to a local clinic. They saw two of the men escort the young woman, who appeared to be about 20 or 22 years old, into the clinic. They were there for about an hour, and the three left and returned to the house. They were able to slip a tracking device on this vehicle, like they did the van, while the three were in the clinic.

The surveillance team returned back to their hotel room and sat around eating a couple of pizzas that they had stopped and picked up on the way back.

"Robert, I want you and Ray to go back after it gets dark and take that eagle thing of Ray's and see what you can find out." Hunter said to the others.

"It's called The Hawk." Ray exclaimed.

"Whatever, and I want to go over some things with Jim while you two are gone." Hunter said as he took a bite out of his pizza.

"Tell me what you know about the three other men and anything else you've found out about Sutton." Hunter asked.

"One of their names is Pavel. He seems to oversee the other two. He's tall, with blond hair, and is of medium build. He hangs mostly with Sutton." Robert said.

"The other two both have a stocky build. One is called Nikolai, and he has short dark hair. The other one is bald-headed. Not sure about his name, but we think it may be Ivan. Both men are tanned and well-disciplined. I'm sure all three are former military." Robert added.

"Russian?" Ray asked.

"Sounds like it. But we're not sure right now. We've not heard them speak anything other than English the few times we were able to hear them." Robert said.

"It's been dark for a couple of hours now. You two start heading over to Sutton's and send in Ray's bird." Hunter said.

Ray and Robert headed out to the van to get everything ready. Ray gave Robert a quick tour of the electronics and the operations of The Hawk.

They drove for about 20 minutes and parked about half-mile from Sutton's house. Ray set The Hawk outside and launched it toward the target. The bird had about 45 minutes of flight time before it had to return.

Ray had the drone take a high pass over the property to get a general view of the layout. He then took the drone and flew slowly just inside of the fence line about 30 feet off the ground.

He brought the drone back to the van and replaced the battery with a new one. He then returned the drone back to the target and continued mapping out the entire property, including the outside of the house and dock area. He had to make several return trips back to the van to change out the battery. This had gone on for several hours when they spotted one of the men doing his nightly patrol. Ray landed the drone on the rooftop of the main house and followed the man with both the night vision and thermal cameras.

Shortly after Ray and Robert left, Jim and Hunter were talking about the last ball game when Jim suddenly changed the subject.

"What's the big interest in this Sutton group? We know we're supposed to find out for the client if their daughter is working for Sutton." Jim said.

"Yes and?" Hunter replied, looking Jim in the eyes.

"Well, Hunter, Robert, and I have put two and two together." Jim paused for a second.

"And what number did you two come up with?" Hunter asked.

"You had us on the Macon account along with doing work on the New Orleans data that led us here." Jim said, looking down at the floor.

"Yes, leg work for clients, you've done it before. What's the problem?" Hunter asked, staring intently at Jim.

"All of which has something to do with sex trafficking." Jim said.

"That's a growing problem." Hunter said, still looking at Jim.

"Robert and I both know what happened to Shay when she was little." Jim said cautiously.

"Where are you going with this, Jim?" Hunter asked, leaning back in his chair and crossing his legs.

"Well, there's the fact that you put Ray at VPI Group a few weeks ago. We know there is something up." Jim said, and he leaned back, matching Hunter's posture.

"What are you asking me, Jim?"

"You add Jack, Tony, Ray, along with all this special training, and things really don't add up to business as usual."

"We're trying to keep up with the times and technology. What's wrong with that?" Hunter replied as he leaned forward, placing his elbows on his knees.

"Also, with the Macon, New Orleans, and Florida cases, we noticed that a few of the people we were assigned to investigate ended up dead."

"What are you saying, Jim? That we had something to do with those deaths?" Hunter shot back, now showing some anger in his voice.

"Hunter, I'm just saying."

"You're just saying what. That we are out killing people?" Hunter interrupted.

"Look, Hunter, we go back several years. Robert and I feel that there's something bigger going on." Jim leaned forward and grabbed himself a beer.

"Bigger like what? And you're not going to offer me one? Hand me a beer." Hunter responded, leaning forward and reaching for the beer from Jim.

"Robert and I feel that you're going after these sex gangs and eliminating them."

"And?" Hunter replied.

"We want in." Jim said as he sat his beer on the table.

"You two want into this hit squad that you think we're running?" Hunter asked, looking at Jim.

"Yes."

"Does Robert feel the same way?"

"We've both been talking about it for weeks. He and I were going to talk to you about it when we heard you were coming up here."

Hunter sat there staring at Jim for a couple of minutes, not saying a word. Jim was starting to feel uncomfortable, not knowing what Hunter was going to say.

Was he going to fire them both? Had they been wrong about the entire situation? Were they going to be the next to be executed? All this was rushing through Jim's mind.

"Ok." Hunter said.

"Ok, what?" Jim asked.

"Ok, you two are in." Hunter said, leaning in towards Jim.

"But understand this. If either one of you talks about this to anyone outside of the group, you'll be joining the others. Do I make myself clear?" Hunter said as he reached out to shake Jim's hand.

About an hour passed as the two sat watching TV when Ray and Robert arrived. Hunter stood up and asked how the bird did. Ray and Robert spent about ten minutes going over the new information that they had gathered.

"Great job, you two. But it's late, and I'm tired. Let's meet back for breakfast tomorrow morning at eight." Hunter said as he walked to the door of the hotel room.

Ray stood and followed Hunter to the door. Hunter stopped before opening the door and looked back at both Jim and Robert.

"Welcome to Omega Group." Hunter said as he opened and exited into the hallway.

Ray looked at them both, nodding and smiling as he followed Hunter out of the room and into the hallway.

As soon as the door was closed, Robert looked at Jim and said, "So we were right?"

"Yes, looks that way." Jim replied.

Once they got back to their room, Hunter called Vicky and filled her in on his talk with Jim. He told her that he was going to use them on the Sutton assignment. Hunter said that they were going to meet in the morning and have breakfast, then head back afterward. He was going to bring back Jim and Robert and have them meet the team.

After breakfast, Hunter told Jim and Robert to pack it up and follow him down to Coulter Airfield.

It was over a five-hour drive back to Omega headquarters. Hunter called to let Vicky know when they were about an hour away.

They pulled up in front of the building housing the Omega headquarters and got out of their vehicles.

Hunter walked over to the entrance, and Ray followed. Jim and Robert walked close behind, checking out the building and area as they walked.

Hunter led them into the conference room as Ray excused himself to take some things up to the communication area.

"Have a seat, guys. The others will be here any minute."

The two new Omega members anxiously took a seat at the conference table as they both took in the new environment.

"Afternoon guys." A voice sounded from behind.

"Vicky!" Jim and Robert said at the same time.

"You're part of this group?" Robert asked.

"Well, yes, I sort of started it and run it." She said with a smile. She took a seat directly across from the two of them. "I'm sure you have a ton of questions."

"We thought Hunter was the head of this group." Jim said as he looked at her.

"He only thinks he is." She replied with a laugh.

About that time, the door opened, and Tony and Kevin walked in.

"Hi, guys. I'm Tony." He reached out and shook their hands, and took a seat.

Jim looked at Tony and said, "Aren't you with the FBI?"

"Yes, but don't hold that against me." He said with a slight smile.

"Good to see you again." Kevin said as he nodded at them both.

The door opened, and Jack walked in, and he also introduced himself and took a seat.

Shay entered the room about a minute later, and both Jim and Robert looked at each other.

"Shay! You're part of this group too?" they said with a surprised look on their faces.

"She's our little mascot." Jack replied.

"And you're my bitch, remember?" she replied.

"Wait what?" Robert asked.

"Long story." Hunter said.

"Yelp, it will take a lot longer to tell it than it actually took." Shay said with a big smile.

Everyone started laughing as Ray entered the room. "What did I miss?" he asked.

"Nothing." Vicky said, "Now that we're all here, let's get down to business."

Chapter Eleven

Keeps Getting Bigger

"Welcome to America, my name is Pavel, and you must be Bohdana Kovalenko." Pavel said in Russian.

"Here, let me take your bags. Did you enjoy your flight from Ukraine?" he asked.

"Yes, very long," Bohdana responded.

They had a pleasant conversation as they went to pick up her baggage and proceeded out to the car. They talked about where she grew up, her family back in Ukraine, and how she dreamed of becoming an American model.

"Well, we don't have far to go. You can rest then." Pavel said as they reached the car.

"This is Ivan. He'll be driving us to where you'll be staying and meeting your new agent."

"This is so wonderful. I can't believe this is happening to me. It's something I've dreamed of since I was a little girl." Bohdana said, showing her excitement.

Ivan greeted Bohdana and opened the door of the SUV for her. "Please get in."

During the short trip from the Texarkana Regional Airport, Bohdana looked out the window of the SUV. She was very excited about her new adventure in America. Her dream of becoming an American model was about to come true.

As they pulled up to the gate of the Sutton compound, she marveled at the size and beauty of the house.

"I have never seen or been in such a home." She said with excitement.

"Get used to it, Bohdana. This is your future." Pavel said with a big smile. "You're going to experience things you've never dreamed of before."

"I will show you your room. Get some rest, and I'll introduce you to the boss tomorrow." Pavel said as they approached the garage.

They pulled into the garage of the Sutton house, and the door slowly closed behind them.

Vicky entered the communication room of Omega and saw Ray sitting in front of his computer.

"You're here awfully late, Ray."

"I just wanted to get some of this data we retrieved from New Orleans and Sutton's place decoded." He replied in a tired voice.

She walked over and stood behind him, "What have you been able to get so far?"

"I've been able to tie the phone that Sutton uses to the other three guys' phones. And I've located the bank account the New Orleans group used and a couple of money transfers to and from an account used by Young Import and Export." Ray said, turning to face her.

"The New Orleans account had $384,520.03 in it."

"You said had?" she asked suspiciously.

"Yes, if you check the Omega operational account, you'll see a slight increase." Ray replied, smiling.

"Can that money be traced back to us?"

"Vicky, Vicky, Vicky, I'm shocked that you would even ask. I bounced the transfer around to several banks around the world before it ended up in the operations account."

"What about the Young account?"

"That one will be a little harder to move. More security on that account, but I'll be able to move that money maybe sometime tomorrow."

"How much is in that account?"

"Let me look." Ray brought up another screen on the wall monitor and entered a few keystrokes on the computer.

"There it is."

Vicky walked around to get a closer look at the amount shown at the bottom of the screen.

$23,754,188.75 was the total shown.

"Impressive. Hold off on transferring that money for now."

"We are good on funds. I just moved a couple million into the general account the day before yesterday."

"I'm afraid to ask where this money came from." She said, looking back at Ray.

"I've been watching this mid-level drug dealer's account in South America. It looked like he had just made a big sale, so I moved the money."

"He's going to be pissed when he finds out." Vicky said with a slight chuckle.

"Not as pissed off as his boss is going to be when he doesn't get his cut of the money."

"I'm going to get everyone together tomorrow so we can go over the information we have on Sutton. We can wait on the other data we have and what we can get from Sutton's place. Go and get some rest." She said as she exited the room.

The next day, everyone got together in the conference room. They wanted to review what data they had and come up with a plan to hit the Sutton place.

Vicky called the meeting to order. She wanted to get everyone up to speed on what they had uncovered so far.

They discussed the comings and goings of the three associates of Sutton, their patrol schedule around the property, what weapons they are using, as well as information about the deliveries that would come two or three times a week.

Other than the one girl that was taken to the clinic, no one else was spotted outside of the house.

Ray's drone was able to map out the entire property and the outside of the house in detail. Very few pictures of the inside were gathered due to the curtains being drawn on almost all of the windows.

The one thing that was pointed out was the fact that two of the associates would always go to a local bar every Friday night. They would be gone for several hours, and this seemed to be the best time to hit the house.

"Does anyone have anything new you want to add?" Vicky asked, looking around the room.

"I've got something I'd like to add." Ray said, "I placed two Baby Hawks on top of the roof of Sutton's house."

"I know I'm new, but what the hell is a Baby Hawk?" Jim asked as he looked at each person.

"Man, Ray showed me some badass toys he's got." Robert replied. "He showed me some stuff that night in the van that would blow your mind."

"You going to tell us?" Tony asked.

"It's nothing really exciting. A Baby Hawk is just a small solar-powered drone with a Wi-Fi camera. I call them Baby Hawks because I can deliver them using The Hawk to save energy. Then they can fly off on their own."

"Can we watch what is going on right now at Sutton's?" Vicky asked.

"Not a live feed. They'll load everything up to the cloud every two hours. I was able to hack into the neighbor's Wi-Fi signal and use it to transmit. They had an easy password to hack. I put one watching the front and one watching the pool area."

"Did you get a chance to look at the video yet?" Vicky asked.

"Everything looks normal as far as the coming and goings from before." Robert said, "Nothing that would raise a red flag except..."

"Except what?" asked Hunter.

Ray pulled up a video clip from the previous day's recordings and displayed it on the wall monitor.

"This right here is the pool area. I think we all recognize our friend Sutton." Jim said.

As the video continued, it showed Craig getting up and greeting a young girl. She looked to be in her early twenties and very beautiful by all accounts. They both talked for a few minutes and looked like they were having a friendly conversation.

Then things turned bad. Craig grabbed the young girl's face with one hand and turned it from the right to the left. It looked as if he was checking her face out like someone would do if they were about to buy some livestock.

The young girl pulled Craig's hand away and took a step back. Craig took a step toward her and gave her a backhand to the face. She turned and fell to the ground on her knees.

"Sorry, guys, but the audio is not very clear at all." Ray said.

It then showed Ivan and Nikolai coming over and picking her up, and carrying her into the house. Craig followed the three into the house and out of camera view.

Vicky and the others sat there without saying a word. You could see her eyes starting to water up. She cleared her throat and said, "Ok, guys, this is what we're here for."

Shay said in a low and stern voice, "I want him. That Craig guy is mine!"

"Ray, keep an eye on things with those little drone things of yours. Let's make sure they stay to their pattern, and in a week, we'll go in. Any questions?" Hunter asked.

The entire team spent every day reviewing the notes and videos of the property. They studied the schedule of the three people they assumed to be guards.

They had decided that Jack, Shay, and Jim would go in after two of the guys left on their Friday night trip to the bar. The three of them worked together for hours practicing room clearing and backing each other up using the Vickers Ranch house and Omega HQ as a model.

Ray and Hunter had installed, in the firearms training area of the Omega building, a high-tech firearms training simulator. Each member of the Omega group was trained in hostage, room clearing, and other situations. This also included Vicky and Ray, who normally would never be in on a raid or needed to be armed.

Robert and Kevin would follow the two guys to the bar. Hunter and Ray would stay in the van to watch the electronics and control everything.

Tony and Vicky would watch, like last time, back at Omega.

No cameras or electronics were seen outside of the house, so that was not a real issue to worry about. The only camera that was discovered was the one at the front gate. They assumed that with the two Pitbulls, cameras were not needed.

They all felt and agreed that entry onto the property would be best from the lakeside since it didn't have a wall to overcome.

The three going in were going to stun the dogs with their Tasers. Once the dogs were down, they would inject them with Etorphine M99 tranquilizer. This would knock them out for a couple of hours and not harm them.

They would each be carrying the same firepower as they did when they entered the New Orleans house. But this time, they had Jim along to help with anything that they might run into unexpectedly. They each carried two syringes filled with Etorphine M99 in case they needed to sedate someone or, in this case, two Pitbulls.

The day of the raid had arrived, they all met in Hunter's hotel room to go over any questions and to make sure everyone knew what to do.

They each went over their equipment to make sure everything was in order and operational.

It was 11 p.m., and Robert and Kevin had verified that two of the men had left the Sutton property.

They followed them to the same bar that they had been going to. They then placed a tracking device on the underside of the vehicle and waited.

Once the operation began, Jack and the others entered the property. Robert and Kevin would take up positions about a mile from Sutton's but still be able to see if the two guys left early and came back.

Once Kevin and Robert reached their position, they radioed in. It was now time for the others to move into position.

It was a dark night with a thin layer of clouds covering the moon. This gave enough light to make their night vision work but turned everything green and two-dimensional.

As Jack, Shay, and Jim were creeping up to the lakeside wall of Craig's property, they could hear the sounds of a party going on across the lake. This would cover any noise that the three would happen to make.

Jack looked back at Shay and then looked up. About ten feet behind them and eight feet in the air flew the drone. It had been following them from the moment they got out of the van a hundred yards back.

"That thing is freaking me out. What does Ray call it?" Jack asked.

"The Hawk, I think." Shay replied.

"You know I can hear you, right?" came Ray's voice over the com unit.

"Any sign of the dogs?" Jim asked.

Ray piloted the drone up and over to the other side of the wall, "Yes, I see them. They are stalking you just on the other side."

Jack had reached the end of the wall about three feet out into the water. The water came up to just below Jack's knees. The dogs both stood on the other side at the water's edge, just three feet away.

Jim slowly moved up to stand shoulder-to-shoulder with Jack while Shay turned and guarded their rear.

The dogs were torn between watching the drone overhead and the noise just on the other side of the wall.

"Jack, you and Jim move into position, and I'll distract the dogs." Ray said.

Jack pressed his talk button one time to signal that he heard and understood.

Jim and Jack slowly peered around the wall and saw the dogs just feet away. They were both looking up at the drone as it slowly got closer to them.

Jim and Jack had their tasers ready, and both aimed and fired at each of the dogs.

The dogs both cried out and went down. The three quickly came around the wall and gave each dog a shot of M99.

"There now, big dawg, you two sit this one out. You'll be ok in a couple of hours." Jim said, stroking one of the dog's heads.

The three moved slowly in the darkness of the shadows with their suppressed Short Barreled rifles, CZ Scorpions, at the ready.

They soon reached the door that led into the den of the house. Jim took the side of the door with the doorknob. Jack and Shay stood on the other side, ready to enter.

Jim checked the doorknob to see if it was locked. To his surprise, it was unlocked, and he slowly opened the door.

As the door opened, they heard a beep that lasted only for a second. The three entered the room and took up positions on one knee. Jack went in first, followed by Jim and Shay. The three stayed there motionless for about three minutes to see if anyone had heard the beep and came to investigate.

There were two open doorways leading out of the den. Jack pointed at Jim and signaled him to move to one of the doorways and to hold the position. He turned and did the same for Shay to do the same with the other doorway.

Jack moved slowly over and took position on the other side of the door from Jim. They both peered into the room to see if it was clear. This room looked to be the dining room. Once they were sure it was clear, they entered and moved into the room and took position on the other door leading out.

They could tell that this next room was the kitchen, with a waist-high bar dividing the kitchen and breakfast area. The two of them moved into the kitchen and saw two doors. One door on the left led out to the garage, and the other on the right down a long hallway.

After clearing those two rooms, Jack motioned for Jim to hold his position there.

He contacted Shay on their com unit, "Viper, one coming your way down the hallway." Jack wanted to let her know he was coming so she wouldn't shoot him.

"Jack, give us an update. Vicky is busting my balls over here." Hunter asked over the comms.

"Three rooms cleared, no contact." He replied to Hunter.

"Jim's posted in the kitchen to watch the first floor. Shay and I are going to finish clearing the first floor and head up to the second."

"Keep an eye out for that girl. She's somewhere in that house." Hunter said.

"Copy." Jack replied.

It took about five minutes for Jack and Shay to clear the rest of the first floor. Before heading up the stairs to the second floor, they both switched from their CZ Scorpions to their suppressed 9mm handgun CZ P-10s.

Shay led as they slowly crept up the stairs leading to the second floor, guns at the ready.

At the top of the stairs, they both stopped, and Shay peeked around the corner and down the hallway.

She saw nothing but four doors that led into what could have been bedrooms.

Where is he? She thought to herself. She was referring to the guy that stayed behind, the third guy. Was he waiting behind one of the doors, or was he sound asleep still? This was the most stressful part of this job. Not knowing where your prey was or wondering if the prey was stalking you also.

Was he waiting behind one of these doors with his gun drawn, ready for her to open the door and enter?

Did they still have the element of surprise? Was the bell sound announcing their entry enough to alert him?

Her heart was racing, and her hand was beginning to shake a little. This was worse than the New Orleans operation. There they were in and out in a matter of a couple of minutes. This time, they had already been in the house for over 15 minutes.

She was just two feet away from the first door, and she was plastered up against the wall as tight as she could get.

She heard the door, now just inches away, creak as it slowly opened. She quickly held up her fist to signal Jack, who was less than a foot behind her, to stop.

Three shots shattered the wall just inches above her head as the person inside the room started firing through the wall into the hallway.

Sheetrock and dust flew all over the two of them as they both hit the floor. Simultaneously Jack and Shay pointed their suppressed CZ P-10s and emptied both their magazines into the wall.

Still lying on their backs, the two quickly reloaded and held their guns aimed at the door. They both had dust and chunks of sheetrock all over them.

They could hear Hunter screaming over the com units for a status.

"Report! Shay! Jack! Jim! What the hell is going on?" Hunter screamed out.

"Hunter, what happened? Are they ok? SPEAK TO ME!" came the screams from Vicky.

"Hunter, this is Jim. I heard shots up on the second floor, I don't....... SQUIRTER!" Jim called out, "We've got a runner out the back door!"

"Jim, let him go. Ray's got him on the drone's camera. Go and check on the others." Hunter instructed.

"Copy that." Jim replied.

"AND GET ME A FUCKING STATUS ON THEM!" Hunter yelled out over the comms.

"He jumped into the boat at the dock, and he's heading to the ramp area." Ray yelled out to Hunter.

"Kevin, Robert, he's heading your direction. Grab him." Hunter called out over their coms.

"It's Sutton." Ray said, "But the drones only got about ten minutes of airtime left."

"Kevin, I want him alive." Hunter said.

"Hunter, what is the status of Shay and Jack?" Vicky called out. She and Tony had been listening to everything that was going on. They could hear but could only talk to Hunter. This cut down on getting unnecessary talk over the coms and allowed Hunter to direct everything. Vicky could only communicate with Ray and Hunter in the van.

"Jim, report." Hunter said.

Up in the hallway, Jack and Shay still lay there with their guns pointing at the door. The door slowly started to open, and there stood a man just inside the room.

The dust had clouded the lenses of Shay and Jack's Night vision, but they could still make out a person standing in the doorway. He slowly staggered forward and into the hallway. They could see that he had several gunshot wounds to the chest.

The man dropped down to his knees and then fell face-first onto the floor.

Just then, Jim entered the hallway from the stairs, "Jack, Shay, are you ok?"

"We're good." They both called out.

"Hunter, I've got Shay and Jack. They're both ok."

"Thank God." Vicky said. She hugged Tony and wiped the tears out of her eyes.

Jack reached up with his hand as Jim approached the two still lying down on the floor. Jim stepped across Jack and reached down to help Shay up.

"Thanks, man, for the help up." Jack said as he stood and brushed off the dust from his clothes.

After Jim helped Shay up to her feet, he knelt next to the man lying face down on the floor. Jim checked his neck to see if he could feel a pulse.

"He's dead." Jim said, looking back at Shay.

"Shay, if you had been three inches taller, he would have blown your head off." Jack said, pointing over at the bullet holes in the wall.

The dead man lay there only dressed in his underwear and with three exit wounds out the middle of his back.

"We have one dead." Jack finally reported over the coms to Hunter.

"Who is it?" Hunter asked.

Jim rolled over the man's body onto his back. "It's Pavel."

Kevin and Robert had pulled in and parked the SUV in a spot just to the right of the top of the ramp. They watched Sutton approach the boat and jump out as he ran the boat up on shore.

Sutton was barefooted and only had a pair of shorts on. Kevin and Robert got out of the SUV and approached Sutton as he limped up the ramp.

"Man, are you alright?" Robert asked Sutton as he approached.

"NO! Someone broke into my house and started shooting!" Sutton said as he turned and pointed back at the lake and towards his house.

"You want us to call the cops for you?" Kevin asked.

"Yes!" Sutton replied. "NO! Just take me into town." Sutton changed his mind, knowing that if the cops came, they would search the house and find what was in the basement.

"Dude, you need to call the cops if someone broke into your house." Robert replied.

"Ok, man, we can run you into town. But if it was me, I'd be calling the cops." Kevin said. "Jump in the back if that's what you want."

Robert opened the passenger side rear door for him, and Sutton got in.

"Where to man?" Robert asked as he and Kevin got into their front seats.

"There's a bar down just outside of town. I've got a couple of friends there, and they can help." Sutton replied.

They had driven toward town for about two miles when Robert, sitting in the front passenger's seat, turned to face Craig.

"Well, Craig, what do you do for a living?" Robert asked.

"Wait. I never told you my name. How do you know me? Have we met?"

"Not in person." Kevin replied.

"Just let me out here. I can walk the rest of the way." Sutton said with a concerned look on his face.

Robert, still facing Sutton, reached around with his right hand in between the front seats.

"What? What is that? What are you..." Sutton cried out as one million volts of electricity knocked him unconscious.

Robert had pulled his taser out and shot Sutton right in the stomach. Robert then pulled out one of his syringes filled with M99 and injected it into Sutton's leg.

"Package is secured." Kevin said over his com.

"Copy." Hunter replied.

Jack and Shay had recovered from their battle and continued clearing the second floor of the house.

"Jim, can you send us a picture of this guy? We need to verify who he is." Hunter said.

About thirty seconds later, a picture popped up on Ray's monitor and the monitor back at Omega.

"Hunter, can you ask Jim to get a closer picture of the tattoo on this guy's shoulder?" Tony asked.

Hunter relayed to Jim the message from Tony. In just a few seconds, a picture of the tattoo popped up on the monitors. The tattoo was that of a sixteen-pointed star. Tony walked up to the monitor to take a closer look at the tattoo.

"That's what I was afraid of." Tony said to Hunter.

"What?" Vicky and Hunter both said at the same time.

"This Pavel guy is a captain in Bratva." Tony answered.

"What is Bratva?" Vicky asked.

"The Russian Mafia." Tony said, replying to Vicky, who was standing next to him, and to Hunter over the communication mic.

Hunter relayed the information to the others as Jack and Shay were busy clearing the basement. Jim had moved back down to the first floor and stood watch.

"We have a slight problem." Shay said over her mic.

"What now?" Hunter replied.

"We found Bohdana."

"Is she ok?" He asked.

"Yes."

"Well, what's the problem?" He replied.

"We found her and two other girls." Shay said they were locked up in the basement.

"Are they all ok?" Hunter asked.

"They appear to be." She said, "What do you want us to do?"

"Shay, you hold them there for now. Jack, you and Jim sweep the house and find anything of value."

"Hunter, we've got Sutton back at the hotel. We tied him up and stuffed him in the bathroom." Kevin reported over the mic.

"We've been listening. Do you want us to help out at Sutton's house?" Robert asked.

"No, sit on Sutton and make sure he stays quiet." Hunter responded.

After about 20 minutes, Jack reported back to Hunter they had completed the sweep and found a couple of laptops, DVDs, cell phones, and the girls' passports.

Things didn't go totally as planned, but what does. They now have Sutton tied up in their hotel room. They have three girls to deal with that weren't in the plan. And they've now stuck their foot in the hornet's nest of the Russian Mafia.

They keep getting deeper and deeper into it. Where will it lead them, where will it end, and at what cost?

All this was rushing through Hunter's mind when Vicky's voice came over the radio.

"What's the status?"

"We're trying to wrap things up here." He replied, "I'll contact you once we get back to the hotel."

Hunter switched his attention back over to the Sutton house." Jim, use one of Sutton's vehicles to get the girls out and take them back to one of the hotel rooms."

"Jack, set the package up as we talked. Then you and Shay get the hell out of there. We'll pick you two up out front in the van."

After the three girls gathered their things together, Jim rushed the three into one of Sutton's vans, and they drove off heading to the hotel.

Ray and Hunter picked Jack and Shay up in the van, and they headed back to the hotel.

Vicky had rented each of the team members a separate room, along with rooms on each side. This gave them the privacy they needed to come and go without notice, hopefully.

Once Jim got the girls to the hotel, they put all the girls in one of the middle rooms, and Shay stayed with them.

Ray sent a copy of the girls' passports to Vicky, so she could find out who they were and where they lived. She and Tony spent the next couple of hours tracking down the locations where these girls were taken from. They had decided since the girls were all over 18, they would just have them flown back to their own country and to their families. She didn't want to involve the police because it may lead them back to the group.

After getting back, Hunter went to check on Robert, Kevin, and Sutton.

"How is our guest doing?" Hunter asked.

"He's been quiet." Kevin said.

Sutton was lying faceup on one of the beds. He was blindfolded, and his arms and legs were tied, one to each corner of the bed. He only had the shorts on that he was wearing when Robert and Kevin had picked him up. His mouth was taped shut with duct tape in case he tried to scream out.

"He's just been lying there, not moved or tried to escape." Kevin said.

Hunter walked over to the bed where Sutton was tied down. He pulled up a chair next to the bed and sat down. Hunter reached over and ripped the tape off Sutton's face.

"Tell me, what's your involvement in this sex trafficking organization?" Hunter asked.

"Fuck you. You and your friends are going to regret the day you ever laid your eyes on me!" Sutton exclaimed.

"You just wait until my friends find me, and when they do." Sutton started, but before he was finished, Hunter stuffed a rag in his mouth and re-taped it shut.

"Perhaps the Surgeon can help with getting the information out of him." Kevin said.

"Who is this, Surgeon?" Robert asked.

"He's done some work for us." Kevin replied.

"Like what kind of work?" Robert asked.

"The kind you never want to be done on you or anyone you know." Hunter said, still looking at Sutton lying on the bed.

"He has his own special way of getting answers out of people." Kevin added.

"I see."

"You'll get to meet him soon enough." Hunter said, looking over at him.

"It's late. You two take turns babysitting our guest while the other one gets some sleep. We've got to sort this mess out tomorrow." Hunter said as he walked to the door of the room.

"I need to call Vicky and fill her and Tony in on what all went down. Talk to you guys tomorrow." Hunter closed the door and walked down to his room.

Ray had ordered dinner for the entire group, and soon after they ate, they all turned in for bed.

It was around 2 a.m. when the two associates of Sutton left the bar and headed back to the house.

Shortly after leaving the bar, the two guys arrived at the Sutton property, and about 30 seconds later, they both entered the house.

The entire house went up into a ball of fire, throwing debris over the entire property and into the property on each side. Windows were shattered in the surrounding houses as car alarms sounded throughout the immediate area.

The explosion was heard several miles away.

Hunter was standing looking out the window of his hotel when he saw the flash from the Sutton house explosion. A few seconds after the distant fireball died away, Hunter closed the curtains of his hotel room and crawled into bed.

Jack was just about to fall asleep when he heard the explosion several miles away. He opened his eyes to the sound and then closed them back. He rolled over to his side, pulled the covers up, and fell asleep.

"Did you guys hear that explosion last night?" Robert asked.

"Yes, I saw on the news this morning that a house blew up and killed several people inside." Hunter said, sipping on his morning coffee.

"I wonder what caused it." Ray asked.

"Guess someone left the gas on when they came home and turned on a light. BOOM, the house blew up." Jack said.

"How do you know that?" Jim asked.

"Just a wild guess." Jack replied as he checked the messages on his cell phone.

Hunter's phone rang, and he reached over the table to answer it. It was Vicky and Tony on the other end.

"How are things this morning?" she asked.

"Everyone is just finished breakfast and meeting over here in my room. I've got Jim, Ray, Jack, and Robert. Kevin stepped over to round Shay and the three girls up."

Kevin had earlier made a run to pick up food for everyone at one of the local diners.

Shay and the three girls were in an adjoining room that connected to Hunter's room.

"Let me speak with Ray." Vicky asked.

Hunter handed his cell phone over to Ray.

"Ray, how fast can you set up an account in each of the girls' names?" Vicky asked.

"I've already got a few emergency accounts set up with about a thousand dollars in them."

"Take three of the accounts and transfer two million from Sutton's account into each one of them."

"What for?" Ray asked.

"Give the account information to each one of the girls." She replied, "This won't make up for what has happened to them, but it may help. Then move the remainder into one of our general accounts. Give the phone back to Hunter."

"I saw on the news that there was a house explosion up there close to where you're at." She said to Hunter.

"Yes, I saw that too. I heard there were three bodies found so far in the debris. Very sad, they were all burned beyond recognition." He replied.

"I agree, very sad. How's our guest?" she asked.

"Kevin gave him something to help him sleep for the next couple of hours."

"Ok, well, there are tickets for each of the girls at the airports will call. Make sure they get on the plane safely."

"I'll make sure. We should be back down at Coulter Airfield in about three and a half hours or so."

"We're going to leave Sutton's SUV at the long-term parking. Oh, one last thing, contact Dr. Wilson and tell him to expect a new patient." With this, Hunter ended the call.

Chapter Twelve

The Brotherhood

Everything was blurry as he slowly opened his eyes. It was hard for him to focus as he thought, "Where am I"? He looked around the room, but everything was a blur. His mind couldn't comprehend what had happened or where he was.

After a few seconds, a figure of a man began coming into focus just feet away. He tried to speak but couldn't.

"What is going on?" he thought.

He squinted his eyes and shook his head, trying to shake the fog out of his head.

A man looking to be in his sixties sitting across from him was starting to come into focus.

"Where am I? Who the hell are you?" he asked, with a slight slur in his speech.

The man didn't reply. He just continued sitting there with his legs crossed and his fingers intertwined on his lap.

He looked around and noticed he was in a small room, perhaps a ten-foot by ten-foot. The floor, walls, and ceiling were covered with what looked to be clear plastic.

"Where am I?" he demanded again.

"Where you are is not important." The other man replied.

"Who the hell are you?" he said as he tried to get up.

"Please don't try and get up. You're strapped down to the chair. You'll only exert yourself." The man replied.

He looked down and saw that he was strapped to a metal chair. There was a strap around his waist, and his hands and legs were handcuffed to the arms and legs of the chair.

He noticed an IV was connected to his arm and attached to an IV bag hanging from the ceiling.

All he was wearing were his boxer shorts. He had been in bed when he escaped the home invasion. Just yesterday, he thought. But how long had he been unconscious?

"Are you going to tell me who you are and why I'm here?" he asked in a heated voice. He was still looking around the room, trying to orient himself.

He noticed a long metal-looking table sitting behind the man observing him. It looked to have several tools and items placed neatly on top of the table.

"If you insist, Mr. Sutton. My name is Dr. Wilson." The man replied.

"And as far as why you're here. Well, let's just say you've done some very bad things. And you're going to have to pay for your actions." Wilson said.

"Do you know who I work for?" Sutton said in an arrogant tone, still trying to break loose.

"Yes, I do, Mr. Sutton. I do know who you work for. Bratva, the Solntsevskaya Organized Crime Group, also known as the Solntsevskaya Brotherhood, a Russian crime syndicate group."

"And when my associates find me, they will kill you, your family, and all your friends." He said, still with an arrogant tone.

Dr. Wilson sat there without saying a word for over two minutes. He sat there looking at Sutton without any sign of emotion or concern.

Finally, Wilson replied, "ви говорите про Каптіан Pavel Volkov, Охоронця Ivan Semenov, та Nikolai Morozov?" (*You're talking about Captain Pavel Volkov, Bodyguard Ivan Semenov, and Nikolai Morozov?*)

Sutton took a long hard look at Wilson and said, "ти розмовляєш українською?" (*You speak Ukrainian?*)

"так, та багато інших, але давайте поговоримо англійською." Wilson replied. (*Yes, and many others, but let's stick to English.*)

"We will speak in whatever language you want. It won't change the fact that you'll die a slow and painful death." Sutton said calmly and with confidence.

"I'm afraid you won't be seeing your associates any time soon." Wilson replied.

"What do you mean?" Sutton asked.

Dr. Wilson pulled out his cell phone and leaned forward toward Sutton. He brought up a video on his phone and showed it to Sutton.

"What is this?"

"You recognize your house?" Wilson asked.

"Yes, so."

"The SUV pulling into the garage, you recognize it also?" inquired Wilson.

"Yes." Sutton said, looking up from the screen at Wilson.

The picture pulled away a little giving a wider shot of the property. After a few seconds, the entire screen lit up into a massive fireball, and then the screen went dark.

"WHAT THE HELL DID YOU DO?" Sutton shouted, now struggling more against his restraints.

"The latest police report stated that three bodies were recovered from the blast and were burned beyond recognition." Wilson said with a smile.

"I assure you, Mr. Sutton, your associates, as you call them, will not be coming to save you." Wilson said as he put his phone back into his pocket.

"However, the three girls and all your records and files are safe and in our hands."

"What are you going to do with me?"

"Glad you asked." Came a voice from the right of Sutton, behind the plastic wall.

"Who is that?" Sutton asked, trying to see who was behind the plastic.

"You're not in the position to ask any questions." Hunter said.

"What are you planning on doing with me?" Sutton asked again, now not so arrogant.

"That is totally up to you." Hunter responded as he pushed back the plastic and entered the room.

"Like what?" Sutton asked.

"Tell us everything you know about your contacts and operations of the sex trafficking ring you work for." Hunter replied as he pulled up a chair next to Wilson.

"They will kill me if I tell you anything." Sutton replied, shaking his head and laughing.

"They think you're already dead." Hunter said as he met Sutton's glaring stare, "Or they could find out that you're a mole for the FBI and still alive." Hunter said as he leaned forward in his chair, resting his elbows on his knees.

"I'm no fucking mole!" exclaimed Sutton as he tried to reach out to Hunter but couldn't due to his restraints.

"I know that, and you know that. But if word gets out that you're still alive, and this file leaks out."

"What file are you talking about?"

Hunter motioned to Ray, standing behind the plastic wall to Sutton's right.

"This is our internet nerd." Hunter said as Ray walked up.

"I've told you I'm not a nerd. I'm a Guru, a Master. I'm not a nerd."

Hunter turned his head slightly and looked up at Ray.

"Show him what you've got, Mr. Guru." Hunter said sarcastically.

Ray turned his computer tablet to face Sutton. On the screen displayed a web page from the Washington D.C. FBI sight. A picture of Craig Sutton displayed on the screen listed him as FBI Special Agent Robert Crawford.

"Well, according to this, you've worked for the FBI for about ten years now." Hunter said as he leaned back in his chair.

"That's fake, and you know it!" Sutton replied, looking up at Ray.

"I know it, and you know it. The important question is, will your Mafia friends believe it?" Hunter said, rubbing the back of his neck.

Ray scrolled to another picture of Sutton/Crawford posing with other FBI and ATF agents, all dressed in tactical gear.

"That picture is fake!" Sutton exclaimed, pulling at his restraints.

"Photoshopped." Ray replied, "But it's damn good if I say so myself."

"One of your SUVs was found at the airport." Hunter said.

"So." Sutton whispered, looking at Hunter.

"All we have to do is drop you off somewhere and ensure the Russian Mob gets these pictures and your location." Hunter replied, pointing over at Ray's tablet.

"What would they do to a mole spying on their operation?" Wilson added.

"A lot more than you could ever do to me."

"Oh, but you underestimate me, Mr. Sutton. I'll consider that a challenge." Wilson said.

Sutton shifted his attention to the table just behind Wilson.

"Now, Mr. Sutton, we can play this one of two ways. You can tell us what we want to know, and you live happily ever after. Or, Two, we give the Mob your FBI file and the location where you can be found, and you take your chances with them. Your choice." Wilson said.

Sutton looked back at Wilson. "You can threaten me all you like. We all know you're not going to kill me. Oh, you might ruff me up some. But in the end, you'll let me go. I've got enough money stashed away that I can disappear forever." Sutton said with a smug look on his face.

"Mr. Sutton, do you know Mad Dog, Rick, and their two associates down in New Orleans?" Hunter asked.

"Never heard of them." Sutton replied, looking down at the floor.

"This is you and Pavel Volkov in this video, right?" Ray inquired, showing a video on his tablet of the two of them in the kitchen of the New Orleans sex house.

"Yes, whatever." Sutton replied as he looked at the video.

"You do know they are dead, along with Rick and Mad Dog?" Hunter said.

"They were eaten by rats!" Ray added, with a slight smile on his face.

"Please, Ray, that was not my best work." Wilson commented, leaning back in his chair and folding his hands behind his head.

Sutton's face went from smug to pale white as he looked over at Wilson and then back at Ray.

"Regarding the $23,754,188 in the Young Import and Export account. That money is gone." Hunter said, still leaning forward in his chair.

"And 75 cents. Don't forget the 75 cents." Ray added.

"How did you get that money? It's, it's..." Sutton asked, stuttering.

"Our Guru here did that." Wilson said, cutting Sutton off.

"Please, Mr. Wilson, that too is not my best work." Ray replied, smiling.

"That's not all my money. Some of it is money I owe to the Russian Mafia." Sutton said, now looking down with a defeated expression on his face.

"I'm sure when your friends in the Mafia find out your body is not in the house. Your SUV being found at the airport, and all that money is gone." Hunter said, looking right into Sutton's eyes. "There will be a contract put on your head so big that the Pope will be looking for you."

"I don't know, man! I'm dead either way I look at it." Sutton said, his eyes starting to water up.

"It's 100% certain if the Solntsevskaya Brotherhood gets their hands on you." Wilson said.

Hunter looked at Wilson and then back at Sutton, "At least with us, you'll have a chance." He said, leaning forward even closer to Sutton.

"Look, Sutton, if you help us, we'll help you disappear. A new identity and enough money where you'll be set."

Hunter looked up as he heard the door into the room open. Ray and Wilson both turned as Jack entered the room.

Jack walked over to Hunter and leaned over to whisper into his ear, "Can I talk to you in private for a second?"

Hunter stood and followed Jack out of the plastic-lined room. Ray and Wilson looked at each other with a puzzled look on each of their faces.

Once in the hallway, Hunter turned and looked at Jack.

"What's so important that it couldn't wait?"

"I thought of another way that we may be able to get Sutton to cooperate." He replied.

"I'm listening." Hunter replied with a curious look on his face.

"We tell the Mob the truth." Jack said.

"The truth?" Hunter inquired, cocking his head to one side.

"Well, some of it." Jack added, shifting back and forth nervously.

"I'm still listening. Let's hear it." Hunter stated, placing his hands on his hips.

"We let the Mob think that a rival gang invaded Sutton's house and that he escaped in fear for his life." Jack said, showing a little excitement on his face.

"Keep going." Hunter said, squinting his eyes a little and pondering the idea.

"After he felt it was safe, he came out of hiding." Jack replied, holding his hands out as if presenting his idea on a silver platter.

"And how does that help us?" Hunter asked.

"Once he's back in, we can use him to gain access to the other parts of the organization." Jack explained with a tone of excitement in his voice.

Hunter looked at Jack and just stood there without saying a word.

The silence was more than Jack could stand. He said, "Well?"

Hunter still stood there without saying a word and just nodded his head.

Jack asked again, "Well, you just going to stand there? What do you think of my idea?"

"This might just work, kid. It just might work." Hunter said as he turned and returned to the room, followed by Jack.

Hunter walked back into the room and took his chair across from Sutton.

"We have another proposal for you." Hunter said, looking at Sutton.

"What is it?" Sutton asked, looking up at Hunter and then at Jack.

"You tell the Brotherhood that you work for the truth."

"What do you mean the truth?" Sutton asked, now confused.

"You tell them that a rival gang raided your house, and you fled for your life. You went into hiding because you feared they would find you and kill you too." Hunter explained, watching the reaction on Sutton's face.

Sutton sat there without answering and glanced at Wilson, Ray, Jack, and back at Hunter.

"What's the catch?" Sutton asked, looking Hunter squarely in the eyes.

"You provide us with the information we want on your operation and the higher-ups. We will set you up with an alibi to your story."

"If I don't accept your deal?"

"Then we drop you in the lap of the Solntsevskaya Brotherhood along with your FBI profile. We'll let you take your chances that you can talk your way out of it." Hunter said with a nod and a not-too-pleasant smile.

"The ball, or should we say, your life is in your hands." Hunter added, standing up from his chair.

Sutton watched as Hunter, Ray, and Jack left the room, leaving Dr. Wilson still looking at him.

Hunter stopped as the three reached the door and turned back towards Sutton, still tied securely to his chair.

"You have until tomorrow to give us an answer." He told Sutton and turned and walked out.

"Wait! You're going to leave me tied up here with this crazy Wilson dude?" Sutton yelled back at Hunter as he closed the door.

He quickly turned back to see Wilson sitting there with a big smile.

"Is there anything, I mean anything, that I can do to help you, Mr. Sutton, to make up your mind?" Wilson asked with an evil smile.

Sutton looked at the tools and items spread out over the table behind Wilson and then back at him.

Hunter's phone vibrated, and he picked it up. "Vicky, I was just about to call you."

"How's it going with our guest?"

"I think he'll come around."

"We may have a problem. Put Ray on the line."

She and Tony had been working on tracking down information obtained by the team from Sutton's place. Kevin and Shay had been restocking equipment at the Omega Office.

Hunter called Ray over, and he placed the phone on speaker.

"Vicky, you're on speaker. I've got Ray here."

"I'm sending you a video. Tell me this isn't who I think it is."

They pulled up the video that Vicky had sent them. It was some news coverage of the explosion at Sutton's house. The footage showed a reporter giving an update on the explosion investigation. As the camera panned away to get a view of the house, it showed a crowd of bystanders in the background.

"Ray, who is that person in the blue windbreaker in the background?" she asked.

"Hold on, let me enlarge it."

Ray opened the link, tapped the screen, and enlarged the view of the man in the blue windbreaker.

"Shit!" Ray exclaimed as he looked over at Hunter.

"Ray, this is Tony. Is that who we think it is?"

"Yes, it looks like Special Agent Roger Basiliano." Ray replied.

"Tony, do you know why he would be at Grassy Lake?" Hunter asked.

"No, it doesn't look like he's there in any official compacity."

"How do you know that?" Ray asked.

"If he were, he'd be all decked out in his FBI jacket. I'm sure the reporters would be all over him with questions too. He's there in an unofficial manner."

"Ray, has your bug flagged anything about the Sutton issue on the New Orleans FBI computer?" Vicky asked.

"No, if it had, it would have notified me." He replied, still looking at the video.

"What about any phone chatter from the burner phones you've been tracking?" Vicky inquired.

"I'll double-check when we get off and see if anything has popped up." He replied as he switched screens.

"This concerns me." Vicky said in a worried tone. "What if he's on to us?"

"I'll send Jim and Robert back up to Sutton's house. They can dig around to see what's up with the investigation." Hunter replied.

"This is getting bigger and bigger every day. I'm worried, Hunter, that we've bitten off more than we can handle." Vicky said in a nervous tone.

"I know you've expressed that concern before. This is where our journey has taken us." Hunter said.

"Keep in mind all the lives we've saved and will save. Children that would not have a life if you had not started this." Hunter added with heartfelt conviction.

"I know, Hunter, keep reminding me of that. Please." She said softly as she disconnected the line.

The following day the three woke up and had breakfast. After they ate, they would head over to see if Sutton had an answer for them.

It was a short drive over to where Sutton was being held, "That's one big ass fancy motor home Wilson's got." Jack said as they pulled up next to Wilson's motorhome.

"His mobile torture chamber on wheels." Ray said as they all three laughed.

Wilson had parked his motorhome at the far end of a small motorhome park just north of Houston, Texas. Although it was well soundproofed, it was far enough away so that no one would be able to hear any screams that may come from the inside.

Once they arrived, the three exited the vehicle and walked up to the motor home. Jack knocked on the door, and the three stood there waiting for Wilson to open it.

"Good morning, gentlemen. Please come inside." Wilson said as he was removing an apron from around his neck.

"Can I offer you three some fresh liver for breakfast?" he asked with a smile.

"NO!" Jack said, looking over at Ray and Hunter.

"We just finished breakfast before we came over." Ray added.

"You're sure? I've made some potatoes and fried up some good old bacon to go with it." Wilson said as he closed the door behind them.

"It's something I fell in love with when I spent some time over in Germany." Wilson said, "Please have a seat."

"How's our friend?" Hunter asked.

"Dead to the world, so to speak. I gave him a slow drip of M99 last night after you left."

"I wanted him to be well rested for today's questioning." Wilson said, "Can I get you fellas anything to drink?" Wilson motioned over toward the refrigerator.

"When will our boy wake up?" Hunter asked, motioning with his head back towards the motorhome's rear.

"I shut off the drip about 30 minutes before you arrived. He should be coming around pretty soon."

Wilson reached over, picked up a TV remote, and turned on a small monitor across from where they were sitting. When the picture appeared, it showed Sutton slumped over. He was still restrained in his chair, as he was when they left the night before.

The four men talked about what they had discovered at Sutton's house and sex trafficking. Occasionally, someone would bring up the ball game from the night before, but it would soon return to the topic of sex trafficking.

After about an hour of conversation, they noticed that Sutton had regained consciousness and started moving around. They allowed him another thirty minutes or so to regain consciousness before they went in fully.

The four stood up and entered the rear room, holding Sutton. He jumped at the sudden sound of the door opening and saw the four men walking into the room.

"Good morning Craig. Can I call you Craig?" Hunter asked.

"Why not." He replied.

"Have you given any of the options any consideration?" Hunter asked as he pulled up a chair.

Ray and Jack each took a corner of the table behind Hunter and sat.

"What's with the dog collar around his neck?" Jack asked, pointing at Sutton.

He hadn't noticed that Wilson had placed a dog collar around his neck while unconscious.

"What the fuck?" Sutton asked, looking at each of them.

"It's a shock collar, Mr. Sutton. I thought we could remove your restraints and allow you to relieve yourself and stretch your legs some." Wilson said as he moved over next to Sutton and removed his restraints.

"Oh, and if you try and leave this room, you'll receive an excruciating shock that will leave you quite unconscious."

Once the cuffs were removed from his wrists, Sutton asked if he could take a piss.

"Sure, the restroom is just to your left behind the plastic."

Sutton slowly stood up, not taking his eyes off any of them, rubbing his wrists and walking over to the door behind the plastic. After he completed his task, he returned to face his fate.

"Sit Craig." Hunter said, as Sutton returned, "Have you eaten?"

"No." He replied.

"Wilson can bring you some liver, potatoes, and fried bacon. Would you like some?"

"Yes, thank you."

"Craig, have you considered our offer?" Hunter asked as he gazed at Sutton. Waiting for a reply.

Sutton briefly looked up from the plate of food Wilson had brought him. He continued to take several more bites as the four others looked on.

"You're referring to the offer where I sign my death warrant?" Sutton replied as he looked up from the plate of food.

"It's totally up to you, Craig. You take the deal we offered you, or you can take your chances explaining your FBI file to your brotherhood." Jack said as he walked over to Sutton's side.

Sutton looked up at Jack as he approached and took a sip of water.

There was silence for over a minute. The kind of silence that caused your heart to beat faster.

Everyone fixed their gaze on Sutton as he placed his plate on the floor.

"Let me clarify something first." Sutton said, leaning back in his chair.

"If I refuse to help. You turn me over to my brothers, along with a fake file saying I work for the FBI?" Sutton said, looking at each of the four, one by one.

"Or..." He paused for a few seconds.

"Or... I tell you everything I know, and you free me and give me my money back, and I take my chances alone?" he added, taking a long drink of water.

Hunter shook his head as he looked at Sutton.

"Regarding the money, we gave a good part to the three girls we freed from your basement." Ray said as he looked at his tablet and leaned against one of the walls beside Wilson.

"Don't worry. You'll have enough to start a new life anywhere and live comfortably." Hunter said.

"Well?" Jack asked.

Sutton looked sharply up at Jack and then turned his eyes to Hunter.

"What do you want to know?" Sutton said, looking down at the floor.

Ray had patched in all the team members via their earbuds before they had entered the room.

Vicky, Tony, Kevin, and Shay were listing at Omega Headquarters. Robert and Jim were also online at their location near Grassy Lake. Everyone was online to hear what Sutton had to say about the enterprise he helped run.

"Tell us about this Young Import and Export business you run." Hunter said, leaning back in the chair with his legs crossed.

"It's a shell company set up to finance the buying and selling of the sex slaves." Sutton started.

"What's your part in the organization?" Jack asked, pulling up a chair next to Sutton.

"Sort of the middleman broker, I guess you would say." Sutton replied.

"Go on." Hunter said.

"They would contact me with an order, and I would fill that order."

"Who is 'they', and how does it work?" Hunter asked, motioning with his hands.

Sutton looked up at the ceiling and then back at Hunter. For the first time, the team saw a bit of remorse on the face of the man that they had before them.

"Other Brokers and Farms." Sutton said softly as he lowered his head.

"Farms? What do you mean by 'Farms'?" Jack asked as he knelt beside Sutton.

"The Farms, where they take new potential higher-end merchandise and grow them." Sutton replied, still looking down at the floor.

The group sat there for what seemed like forever, looking at this monster sitting before them. A monster that treated young, innocent children like some commodity to buy and sell. How could one 'human' treat another human like that? The hatred toward this person before them started to grow with every second that passed.

It took everything he had for Jack, and for that matter, each of them, to not just turn this monster over to Wilson and let him do his job on him. But they needed more information. More sick and demented details on this group of people that ran this sex trade business.

"GROW?" Hunter growled menacingly as he stood and took two steps toward Sutton.

"Hunter, let him finish. Please sit back down." Wilson said in a calm voice.

Hunter turned and took a long hard look at Wilson and then back at Sutton. Sutton looked up at Hunter with terror and was cowering in his chair. Hunter returned to his chair and sat, locking his eyes on Sutton.

"Please excuse my friend's outburst. Mr. Sutton, please explain to us what you mean by 'grow' and the function of the 'Farms.'" Wilson said, trying to defuse the situation.

Vicky, Tony, and Kevin sat there listening to everything happening before them. Their mouths were hanging open, and tears streaming down their faces. Everyone but Shay. She had pure anger and rage running through her body.

"Aunt Vicky, I'm going there. I want to ask this piece of shit some questions." Shay said, with a tone of revenge in her voice.

"No! you're staying here." Vicky said, looking over at her.

"You'll have your chance later. They don't need you there adding to the tension."

Finally, Sutton looked up at Wilson and, with a shaky voice, said, "The farm is where girls and sometimes boys are taken and tested to see if they have what it takes to pass."

"Continue." Wilson said.

"Each farm has a 'Madam Overseer'. The Overseer teaches the new...." Sutton paused and looked over at Hunter and the others. "She decides who passes and who fails."

"What next?" Jack asked.

"The ones who pass are further trained on the proper ways and expectations of their roles." Sutton said. "The ones who don't make the grade get shipped off to a lower group or traded for someone else."

"We saw you down in Florida and then again in New Orleans. Where do these places fall into your organization?" Hunter asked, finally regaining his composure.

"Think of the professional baseball structure. New Orleans would be the minor leagues, Florida would be the single A team."

"Single A? Like back on the street hookers?" Ray asked, still sitting on the table relaying messages from the ones at Omega.

"No, not directly. They are used as high-priced 'Call Girls'. They get more than your typical street workers."

"What if they don't make it there?" Hunter asked, leaning forward in his chair with his elbows resting on his knees.

"If they don't make it there, they usually end up on the streets. That's up to their handler." Sutton replied.

"The ones in the minor league? Where do they fit in?" Jack asked.

"They fill some of the brothels or are used by higher-end customers." Sutton said, now not feeling as threatened as he did just a few minutes ago.

Sutton was starting to feel a sense of relief as he revealed these dark secrets he had stored inside.

"Are you the 'Major League'?" Hunter asked.

"No. that would be the 'Farms'." Sutton said, matching Hunter's gaze.

"The ones at the farm. The ones who pass your test and graduate. Where do they go?" Ray said, passing on a question from Vicky.

"Can I have another bottle of water?" Sutton asked, looking over at Jack.

Jack opened a small cooler beside him and passed Sutton a water bottle.

Sutton opened the bottle and took a long drink, almost downing the entire bottle. He lowered the bottle and placed the cap back on it. He then cleared his throat and continued.

"The ones that graduate the farm are sold to or provided short term to a more discreet clientele."

"Like who?" Ray asked.

"You'll be surprised when you hear who some of the clientele is." Sutton replied, leaning back in his chair.

"Give me an example." Jack asked.

Sutton paused and looked at Jack and smiled. He leaned back in his chair and placed his hands behind his head, interlacing his fingers.

"It's going to cost you something for this information." Sutton said with a smug look on his face.

"We had a deal." Hunter said, looking hard at this smug-looking piece of shit before him.

"Sorry." Sutton replied.

Hunter looked over at Wilson and gave him a short nod.

Wilson reached over, picked up a small TV remote-looking control, and pressed one of the buttons.

Jack and Wilson sat around the table while Hunter and Ray were outside talking with Vicky and the others on the phone.

"He's coming around." Jack said, leaning out the door of the motorhome.

"Got to go, Vicky. Our boy is waking up from his nap." Hunter informed Vicky over the phone.

Wilson was already in the room with Sutton as the others entered.

"You enjoy your nap?" Hunter asked, walking over and pulling up his chair.

Sutton was sitting on the floor, leaning against the wall. He looked up at Hunter and the others as they entered the room.

"Fuck you man." Sutton said and flipped him the bird.

"Why did you do that? What did you do, kick me in the fucking face?" he asked, wiping some blood off his face.

"Nope, you did a face-plant when the shock hit you." Ray said, laughing.

"It was funny as hell watching you twitch there on the floor." Jack added.

"We agreed that you would tell us what we wanted in exchange for your freedom, and you went back on our deal." Hunter said in a matter-of-fact tone.

Hunter sat there staring at Sutton without moving.

"OK, fine." Sutton said, still sitting on the floor.

"Let's start again with the farms." Hunter said, leaning back.

"What do you want to know?"

"Start with who runs it, what's their function, and where is it located?" he replied.

"The who is Michael Clinton, he runs the ranch here. Then there's Kay Griffith. She's the Madam Overseer at the ranch." Sutton replied, looking at each of the captors.

"Ok, tell us about this Clinton guy." Hunter asked.

"Wait!" Ray said, "Tony wants him to clarify what 'runs the ranch here' means."

Hunter looked back at Ray and gave him a slight nod, "You heard him. Explain what you mean by 'runs the ranch here.'" Hunter said, turning to look at Sutton again.

"Clinton runs the ranch here in this country." Sutton replied.

Ray looked over at Jack. He also turned and looked over at Ray. Jack mouthed the words, "What the fuck." at Ray. Ray just shrugged his shoulders in response.

"How many of these 'ranches' are there?" Hunter asked.

Sutton looked up to the ceiling as if he were thinking to himself.

"I believe currently there are six that I'm aware of. And each ranch has a broker, like me, to make their trades and resupply their merchandise."

"Are all these 'ranches' located here in the United States?" Hunter asked, with an astonished look on his face.

"No, there's only one here in the United States, two in Europe, one in Asia, one in South America, one in the Middle East." Sutton replied, now looking at the surprised look on Hunter's face.

"Are they all independent, or do they report to someone else?" Ray asked, relaying another message from Tony.

"To my knowledge, they all report or answer to one person or group. They refer to it or them as The Dynasty."

"And don't ask me anything about it. I don't have a clue where they are or who runs it. It could be the Russians or the man from Mars. I can't help you there. You can shock me all you want, but it'll do no good because I don't know anything about it." Sutton added, looking at each of them with a concerned look on his face.

Hunter motioned for the others to follow him outside. As they started out the door, Ray stopped.

"Vicky wants to know who the clientele is." Ray said, and all of them looked back at Sutton.

He looked up at the four men standing next to the door and said with a smile, "The clientele for the ranches include Presidents, millionaires, politicians, movie stars, Kings, Queens, and anyone with the money or power. The list is larger and more powerful than you could ever imagine, and you would recognize many of the names on the list."

The four looked at each other and continued out of the room.

Sutton sat on the floor for a few seconds after the four left. Then he stood up, walked over to the ice chest, got himself a bottle of water, and went and sat down in the chair.

Chapter Thirteen

The Recon

It was about one in the afternoon when Jack, Hunter, and Ray left Wilson's motorhome. They wanted to grab something to eat and discuss what information they would need to get from Sutton next.

Wilson took a cot and bedding into Sutton's room so he could rest. He also brought in some food and drinks so that when Sutton got hungry, he could grab something.

Sutton was settling into his new home, or you should say prison cell. At least he had a bed, food, and water now. His restraints had been removed, so he was free to move around in his little ten-by-ten-foot world.

He could hear someone on the other side of the wall moving around. He assumed it was the crazy guy named Wilson.

He pushed aside the plastic in front of the door, and he slowly turned the doorknob to open the door.

As he opened the door, he heard the voice of one of his captors, "Good afternoon Mr. Sutton. I hope you got some rest. The others will be here soon." Wilson said.

Sutton continued to stand at the door, fearful of taking a step on the other side.

"Please, Mr. Sutton, you may come in. I've extended the area that you can go."

"I'm not going to get the shit shocked out of me if I walk out of this room, am I?"

"No. As long as you stay within the confines of this unit, you'll be fine. However, if you choose to walk out the door, I'm afraid you'll receive a shock much worse than the one you received before." Wilson said as he sat at the table.

He motioned Sutton over to the table with a wave of his hand.

"Please come and have a seat. We can wait on the others together." Wilson encouraged.

Sutton slowly stepped through the door and walked over to the table, and sat down. He looked around at his new surroundings.

Looking over at Wilson. He asked, "What's the plan for today?"

"Well, when the others get here, I'm sure they're going to have many more questions for you." Wilson said as he motioned to some cookies sitting on the table.

"Please have a cookie, I baked them last night."

Sutton reached over and picked up one of the chocolate-chipped cookies and stopped short of taking a bite out of it. He looked at Wilson with a questioning look.

"You didn't poison these cookies, did you?" Sutton asked, staring at Wilson.

Wilson reached over and took the cookie from Sutton and plopped it into his mouth.

Wilson smiled. "If I wanted to poison you, Mr. Sutton, I had plenty of chances to do so before now."

Just about that time, the door to the motorhome opened, and Jack walked in.

"Having cookies and milk, girls?" he asked as the other two entered behind him.

"Just sitting here, waiting on the goon squad to get here." Sutton said with a slight smile.

He shifted back in his seat as Hunter entered through the door.

"I'm assuming you have a few more questions for me?" Sutton asked, looking at the three new arrivals.

"Yes, a few." Hunter replied as he placed a map on top of the table in front of Sutton.

"Show us where this Clinton Ranch is located." He told Sutton as he pointed at the map.

Sutton looked down at the map and rotated it so it faced him. He took a few seconds and then pointed at a small town on the map.

"Clinton's place is just west of this small town of Centuryville."

Ray turned the map around so that he could see the map more clearly.

"I'll check it out and see what I can find on the surrounding area and Clinton's place." Ray said as he retrieved his tablet from his backpack.

"Tell us everything you know about this place." Hunter said, pulling up a chair next to Sutton.

Sutton leaned back in his chair and started spilling his guts on everything he knew about the ranch.

"The house is a 35,000 sq ft. two story rustic home and sits on..." Sutton began and then paused, looking over at Jack and Wilson.

"You're going to write this stuff down, right?" Sutton asked, looking over at Hunter, who was just setting there with his arms crossed and head cocked slightly to one side.

"It's being taken care of." Jack said, referring to Vicky, Tony, and the others back at Omega, who were taking notes and recording every word.

"Ok, the total property is about 375 acres of hills, flatland, and a lake that makes up the Clinton ranch, 150 acres of which is manicured land with a lake in the front."

"The main House sits about 1/2 mile off the main road. The lake is about 80 acres with a 2-acre island in the middle. It's fed by a 30-foot-wide mountain stream running through the front part of the property just outside of the fence." Sutton paused for a second to take a long draw from his drink.

The others just sat there, waiting for Sutton to continue. Ray had put down his tablet to focus on what Sutton was saying.

"The lake has a boat dock for six boats. There are three-speed boats and a 30-foot custom pontoon boat. What else?" Sutton asked, looking at Hunter.

"Every last detail." He replied, not moving a muscle.

"It's surrounded by hills on the back side of the house and, as I said, a lake and wide stream in front. An Olympic size outdoor heated pool behind the house. There's a small indoor pool and Gym. Two fireplaces on each side of the main house, with a catwalk around each chimney, for a guard tower." Sutton paused again as he took a bite of one of the cookies that Wilson had made. He followed it up with a quick swig of his drink, and then he continued.

"There's a horse stable to the right rear of the house and a heliport for one helicopter on the opposite side of the house." Sutton continued as he leaned back and placed his hands behind his head. He was starting to relax as he spilled his guts about everything he knew.

"The property is fully fenced in. With a 15-foot stone fence along the front 300 yards of the property. A 15-foot chain-link fence around the remainder. With a 25-foot buffer on each side of the fence."

"Any cameras?" Jack asked as he leaned forward.

"Yes. There are cameras, both thermal and night vision, along the perimeter of the property. Also, cameras along the outside of the house and inside on the main floor and basement. Oh, and there are motion sensors on the main and basement floors too." Sutton replied, looking over at Jack.

"Anything else?" Hunter asked, remaining motionless.

"There's one main road onto the property. It has a guard post and gate. It sits about 100 yards off the main road. The property has an Auxiliary power source that is housed in the horse stable."

"The power source, how long before it kicks in if the power goes out?" Ray asked.

"Not sure, never been there when the power went out."

"What about the staff and guards?" Hunter asked, finally moving and reaching over to the table to retrieve a drink.

"Normally, there are three full-time staff members. There are fourteen-armed security guards, seven on two rotating shifts, and one ranch hand that lives in the stable and takes care of the property. The full-time staff consists of two kitchen staff and one housekeeper." Sutton paused again to take another bite of his cookie and swig of his drink.

"They will bring in more part-time staff as needed. When there are no visitors at the ranch. The security crew consists of three during the day and four at night. However, when there's a party going on, security will double or triple. Depending on who and how many guests there are." Sutton concluded, looking at each of the four men.

"This ranch sounds more like a fortress." Jack said, looking over at Hunter.

"The ranch is designed to keep people in more than to keep people out." Sutton said, looking at Jack.

"Those guards, are they local rent-a-cops, or are they trained?" Hunter inquired, looking at Sutton.

"Bratva Brotherhood. Mostly former criminals and thugs the like." Sutton said, shifting his eyes over to Hunter.

Jack glanced over at Hunter, who still had his eyes locked on Sutton.

"Don't worry. I'll give you their names and shift times." Sutton said, returning Hunter's stare.

"That's fine. Tell us about some of the other key players." Hunter said, still locked onto Sutton.

"Michael Clinton, he's what we call an Overseer. He's in charge of the ranch and is the main person in the North American operation. He answers to the Dynasty directly. He's the one who would contact me for special orders and requests." He replied, now looking down at the floor.

"Who else?" Ray asked, sitting over to the side, now with his tablet on and entering Clinton's name into his search program.

"The next one would be Kay Griffith. She's the Madam Overseer. She trains and disciplines the products based on needs. She's attractive but very cold and heartless. I've seen her being very cruel and sadistic towards some of the girls." He added, still looking down at the floor, leaning forward and resting his elbows on his knees.

Jack stood up and walked across the floor to the window. It was all he could do to keep from laying into Sutton and beating him to death.

Hunter looked over at Jack and Wilson and let out a deep breath. "Let's all take a short break, I need to get some fresh air." He said as he stood up.

"Oh, I almost forgot. The local police chief, Brandon Flynn, is in Clinton's back pocket." He added as he watched Hunter and the others start to walk out of the motorhome.

"He's attended some of the parties at the ranch, also."

"Anything else?" Jack asked without looking at Sutton.

"Two German Shephard dogs. The guards use them to patrol the grounds and to alert them if anyone is outside." He said, looking over at the three.

Ray and the other two stopped briefly and looked back at Sutton, who was looking at them with a look of sorrow. After a couple of seconds, they continued out of the motorhome.

Sutton watched as the three exited. He then glanced over briefly at Wilson and then looked back at the door. A cold chill ran throughout Sutton's body as he slowly looked over at Wilson again.

Wilson sat through the entire exchange of information without saying much at all. He sat there looking at Sutton with no expression whatsoever on his face. Not taking his eyes off him, not uttering a word. Just a bone-chilling stare that would send chills down the strongest man's spine.

Once outside, the three walked over to their SUV. They needed to discuss what they had learned so far. They also needed to take a break from the sickness that they had listened to for the past hour.

Ray took his tablet and placed it on the hood of their SUV. He brought up a screen and started a video conference call with Vicky and the others at Omega. They also conferenced with Jim and Robert, that were on their way back from the Grassy Lake area.

"Did you guys get all of that?" Hunter asked Vicky when they all were connected.

"Yes, we did." She replied with a noticeable sign of concern in her voice.

Vicky, Tony, Kevin, and Shay had been listening to the conversation from the very beginning and had been engaged in researching the area and the surroundings of the ranch. They were able to retrieve court documents of the property and some background information about Michael Clinton and Kay Griffith. Neither of them had any criminal record or had ever shown up on the FBI's radar.

"Ray, have you uncovered anything on this operation based on the new information?" Vicky asked.

"No, but when I get back to the office, I'll be able to focus more."

"Well, get back here as soon as you can. I need you, Shay, and Robert to get over to Centuryville and find out everything you can."

"Oh, Ray, have you been able to find out anything else on those burner phones?" Vicky asked.

"I've contacted some of my former 'Black Hat' colleagues. I've offered a finder's fee to anyone who can crack the owners or location of the calls." Ray replied, looking at Vicky on the tablet screen.

"Any success yet?" she asked.

"None to speak of yet. They are what you'd call the alphas of the nerd community. They are very competitive with each other. If anyone can break it, these guys can." Ray said with an air of pride and confidence.

"Ok, while they are working on that, I need you to focus on this new problem." She replied. "Ray, I'm sending Shay there to pick you up. She should be there in about an hour."

"I'll be ready."

"We're going to stay here and see if we can find out anything else from Sutton." Hunter chimed in.

"Ok, but don't let Shay in the same room with Sutton. I don't know what she will do. I can see it on her face." Vicky warned.

"What do you want us to do with Sutton?" Jack asked, leaning against the SUV.

"Stay there and see if you can get anything else out of him. Make sure you keep him on our side for now."

"Based on what we already know, we're going to need additional firepower." Hunter said, nodding his head slightly as he spoke.

"I guess we need to bring in Nicholas and Christopher, then." She reluctantly said.

"We'll wrap things up here this afternoon and get back there. I'll talk to them tomorrow. I think Wilson can watch over Sutton until we decide what to do with him." He said as they ended the conversation.

They entered the motorhome and saw Wilson and Sutton sitting there in total silence. Sutton was sitting at the table finishing off a sandwich that he had made himself. Wilson was just sitting there in complete silence, looking at Sutton.

"Did you two behave yourselves?" Jack asked, looking over at Sutton.

"That guy has not said a word since you left. He's creeping me out." Sutton replied, looking over at Wilson.

Hunter grabbed a couple of pieces of paper and gave them to Sutton. "I need you to draw a diagram of the house and the property layout. I want the locations of every camera and alarm system on the property. Draw me a floor plan in as much detail as you can of the house, barn, and anything else you can think of."

Sutton sat there for a few seconds, just staring at the paper in front of him. He soon reached for a pen that was sitting next to the paper and started drawing an outline of the property.

They all sat there in silence while they watched Sutton sketch out an overhead view of the property. Every few minutes or so, one of them would ask Sutton something about a part of the diagram in front of them.

Ray kept a watch out the window for the arrival of Shay. He had all his equipment packed and ready, so he could bolt out the door as soon as he saw her.

Wilson never got up from his chair and just sat there watching Sutton draw out his diagrams. Every now and then, Sutton would glance up, only to meet the dead stare of Wilson.

What was Wilson going to do when the others left him alone with him? This constantly went through Sutton's mind.

Shay arrived to pick up Ray without incident. They both headed back to Omega, so they could get ready to go and scout out the Clinton Ranch. During their one-hour drive, they talked about nothing but the information that Sutton had given them.

Shay was very eager to take down this major player in the sex trafficking world. They all knew that this time, things wouldn't be so easy. They were going up against some major firepower.

Shay and Ray arrived back at Omega about 45 minutes before Jim and Robert arrived.

They took time to get cleaned up and pack about a week's supply of clothing and equipment that they would need.

Kevin would fly Shay, Ray, Jim, and Robert to an airfield close to Centuryville and drop them off. He would then return and help with the gathering of information.

After about four hours, Sutton finished the diagrams of everything that he could remember on the Clinton Ranch.

Hunter took pictures of the drawings and sent them to Vicky at Omega. He would bring the originals with him when he returned. He wanted the team to get a head start on the review of data as soon as possible.

Vicky and Tony were reviewing and categorizing the data on the Clinton ranch. Meanwhile, Ray, Shay, Jim, and Robert were gathering what they needed together to run their reconnaissance on the property.

Ray packed several of his Hawks and Baby Hawks to assist in the recon. He had equipped one of the Hawks with electronic recording devices. The same type was used in New Orleans to retrieve the electronic signals and codes of the cameras.

Each person would be fitted with NVGs, standard Night Vision Goggles, and communications devices, a suppressed CZ P-10c 9mm pistol equipped with laser sights and lights, a standard IFAK, Individual First Aid Kit, and four spare magazines for their pistol. They carried an Ari B'Lilah knife, and each wore a level III light body armor vest.

Their rules of engagement would be that of RECON only. No engagement whatsoever unless they were compromised or their life was threatened.

They were to spend as much time as needed to map out and find out everything they could about the ranch.

They would be driving two vehicles, one SUV and a van that Ray used to run his Hawks and electronics from.

They would be staying in a hotel just outside of Centerville, so they could learn their way around the town.

If all went well, the team would spend a week doing the recon on the ranch. It would take about a week or two to come up with their plan to take down the ranch. If all went as planned, that is.

Hunter and Jack would be leaving Sutton in the care of Wilson at his motorhome. They ensured Sutton that after they had completed their plans with the Clinton Ranch, he would be freed according to their agreement.

They would head back to the Omega Headquarters and help with reviewing all of the data they had collected, as well as the new data that the team would be sending from Centuryville.

The weather in that area was starting to turn cold. They would also have to contend with freezing cold temperatures at night, with a greater chance of snow-covered ground if they waited too long.

After they settled into their hotel rooms, they got together in Ray's room to come up with a plan. They would all take the SUV and recon the town and then drive up to scope out the area surrounding the Clinton ranch.

Centuryville was a small picturesque little town with a total population of about 4,000. It had two major banks, five churches, one hotel, several mom-and-pop restaurants, two bars, two Dollar Generals, and a Mcdonald's.

It was a great place to be from if you were young and a great place to retire to if you wanted to retire. There was one small fire and EMS station that was mostly manned by a volunteer force and a police force of only eight full-time officers.

The crime was next to nothing in the community. Other than an occasional fight at the local bar, and every now and then, some of the local teenagers would toilet paper one of the neighbor's yards.

You could leave your doors unlocked, windows opened, and the kids could play outside without fear.

The community consisted mostly of middle-aged folks and retirees. An 800-acre lake just outside of town and several streams provided some great fishing. The surrounding area, mostly woods and hills, consisted of many varieties of game animals for hunting.

The Clinton ranch was about eight miles north of the town, off one of the rural roads that ran throughout the area. The closest neighbor was over half a mile away, as the crow flies. The land surrounding the Clinton ranch was mostly hunting property that was leased out to one of the hunting clubs in the neighboring town.

They picked up some information on a couple of the local Airbnb's in the area from the hotel lobby where they were staying. They thought it would be a better place to run their operations when the time came.

It was about two in the afternoon when they headed up to check out the Clinton ranch. They wanted to get a good look at the area before returning later that night to start their recon.

They noticed several dirt roads and fire breaks in the area near the ranch that might be useful if the need arose. Two of the dirt roads led to hunting camps, which were not currently occupied. One of the camps was located close to the ranch's property line. This, they agreed, would be a good place to park and hike the rest of the way.

Once they got close to the entry of the ranch, they slowed down the SUV so they could take pictures of the entry.

The entry consisted of a five-foot-tall stone wall on each side of the driveway. It ran for about 30 feet out towards the road. A double iron gate that opened and closed remotely blocked the drive. It had your standard camera, speaker, and card key entry that granted access through the gate.

They drove up the road for about 200 yards past the entry of the ranch. The bridge crossed over a 30-foot-wide stream that ran across the front of the property.

They had printed several satellite screenshots of the ranch and surrounding area taken from Google Maps. This gave them an idea of the area, and they made notes on the maps as they drove along.

There was no real easy access to the rear of the property, which was made up of mostly woods, rocks, and steep terrain.

They drove another half mile past the bridge and turned around back towards town. Once they reached the bridge again, they pulled over, and the four of them got out of the SUV.

"Let's check out this stream." Jim said as he headed down to the stream under the bridge.

The other three followed, and they soon found themselves standing next to a beautiful stream with grassy banks on each side for about a hundred feet, and then it turned into deep forest trees.

They followed the stream towards the ranch for about one hundred fifty feet past the bridge. They spotted a chain link fence that stood about fifteen feet tall along the left side of the stream. Along the fence and on several trees on the opposite side of the stream were signs that read Private Property Keep Out, in big red letters.

There was a narrow dirt path just on the inside of the fence that looked to be a service path for 4-wheelers to patrol the fence line. The stream ran for another 100 yards or more through the woods. There was a small bridge that crossed the stream next to the guard post. The stream was between the guard post and the main road. Any frontal assault on the ranch would require crossing that 30-foot stream.

Robert stopped and motioned with his head over to the fence, "Something looks strange about the top of the fence." He said to the others.

The top of the fence was lined with razor wire, which wasn't what was strange about it. It was the position of the wire on the fence. It seemed to confirm Sutton's claims that the ranch was designed to keep people in and not so much to keep people out.

"I brought 25 Wi-Fi trail cams with us to use." Ray said as he reached into a backpack that he had with him.

"I have five of them with me. I'm going to place one right here on this tree facing downstream." Ray said as he secured the trail camera to the side of a tree.

"Well, we don't have to worry too much about snakes. It's too cold for them right now." Shay said, looking over at the others.

"Snakes?" Robert exclaimed, "No, I don't do snakes!"

Shay laughed and said, "You don't need to worry about the snakes. It's too cold for them. You just have to worry about the bears and mountain lions."

The others turned and looked at Robert as he stood there with a 'Go to Hell' look on his face.

"I didn't sign up for this shit. Guys with guns, I can handle. But snakes, bears, and big ass cats. Nope!" Robert said as the four of them started walking back to the SUV.

Once back to the SUV, they headed back to their hotel rooms. It was starting to get dark. They would do most of their recon work in the cover of darkness. But tonight, they wanted to get a feel for the nightlife in the town of Centuryville.

The next morning, Ray and Shay set out to do some recon of the fence line with some of Ray's Baby Hawks. They drove to the hunting camp that they discovered on the satellite map and set up there.

Ray had equipped his Baby Hawks with an HD camera and Wi-Fi signal tracker. They would be able to get a visual recording of the fence line and possibly pick up any Wi-Fi remote cameras that were placed along the fence line. Each Baby Hawk had about a 45-minute flight time, so it would take several trips and Baby Hawks to map out the fence line.

He would use the larger Hawk drone after dark to scout out the inner property and around the house. He also could use some of the Baby Hawks to get a closer view of the house and guard post due to the fact they were smaller and much quieter than the larger drone.

Due to the thick forest and occasional limb hanging over the fence, Ray had to take the drone fence recon slower than he had first planned. He would stop at times to check out possible breaching points in the outer fence.

The sides of the property were mostly woods and brush covered, with a slight incline. The property got steeper as it got closer to the rear of the property. At one point, the patrol path went from being accessible by ATVs to only a footpath.

The fence line was slowly going from tree covered to open rocky terrain the higher the drone climbed. A warning light started flashing on Ray's tablet, indicating that the small Baby Hawk drone was about to run out of power. He knew that some of his babies wouldn't return home, but that was the price he had to pay.

Ray had named each of his little friends and felt a little saddened when one went down. He was able to land this drone on top of a rock that overlooked the property below. Although the small drone would not have the power to fly again, the solar power panel on its back would supply enough power to run the onboard camera.

The tiny drone would provide an overwatch of the rear of the ranch property. The distance from the large boulder that the drone rested on was about three hundred yards from the rear of the main house.

Two of the drones had already landed due to running out of power. However, because of the forest tree cover, there wouldn't be enough sunlight to provide any power for their solar-powered cameras.

Four of the team members had taken turns on night recon. They recorded the activity on the property and noted the arrivals and departures of the guards and staff.

They needed to get an inside view of the guard's gatehouse. This was something that the Hawks couldn't get. They needed to come up with a plan.

It was a cool crisp morning. The sun had been up for about an hour. Shay and Ray slowly walked through the woods along the cold stream. They could hear the faint sound of a woodpecker getting an early start to its day on a distant tree. The soothing sound of the stream ran past them only five feet away. Every few minutes, they could hear the scurry of squirrels scampering through the fallen leaves, gathering food for the coming winter.

"I'm going to stop here. I'll meet you on the other side." He said, eyeing the surrounding woods.

"Give me about an hour and a half. If all goes well, I'll meet you at the bridge." She replied as she adjusted her backpack.

"Please be careful." Ray said as he slowly made his way back to the van where Robert was waiting. Jim had remained back at the hotel as a backup just in case they needed something. They didn't want to run the chance of all four of them getting captured.

"Always." Shay smiled and started her way through the woods towards the Clinton guard post.

After about ten minutes of following the stream, she came to an opening and spotted the ten-foot brick wall that ran along the front of the property. It was an easy walk after that. The ground slowly ran downhill from the wall to the stream. The grass was about three inches tall and had a coating of dew that gave it a light green tint.

She continued to walk along the wall noting the surroundings and the structure of the wall. She could see the trails of small animals on the dew-covered grass that went along the stream bank and into the stream.

She was able to make out the guard post through the early morning fog that was rapidly dissipating.

As she got closer, she could see movement inside as someone was watching her approach through a side window.

The sound of the forest was beginning to be drowned out by the rushing water running over the rocks to her left. The closer she got to the guard post and driveway, the harder the terrain was to maneuver.

She had to watch her footing as her approach was slowed by the rocks, and she lost sight of the man that had been watching her.

She moved closer to the wall, where the ground was a little bit easier to walk. She had placed her right hand on the wall to help steady herself.

"Hey! Where are you going? You are not supposed to be here. This is private property." Said the man standing outside next to the post.

His English was particularly good, but she could tell that it had a strong Russian accent to it.

"Hey." Shay replied, still making her way the last ten or so feet to where the man was standing.

"You're not supposed to be here. This is private property. Didn't you see the signs?" he asked as he threw his hands in the air.

She stopped and shrugged, "I didn't see any signs, sorry." Shay said as her hands squeezed into fists.

He started pointing his finger at her and ordering her to come to him. "You come here." He said in an obviously angry tone.

"Sorry, I didn't see any signs. I was watching the birds and other little animals in the woods." She said in a childlike innocent voice.

She walked to within six feet of the man. She could tell that he was putting on more of a show of authority than anger.

"Do you have a bathroom in that building there? I've got to go really bad." She said, giving the man a poor little me look.

"What's your name, little one?" the guard said, looking her over.

"Lynn, what's yours?" she asked, looking up at him and trying to control herself.

The guard paused a second and looked her over from head to toe. "Aleksander. What's in the bag?" he asked, pointing to the backpack she had on her back.

"Oh, just some water and trail mix I brought along with me." She replied and removed it from her back.

"Open it. I must see inside." He said, eyes narrowed.

She held the bag in front of her and unzipped it, and opened it. "See." She said, smiling and looking up at him.

"What is that? I must see it." He said, pointing to a small box inside her bag.

She reached inside her bag and pulled the box out. "They are tampons. You need one?" she asked, holding them out for the red-faced man to take.

"NO! You go do your business and get out of here." He said, waving his hand dismissively.

"OK, it'll only take me a couple of minutes." She replied and walked into the guard post. She slowly turned and noted everything she saw inside the ten-by-ten room. She wanted to make sure that the small lapel camera that Ray had attached to her jacket got a good view of everything inside. She saw the bathroom door in the back corner of the room.

While she was talking to the guard, her cellphone was paring with his cellphone and loading a program that Ray had received from one of his Black hat friends. This program, once loaded onto a phone, allowed someone to turn on the microphone on the targeted cellphone. It also, once it came within three feet of another cellphone, loaded the same program onto that device. This process would then spread to any cellphone that came within range.

The program also allowed for tracking the location of the cell phone that was infected with the program. Ray would be able to soon eavesdrop on each phone within the Clinton Compound and locate it.

Once inside, she removed the tampon box from her bag. Inside were four tampon holders. Only one contained the real thing. The others held two small radio transmitter detection devices and a mini camera.

The bottom of her water bottle unscrewed and held a small radio jammer. The tricky part was going to be how would she hide the camera in the guard post without the guy seeing her.

It was easy for her to hide the radio jammer and transmitter detection device in the bathroom. Luck would have it that the radio equipment master unit was located inside the bathroom. After she had placed the devices, she flushed the toilet and exited the bathroom.

She saw that the man had followed her into the guard post and was sitting at a table that lined the front of the building. There were two monitors sitting on the table that displayed six different camera locations each. Two laptop computers were on the table, and a rack that held two AR-15 semi-auto rifles was located next to the door. A kitchenette was in the back corner opposite the small bathroom.

A second guard arrived as she was exiting the bathroom. This made it next to impossible to place the mini camera in the front part of the guard post.

However, it did give her the opportunity to download the cellphone program onto a second guard's device. All she had to do was to stand within three feet of the person for about 60 seconds. This would give the program time to infect the second guard's phone.

Getting close to the guard was easy. Shay put on her flirtatious charm and had no problem getting in close to the guards. The problem would be getting away. The fear that Ray and Robert had was what if they grabbed Shay and took her as a new sex slave.

"Hey, I'm Lynn. What's your name?" Shay asked the second guard.

"Why you here?" asked the new guard, as he, too, checked Shay out from head to toe.

"I told your friend here, Aleksander, that I was hiking and needed to use the bathroom." She said, smiling at the second guard.

Ray had an idea. He picked up his cell phone and dialed Shay's cell.

Her cell started to ring, which startled her. She reached into her pocket and pulled it out. She noticed on the caller ID that it was Ray. She answered it with, "Hello darling."

"Where you at?" Ray replied, playing the role of Shay's concerned boyfriend.

"I'm standing here talking to two gentlemen about a mile down from the bridge. I'm about to leave. I had to stop and take a pee." She looked at each of the guards and smiled. "These two gentlemen allowed me to use their little guard building's bathroom. I'll meet you at the bridge in about fifteen minutes." She ended with, "Love you." And put the phone back into her pocket.

"I've enjoyed our little visit, guys, but I've got to go." She said, looking at the two men.

She took a step towards the door but was blocked by the second guard. She stopped about two feet from where the giant of a man stood, blocking her way.

She looked up at the six foot-six 275-pound man and said, "Excuse me."

He looked down at Shay and gave her an evil-looking smile, "Sure thing, little one." And he moved over to his right, giving Shay just enough room to squeeze through.

The two guards followed her out of the building. As she started to cross the driveway bridge and head back down the hill towards the creek. One of the guards shouted out, "NO! You go up the driveway and walk up the road to the bridge."

Shay stopped and turned toward the two guards watching her, "Sure thing. You guys have a nice day. Oh, you never told me your name." She gave them a smile and wave and turned and walked up the driveway towards the road.

"Boris." He replied. "You have a nice ass little one. You come back, and we party." He said as Shay started walking towards the road.

She didn't reply or even acknowledge the comment. She just kept walking.

After she reached the road, she turned and walked up toward the bridge. She had walked about a hundred yards when Ray's van pulled up next to her with Robert in the driver's seat.

"You do have a nice ass." Ray said as they pulled up next to her.

She flipped Ray the bird, opened the side door, and got in.

"Those guys gave me the creeps." She said.

"We thought you were about to beat the shit out of both of them when the big guy wouldn't move." Robert added, smiling as he looked back at her.

"They will get theirs soon enough." She said as she clenched her fists. "Sorry, I wasn't able to plant the camera."

"No problem. We were able to get some good footage from the button camera you wore." Ray replied, looking over his left shoulder at her.

"I think we've gotten everything we need for now. With the cellphone hack, we'll be able to track them and hear everything everyone says." Ray said with a look of satisfaction on his face.

"I'll give it a week, and every cellphone in the place will be infected with the program." He added.

"Let's head back to the hotel, I need to shower and wash this pervert scum off." Shay said as she looked at Robert.

"I'll call Vicky and let her know that we'll be heading back this afternoon." Ray said, turning back towards the front.

Chapter Fourteen

Sutton Heads South

Everyone was assembled at Omega's conference room. Jack had just finished showing the two new members, Nicholas, and Christopher Adams, around the facilities.

"I think we're going to need a bigger room." Vicky said as she looked around at the team and smiled.

"Let's review everything we've got on the Clinton place." Hunter said.

They spent the next two and a half hours looking over all the information they had retrieved from Sutton and the recon that Shay and the other three had brought back with them.

"Well." In a disappointed tone, Jack said, "I don't think we're going to be ready in two weeks like we had planned."

"No, this is much bigger than anything we've done in the past." Vicky said, looking over at Jack.

"Agreed." Hunter said, "This will take a lot more planning than we needed on the other jobs."

"And it's a lot more dangerous, too. This time, we're going up against a trained and much more heavily armed group." Kevin said, looking around at the group sitting around the table.

"With our group growing, we're going to spend some additional time working together before we tackle this project." Tony said, looking at Vicky and then at Hunter.

"I'm going to contact Stan and see if he can hook us up with additional training." Hunter replied, looking at Tony.

"Nicholas, I understand you are a former Olympic long-distance shooter?" Tony asked.

Nicholas looked at Tony and replied in a prideful tone, "I don't like to brag, but it was multiple Olympic Gold Medals in long-distance shooting. I also assisted in training our Navy SEALs and Army Delta Force snipers too."

"If'n ye head get any bigger, it'll pop." Christopher said, with his Scottish accent.

Nicolas and Christopher locked eyes with each other, and at one point, the team thought they were about to get into a fistfight.

"You're just jealous because you can't hit the side of a barn at a hundred feet with a gun." Nicolas responded back at Christopher.

"Aye, ah lik'th' up claise 'n' personal." (*Yes, I like up close and personal*) Red replied, "I'd rather gut ye with me knife."

"Gentlemen, is there going to be a problem with you two working together?" Vicky asked with a concerned look on her face.

"No, ma'am, we have been going at each other like this for over 25 years." Nicholas said with a grin.

"Aye." Replied Red.

"We're all talk, Ms. Vickers. Well, at least Red is." Nicholas said, looking over at his old friend Red.

"Getting back to business." Vicky said, looking back and forth at the two new additions to the group.

"Hunter, I agree. We're going to have to do some additional planning on this job. It will be a lot to take on in our current status." She said, meeting eyes with each of the team members.

"Our biggest advantage is surprise." Tony said, leaning back in his chair, "If we lose that, then the job will go south fast."

"We'll need to train hard and build our team's strength. If we need to delay it for two or three months, then that's what we'll have to do." Jack said, leaning forward, his elbows on the table and head resting on his fists.

Vicky looked around the room as everyone nodded in agreement with what Jack had said.

"Ray, do you have any new toys you're working on that will help?" Hunter asked, looking over at Ray, who was leaning against the conference room wall.

"Well, if I can get a couple of guys to help, I can have those night and thermal vision units ready in a week or so. All I need is some help putting the units together." Ray said, scanning the group for any volunteers. "I've also picked up three Range-R units for the group."

"What is that?" Shay asked, looking at Ray with a smile that one might see Christmas morning on a child's face waiting to open her gifts from Santa.

"Glad you asked." Ray replied.

"The Range-R is a hand-held radar device capable of detecting motion through solid walls. It operates like a motion detector, using radio waves to detect the presence of people and movements at 50 feet or more." He added with the same pride he displayed with all his new toys.

"I've seen one in action." Tony said, "We've used them before, in the Bureau during raids. We were able to detect where the bad guys and hostages were. A very useful tool, I might add."

"Let's get those thermal units finished. I want to have everyone on the team equipped with one before we start any major training. Can you do that, Ray?" Vicky asked.

"Yes, I've got all the parts. All I need is some help putting them together. Maybe three or four days at most, with enough help."

"Ok, Kevin, Robert, Jim, you guys help Ray prepare these units and whatever else he needs. I'll contact Stan and see if he can hook us up with some training." Hunter said, leaning back in the chair with his legs out and crossed at the ankles, hands behind his head.

"The rest of you, I want you to work on the plan to get in and out of there. We need a plan and several backup plans. Make a list of what you think we'll need. What we don't have, get it. Any questions?" Vicky asked the group.

"I've got one." Nicholas replied.

Everyone stopped and looked over at him.

"Yes, what is it, Nicholas?" Vicky asked.

"I may be speaking out of turn, but all this stuff costs a lot of money. Who pays for it?" He asked, waiting for a reply of none of your business.

"Ray sees to that." Jack said, "He's a master of robbing Peter to pay Paul. He's like Robin Hood."

"I like that. Robin Hood." Ray said.

"Robin Hood?" Nicholas replied.

"Ray hacks into drug cartels and our previous job's bank accounts. He moves their money into Omega's operating account." Jack said.

Red reached into his hip pocket and pulled out a silver flask, "A toast to our success." At which, he turned up the flask and downed a couple of swigs.

Everyone stopped, looked over at Red as he finished, and placed the half-empty flask back in his hip pocket.

"Red, do you have a drinking problem? Now is the time to tell us." Kevin asked with a concerned tone and look on his face.

"No, not a problem at tall. I keeps me flask filled with me best Scottish whisky I can find, which reminds me. Nick, we need to stop at the market so I can pick me up some." Red said with a wink and a smile.

"Don't worry, guys. Red's been drinking since he was eight years old. He functions better when he's had a swig or two." Nickolas said, looking at Kevin and then at Vicky.

"Aye." Red said, "It's like you drinking water. I promise on me dear mum's grave, there isn't a problem."

"Don't worry, guys. In the over ten years I've known Red, I've never seen him where he's had too much to drink." Nickolas said in a reassuring voice.

Everyone stood from their seats and exited the conference room to start their new tasks. As Red and Nickolas exited the room, Red turned back to Nick and said, "Well, there was that time when I wrestled that big Angus bull, and we ended up finishing off me bottle of whisky together."

"The last time I heard you tell it, it was a grizzly bear. And I still say it's bull shit." Nickolas said as the two left.

The door closed behind the team and left Vicky and Hunter sitting in the room.

"What do you think?" Vicky asked, still looking over at the door.

"About what?" Hunter replied.

"Everything. The mission, the team, Red, everything." She said, turning to face him.

Hunter reached over with his right hand and pulled at his left ear several times, "I think the team is solid. They definitely need some additional training. Red's going to be fine.

He brings some special skills to the team. The Clinton ranch will be tough, but I think we can pull it off."

Vicky looked up at one of the monitors on the wall. It displayed a picture of the Clinton house taken from one of Ray's drones.

"Vicky, I know you worry about Shay. She's more than your niece. She's like your daughter. You're worried that something will happen to her." Hunter said softly, placing his hand on her arm.

Vicky turned away with a tear streaming down her face, "They are all my children. If any of them gets hurt, or God forbid, gets killed, I'll never forgive myself."

She looked at Hunter and wiped the tears off with her sleeve.

"I understand, but they're all adults and know the risks."

"That doesn't make it any easier." She replied.

"Well, what do you want to do about Sutton?" he asked, changing the subject, "Wilson can't hold him forever. It will be a month or more before we're ready."

She looked at him, and her expression instantly changed, "I don't give a damn what he does with that scumbag. He's part of the problem that we are trying to solve." She stood up from her chair and walked towards the door.

"Take him down to South America somewhere and drop his ass off. Tell the locals that he's DEA. Maybe they'll give him the same treatment." She paused, "The same treatment that he gave those children he destroyed."

"You know they'll kill him." Hunter said, looking at Vicky as she stood in the doorway.

"I'm sure they will. But maybe they'll beat, torture, and rape him before they put him out of his misery." And with that, she walked out.

Hunter entered the building, walked over to the office door, and looked inside. Stan Rosberg was sitting behind his desk reading a martial arts magazine and looked up and saw his old friend standing at the door.

"Come in, my friend. What brings you here?" he asked as he stood and extended his hand.

Hunter walked over and took Stan's hand with both of his; he shook it.

"Can we close the door?" Hunter asked, turning slightly and pointing at the door.

"So, it's one of those visits? Please close the door, and make yourself at home. Can I get you something to drink?"

"No, I'm fine, thank you." Hunter took a seat across from Stan's desk. He leaned back and crossed his legs with his ankle over his left knee.

"Tell me, my friend, what brings you to me?" Stan asked, removing his glasses and placing them on his desk.

"I need your help." Hunter began.

"Ask, and if it's within my powers, consider it done." Stan said, opening his arms.

"I need someone to give a group of friends some special training." Hunter said, leaning forward now with both feet on the floor and elbows resting on his knees.

"I'm assuming since you came to me, you're not needing a class in cross stitching or basket weaving."

"No, more tailored towards the commando and SWAT-type training."

"And for how many?"

"A dozen or so."

"Are we referring to Jack, Tony, and my darling Shay as being part of this group?" Stan asked, folding his hands together, forming a temple in front of his face.

"Yes, and a few more new members."

"And what is the experience of the group?" Stan inquired.

"We'll say intermediate. Is that going to be a problem?"

"Oh no, it will only affect the time and cost associated with bringing this team up to the level you are asking for."

"Cost is not an issue. Let's say a month, give or take a week." Hunter said.

Stan took a deep breath and looked up at the ceiling, "I have a former acquaintance I've done business with before. He's very good at his trade and has a nice facility. I think he'll be the right person." Stan said with a slight nod.

"You can trust him?"

"Yes, or I wouldn't have suggested him. He's worked with groups before for various countries and agencies. He'll be fine with your group." Stan said, assuring his friend.

"Where is this place at?"

"East."

"Middle East?" Hunter asked, with a confused expression on his face.

"Oh no, my friend, East as in North Carolina." Stan said with a chuckle.

"Let's do it." Hunter said as he stood.

"I'll make a phone call and let you know by the end of the day today." Stan said as he stuck out his hand.

The two friends shook hands, and Hunter left and returned to Omega.

Hunter picked up his phone and dialed it; a menacing voice came on the other end. "Yes."

"Dr. Wilson." Hunter said.

"Speaking." came the reply.

"Get Sutton ready. He's taking a trip down South. You and Kevin will drop him off with some friends down in Celaya, Mexico."

"Fine." Wilson replied with a hint of disappointment in his voice.

"What's wrong?" Hunter asked, sensing the disappointment in Wilson's voice.

"I had just picked up a new cordless nail gun, and I was hoping to try it out." Came a disappointed reply.

"Sorry, but there will be others soon enough. But we need Sutton, all intact. You'll be turning him over to a contact in Celaya. Then he'll be handing Sutton, I mean FBI Special Agent Robert Crawford, to the Jalisco drug Cartel."

"Fine." Replied Wilson.

"I'm sure they will take good care of our friend. I'll also have some fake credentials and data to turn over to the contact." Hunter said, still hearing the disappointment in Wilson's voice.

"He'll be ready." Wilson replied.

"Hello." came the reply over Stan's cell phone.

"Mr. McKenny, Stan Rosberg here."

"It's been a long time since we've talked." McKenny replied.

Charles McKenny, his close friends called him Chuck, was a former SEAL Sniper. After retiring from the SEALs, he started an exclusive training center specializing in training various law enforcement agencies, executive protection, and other groups worldwide.

"How's your schedule look?" Stan asked.

"Staying busy, why?" he replied, in a curious tone, "You got something for me?"

"I think so. It's a time-sensitive job."

"Let's hear it."

"It's a group of about twelve, medium experience. They need to start ASAP and get up to operation status in a month." Stan explained.

"What kind of operation are they training for?" he asked.

"You know, breaching, moving, sweeping, close order combat, and some countermeasures."

"Equipment?" Charles asked.

"They'll be bringing their own toys. That's really all the information I can give you."

"Are they government or private?"

"They are dark, off the books."

"That's fine. Oh, since your last visit, I've built a new three-story shoot house."

"Love to see it sometime, but I will not be making the trip."

"Getting back to the scheduling. I've got some groups coming in the next few weeks, so the earliest I can work them in is four weeks from now. And for a month for the training that you said. We'll say $50 thousand per person. That includes food and housing." Charles said.

"As I said, it's time-sensitive, and they're needing to start in a week."

"Don't know what to tell you man." Charles said, sounding somewhat disappointed.

"Can you make it work for $75 thousand a person?" Stan asked.

There was a long silence over the phone.

"$75 thousand for twelve people for a month of off-the-books training." Charles said, not as a question but more of a statement.

"Yes, twelve plus or minus." Stan replied.

"Let me make some calls and get back to you. If I can reschedule the other three groups, then you've got a deal." Charles said and disconnected the line.

About six hours later, Stan's phone rang, and it was Charles on the other end.

"Well, what's the verdict?"

"I was able to reschedule two of the three."

After a slight pause, "And?"

"I think I can work the other group into your group's training. It will give them some good measure of where they stand in their training after the first two weeks." Charles explained with some excitement in his voice.

"Interesting, and who is this other group?"

"They are an executive protection group, and there'll be six of them."

"I'll run it by my contact. They'll be at your place on Saturday." Stan replied.

"Sounds good. Looking forward to meeting this group of yours. Later man." Charles said, and he disconnected the call.

Hunter received a call from Stan later that afternoon, explaining the cost and contract information that Charles had given him. Hunter agreed to everything and would meet Vicky at her house to go over the details.

"Everyone is going. Including you, Vicky." Hunter said, sitting on the couch next to her.

"Why do I need to go?" she asked, looking back at him with a puzzled look on her face.

"It's not going to hurt for you to know what's going on. Besides, you never know when some of this training will come in handy." Hunter replied, reaching over to the end table to retrieve his drink.

"I don't see me anytime soon, running through buildings with a gun and shooting." She shot back.

"Maybe not, but you'll be able to see how things move and will be able to communicate with the team better if you know what they are running into."

"When do we leave?" she asked, standing up from her seat.

"Saturday, Kevin will fly us and our personal belongings there. Jim and Robert will drive a truck with the equipment, and Ray will follow in his electronics van. They'll leave Friday and meet us there at the airport." He stood up and followed her into the kitchen. "At the airport, we'll have three SUVs rented that will drive to the training facility."

They both placed their glasses into the sink, and Hunter leaned against the counter.

"Kevin and Wilson are taking Sutton down to Celaya, Mexico. They'll be handing Sutton over to a contact. He'll then turn Sutton over to the Jalisco drug Cartel as FBI

Special Agent Robert Crawford." Hunter said, looking at a bowl of apples sitting on the counter next to him.

"Good, that's one less thing we have to worry about." She said, looking out the window at one of the horses.

"It doesn't bother you to send a person to his certain death? And I might add, a long and painful one at that." he asked, looking over at her.

"No. He will be getting what he deserves. Those children he trafficked didn't deserve what they got." She replied, without a bit of emotion.

Hunter nodded in agreement, reached over, picked up one of the green apples, and took a big bite out of it.

"By the way, Wilson won't be making the trip with us to North Carolina. I don't think this place has anything to offer him."

Vicky finally cracked a smile and said, "Probably not." as she turned and looked at Hunter.

It was almost 11:30 a.m. Saturday morning, the sun was bright in the sky above, and the temperature was in the mid 40's.

"Base to Yang." Charles called out over the radio.

"Go for Yang. "Came the reply from Phillip Yang. Phillip was a former DELTA force and now worked with Charles McKenny at his training facility.

"Our guests should be here in about 15 mikes."

"I'm just finishing up in the shoot house. I'll be there in 10." Yang replied over the radio.

"Copy."

Phillip arrived back at the office and grabbed himself a bottle of water out of the refrigerator in the breakroom.

"Don't forget, this group coming in are black ops, so not a lot of questions on their background. We're here to work with them on a special operation they have coming up." Charles said, getting up from behind his desk.

"Not my first rodeo bro." Phillip responded as he took a big swig from the bottle of water.

"I know, but Stan always sends us some good business and usually some highly covert operators. Don't see why this would be any different." Charles explained.

In about 30 minutes, the caravan of vehicles arrived at their destination. They pulled up in the dirt parking lot in front of Charles's office, leaving a dust trail behind them.

Hunter exited the lead vehicle and walked towards Charles, who just walked out of his office, followed by Phillip.

Hunter was dressed in olive drab pants with a sand-colored long-sleeved shirt and black boots. Charles and Phillip were both dressed in a similar manner with black cargo pants and grey shirts.

"Hi, my name is Charles, and this is Phillip." They both stuck out their hand toward Hunter as he approached.

Hunter grabbed each man's hand and gave them a strong shake.

"I'm Hunter, Stan tells me that you can teach my group here a thing or two." Hunter said, motioning back towards the caravan of parked vehicles.

"I think we can oblige you and your group." Charles said, looking over towards the vehicles.

The three started walking over to where the vehicles were parked.

"Where can my team unload their equipment?" Hunter asked, looking back at Charles and Phillip.

"They can offload all their personal items here. They'll be staying in a bunkhouse through the main office there." Phillip said, pointing back over his shoulder with his thumb.

"As for the other equipment, you can pull your truck and van around back into the building behind the bunkhouse. It's secure, so you won't have to worry about your things." Charles said, stopping and turning back towards the office. "It should hold all your vehicles if you prefer securing them all."

"No, the Truck and Van should be the only ones." Hunter replied as he turned and motioned for the others to get out of their vehicles.

Vicky, Tony, Jim, Robert, Kevin, and Nicholas all were dressed in a similar fashion as Hunter. More fitting for the occasion.

However, the other four had their own style. Ray had his nerd vibe going, black dress pants, a white shirt, with a tan Calvin Klein jacket on.

Jack had on a pair of blue cargo shorts and a long-sleeved New Orleans Saints jersey, and a Saints baseball cap over his unkept hair and was wearing brown sandals.

Shay had on her favorite jeans with rips up and down the legs, sporting a black hoodie and rose-colored sunglasses, topped with a red baseball cap turned around backward.

Then you had Red. He stepped out of the vehicle wearing a green and black tartan kilt that he wore just to mess with Nicholas. Black flannel shirt, flip flops, and his red beard were done up into two beaded ponytails.

"What kind of clown show is this shit?" Phillip whispered to Charles as he turned and tried to hold in a laugh.

Hunter turned slightly towards Charles and Phillip and let out a long breath nodding his head. "They're not much to look at, but they get the job done. SO! Lead us to our bunks where we can get settled." Hunter said, walking towards the office with Charles and Phillip.

After the group got settled, Charles ordered pizza and burgers for the group. While they sat around, Charles asked if they could introduce themselves to him and Phillip and what part they played in the group.

"Hunter, tell us what you can about your group here and what you're looking to get out of this training." Charles said, looking around at the group finishing up their meal.

"You've met me. I'm the on-the-ground control and command. I guess we'll say."

Pointing at Vicky, "Vicky here is the head of this outfit. She's really the boss, and she stays behind in the operations center and helps direct things.

"Tony helps with the planning and assists Vicky and Ray with the operations." He said, pointing over at Tony.

"Ray is our resident techno guru. He handles all the electronic stuff and computer things. That shit is way over my head." Ray gave a wave and nod to Charles and Phillip.

"He also handles our drone recon." Hunter added, looking back at Ray.

"Drones, you fly the Reaper or Avenger, man? Those things bailed my ass out many times." Phillip asked, starting to warm up to the group.

"No, sorry, I fly mostly the Hawks." Ray said with a smile.

"Never heard of that one, must be some secret squirrel thing or something." Phillip said.

"Or something." Ray added, leaning back in his chair.

"Kevin, here is our transportation guy, anything from fixed wing, chopper, or land vehicles, Kevin's your man." Kevin nodded at the two men.

"You get your training in the military, Kevin?" Phillip asked.

"Yes, I flew Cobras for a while and then ended up flying the A-10 for about six years. Did four tours in Afghanistan." Kevin said with a big smile.

"Bro, we need to talk. We may have crossed paths." Phillip said.

"He can handle a gun too." Hunter added.

"Jim and Robert both are good at surveillance and can handle themselves when it comes to firearms."

"Nicholas is our long gun expert." Hunter said.

"Have we met?" Charles asked, looking hard at Nicholas, "You look very familiar."

Nicholas cut his eyes over to Hunter, who was shaking his head slightly.

"Don't think so." Nicholas replied.

"You look like this guy I met in sniper school. His name was, well, we called him Shadow. You sure do look a lot like him." Charles said, now thinking that if it was, in fact, him, he wouldn't admit it anyway.

"This brings us to Jack and Shay; they generally work together as a team. Jack does more of the long-range stuff so far and has some close-quarters experience. Shay is more close quarters and spent time in the Marines as a self-defense instructor." Hunter said.

"Marine self-defense instructor. What are you, 100 pounds wet?" Charles asked, winking and smiling at her.

"We can go outside if you like to find out." Shay shot back as she moved to the edge of her seat.

"No offense Missy, you just don't look like a former Marine self-defense instructor." Charles said, holding up his hands to surrender.

"Like I said, we can go outside, or I can show you here." Shay repeated.

"Feisty, isn't she." Charles said, motioning towards her with his head.

"Well, she can back it up, so I wouldn't push her too much." Jack said, leaning forward with his elbows on his knees.

"Let's get back to the introductions." Hunter said, cutting in.

"This leaves us with our colorful team member Christopher." Hunter started before being cut off.

"Ye can call me Red. I'm a tracker stalker, outdoors survivalist, and hunter. Good with me knife and longbow and me fists. I prefer up close and personal." Red finished and looked around at his teammates.

"Red is like a bull in a China shop." Nicholas added with a grin.

"Interesting." Charles added.

"Almost everyone here has some sort of military background except Vicky, Jack, and Ray." Hunter said, looking at each one of the team members.

"Vicky and Ray need some firearms training. I don't think either one is very proficient in firearms." He added, looking at Charles, who had stood up and leaned against the wall.

Ray raised his hand, "I don't do guns." He said, shaking his head.

"You're going to do guns, like it or not." Hunter replied, meeting the gaze from Ray.

"We need you guys to bring us together as one. Some of us have worked together on previous endeavors, but we've never all worked together as one team. That's where we need your help, teaching us to operate together." Hunter said.

"Hunter, why don't you and Vicky stick around a little so we can outline a plan to accomplish what you're looking for." Charles said, looking at him and Vicky both.

"You other guys can unpack and get some rest. We'll get started tomorrow morning at 0500, so be dressed and back here. We'll go over our plan for the day then." Charles announced to the group.

"Have your KITs ready and proper dress for the training. No flipflops or shorts." Hunter said, looking at Red and Jack.

"0500? Isn't that early? The sun hasn't even come up yet." Jack replied.

"What's wrong, Jack? You going to miss out on your beauty sleep?" Ray said as he stood up from his seat.

"He could sleep for a month straight, and it wouldn't help." Shay said, laughing.

"Guys, while we're here, Charles and Phillip are in charge. We're in their house, so we're following their rules. Do I make myself clear?" Hunter said in a not-so-nice tone.

The team, minus Hunter and Vicky, exited the meeting and retired to their sleeping area. They spent the next hour getting their KIT's together and clothing ready for the next morning.

Hunter, Vicky, Charles, and Phillip stayed for two hours going over what they were looking to achieve, as well as working on their plans for the Clinton mission.

Hunter wanted to get as close to what they would expect when going after the Clinton ranch without letting Charles and Phillip know of their real goal.

After their meeting, Hunter and Vicky headed back to join the others and prepare for the next day.

"What do you think?" Charles asked, looking over at Phillip.

"It's going to be an interesting four weeks." Phillip replied as he got up and headed towards the door.

"See you at 0430." Phillip said, throwing up his hand as he exited the room.

Charles leaned back in his chair and thought about the next day's training.

Chapter Fifteen

TRAINING DAY

It was about 0430 the next morning, and Charles and Phillip were preparing for the first day of training. They had been discussing the odd group of alleged operators that had booked a month of training.

Were they some black ops group from some off the book's government agencies? They were more like a group of corporate employees on a team-building retreat. But Stan wouldn't do that to them, Charles thought. So, who are they?

Phillip brought up the idea that they were operators without official ties to a government for which they worked, or NOC's, non-official cover, as they referred to them in the day.

And that Nicholas dude, Charles thought, he was sure he had met him before. But if he was black ops operator now, it wasn't any of his business. It was just something about the group that kept eating away at him.

"Our group will be here soon." Phillip said, snapping Charles out of his thoughts and bringing him back to the present.

Charles took a long drag from his coffee cup and walked over to the coffee pot to refill it.

"This is going to be interesting." Charles commented to Phillip, who was placing a packet in front of each of the chairs facing the table.

Just before 0500, the door from the bunkhouse opened, and Tony, Jim, Robert, and Kevin came strolling in.

"There's coffee over here gentlemen." Charles said, moving over toward the front of the room.

The others soon followed, and pulling up the rear was Jack. They all took a seat at the table and started looking at their packets.

"We've got some coffee, doughnuts, bagels, and sausage and biscuits over here if you want something." Charles said, pointing at a table set up over on the side of the room.

"There's a town about 10 miles south of here. They have a few fast-food places and a couple of diners. But breakfast and lunch will be here. There's a kitchen behind the bunkhouse if you want to pick you up some stuff and keep it here." Charles said, referring to a map of the property in their packet.

"However, there will be days where we work through lunch or even dinner. So, plan accordingly. Take along some snacks that you can stuff in your KIT or cargo pockets. Keep your camelbacks full and drink plenty of water throughout the day. I'm sure this is nothing new for most of you, but it's something I must cover. Any questions?" Charles looked around, and of course, Jack raised his hand.

"Yes, Jack, what's your question?" Charles asked, pointing over at him.

"Does anyone deliver here?" Jack asked.

"Yes, it's in your packet. And by the way, you don't have to raise your hand here." Charles said, "Any more questions? If not, then Phillip will meet everyone out back in 20 minutes. Bring your sidearm, holster, ear, and eye pro, along with at least 300 – 400 rounds of ammo each. That should take us to before lunch. If there's nothing else, see you in 20." With that said, Charles and Phillip left and headed to get KITed up themselves.

KIT is a military term referring to each Soldier's equipment that they wore. Their "full kit," or plate carriers with plates, ACH (Army Combat Helmet), eye protection, gloves, hydration system, boots, ammunition magazines, individual first aid kit, etc. And whatever they might need for that mission.

The others went back to the truck that temporarily stored all their equipment, so they could retrieve their weapons. Once they were ready, they all met up behind the bunkhouse for their instructions.

"When you return to the bunkhouse, there's a ten by ten armory in the back corner, opposite the restroom, in which you can store all your weapons. It's well secured, and we'll issue you guys a key and new lock to the door." Phillip told the group.

Most of the Omega group was looking forward to firing their weapons, but Vicky and especially Ray were very hesitant.

They spent the next three days on the pistol range, receiving one on one instruction from Charles and Phillip. All morning they didn't stop firing their weapons, breaking only for lunch, then back at it again. They would stop around Sixteen hundred (4 p.m.) in the afternoon and spend the next couple of hours cleaning their weapons and receiving classroom training on handgun tactics, including learning various other weapons.

By the end of the third day, most were hitting their targets at 50 feet, punching a hole the size of a tennis ball in their targets.

On the fourth day, they switch to their Short-Barreled Rifles and repeated the process just as they had done with their handguns. This went on daily for the next four days without a day off.

On the eighth day, with still no break, they started their training with both the short-barreled rifle and their handguns. They would fire one weapon and then transition over to their other weapon. They repeated this drill for the entire day until it got to be second nature to them.

On day nine, Charles took them out to a larger range, where they learned how to shoot while moving. They learned how to shoot on the move and from different firing positions. This went on every day for three more days. Each day ended the same, cleaning their weapons, more classroom lectures, and learning more about other weapons.

On the night of the eleventh day, Charles made an announcement.

"Tomorrow, you guys can sleep in. We're not going to get started till Thirteen hundred (1 p.m.)." Charles said with a big smile.

"You guys can sleep late, go into town, do whatever you want to do, as long as you're back by noon time and KITed up by thirteen hundred."

"We're going back to the range tomorrow afternoon for some additional drills, and tomorrow night, we're going to be doing night drills. So, get some rest." Charles ended to the sounds of moans and groans from the group.

They shot hours into the night, using handheld lights and rail-mounted lights. Moving and shooting, shooting and moving. This went on for two long days and nights, ending about midnight.

Charles divided them into two groups, long-distance shooters, those that could hit their targets past 300 yards, and those who were below that range. Phillip would work with the ones who weren't able to manage good target placement past 300 yards, and Charles would take the ones who were better shooters past 300.

This put Nicholas, Jack, Hunter, and Jim into the group with Charles. Phillip took the remainder and worked with them.

Hunter and Jim were good out to between 450 and 500 yards. However, it was head-to-head with Nicholas and Jack out to around 1,000 yards. This is where Nicholas pulled ahead of Jack with his accuracy.

Nicholas, Jack, and Charles were up in a 4-story tower looking down. Jack and Nicholas each were wearing reactive helmets and vests. They would make a buzzer sound if one of them is hit with a laser. They were not aware that Phillip was hiding about 200 yards away with the same equipment.

Nicholas and Jack were sighting in on their target below, about 400 yards away, when Jack's and then 2 seconds later Nicholas' buzzer started to sound. Phillip had shot each in the head with his laser rifle. Charles warned them that they may not be the only snipers out there and that there may be counter-snipers that are looking for them too.

Jack was sighting through his scope on his target from the 4-story tower. The target was down a hill, which made it about equal to shooting from an 8-story building. He calculated the range to be 600 yards. He fired and overshot his target by several feet. He tried again with the same results.

"Remember, Jack," Charles said, "your rifle is zeroed and based on a flat trajectory at 100 yards."

"Jack lifted his head up from his scope. He looked to the side where Charles was spotting him through a spotting scope.

"Gravity is going to work against you if you're shooting at a zero angle. Your bullet is going to drop more." Charles continued, making an arching motion with his hand.

"Whereas, if you're shooting downhill, your bullet is not going to drop as much. You've got to adjust for that. It's science."

"What's your angle to target?" Charles asked.

"About a 30-degree angle." Nicholas replied. He was to the right of Jack and looking through his scope at the same target.

"Correct. So, your target is 600 yards at a 30-degree downward slope. Your effective range is 552 yards. Now adjust your aim and try again." Charles said, looking through his spotting scope.

Jack squeezed his trigger, and the report of his rifle echoed throughout the area. The round hit on target but about six inches to the right.

"Good shot." Charles said, "But you didn't adjust for the crosswind coming in from your left down near the target." Charles took his hand and made a left-to-right motion.

"How did you know that?" Jack asked, with a surprised look on his face.

"Years of training and sending hundreds of thousands of rounds down range. Also, look at the grass between you and the target." Charles replied. "Do it again. This time adjust your aim for the crosswind."

Jack took aim and made the adjustments through his scope, and fired another round. This time Jack was right on target.

"Great!" Charles said, patting Jack on the back of his shoulder.

"Here's what I want you to do, download this app on your cellphone. You place your phone on the barrel of your gun, and it gives you the angle to your target. It will also give you the adjusted range to target based on that angle." Charles explained.

"There are also a number of high-tech scopes out there that are linked with a range finder that will calculate the distance and angle to target and adjust your scope automatically for you. But don't get lazy and rely on those two options; you'll need to be able to adjust on the fly." Charles said.

Nicholas and Jack spent the next several hours aiming, adjusting, and firing. Charles would have them switch targets, which forced them to recalculate everything.

The next day he had Jack and Nicholas repeat this drill for two hours before moving on to the next drill. Now, the three targets, numbered 1, 2, and 3, are all set up at different distances.

"See the targets numbered 1, 2, and 3? I'll tell you which target to shoot and in what order. You'll have six seconds to hit all three targets." Charles instructed.

"Ready, Nicholas?"

"Ready."

"3, 1, 2." Charles shouted, and Nicholas fired.

"3, 3, 1." Charles shouted again.

This went on for several hours, with Nicholas and Jack switching out every few minutes.

Charles split those two days working with Nicholas and Jack on the longer distance ranges and Hunter and Jim on the shorter long-distance targets.

Hunter and Jim were shooting off the same tower as Nicholas and Jack but were on different levels and shooting in a different direction at closer targets.

During those two days of shooting, Phillip had the others training on a much shorter 100-to-200-yard distance. They were not shooting from the steep angles that Jack and the others were doing with Charles.

Later that evening, after the group finished their second day of long-distance shooting, they did what they did every night; cleaning their weapons and recapping the day's training with Charles and Phillip.

"Ok, guys, tomorrow you all have the day off." Charles said and was met with cheers and applause from everyone.

"Starting the day after tomorrow, we're going to be in the shoot house. So, get some rest. You're going to need it." Phillip said before the group retired to their bunks and fell asleep from exhaustion.

The next day most of the team stuck around and just relaxed in the bunkhouse. A couple drove into town, checked out the local diners, and picked up a few items at one of the stores.

The next morning the team met again in the conference room to go over the day's training. They reviewed the safety procedures and what would be covered on the first day in the shoot house.

The shoot house was a three-story structure with various rooms and hallways on each floor. It had two staircases on each floor and one leading up to the roof.

Each room had two Wi-Fi video cameras with sound that connected to the main operations center just off from the shoot house.

From this operations center, they could watch each room and hallway to see the progress the class was making. They could also control the power and other special effects that were used for various training scenarios.

Charles issued each team member a blue training pistol and a blue training MP5-style rifle. The team had access to other training equipment, such as flash bangs, nine-bangers, smoke grenades, blue training shotguns, and knives.

The first several hours were spent, in the classroom, going over door breaching and room entry, along with how to cover your part of the room when the team made entry and how to exit the room once it was cleared. They trained to work in two, three, four, five, and single-person entry teams.

After several hours sitting in the classroom, they moved to the shoot house, and Charles and Phillip broke the group into small teams, working with them on what they had covered in the classroom.

Charles took Nicholas, Jack, Jim, and Hunter outside and spent a couple of hours on providing overwatch for the team.

Although Vicky and Ray wouldn't ever be put into the position of room clearing, it was still good training for them to understand the dynamics of the procedures.

This training went on for two long and exhausting days. On day three of the shoot house training, Phillip issued them all several boxes of UTM training rounds for their guns that they would be using in real life.

This UTM round, although not lethal, would hurt like hell if you were hit on any area of the body that wasn't protected. Phillip would inspect each person as they loaded their magazines with the UTM rounds to make sure no one accidentally loaded a real round into one of the mags.

They spent the next two days training with this UTM ammo, shooting dummies that were set up in the rooms. Some of the dummies were deemed as hostages or non-combative and were not to be shot.

Charles and Phillip would take turns standing in the rooms and providing a distraction to the team when they would breach a room. They were used to being shot during this training exercise, and this time was no exception. They were well padded and protected from any UTM round that found their mark.

"What's up Hunter." Charles said as he watched Hunter approach.

"That's some good training you've put us through. I've seen some great improvement in my guys since we've been here." Hunter said as he turned and faced the same direction as Charles.

The two of them were looking out at the team as they all were taking their equipment off for the day.

"I've got a favor to ask." Hunter turned slightly towards Charles.

"Shoot." He replied.

"I'd like to see if the team could train tomorrow with their additional equipment." Hunter asked, now fully facing Charles.

Phillip walked up and faced Charles and Hunter, "What's up, guys?" he asked.

"Hunter wants to train some with their other equipment tomorrow." Charles replied, looking at Phillip.

"What equipment is that?" Phillip asked.

"Ray would like to try out their new headgear and drone." Hunter replied, looking at both Charles and Phillip.

"You guys going to fly in a drone?" Phillip asked, with a puzzled look on his face.

"That's all on Ray. He's the tech guy. I don't understand anything he does. But he's good at what he does. I'll give him that." Hunter said, seeing Ray hobble off towards the bunkhouse with his gear in tow.

"He's definitely not a fighter." Phillip added, taking a glance over toward Ray.

"Nope, but he's damn good at that technical shit." Hunter added with a slight smile.

"We'll have to check out that equipment before you use it." Charles said, looking over at Hunter.

"That's not a problem. We'll have it tomorrow morning for you two to check it out." Hunter replied as he started to head off toward the bunkhouse. He threw up his right hand to signal bye to the two men and picked up his gear, and followed the others into the bunkhouse.

The next morning Charles and Phillip entered the conference room, surprised to see that Ray was already there. He was placing square boxes in front of each of the chairs. He had also stacked 2 suitcase size containers next to where he sat.

"Good morning gentlemen." Ray said, giving each one of them a short nod of his head.

"You're up early today." Phillip replied, walking over to pour a cup of coffee.

Phillip made a motion towards Ray with his hand, asking if he wanted a cup of coffee.

"No, thank you, I've had two cups already this morning." Ray replied, holding his hand up.

About that time, the door opened into the conference room, and the remainder of the team walked in. They stood around the breakfast table for a few minutes, piling everything they could on their plates.

After a few minutes, they began taking their seats and getting ready for the day's briefing.

"Ok, guys." Hunter began as he walked to the front of the room.

"Ray's going to go over our new headgear. Some of you have seen it and helped assemble them. But today, we're going to do our training with the assistance of Ray and his helmets." Hunter said, pointing over at Ray to take over.

"Open your box and take out your helmets and cellphone controller." Ray instructed as he did the same with his container.

"May I see one?" Phillip asked, looking at Ray and down at one of the boxes containing one of the units.

"Sure, help yourself." Ray replied, motioning at one of the extra containers.

Everyone pulled out their helmets and controller and began looking them over.

"Power your controller up. There's a small switch on the right side of the helmet to power it up. They will automatically sync together. Once they are powered up and synced, put the helmet on and place the controller on your wrist." Ray instructed them as he did the same with his.

Each person adjusted their helmet straps and placed their helmet on their heads. As Ray did the same, he also powered up two of his laptops sitting in front of him.

"You'll see several colored squares on the controller screen. Now pull down your clear face shield display screen. Charles, could you turn off the lights." Ray asked.

As the lights went out, the display on the controller display dimmed.

"Press the green square." Ray instructed, and the small green square filled the controller display screen.

"You'll see that the green square is now divided into three sections. With an R, B, and L on the squares. If you press the R, the display will be on your right side, L for the left side, and B will display on both displays in front of both eyes."

"Press the B." Ray instructed, immediately a heads-up display projected on their face shield.

"You are now in the night vision mode." Each of their screens displayed a green two-dimensional view of the room and everyone sitting around the room in front of their eyes.

Everyone sat looking around the room at the new view of the world.

"Now press the red square. The screen will now switch to infra-red display." The group followed his instructions.

Several made comments of acceptance and how cool the units were. As they looked around the room, switching from night vision to infrared.

"Now press one of the red or green buttons twice. Now you have both night vision and infrared displayed on your screen." Ray said as he looked over the room at the class.

Ray placed his hand on top of one of the laptops and spun it around so the class could see, "I can also see on this laptop everything that each one of you is seeing."

"Let me get this straight. You can see everything from the command post that we are seeing out in the field?" Hunter asked in an uncommonly delighted voice.

"Yes, and that's not all." Ray replied, "Now press the blue square."

Everyone pressed the blue square on their controller, and a green display of the outside view of the building popped up on their displays.

"You are now seeing the building from 200 feet up, from the camera on Mother Hawk." Ray said, "I've equipped Mother Hawk with both night vision and infrared."

"Damn!" Phillip said in a more than surprised voice.

"What's the grey square for?" Shay asked.

"Go ahead and press it. You'll now see a grey square like the others with two added options, a Plus and Minus symbol. You also have a 4k camera, just like the one on your cell phone. This is mounted front and center of your helmet. Pressing the Plus will zoom in on your target, and the Minus will zoom out." Ray instructed the class. "It will display in front of you as if you're looking through binoculars."

"This thing is kick-ass." Jack replied, and several others expressed their approval too.

"The helmets are all equipped with communication units too. So we'll be able to talk hands-free with each other. I'll be able to control your displays if your hands are tied up for some reason and can't use your controller." Ray said.

"I'm sure these units cost the government millions each." Charles commented, now wearing the unit that Phillip had previously worn.

"Not really." Ray replied, "The government had nothing to do with these."

"Ray developed them himself." Vicky replied.

"No shit." Phillip said, looking over at Ray, who was beaming with pride.

"They weren't that expensive once I worked out the kinks."

"Really?' Charles replied with an inquiring expression on his face.

"Yes, all in all. I'd say about $5,000 each, and I got most of the parts off eBay. Some of the parts were made with my 3D printer."

"Ray, you think you could hook Charles and me with two of these?" Phillip asked, smiling at Ray.

"Well." Ray started.

"They are proprietary." Hunter said quickly, cutting off Ray.

"And you didn't see them." Hunter added, looking at both Charles and Phillip.

Charles and Phillip both nodded in disappointment.

"We know, secret squirrel shit, they get all the cool stuff." Phillip said, looking over at Charles.

"Getting back to these units." Hunter said, "You'll be able to see everything each person sees. And they'll be able to see what the drone sees also?"

"Yes." Ray replied, "But, it's going to take some practice walking around with these things on. Your depth perception is going to be off some."

"These things are going to be a game changer." Kevin said, raising his visor up.

"You'll be able to customize the setting on your units to fit your liking." Ray said. "Also, there is a texting mode, where you can send and receive text messages from each other or command. It will also work like a regular cell phone. It's tied into your helmet's communication set."

"We're going to be training with them for the next two days." Hunter said, addressing the group. "Let's take a short break, get your KIT's together and meet outside the shoot house in 45 minutes."

The next two days, they trained with all their new equipment, putting what they had learned the past several weeks to work.

The first day was more about getting used to the new helmets and learning how to not walk into walls while using them. On the second day, everything was coming together. Man and equipment were becoming one. The team was becoming one also.

At the end of the second day of training, Charles addressed the group during the evening hot wash.

"I've got an executive protection team coming in for two days to work on an upcoming event. I'm going to pit your team against them to see if they can protect their asset while you are trying to penetrate and capture the asset. It should be a good test of both of your skills." Charles said.

"On their first day, you guys can hang out in town or do some planning on your next day's assault. I'll be giving you a little information on the target and team protecting him to help some with your planning."

"What about using a sniper against one of their guys outside of the building?" Nicholas asked.

"Good question." Phillip replied, nodding his head.

"No live ammo will be allowed anywhere near the exercise, and the UTM training rounds would not be that accurate for anything over 50 yards." Charles replied, "Why, what did you have in mind?"

"How about if I take several practice shots at targets on the roof and around the building? I can do this before they arrive. If I can hit the targets 100% of the time during my practice shots, and then if I get a clear scope shot on one of them during the exercise, we can call it a hit." Nicholas explained, looking at both Phillip and Charles.

"That may work." Charles said, nodding his head in agreement, "Phillip, what do you think?"

"Sure. Where do you plan on setting up?" Phillip asked Nicholas.

"On the middle platform on the shoot tower." Nicholas replied, "I'll use Kevin as my spotter."

"No." Hunter said, "You'll do this solo. You'll need to see if you can do it without a spotter."

"Good idea." Phillip replied, looking at Hunter.

"You're talking about an 800-yard shot and changing angles possibly with each shot." Charles replied.

"Yes, if a target presents itself." Nicholas said.

"And what if they spot you first?" Phillip asked.

"Then I'm out of the exercise." Nicholas said with a smile.

"Ok, we'll do this first thing in the morning, before the other group gets here. Phillip will work with you on setting it up." Charles said, glancing over at Phillip, who gave him a nod back.

"The other group won't be here till between 1100 and 1200. So, you'll have plenty of time setting up your shot." Charles said, "This is something that if they haven't planned for it, they'll need to in the future."

"Isn't that why we're all here? To make our mistakes now and not when it really counts." Vicky said, looking at Nicholas and then back at Charles.

"Very true, good point." Charles replied.

"Let's call it a day and get some rest. Nicholas, you and Phillip hit the tower at 0800 tomorrow. That'll give you plenty of time to set up and execute your plan." Charles said. The group then left the conference room and went to their bunkhouse.

Chapter Sixteen

A New Omega Is Born

The Tag group arrived just passed 1100 (11 a.m.) as scheduled. They immediately checked in with Charles and Phillip and proceeded to the shoot house to put together their plan to protect their asset.

They spent about two hours checking over the route to the shoot house and putting their plan together.

Once they were ready, Charles had the two teams, Omega and Tag Personal Protection, gathered in the conference room to review the rules.

"Listen up, guys. You'll be using the UTM training rounds for this exercise. You'll still need to wear your KITs and head protection and protect any other area you don't want to be bruised. These rounds, even though they are non-lethal, if they hit anything that's not well protected, will still hurt like hell."

"Phillip will be issuing you the rounds and checking each gun, mag, and person to make sure no one has any live ammo. This is for your protection." Charles added.

"Whatever team or personal equipment you think you'll need for this exercise, get it and use it." Phillip said, "But I'll need to check it out first."

"You each will be using your own secure coms, but you'll need to give me and Phillip a unit so that we can communicate with your teams."

"Can the young chick be on our team?" Jason from Tag Personal said, referring to Shay. "I'll be glad to protect her, so she won't break a nail."

The entire Tag group broke out into laughter. Jason stuck his right hand out to get a high-five from his teammate Robert.

The Omega team all looked over at Shay after Jason had made that comment.

Red leaned forward in his chair and started to get up, but Nicholas placed his hand on Red's knee and quietly said, "Not now, my friend, not now."

"Jobby heid, shut yer puss. (*Shit head, shut your face*)." Red said, his face turning as red as his beard.

The Tag team just laughed even harder.

Shay didn't bat an eye or even acknowledge the comment in any way.

Jack leaned over and lightly slapped Hunter on the arm to get his attention. He pointed over at Shay, "Oh shit, you see Shay's jaw jutting out. I think that Jason dude is going to have a bad day before it's over." Jack said with a muffled laugh.

Hunter just stared ahead and slowly nodded his head.

"That's enough, guys. We're here to learn. So, let's break now, and we'll start the exercise in two hours. That will put the start time at about 1700 (5:00 p.m.)." Charles said, trying to defuse the friction in the room.

"Tag, you'll enter your vehicles from the gate. The opposition team, you'll have those two hours to set up. We'll end the exercise when and if the target is captured or if the time runs out at 0800 (8:00 a.m.) tomorrow morning. Good luck to both teams." Charles said, ending the meeting before things got out of hand.

"By the way, Phillip and I will be wearing a red helmet and red jumpsuit; do not shoot us. One or both of us will be in the building acting as judges. If we tell you you're out, then you're out of the fight. We will NOT help either side in any way. Pretend we are not there." Charles said, looking at both groups.

"If there aren't any questions." Charles paused for a second, "Good luck."

With that, the Tag group stood and started for the exit.

"It looks like they recruited from the local high school and retirement home for their team." One of the Tag team members said as the door closed behind them.

Hunter and the others gathered in their bunkhouse for a final briefing before the exercise started.

They had set up their command post in the bunkhouse the night before, and they were up and running.

"Ray, did you get the frequency of Charles and Phillips radios?" Hunter asked.

"Yes, but their cameras in the shoot house are hardwired, so I didn't have time to tap them." Ray replied.

"I also accessed the Tag communications as soon as they arrived. So, anything they say, we'll know, and I can cut their communications too if we need to." Ray said with an evil playful smirk.

"Great, can you record some of their radio traffic so we can do that playback thing you do?" Hunter asked, looking over at Ray.

"Excuse me, have you forgotten who I am?" Ray replied.

"Nicholas, you'll be Sierra. Get your stuff and head up to the sniper hide now before they get started." Hunter said, pointing at Nicholas. "Take whatever you'll need. You're going to be up there for a long time."

"Copy that." Nicholas grabbed his equipment and headed to the tower.

"We're not going to move on them until it gets dark. Until then, I want those Hawks up and getting whatever intel we can get. I want to know where each one of those assholes is at all times." Hunter looked at each member of the team.

"That Jason is mine." Shay said, looking over at Hunter. "Anyone touches him. I'll shoot you myself." She added, in a low tone.

"You heard the lady." Hunter said.

About 20 minutes later, "Command, this is Zeus. I'm in position." Came the voice of Nicholas over the radio.

"Copy, Sierra, read you loud and clear." Tony replied.

"Zeus." Replied Nicholas, "I'm Zeus."

"How come he gets a cool name, and I'm stuck with Alpha One?" Jack asked.

Hunter glanced over toward Jack and looked over at Vicky.

Vicky just rolled her eyes and shook her head.

"I mean, Shay has Viper, Nicholas now has Shadow and Zeus, Kevin has Eagle, and Christopher is Red. Even Ray's drones have cool names, Mother Hawk and Baby Hawk." Jack said in a low voice but loud enough for the others to hear.

"Ray, I want one of those Hawks up now and following their vans." Hunter said, looking back at Ray.

"Already got Baby 1 up and hovering at five hundred feet over them now. Looks like they've got three SUV's. Two tangos in the first and third SUVs and three tangos in the middle SUV." Ray said, looking over his shoulder at Hunter.

"How about The Destroyer?" Jack said, looking at Jim and Robert.

"Sounds good." Robert said, trying to pacify Jack.

"Shut up Jack." Tony said, "Or I'll tell them what I called you when you were five." He looked over at Jack.

"Today you're Alpha One." Vicky said, pointing at Jack with her right index finger.

Shay, sitting on her bunk bed, finally cracked a smile.

"Tony, you're going to have to tell me what you called him." Shay said, now with a big smile across her face.

"Angel 1 and 3, let's roll." Came the voice over Ray's audio monitor.

"They are on the move Hunter." Ray said, now with some excitement in his voice.

"Have you got them identified yet?" Hunter asked.

"Angel 3 is Robert, Angel 4 is Matt. They are in vehicle 1. Angel 5 is Mike, and Angel 6 is Steven. They're in the last vehicle. Angel 2 is Tyler, and Shay's friend Jason is Angel 1. They are in the middle vehicle with Todd, the package." Tony replied, reading off the information displayed on one of the monitors.

"I'm recording all their radio communications and assigning their traffic to each person for audio playback." Ray said.

"I don't understand." Red said, looking at Ray.

"Once we record enough radio traffic, we'll be able to respond to their communications as if we were one of them." Tony explained.

"Jobby ye dunt say, (*Shit you don't say*)." Red replied with a chuckle as he kicked back on his bunk bed.

"It's now 1800 (6:00 p.m.) I want everyone to get some rest, Ray and Tony. You two switch shifts listening to our friends." Hunter added.

"Let me know when you've figured out the shift changes. We'll plan on hitting them just before they rotate shifts. That way, the ones getting ready to come off shift are tired, and the replacements are still asleep and will be slow to react." Hunter instructed.

"Ray, let Nicholas know that we are not moving until sometime after midnight and get some rest." Hunter instructed and headed to his bunk bed.

"Hunter. Hunter, wake up." came the voice of Tony as he stood next to Hunter's bunk.

"What is it?" Hunter asked as he lifted his head up and looked at Tony.

"They're going to do another shift rotation at 0200 (2 a.m.)." Tony said as he turned and headed over back to the communications desk.

"What time is it now?" Hunter asked, trying to get his brain back up to speed from his nap.

"Little after 2400 (midnight)." Tony replied.

Hunter stood up and walked over to where Tony was sitting.

"What do we have so far?" Hunter asked as he sat down next to Tony, still trying to get his brain back to fully functioning.

"Angels 3 and 4 are on watch now. Angel 3 is on the roof, and 4 is walking around the building. Angels 5 and 6 are asleep in the room next to the stairs on the 3rd floor." Tony said, pointing at one of the display screens.

"What about 1 and 2 and the package?" Hunter asked, now almost fully functioning.

"Angel 2 is posted outside the package's room. The package and Angel 1 are asleep in the room." Tony replied.

"What room are they located in?" Hunter asked.

"They are in the middle room between the classroom and the room Angels 5 and 6 are currently sleeping in." Tony replied, pointing to a floor diagram on the table.

"Ok, great, let's get everyone up and get ready. We'll go at 0115 (1:15 a.m.)." Hunter instructed.

Tony went around and woke everyone up; as Hunter made a fresh pot of coffee. The group slowly made their way into the conference room, where Hunter was preparing to review the plan.

"Everyone, grab yourselves something to eat and take a seat. Ray, make sure Nicholas is in on this conversation." Hunter said as he took a sip of his coffee.

Hunter updated everyone on the intel and location of each member of the Tag group.

"Nicholas, are you there?" Hunter asked over the comms.

"Zeus is here and looking down over his dominion." Nicholas replied.

Jack threw his hands up into the air, "See! Why does he get a cool name?"

"Nicholas?" Hunter started to say.

"Zeus." Came the reply over the comms from Nicholas.

"Ok, Zeus. You're going to kick things off. Once we get set up in our positions, I'll give you the command, and then you will take your shot on the guy on the roof. They should be doing a radio check at around 0115 if they keep to their schedule. Once Angel 3 radios that he's clear, I'll give you the word, and you take him out." Hunter looked at each of the team members and took a sip of coffee.

"We want to take down the ones that are on watch before the others are awake and ready. If we can catch the others still asleep or in the process of getting ready, that would be great." Tony added.

"Nicholas, I mean Zeus, you clear?" Hunter asked.

"Zeus is clear and ready to strike down the mere mortal below." Nicholas replied.

"Teams will hold back away from the building until he takes out the guy on the roof. As soon as he takes the shot, we move in. Alpha team, you'll go in through the front door, and Bravo team, we'll go in the back door. Everyone clear?" Hunter asked.

Each one nodded, indicating they were clear and understood.

"Ray, as soon as Nicholas takes down his target, I want you to jam their radios." Hunter said, looking over at Ray.

"Got it." Ray replied with a thumbs up.

"Tony, I'm going to need you out there with me." Hunter said, looking over at Tony.

"What do you need me to do?" Tony asked.

"When Nicholas takes his shot, I need you to break from us and head to the power source for the building. And when I give you the word, I want you to cut the power to the building." Hunter said, placing his coffee cup on the table.

"No problem." Tony replied.

"We'll have roughly 15 minutes from that radio check. They'll make their last check before the shift change. We want to end this thing before then." Hunter said, looking at each person one by one.

"Vicky, you and Ray will keep us updated on anything you see. I want those drones up in the air watching over us." They both nodded.

"Once we breach, keep the chatter and noise down. Until we take down the rover, we don't know where he's going to be in the building." Hunter instructed.

Each team member sported their new helmets, KITs, Suppressed CZ Scorpion EVO 9mm with night vision optics, and a CZ P-10c 9mm pistol, suppressed and with laser sights and lights on both the EVOs and pistols. Each weapon was loaded with the UTM training rounds, which was verified by Phillip, along with several spare magazines for each person. One person on the team carried the Range-R hand-held radar device.

They all wore black tactical pants and black long-sleeved shirts. They sported black hoods over their faces, black gloves, and black boots with matching elbow and knee pads. They looked the part of real operators.

The remaining question was, did they live up to the task?

Just before 0115, the teams moved into their staging position, which was just out of sight of the roof of the shoot house.

"Zeus, we're in position. You've got a green light." Hunter said over the radio.

"No, go on the target. He's not in the target zone yet." Came Nicholas's reply.

Nicholas and Phillip had agreed on a target area the morning before. What if the person was within that target area? Then Nicholas's shot would count.

Five minutes had gone by, and already their plan was behind schedule. Both teams held their position, waiting on word from Nicholas. And the confirmation from Phillip that the target was down.

"What the fuck!" Angel 3 yelled out as his armband started to vibrate, and two little red lights started to flash.

"Target is down." Nicholas said, followed about three seconds later by Phillip's confirmation over their team's radio.

Phillip had issued an armband to each person. This armband would vibrate, and two small red lights would start flashing if they had determined the person was dead or out of the fight. The armbands could be activated remotely by Charles or Phillip.

Each person was instructed that if their armband were to go off, they were to stop what they were doing. They would either sit down or lay down where they were when the armband vibrated. And no communication of any kind was to occur with any of their teammates.

"Ok, let's go. Take it slow." Hunter instructed over the radio.

Both teams moved in two different lines from two different directions toward the building. There was still the chance that the roving guard could look out of one of the windows and spot their advancement.

In a matter of just over a minute, both teams were positioned just outside the front and back doors of the building.

"Alpha in position." Jack called over his mic.

"Bravo in position." Hunter echoed into his.

Hunter signaled for Tony to go around and take up the position at the power box of the building. He then gave the word to the Alpha team to make their entry into the building.

The lights were out on the first floor, so the teams continued using their night vision on their helmets.

"Take it slow guys." Vicky said into her mic.

About 30 seconds into Alpha's entry, they heard, "FREEZE!" the voice of Ray, over everyone's earpiece.

Everyone on both teams froze in their steps.

"What is it?" Hunter whispered into his mic.

"I detected through Jack's monitor a slight flicker of an infrared light beam across the hallway about three feet in front of Jack." Ray said over the radio.

"Jack, you see it?" Jack looked down slightly and noticed the light beam through his night vision display.

"Got it." Jack replied in a whisper, "It's about two feet off the ground."

"I can crawl under it." Shay replied into her mic.

Shay took off her vest and quietly placed it on the ground. She dropped down to all fours and rolled over onto her back. She slowly inched her way toward the invisible infrared beam. Taking it very slowly so as to not make any noise. Her heart was racing because she knew that the roving guard could come around the corner at any second.

Jack and Red had moved up as close as they could to the invisible beam of light. They both had their CZ Scorpions up and were scanning the area for any other infrared beams in anticipation of the guard appearing.

Jack looked down to check on the progress of Shay's crawl under the beam. She had inched her way about a third of the way under the beam.

"Take it slow." Vicky said over the radio.

The entire Omega team was all tense, waiting for Shay to clear the beam. They all knew if she accidentally broke the invisible beam of light that, it would set off an alarm, and their surprise entry wouldn't be a surprise anymore.

Jack was watching the flickering of the infrared beam through his night vision. He looked down at Shay slowly, inch by inch, making her way under the beam.

Jack looked at the small box on the wall that was emitting the beam. He cocked his head slightly to the left. He lowered his CZ Scorpion down and let it hang off the sling on his side.

He removed the glove of his right hand and slowly reached over the top of the small white box.

Jack then felt the other side of the two-by-three box and found what he was looking for.

"Got it." Jack said and walked past Shay, that was lying on her back at his feet.

"What did you just do?" Vicky asked in a shocked and puzzled tone.

"They sold models just like this at a hardware store I shopped at when I was a kid. I remembered that they had an on-off switch on the side." Jack whispered into his mic.

Jack looked down at Shay, who was still on her back, lying on the floor. He gave her a slight smile and reached down to help her up to her feet.

Shay raised both her hands into the air and flipped Jack the bird with both hands. She then rolled over to her knees and slowly stood up.

Red reached down and picked her vest up, and handed it to her. She quickly put the vest on and retrieved her Suppressed CZ Scorpion that Red was holding and looked up at Jack.

Jack looked back at her, "She is doing that thing with her jaw again." Jack whispered into his mic.

"Ok, kids, get your heads back into the game. We just found one of those infrared boxes on our side and switched it off. Keep moving. We're behind schedule." Hunter said in a whispered but noticeably irritated voice.

"We're coming up on another radio check." Ray said over the radio.

"You know what to do." Hunter replied.

Ray turned off the jamming device and prepared for Tag's radio check.

"Status check." Came the voice of Angel 2 over the radio.

Ray pressed a key on the keyboard, "Angel 3 clear." Came the prerecorded voice of Angel 3.

"Angel 4, second-floor clear and heading down to one." The rover responded.

"Angel 2 copy all clear." And with that reply, Ray turned the jammer back on.

They now knew the location of the roving guard, and he was heading right for them.

"Alpha, our stairway is blocked, so the rover will be coming to you." Hunter said.

"We're heading your way. We'll both have to go up through that stairway." Hunter added, as he and the rest of the Bravo team, slowly walked down the back hallway to join up with the Alpha team.

Jack keyed his mic two times to signal that he had received the message. He didn't want to talk into the mic, not knowing how close the roving guard was.

Jack and his team were tight against the wall just inches from the bottom of the first-floor stairway landing. Waiting with anticipation, heart rate increasing and adrenaline rushing through their bodies. They each waited for the rover to step onto the first-floor landing.

Bravo team had reached them and set up just around the corner of the stairway. They didn't want to end up in the line of fire of their Alpha teammates when their prey entered the kill zone.

Jack had switched from his CZ Scorpion to his suppressed CZ P-10c 9mm pistol. Jack held his CZ, pointing downward, flat against his body in his right hand, finger along the slide of the gun. He wanted to make sure the end of his suppressor would not be seen by the approaching rover.

He placed the back of his left hand about shoulder high, just inches from the corner of the wall leading to the stairway. His back pressed so hard against the wall that he thought he might press right through it.

Then he heard the steps of the roving guard stepping down on the top step. Then another step and another step closer.

How many steps were there, Jack thought to himself. He was trying to remember. Were there ten or fifteen?

Another step. He's getting closer. Jack readied himself and shifted his weight on his feet.

Shay was much better at this close hand-to-hand shit, he thought to himself. But he was the team leader. It was up to him.

Another step and then a pause. Why did he stop? Did he see or hear something? Jack's heart was about to beat out of his chest.

Shay reached up with her left hand and gave Jack a light squeeze on his right shoulder. She was trying to let Jack know that he had this, and she was right behind him.

Jack could now see the man's shadow slowly growing bigger on the first-floor landing. A red glow of a flashlight suddenly appeared from the stairway as it scanned across from the opening of the first floor.

Jack took a deep breath; this was it. The figure of a man appeared from the stairway, and Jack pounced. He grabbed the man's right arm just below the elbow with his left hand and pinned the man against the wall. Jack brought his suppressed CZ up and pointed it at the right side of the man's helmet.

"Don't make a sound." Jack whispered to his captive prey.

"If you do, I'll blow your freaking head off., Jack added in a low but commanding voice.

Jack knew that the training ammo loaded in his gun would only leave a mark on the man's helmet, but it sounded good.

About two seconds later, Jim from the Bravo team grabbed the man and pulled him around the corner to where the others were standing.

Suddenly Angel 4's armband started to vibrate, and the red lights on the armband began flashing.

"Why don't you set this one out." Robert said as he helped lower the man to the ground.

Jack took a few steps back and leaned against the wall, and closed his eyes. It was over for now, but there were still five to go before anyone could relax.

"Great job guys." Came Vicky's voice over their coms.

"Still no updates for you." Ray added, "As far as we can tell, the others are still in their last known position."

It was slowly approaching the final radio check and a wake-up call for the other team to get ready and take over the next watch.

"We've got to move now." Hunter said in a whisper over the coms.

"Bravo will take the lead. Alpha, you break left at the top of the stairs and clear that side, and then position at the steps leading up to the third floor. We're going right and clearing. We'll index back with you when we've cleared." Hunter instructed as he moved into position leading the team up the stairs.

Everyone gave him a thumbs-up, and they moved together slowly up the stairs.

Once the second floor was cleared, they started their ascent toward the third floor. The Alpha team took the lead this time. Once they reached the top of the stairs, the hallway took a right turn and then another right turn shortly again.

Both teams paused at the top of the third-floor landing.

"Guys, it's almost time for their final radio check and wake-up call." Ray said, with a little stress in his voice.

"Ray, keep their radios jammed. I'll give you a thumbs up in front of my screen when I'm ready for Tony to kill the lights, then let Tony know. Alpha and Bravo, no more talking till we breach the rooms." Hunter quickly said in a whisper over his mic.

"Copy." Ray responded.

"Ready." Came Tony's response.

"Alpha, move into position." Hunter said.

The Alpha team slowly moved from the top of the stairs and reached the final turn of the hallway. The sleeping Angel team members, 4 and 5, were hopefully still asleep in the room that was now directly across from them.

The light was on in the hallway, and Jack slowly peeked around the corner. He could see the Angel 2 guard sitting outside the room that housed their target.

The challenge was to take down this guard without alerting the other two rooms. Then breaching the two rooms, catching the others asleep or off guard.

Hunter's Bravo team had held back at the stairs, so he could give the final instructions. He wanted to get any final updates from Ray, Tony, and Nicholas.

Nicholas could see the windows of the two rooms from his sniper nest. He reported that the lights were still out, and everyone appeared to still be asleep.

"Bravo team, switch to infrared on one side and night vision on the other side. When we hit the sleeping quarters, I'm going to throw in a smoke bomb first. The night vision will not be any good in the smoke. We'll still be able to see them with the infrared."

"Once in position, we're going to hold for about two minutes. Keep your eyes closed during that time to allow your eyes to adjust some to the darkness." Hunter added.

"Alpha team, keep with the night vision. When Tony kills the lights, you'll still be able to see and then move on the guard in the hallway." Hunter instructed; he then moved his team to the hallway next to Jack's team.

After about two minutes, Hunter held his hand up in front of his helmet camera. He gave Ray the thumbs-up to let Tony know to kill the lights.

About two seconds later, the lights went out in the entire building.

As soon as the lights went out, the guard, Angel 2, keyed the mic on his radio.

"Angel 3 and 4, report." The guard said into his mic.

No answer. And again, the guard called out to the other two Angel guards, with no reply.

He was so focused on trying to get in contact with his two team members that he didn't notice Jack's team slowly approaching in the dark.

Jack had his CZ P-10c 9mm pistol out front, pointing at the Angels guard's chest. The guard turned to his right and notice three dark figures just four feet away.

The guard screamed out, "GET UP, THEY'RE HERE!" But his scream was drowned out, by the explosion of the smoke grenade, in the sleeping quarters of his fellow Angel team members.

Jack pushed the Angel 2 guard against the wall as Shay and Red got ready to bust through the door of the room that housed their target.

At the same time, Hunter and his team breached the sleeping quarters of the other two Angel guards.

As soon as the sleeping guards heard the explosion, they both sat up from their cots and were immediately grabbed by Hunter, Jim, Robert, and Kevin before they knew what was happening.

Red, using his brute force, slammed his shoulder into the door, and it went flying across the room. Shay then entered directly behind Red with her Suppressed CZ Scorpion raised and ready to fire.

Red's momentum took him right towards their ultimate goal, the person that the Tag group was guarding.

Todd was rising from his cot and had a gun in his right hand. He pointed his gun at the approaching grizzly of a man. But before he could get a shot off, Red landed on top of him, causing the cot to collapse, and the two men fell to the floor.

Jason, Angel 1, jumped up from his cot and took aim at Red but couldn't shoot out of fear of hitting his own man.

He then saw Shay moving towards him from the other side. He turned to face her and sighted his gun on the approaching figure.

He fired, barely missing her right side. She turned as the UTM round hit the wall behind her and splattered into a blue paint blob.

Shay spun around and fired four rapid shots from fifteen feet away at Jason. Two shots dead center of his forehead, and two shots hit his genitals. Jason bent over in pain as he grabbed his crotch and dropped to his knees in pain.

Shay turned and blew a bubble between her lips with the bubble gum that she had been chewing.

"Still got my nails." Shay said as she walked up to Jason, still balled up on the floor in pain.

In the adjoining room, Charles had been watching the entire event go down on camera. The cameras were not affected when Tony killed the lights due to being on a battery backup system.

Charles stepped out of the adjacent room moments after Jason hit the floor. He walked over to where Red had finally gotten to his feet, holding the arm of his captive prize.

"She definitely has some anger issues." Charles said, looking over at Red.

"Aye, she's wee heid." (*Yes, she's little crazy*) Red replied.

Phillip had followed the Omega team up the stairs but stayed back so as to not interfere with any action that occurred.

He entered the room that Hunter and his team had taken to see who was still standing and who was out of the game.

He saw through the still smoke-filled room that Hunter's team had captured the two Tag members still in their cots.

He then went to the room where Jason and the package was. Only to see Jason still on the floor groaning and holding his crotch.

"Get the first aid kit." Charles said to Phillip.

"What happened?" Phillip asked, looking down at Jason.

"Well... Shay happened. I told them to wear safety protection on anything they didn't want hurt or bruised." Charles replied, looking down at Jason, that was now trying to sit up.

"Paybacks a bitch, isn't it Jason." Phillip said with a smile.

"I'm going to get that bitch!" Jason said as he was trying to finally stand.

"I'd leave it be if I was you." Charles said as he reached down and helped Jason stand.

"You started it." Todd said as he walked over to help his teammate.

"Aye, laddie, if ye dunt want any more embarrassments or further injury. I'd leave the lass alone." Red said as he walked up to within inches of Jason's face.

"Ok, if both teams can play nice, we'll have a hot wash at 0900 later this morning. You guys get some rest." Charles said and walked out of the room.

At 0900, the Tag Personal Protection group walked into the conference room. Only to see Vicky and her Omega group already sitting and eating breakfast.

"Come on in." Tony said, motioning to the new arrivals.

The Tag group walked in, not as cocky as they were before. They all walked over to the table with the food and started filling their plates.

Jason was the last of the group to enter the room. He was walking very slowly and gingerly as he walked towards the table.

After putting on as much food as they could on their plates, they walked over and took a seat. Some of them took seats next to members of the Omega group and started congratulating them on their success.

All but one. Jason, who was sporting a large golf ball size bruise and a lump on his forehead, stood alone against the back wall.

Charles and Phillip entered the room from Charles's office.

"Good morning to everyone. Hope you got some rest after our little competition earlier." Charles said as he took his position in front of the whiteboard.

Phillip walked over to the table and picked up a sausage and biscuit. He poured a glass of orange juice and took a sip, and placed it down on the table. He turned around and leaned against the table, nodding and smiling at some of the class members.

"I hope everyone learned something over the last 24 hours." Charles started, looking over the group.

"I think we all will agree that Vicky's group won this encounter." Charles said, taking a slight bow towards Vicky.

The entire class applauded as Vicky, red-faced, gave a slight wave to the group.

"All the credit goes to the team. They did it all. I just sat back and watched them work. I'm proud of what they have achieved." She said and gave Shay a wink and a smile.

“Not bad for some old people from the local retirement home and high school.” Robert said, leaning back in his chair.

“Yes.” Todd said, “I think our first mistake was underestimating you guys. You have my utmost respect.”

“We’ll never assume that because a person doesn’t look like they’re a threat, that they’re not.” Jason said.

“This is something that we’ll never forget, and we hope it’ll never happen again.” He added.

“I think everyone will take away something from this training; lessons from the things they have done wrong and things they will do differently in the future.” Kevin said, looking around at the class and raising his cup of coffee for a toast.

“This is where you make your mistakes.” Phillip added and took a bite of his biscuit.

Most of the class nodded their heads in agreement.

“I want to apologize to your young team member. I believe your name is Shay?” Jason said, looking directly at Shay, who turned and made eye contact with him for the first time.

“I grossly underestimated you and disrespected you. Again, I’m sorry.” Jason said, placing his right hand over his heart.

“No problem.” Shay said and smiled, “And I’m sorry about the shots to both heads.”

Several of the class members burst out into laughter.

"Cumhachdach gear comes in sma' bulk", Red said, giving Shay a wink.

“What did he say?” Mike from Tag said, looking around at the group.

"My brother in arms said... Powerful things come in small packages." Nicholas replied.

“If no one has any questions, we’re finished. Except for your group Vicky. I need you guys back here at 0500 in the morning.” Charles said.

The class stuck around for another hour or so, talking and laughing together.

Todd, the leader of their group, spent some time talking to Vicky and Hunter.

“Vicky, Hunter. Here’s my card. If you ever need any help, please don’t hesitate to give me a call. But somehow, I think you’ll be fine.” Todd said and shook each of their hands.

The Tag group soon packed up their bags and equipment and headed out.

They had gathered again at 0500 in the conference room to start the new day. What was in store for them next? More handgun drills at the range? More training in the shoot house? Or were they going to break down every gun they owned and clean them and put them back together blindfolded?

They spent the first couple of hours going over how to blend in with the crowd. How to change their appearance and hide themselves from camera view. How to look non-threatening and detect threats would lead them up to the next topic.

"I've got a special guest instructor." Charles said, "He'll be conducting the next two days of training. He's one of the best hand-to-hand combat instructors I've ever met. A former Israeli Defense Force instructor. He's a master in Krav Maga and several other martial arts. Some I've never heard of. I also understand that he's a friend of Hunter's and that they both go way back. I'd like to introduce you to Stan Rosberg."

Stan entered the room from Charles's office and walked over to the front of the room next to Phillip.

"You're going to learn how to defend yourselves in close hand-to-hand combat. We'll use the training handguns and knives that you've been training with so far. In the event an attacker grabs your gun, or grabs you from behind, or has you down on the ground, you'll know how to eliminate that attacker with the use of your hands, knife, or gun." Stan said as he walked back and forth in front of the room.

"This is up close and very personal. It's nothing like killing someone with a weapon from 50 feet or 300 yards away. You'll be in physical contact with the attacker, even feeling his breath on your face. At that point, it's kill or be killed. You'll see the life drain from his eyes. And before it's over, you'll have his blood all over you." Stan paused and looked at each member of the group.

"Some of you have already been put in this situation, and you stand here today because you won. You had trained for it, and you were able to walk away to fight another day."

"Charles, Phillip, Hunter, and myself, and maybe a couple of others are here today because we were trained and came out on top. That's why I'm here for the next couple of days, to make sure you walk away to live another day. Questions?" he asked, scanning the group.

"How many of you have heard of the OODA Loop?" Stan asked, glancing at each person.

No one from the group raised their hand.

"OODA stands for, Observe, Orient, Decide, Act." He looked at their faces to see if anyone showed any indication of following what he was saying.

He knew that Shay had it down by heart. He taught it to her himself. He wasn't sure if she was still shocked seeing him there or if she was just playing dumb.

"The Observe means you observe your surroundings. You're looking for anything out of the ordinary." He turns and writes the word OBSERVE on the whiteboard.

"The Orient means you adjust yourself and take note of the surroundings and where the threat is." He writes the word ORIENT under the other word.

"Next, you must Decide what action you're going to take based on what you've observed and the threat." He adds that word to the whiteboard.

"Finally, you Act based on the information from the previous three observations." Adding the final word to the board.

"The predominant factor in the OODA Loop is to observe first and move through the loop faster than your adversary. So that your adversary is responding to information that is no longer relevant because the situation has already changed." He said, looking again at the faces of the group.

"Let me give you an example." He turns back to the whiteboard and draws an overhead view of a street. And running off that street, he draws a narrow alleyway.

"Here, you have a street and an alley running off that street. And right here, you have a mugger." He draws a little stick figure just inside the alleyway.

"Here we have you walking down the street, not a care in the world." He draws another stick figure on the street.

"Your attacker has already completed the first three steps. He's observed you. He's oriented himself to the area and where he's going to hit. He's made his decision on what he's going to do and when. All he's got to do is act when you've reached the point he's picked." Stan turns and looks at the group.

"All you have to do is change direction, and the mugger has to start his OODA loop all over again." Stan said, placing the marker on the desk.

"The same thing applies when you're in a fight. The faster you move through your own OODA, the more your opponent must interrupt his OODA and alter his plan. Do we understand now?" he was getting a few nods now.

"It'll become clearer when we put it into action."

They spent the next two days training in the sand pit. They worked on grappling techniques, Judo, Krav Maga, and other forms of hand-to-hand combat. They used rubber knives, guns with blanks, and UTM training rounds. It was the hardest two days of their training.

The realization was that the past several weeks weren't about just shooting targets, training, moving, and working as a team. It all came down to this; kill or be killed.

Sure, some of them have taken a life, but somehow things were different. They were a team now. They had grown in the last several weeks from individuals to a family. They were now one team.

The next day was graduation day, so they could sleep till 0800. They assembled for the last time in the conference room. This was the end of a long, painful, exhausting, and fulfilling month.

"Great job, gentlemen," Charles paused, "and ladies. This is not the end of your training, but the beginning. We've given you a good foundation to start. It's up to you to continue the training. Don't leave here without committing yourself to practice some, if not all, the drills you have gone through. It could mean the difference between your life and the lives of your team members. Success or failure." Charles paused again, looking at each and every one.

"Hunter, Vicky, your team has impressed me totally. When I saw you that first day, I didn't think much would be accomplished. But you've proved me wrong. I don't know what you have coming up in the near future, but I'm glad I'm not on the receiving end. God's speed to you all."

The long trip back to Omega was a quiet one. No one hardly said a word. Each one reflected on the past month's training and what was to come. They felt a new closeness to their fellow team members. Something few would ever feel. The understanding that this next mission to the Clinton compound may be the last for some of them haunted their thoughts.

Chapter Seventeen

A Shocking Arrival

It had been almost two weeks since the team had returned from Charles' training camp. Ray, Jim, and Robert poured over the information that was still being gathered on the Clinton ranch.

There were weeks and weeks of recordings of the radio traffic that they had to review and log.

They assigned those voice conversations to the appropriate person for playback on the computer.

They noted that one of the guards had left, and a new person replaced him, but all in all, everything was just as they left it.

The phone trap and tracker list were larger than expected. Fortunately, the program wouldn't start tracking the phone unless a person visited within a certain GPS grid point. If the phone visited two or more times or stayed within that set grid for more than one hour, it would log their phone number. This would eliminate anyone making deliveries to the ranch if they only stayed long enough to drop something off and leave. Without setting these parameters, the cell phone bug would have spread to millions, if not billions, of people around the world. But still, this resulted in thousands of phone numbers.

Phones that were infected wouldn't pass the bug onto another phone once it was outside the GPS perimeter. This program was a creation of a black hat hacker that Ray knew. Several phones ended up in other parts of the country and other parts of the world.

A few of the phones were tracked to Washington, DC, and other state capitals around the country.

Several guests coming in to take advantage of the sex slaves were collected. Their names were logged, and background checks were performed on each person. Several phones were not identified as belonging to anyone and were assumed to be burner phones.

The Baby Hawk that Ray had placed to observe the property had failed due to weather or some unknown issue.

Vicky was sitting behind her desk at Omega headquarters, deep in thought, when she heard a knock at her door.

"Come on in." Vicky said, snapping out of her trance.

"Vicky." Jim said as he entered her office.

"What have you got." She replied, looking up at him.

"I've found a hunting property with a cabin that butts up to the back of the Clinton property." He said, with some excitement in his voice.

"That's perfect." She said with a smile, "Tell me about it."

"The cabin is about a mile through the woods from the back of Clinton's property. It's got a dirt road from one of the county roads that leads up to the cabin. Two bedrooms, one bath, kitchen, and den. It's small, but I think it will fit our needs." Jim said, placing a map of the area on her desk.

"Here's the cabin, and here's the Clinton property." He said as he pointed the two locations out on the map.

"I've located a larger remote lodge. It's off the same road as the Clinton ranch and about two miles down the road. It sits about a hundred yards off the road. It'll be good for our main operations to set up there. It's got everything we need, water, power, Wi-Fi, Central heating, full kitchen."

"The first one you mentioned, the cabin in the woods?" she asked, looking up from the map.

"What about it?"

"Does it have power, heat, and stuff?" she inquired, leaning back in her chair.

"Well, no. It has well water, no direct power, except for a gas generator, and it's heated by two wood-burning stoves." Jim said in a low voice.

"But it will be a good staging area to approach from the rear of the property." He added eagerly.

"I agree." Vicky replied, "We're not out there for a vacation. We shouldn't need it for more than a few days at most. We'll do the last-minute planning and hold everyone at the lodge. We'll use the cabin as an entry point." She said, giving Jim a big smile, "Go ahead and reserve the two places."

"I'll get on it right now." Jim said as he stood to walk out of her office.

"Get with Hunter and see when he thinks we'll be ready, and have Ray make the financial arrangements."

"Will do." He replied.

"Oh, and great job." Vicky said. She nodded and smiled at him as he walked out.

Once Hunter got the news of the lodge and cabin, he notified Nicholas, Jack, and Kevin.

They planned a trip the following day to check the locations out in person.

Ray was able to quickly check and made sure the two locations were available and made the necessary payment arrangements.

The others stayed behind to continue with the planning and the checking of all the equipment. Their plans were to hit the Clinton ranch in a week, so time was rapidly running out.

Vicky, Ray, and Robert continued to pour through the data that was collected. They would also need to check the new data that Hunter and the others would feed to them from the onsite visit near the Clinton property.

Shay and Red spent all their time working on the team's KITs and making sure everyone's equipment was ready.

Once they arrived at the Lodge, Hunter, Jack, and Jim spent time checking out the accommodations and where best to set the communications equipment.

Nicholas and Kevin made their way up to the cabin behind the Clinton property to scope out that location. They both loitered around until it started getting dark and with their night vision goggles, they headed through the woods towards the back of the Clinton property.

Ray had given them some modified trail cameras to place in key locations around the back of the property.

Nicholas found a good nest to build his sniper's hide that overlooked most of the rear of the property.

"Nicholas, this is Jim. How do you copy?" came the voice of Jim over Nicholas's earpiece.

"Loud and clear." Nicholas replied.

"Report." Jim requested.

"I'm set up in my overwatch position." Nicholas said in a low voice. He knew that at night and when the air is cold, a person's voice would travel further.

"What's your field of view from your overwatch position?"

Nicholas took a small spotting scope and range finder out of his right cargo pocket.

"I'm approximately 300 yards behind the main house. I've got a full view of the back of the house and pool area. The stable to the left is about 200 feet from the main house. To the left of the stable, I have nothing but trees. To the right of the house, I have an open field of view for about 800 yards. I've got a clear line of sight of the two guard post positions on top of the main house." Nicholas replied.

"Copy that." Jim replied, "Any view of the lake or driveway leading up to the house?"

"Negative." Nicholas replied, still speaking in a low voice.

Kevin had moved down the fence line to the right of Nicholas to see if he could set up one of Ray's trail cameras.

"Kevin, this is Jim. How copy?"

"Loud and clear. I'm about 200 feet down and to the right of Nicholas's position behind some rocks.

"How's your view?"

"I can see the side of the house and pool area. Nothing much more. I only can see one of the rooftop guard posts and part of the lake in the front." Kevin added as he knelt down behind a large rock.

"Kevin, I've got movement in the back of the house and on the roof." Nicholas urgently said over his radio.

A guard appeared from the back of the house and started walking in the direction where Kevin was hiding.

"Kevin, I've got a guard heading in your direction!" Nicholas said.

"Got him!" Kevin replied in a whisper.

"Kevin, get down! The guard on the roof is looking through what looks like night-vision binoculars. He's looking in your direction!" Nicholas said, now with much stress in his voice.

"What's going on?" Jim asked over the radio.

"Hold on." Nicholas replied, "Kevin, the guard on the roof has what looks like an AK, and he's aiming in your direction!"

Suddenly a shot rang out that echoed throughout the area. The shot was loud enough that Jim and the others could faintly hear it at the lodge only a couple miles away.

Nicholas's heart stopped as he looked over toward where his friend was. He couldn't see whether Kevin was hit or he was ok.

"Kevin! Kevin!" Nicholas repeated several times into his radio. But there was no answer.

The guard on the ground started running over to the area where Kevin was.

"Nicholas, Kevin. Someone tell us what's going on." Came the loud voice now of Hunter over the radio.

"I've got two more people outside standing next to the pool." Nicholas reported, his voice a little shaky.

"I can see what looks to be a body lying on the ground just on the other side of a tree." Nicholas said over his radio.

"Is it Kevin? Can you tell if he's alive?" Hunter asked in a hurried voice.

"Negative. The tree is blocking my view. The guard is approaching and stopped about ten feet away from the body. Wait! He's pointing his gun at the body on the ground." Nicholas said, in not much more than a whisper now.

Suddenly the report of the guard's gunshot echoed through the area.

"They just shot him again." Nicholas said over his radio.

"Jack, grab your gear and get ready to head up to that cabin to see what's going on." Hunter said as he turned towards Jack. Jack had been standing next to him, listening to the radio traffic.

Jack turned and hurriedly grabbed his rifle along with his KIT and headed towards the door.

"Nicholas, do they see you?" Hunter asked over the radio.

"Negative." Nicholas replied.

"I'm sending Jack your way. He should be at the cabin in ten minutes." Hunter informed Nicholas.

"Copy that. I'll hold this position until he arrives." Nicholas replied, still lying motionless in his sniper hide.

It had been about five minutes since the last shot was fired. A couple of other guards and staff members of the Clinton ranch had gathered around the body lying behind the tree.

All Nicholas could do was lay and watch the crowd gather around his friend. There was nothing that he could do. All he had brought was his spotting scope, camera, and handgun.

He kept scanning the area to make sure that he himself had not been spotted by one of the guards on the ground or on the roof of the house.

One of the guards close to the body had a German Shephard on a leash. He was doing his best to keep the dog from the body, as the dog kept barking and trying to get closer.

Tears started to roll down Nicholas's face as he lay there watching and unable to help his friend.

"Psst, Psst," came a faint sound from behind Nicholas.

Nicholas turned his head slightly and looked over his right shoulder toward the sound.

"Nicholas, it's me. Let's get the hell out of here." Came the whispered voice of Kevin.

"What the fuck, man! I thought they shot you!" Nicholas replied, still in shock, looking over his shoulder.

"No, man, they shot a mountain lion." Kevin replied as he motioned for Nicholas to follow.

"That son of a bitch was in a tree about 40 feet from me. I didn't see it until the guard shot it out of the tree, and it hit the ground." Kevin said as Nicholas crawled towards him.

"Why didn't you answer your radio?" Nicholas asked in a somewhat angry tone.

"When I heard the shot, I hit the ground and started crawling up a ditch behind me. I must have lost it somewhere." Kevin said sheepishly.

At that moment, the voice of Hunter came into Nicholas's ear.

"Nicholas, can you see Kevin?" Hunter asked, still with an angry, stern voice.

"Yes, he's right here with me. He's fine. The guard shot a mountain lion that was about to chew our boy's ass up." Nicholas replied, with laughter in his voice.

"Did the lion chew his radio up, too, so he couldn't answer?" Hunter said, now relieved but irritated.

"No, Kevin said. In his panic, he dropped his radio and went screaming like a little girl through the woods." Nicholas said with a chuckle.

"Shit, man, I didn't say that." Kevin said, looking over at Nicholas as they walked towards the cabin.

"Ok, you two, grab your things and get back here ASAP. We'll talk about it when you two get here."

"Copy that, we are almost back to the cabin, and we should be heading your way in about 20 mikes." Nicholas replied to Hunter over the radio.

"Jack, you copy?" Hunter asked.

"I copy and am returning back to the lodge." Jack responded in a relieved voice.

Nicholas gave Kevin a hard time on the way back to the lodge. He went on about if something had happened to him, he would have to be the one to tell Vicky. He didn't want to have to be the one to do that.

After returning to the lodge, Kevin had to hear it all over again from the others.

"Maybe we need to change your code name from Eagle to Scaredy Cat." Jim said with a big laugh.

Kevin knew the next few days were going to be long and filled with jokes and puns. But he knew just how close he was to being cat food to some wild mountain lion. He was just thankful that that day was not his last.

"Jim, I need you to stay here at the lodge; we're going to head back. I'm going to have Robert come and bring some of our equipment. You and him hang out in town and poke around and see what you can dig up on the Clinton operation." Hunter said.

The next morning Hunter, Nicholas, Jack, and Kevin headed back to Omega to help the others with the last-minute details.

It was about 8 p.m., and Jim heard a car pull up outside. He walked over to the window to see who it was. It was Robert with some of the equipment.

Jim met Robert out where he had parked the SUV and small trailer. He proceeded to help Robert bring in the food and supplies that were packed away in the trailer and SUV. There was enough food to feed each team member for about a week. Ray had also sent some of his electronic equipment so that the two could have things set up when the others arrived. There were several weapons that were checked out by Shay and Red that had been sent ahead.

The next morning, Jim and Robert got up and headed into town to get some breakfast at a local diner.

As they entered, they noticed two of the Clinton guards, Igor Kozlov and Yuri Agafonov, sitting in a corner booth eating breakfast. In the same booth and across the table from the two guards sat Brandon Flynn, the Centuryville chief of police.

Jim and Robert walked over and took a booth about ten feet away from the guards and chief. They were close enough to make out some of the conversations between the three men.

"We've not seen you at the ranch in a couple of weeks Chief." Igor said, taking a sip of his coffee.

"I was planning on dropping by one day this week." Brandon replied, giving the two a smile.

"This is not good week to visit." Yuri replied, motioning with his hand.

"We are having a closed party the day after tomorrow, and we have some special guests attending." Yuri added.

"What kind of party and guests?" Brandon asked, placing his coffee on the table.

"Not your concern." One of the Russians responded.

"You can come after party is over." Yuri added, nodding his head.

"You know you are always welcome. But not this week." Igor said, reaching across the table and patting the Chief's arm. "We have new batch of merchandise." he said, as he leaned back in his seat.

"I think you'll approve." Yuri added, and the three men lifted their coffee cups up in a toast.

"Well, guys, I've got to go and do my job. You know, serve and protect." Brandon said as he stood and threw two twenty-dollar bills on the table.

"Breakfast is on me. Tell Michael I said hello, and I'm looking forward to checking out some of the new merchandise." Brandon said as he placed his hat on his head and walked towards the door.

Jim and Robert sat in disbelief. Neither one said a word to the other for a couple of minutes. They couldn't believe the conversation between the chief of police and two of the sex trafficking guards.

This was big news and very unexpected information which they had not planned.

Luckily, they had brought along some of their surveillance equipment. They were able to record the conversation. They had used this equipment on many occasions while working on some Vickers Private Investigation cases.

After they finished their breakfast, they both headed back to the lodge and called Vicky.

Jim and Robert filled Vicky and the others in on what they had learned. They also sent them the audio and video of the chief and two guards meeting for breakfast.

"Ray, dig up everything you can on this Chief Flynn," Hunter said, "he's got to be dirty."

"I'm on it." Ray replied as he opened his laptop.

"Tony, I know you're on an extended leave from the FBI. But do you think you could find something on this guy?" Hunter asked, turning to Tony. Tony had returned after finishing up some work he had back at his office. He had returned back to Omega to help with the raid on the Clinton ranch.

"I've got a friend at the Bureau I can call. He'll get whatever he can on him." Tony said as he took out his phone and left the room.

"We're coming to you tomorrow. We should arrive sometime after 2 p.m.." Hunter told Jim.

"We'll see you then." Jim replied and ended the call.

"We need to find out who these special guests are." Vicky told Ray as she closed her laptop and started to put it away.

Hunter walked over and placed his right hand on Vicky's left shoulder. She looked up at him and gave him a brief smile.

"You ready for this?" Hunter asked, looking down at Vicky.

She took a long deep breath, "As ready as I'll ever be. The question is, is the team up to it?"

She took her right hand and placed it on top of Hunter's hand, and gave his hand a slight squeeze.

Hunter looked over to the corner of the room where Ray had been working.

"Ray, send a message to everyone to be at the jet, packed and ready by 7 a.m. tomorrow morning."

Ray nodded and brought up a screen on his laptop. He sent out a group message for the team to meet in the morning and went back to work.

It was about 1:30 p.m. the next afternoon when two black SUVs and a white van pulled up to the lodge. The entire team was now together, and their lives would change in the next 72 hours.

Every one of the team members had visited the area in the last two months or so. They wanted to get to know the area before they executed their plan to take down the Clinton ranch.

They would spend the remainder of that day checking over their equipment and making sure everything was ready. They would start phase one of their operation tomorrow.

Nicholas and Kevin took one of the SUVs and headed over to the cabin to make sure everything there was secure. Red and Ray wanted to check out the cabin, so they rode with them.

"Did we ever figure out how to breach the front gate without alerting the guards?" Vicky asked, looking in the general direction of the team.

"Ray has the camera taken care of. Jack has a plan to secure access to the gate." Hunter replied.

"Shay and I will take care of that tomorrow." Jack said, giving Vicky a thumbs-up.

"Nicholas and Kevin will take over watch tomorrow night and be in their sniper hide early the next morning." Hunters said, pointing at an aerial picture of the ranch that they had hung on the wall.

"Tell me again, why we're not going in under the cover of darkness?" Vicky asked.

"They used the dogs at night to patrol, and the guards have night vision. They have the security system in the house on at night. Also, in order to get close enough to the house without being seen by everyone, we're going to have to drive up to the house. Doing it at night would alert everyone, so we're going to do it at a normal time when guards arrive." Hunter explained, looking over at Vicky.

"Didn't I go over this with you?" he asked.

"Yes, yes. I'm just nervous and just wanted to hear the plan again." She said, in a nervous tone.

"Don't worry, Vicky. We've got this." Jack said with a big smile.

Vicky returned Jack's smile with a slight smile of her own, but her face had worry and concern written all over it. She was worried about her children. She felt this way every time one of these operations started, but this time it was far worse. She had this feeling deep down that some of the Omega members were not coming home this time.

The next morning started the next phase of their operation. Shay and Jack headed out to take their positions. Jim and Robert followed but stayed about two hundred yards behind.

Shay and Jack reached their predetermined spot on the road about 3 miles from the Clinton ranch heading into town.

Shay pull the SUV over, and they both exited the vehicle. Jack walked around to the driver's side and proceeded into the woods for about fifty feet.

Jim and Robert had pulled onto a dirt road and turned around, heading back out onto the main road.

Shay moved into position about thirty feet behind the SUV and stood looking back down the road.

Ray had been monitoring things back at the lodge. "Here they come." Ray's voice came over the earpiece, "I'm tracking their phones about three hundred yards coming up behind you."

"Copy." Jack replied.

"Shay, it's going to be one of your old friends from the guard house." Ray said with a chuckle.

"Great, which one?"

"Aleksander, at least that's whose phone is in the car." Ray said.

"Can you tell who the other one is?" Jack asked as he watched down the road from behind a tree.

"We have him by the name of Makhail." Ray said, checking his laptop.

Shay was standing by the side of the road as the vehicle approached with the two Clinton guards inside. She flagged down the vehicle, and they came to a stop next to where Shay was standing.

The passenger lowered his window and looked over at Shay. "What's up beautiful? Again, we meet." Aleksander said.

"My car broke down. It just stopped running. Can you give me a ride back to town?" Shay asked as she recognized the man speaking as one of the gate guards she met during her recon.

The two men looked at each other and smiled, "She's the piece of ass I told you about." Aleksander said to the driver.

"And what is your name?" Shay asked the driver, leaning into the passenger's side window and giving them a big smile.

"I'm Makhail, get in. We're heading that way anyway." He said, leaning over towards the passenger's side so he could get a better look at her.

When Aleksander turned back to look at Shay, he was facing a gun pointing directly at his face.

The driver started to reach for his gun, but Shay said. "I wouldn't do that." As she motioned over to the driver's side window.

Makhail turned towards the driver's side window. When he did, he saw Jack with his gun pointing just inches from his face.

"Howdy, how about you two raising your hands?" Jack said with a big smile.

The two Russians slowly raised their hands as they each looked at the guns pointing at them.

Shay opened the rear passenger's door and got into the back seat.

Jack reached in the window and took the driver's gun. He looked at the gun, then looked back at the driver Makhail. "What kind of gun is this?" Jack asked, looking intently at the gun in his left hand.

"It's a Russian Strizh. You Americans call it Strike One." Makhail replied with resentment in his voice.

"It's ugly as shit." Jack said, looking up from the gun and back at Makhail.

"What can I say? I took it off a dead Russian Spetsnaz." The Russian driver said, now with an air of pride.

"What in the hell is a Russian Spetsnaz?" Jack asked with an inquisitive look on his face.

"Russian Special Forces. Don't you know anything?" Shay replied from the back seat of the SUV.

"Now give me your gun sweetie." Shay told her old acquaintance from the guard house.

"Nyet (*No*)!" the Russian said defiantly. Both guards had their hands still in the air.

“I was hoping you’d say that.” She said, reaching down, taking a stun gun from under her coat. She placed it on the back of Aleksander’s neck and pulled the trigger. Over a hundred thousand volts hit him, causing his body to arch upward and then go limp.

About that time, Jim and Robert pulled up beside them. Jack ordered the Russian driver out and into their car. They zip-tied him and placed a gag in his mouth. They then put a blindfold and pillowcase over his head.

Jack and Shay did the same with Aleksander, who was still out cold in the front seat.

They gave both Aleksander and Makhail a shot of Etorphine M99 that Dr. Wilson had provided them. This would keep them unconscious for over an hour until they got the two safely put away.

Jim drove the SUV with Makhail inside; Jack drove Aleksander along with Shay. While Robert jumped into the vehicle that the two Russians were in and followed the others.

The two vehicles with the Russians headed toward the cabin while Robert took the Russian's vehicle to the lodge.

Hunter was already waiting at the cabin for them to arrive. He wanted to get whatever additional information he could out of them.

Once they arrived at the cabin, they placed the two prisoners in two separate rooms.

Hunter tried for over an hour to get additional information from the two with no success.

Jack entered the room where Makhail was being questioned by Hunter. He walked over to Hunter and placed his hand on Hunter’s shoulder.

“Let me try something.” Jack whispered into his ear.

“Go ahead. I’m not getting anything out of them. I wish the doctor was here. He’d get them to talk.” Hunter said in a defeated tone.

“Ok, Mr. Makhail, one last time. Who are the guests that are coming?” Jack repeated the questions that Hunter had asked.

“Go to Hell.” Makhail called out in a defiant voice. Still bound to the chair and pillowcase over his head.

“Ok, suit yourself. Right or left?” Jack asked.

“What do you mean, right or left?” Makhail snarled back.

“Which foot do you like best, your right or your left?” Jack replied.

Jack pulled out a Ruger model 3604 22 from his right pocket and chambered a round.

“Tell us who’s coming and when?” Jack repeated in a stern voice.

"Fuck you, little man. What are you going to do, kill me?" Makhail said and started laughing.

"Ok, right foot then." Jack said as he pointed the Ruger 22 at Makhail's right foot and pulled the trigger.

The 22-round fired out of the end of the gun and struck Makhail's right foot about two inches above the toes. Blood splattered, and Makhail let out a blood-curdling scream as blood started oozing out from around the bullet hole in his foot.

Hunter had a shocked look on his face as he watched Jack apply his form of encouragement.

As Makhail continued to scream, Jack walked over to the left side of Makhail and leaned over to his ear.

"Now, are you ready to answer our questions?" Jack said into his ear.

"GO TO HELL!" Makhail screamed out.

"Ok, left foot it is." Jack replied and moved down towards Makhail's left foot.

"Last chance Bro."

"Tell us when and who will be at this party." Hunter said as he walked over to Jack's side.

"If you don't talk, then after the left foot, I'm moving to the right kneecap." Jack said as he pointed the Ruger at Makhail's left foot.

"The Brotherhood will kill me if I talk." Makhail cried out.

"Not my problem." Jack replied.

"Ok, left foot it is." Jack said as he pulled the trigger again. Sending a 22-round into Makhail's left foot.

Jim entered the room right after he heard the first shot. He stood over by the door and looked at both Hunter and Jack standing next to Makhail.

"Uh.... guys." Jim said, just a second before the shot into Makhail's left foot rang out.

Hunter turned and looked at Jim as Makhail cried out again.

"Aleksander has something to say." Jim said, looking at Jack and then at the bleeding feet of the Russian.

"We'll be right there." Hunter said as he tapped Jack on his shoulder and motioned for him to follow.

"Dude, what the hell?" Jim said as Jack walked past.

"We don't have days to wait around until these guys talk and Doctor Wilson is not here. So, I decided to rush things." Jack said, stopping at the door next to Jim.

"Who's going to clean that blood up?" Jim asked, looking back at the Russian.

Jack looked back and shrugged his shoulders, "I don't know. Didn't think that far ahead." and walked out the door.

Hunter entered the room that Aleksander was tied up in. Shay was sitting at a table next to the wall. She had a piece of paper and was writing names down.

"What's up?" Hunter asked, looking at Shay and then at Aleksander.

"My friend here has changed his mind about not talking." Shay said as she handed the paper to him.

Jack and Jim entered behind Hunter. They both stood there looking over Hunter's shoulder at the paper.

"Is that who I think it is?" Jim asked in amazement.

"Are you sure about these names Aleksander?" Hunter asked, looking over at him, still tied to the chair with the pillowcase over his head.

"Yes, Yes, I am 100% sure. They have been here many times. They give a lot of money to the Brotherhood in order to come and party." Aleksander said, nodding his head franticly.

"Let me get this straight. We have Robert Maxwell, a Senator from California, and former Governor William Rotham. Coming to the Clinton ranch for a sex party?" Hunter said, looking over at Shay, who was leaning against the wall.

"Yes, it's true." Aleksander cried out.

"Who's this James Walters we have here on the list?" Hunter asked, moving his attention back to Aleksander.

"He's a tech millionaire from California. He's a regular here too. He helped set up and fund the security system at the ranch. He's an old friend of Michael Clinton." Aleksander said.

"Please let me go. I've told you everything I know." He added, his voice starting to crack.

"Anyone else?" Hunter asked, looking down at Aleksander.

"Yes, but I do not know his name. I was just told for me and Makhail to be back by nine tomorrow morning. That's when the special guest will be arriving."

"What about the others? What time will they be arriving?" Hunter asked.

"Very soon afterward. One of the guards will be picking the three gentlemen up at the airport and bringing them to the ranch." Aleksander said in a defeated voice.

"This special guest, how is he arriving?" Jack asked, leaning against the wall next to Shay.

"Helicopter, that's all I know." Aleksander pleaded.

"How about staff? How many staff members will be there tomorrow?" Jack asked, taking a couple of steps toward Aleksander.

"None. When special guest come, staff is sent away. Staff prepares food in advance for two days stay." Aleksander added, trying to see through the pillowcase over his head.

"Jim, go and check on Makhail." Hunter said, turning towards Jim, who had moved back next to the door.

Jim left and went across to the other room where Makhail was being kept. About two minutes later, he returned back to where the others were.

"We have a problem." Jim said as he entered the room.

"What is it?" Hunter asked, turning towards Jim.

"Makhail is dead."

"You killed my comrade?" Aleksander said in a low tone.

"No, we only shot him in his feet." Jack said, with some concern in his voice.

"Makhail had bad heart anyway. So, you going to kill me now?"

"No." Hunter replied as he looked back at Aleksander.

Hunter looked over at Jack and Shay and then turned to look at Jim, who was still at the door.

Hunter looked back at Aleksander, who was sitting quietly and motionless.

"What are we going to do with him?" Shay asked, sitting in her chair with her fingers interlaced together atop her lap.

"Shay, you stay here with our friend. Jim, you, and Jack, come with me. We're going to dump Mikhail's body." Hunter said as he headed towards the door.

Little over an hour later, the three returned to the cabin and loaded Aleksander in the back of one of the SUVs, and they all headed back to the lodge. Once back at the lodge, the team added the new information that they obtained to their plan.

"Well, we can't knock off a former governor and sitting Senator." Vicky said, looking for answers from the team.

"Nope." Kevin added.

"What if we just drug them and leave them tied up?" Shay suggested.

"Aye, sounds like a plan to me." Red said, looking over at Shay.

"We'll let the press and authorities deal with their fate." Jack added.

"Vicky, you and Tony alert the local and national press as soon as we are clear." Hunter said, looking at Vicky and Tony.

"I've got a contact that can let the State police and the state bureau guys know." Tony added as he jotted down notes on his notebook.

"So, we're all good to go?" Hunter asked, looking for a response from each of the team members.

"Anything you want to add Vicky?" Hunter asked, looking over at her as she slowly took a sip of her hot chocolate.

"Just everyone, please be careful. I know we've trained hard for this, and we're ready. Remember, we are doing this for the children that are being abused and used as sex toys." She added, placing her hot chocolate on the table.

"Ok, if there's nothing else, Nicholas, Kevin, you two get your stuff and head to the cabin. Get some rest. I want you two to be in position before sun-up." Hunter said, glancing over at Nicholas.

"Eraser." Jack said, just loud enough to get everyone's attention.

"What?" Vicky asked, looking over at Jack and squinting her eyes.

"Eraser, that's my code name!" Jack replied loudly and with some excitement, throwing his hands up into the air.

"Fine." Vicky said as she picked her empty cup up and walked towards the kitchen.

Jack looked around the room at the reaction of the other team members. They were all just going about their business as if nothing was said.

"Come on guy's, what's wrong with Eraser?" Jack pleaded for approval from the others.

"Tony, I still want to know what you called Jack when he was little." Shay said as she started to laugh.

Jack looked at Tony, "Don't you dare. You know people die of friendly fire all the time. Accidents do happen!" Jack said, pointing his finger at Tony.

It was almost 8:30 in the morning, and Nicholas had been in the hide for several hours. Kevin had worked his way down next to the fence, where he had cut a small section big enough for him to slip through.

Off in the distance, the thumping of the rotor blades of the Blackhawk helicopter slicing through the air as it approached the ranch could be heard.

"Control, this is Zeus. The helicopter is approaching about two mikes out." Nicholas whispered over his radio.

"Copy." Ray replied.

About two minutes later, a white Blackhawk helicopter flew just over treetop level and circled the property, touching down about 200 feet from the house.

"Control; chopper has landed." Nicholas said over his radio.

"Zeus! Can you get eyes on who's in that helicopter?" Hunter exclaimed.

"Stand by." Nicholas replied.

Four men jumped out of the helicopter that had just landed on the Clinton grounds.

"I've got three men, all carrying AKs and side arms. The last man getting out appears to be much older and seems to be in charge." Nicholas said.

"Zooming in. Hold on." Ray said over the mic. "Running facial recognition."

Ray had switched over to Nicholas's helmet camera and was watching the men exit the helicopter.

"Got it!" Ray said, throwing his hands up in the air.

"No, can't be." Vicky said with a gasp, "Check it again Ray."

"Who do we have? Someone talk to me!" Hunter said, now very agitated, not knowing who this mystery visitor is.

"I ran it again, and I came up with the same results." Ray said, looking back at Vicky.

"Oh my God!" she said, placing her hand over her mouth.

"Will someone please tell me who the hell we're looking at?" Hunter said, now getting very irritated.

"It's Pedro Alonso López." Vicky said in a low voice, still not believing who she was looking at.

"Did you say Pedro Alonso López?" Tony asked as he moved over behind Ray.

"Affirmative." Ray replied.

"Who the hell is this López guy?" Hunter asked, still sounding irritated that he was left in the dark.

"López became known as the "Monster of the Andes" in 1980. He led police to 53 graves in Ecuador. The victims were all girls 12 years of age. A couple of years later, he was found guilty of the murder of 110 girls in Ecuador. He further confessed to an additional 240 murders in Peru and Colombia." Tony said in a subdued voice.

"So why is this guy not rotting in some South America prison?" Hunter asked.

"In 1998, he was released by Colombian authorities. Interpol ordered his re-arrest by Colombian authorities over a fresh murder in 2002, and he is currently wanted by the police. He hasn't been seen since 2021." Tony paused briefly.

"Interpol and the FBI, along with several other law enforcement agencies, have been looking for him nonstop." Tony added, pulling up a chair and sitting behind Ray.

"He's not leaving this compound except in a body bag." Hunter said in a very matter-of-fact voice.

"You heard that, guys; you have a green light on this López guy. I don't want him leaving this place except in a body bag." Hunter ordered over his mic.

Chapter Eighteen

THE CLINTON RAID

Just before 10 a.m., a white Ford Escalade pulled up to the security gate of the Clinton ranch. Ray had the gate camera pulled up on one of his monitors at the lodge.

"The other guests have arrived." Ray said over the radio.

"Zeus copy." Nicholas replied.

"Eagle copy." Kevin replied.

Jack had a big smile on his face as he pumped his right fist in the air. "Stryker copy." Jack replied, with yet another code name he came up with.

Jack was driving the Russian's SUV that they had taken the day before. In the passenger seat was Red. Sitting in the second-row seat behind the driver was Robert, then Shay in the middle, and Jim sitting behind the front passenger. In the third row was Hunter. Aleksander was out cold, tied up behind the third seat.

"Ok, let's move." Hunter told Jack.

"Control, this is Stryker. We are moving. ETA to the front gate in 1 mike." Jack said over the radio.

"Copy Stryker. We have control of the gate camera. Switching to recording on your mark." Ray replied.

"Pulling in now." Jack said.

With that, Ray switched the camera to a previous recording of Aleksander pulling up to the gate. Jack reached over to the card scanner and scanned Aleksander's key card, allowing the gate to open. They slowly drove on through, heading now towards the guard's building.

"That was easy." Red said, shifting nervously in his seat.

"I don't think the rest is going to go as easy." Shay said as she checked to make sure she had a round chambered in her CZ Scorpion.

"Ok, control, jam their communications." Hunter said over the radio.

"Copy. Their communications are now jammed." Ray replied.

Jack slowed the Escalade as they approached the guard house. Igor was the guard currently working the guard house. He looked out the window and saw that the Escalade had stopped about 20 feet short.

He was unable to see into the vehicle due to the tinted windows and the sun reflecting off the front windshield.

Robert had slipped out of the vehicle as it rounded the last curve in the driveway. He slipped around to the rear of the vehicle and followed it as it slowly approached.

When Igor noticed that the vehicle was just sitting there. He stood up and exited the guard house, still trying to see inside of the Escalade.

Robert stepped from around the back of the Escalade and aimed his suppressed CZ Scorpion at Igor. Robert fired two subsonic 9mm rounds, hitting Igor squarely in the chest. Igor fell backward and onto the driveway next to the guard house.

Robert rushed forward as Jack pulled the vehicle up next to the body lying on the cold concrete. Robert checked to make sure that the Russian guard was dead and gave the others a thumbs up. Jim jumped out of the vehicle and helped Robert drag the lifeless body into the guard house.

"Tango down." Jack said.

Jim returned to the passenger's side of the Escalade as Jack slowly started up the driveway towards the main house.

"Control, guard house secure." Robert said over the radio.

"Copy." Ray replied.

Robert stayed behind in the guard house, just in case someone unexpectedly arrived. He found an extra jacket and hat that was worn by the guards. He put them on and took his position behind the desk.

The Escalade slowly moved up the driveway towards the house. Jim ran along the side, keeping out of the view of the guard on top of the house.

"Zeus, take the shot." Hunter called out over the radio.

Nicholas sighted in on the back of the guard's head and slowly exhaled. He gently squeezed the trigger of his suppressed M25 Sniper rifle, firing a 7.62 round at supersonic speed directly into the back of the guard's head. When the round hit the guard, a pink mist cloud formed where his head used to be as the body dropped straight down.

Nicholas's M25 rifle was fitted with a suppressor, which reduced the sound of the 7.62mm NATO round being fired from the weapon. However, with a distance of just over three hundred yards, Nicholas was not able to use subsonic rounds. This left the crack of the 7.62mm round audible when the round hit supersonic speed.

"Control, this is Zeus, Tango down." Nicholas said over his radio.

"Copy." Ray replied.

"That's a total of four guards down, counting Aleksander and Makhail." Hunter said over the radio.

"There should be three more guards plus the three Lopez guards." Shay said to Hunter.

"Let's hope that we've accounted for everyone. But let's assume there are more than six guards left." Hunter replied as he looked out the side window of the nearing Clinton ranch home.

"We can't rule out Clinton or the other guests. They may resist or be armed too." Jack added as the vehicle carrying the team was now within 100 yards of the front door.

Jim slowed his trot alongside the Escalade and allowed it to pass. Once it was clear, he took cover behind one of the many boulders that lined the driveway. In this position, he could cover the front of the house and the left side.

Tony now had two of Ray's larger mother Hawks up in the air flying over the property. They would be looking for anyone else that might be outside.

Vicky, Ray, and Tony were now able to see an aerial view of the mission along with the helmet camera views from each of the team members.

Things were starting to get busy with Ray, Vicky, and Tony back at the control center. Although they weren't in danger as the others were, they had a lot going on.

Ray was keeping track of all the helmet cams and communications, both the teams and Clintons. Tony was keeping an eye on the mother Hawks and monitoring the local law enforcement radios, and helping Ray with the monitoring of the security cameras inside and outside of the house.

Vicky took over the communications between the command and the team members at the ranch. She stood behind both Ray and Tony, taking in everything and relaying the information out to the team.

"Omega, this is Mother. I now have command." Vicky informed the team over the radio. Letting them know that it will now be her and not Ray, relaying the information.

The team didn't know if someone inside the house was aware of Nicholas' shot or not.

"Control, do you see anything out of the ordinary inside of the house?" Hunter asked over the radio.

"Negative. Doesn't appear that anyone heard Zeus's shot." Vicky replied, standing behind Ray and Tony, looking at each one of the monitors.

"Do you have a visual on everyone inside of the house?" Hunter asked as they pulled up to the front door.

"We have Michael Clinton, Robert Maxwell, James Walters, and one of the guards in the den area. They appear to be talking and having a few drinks." Vicky replied.

"Hold on." Vicky said into the radio.

"We have Kay Griffith, Lopez, one Clinton guard, and the three Lopez bodyguards located. They are in the basement area, where they keep the girls." Vicky relayed the information to the team.

"There's one guard unaccounted for; we're not sure where he is." Vicky added.

"Copy." Hunter said as the Escalade came to a stop, and the team exited the vehicle.

As soon as Nicholas took out the guard on top of the house, Kevin made his way through the opening in the fence. He slowly moved to the back of the house, keeping in the shadows the best he could.

"Control, this is Zeus. Eagle is in position." Nicholas said over the radio, keeping an overwatch of the area.

"Copy." Vicky replied.

"Control, this is Stryker. We are breaching the front door in 3, 2, 1." Jack replied over the radio.

"Vicky!" Ray cried out, pointing at one of the monitors showing the front entry foyer of the house.

The missing guard was walking towards the front door. And then they saw the front door burst open, and Red, Jack, Shay, and Hunter coming in.

The guard looked at the four coming through the door and raised his AK-47 up, and opened fire. The report of the unsuppressed AK firing echoed throughout the house, alerting the others.

Vicky and the others watched as automatic fire riddled the front door from the guard's AK-47.

Red, the first through the door, fell as one of the rounds found its mark just above his body armor. It tore through his right shoulder.

Jack fell to the ground backward as he was trying to get out of the way of the wall of bullets heading in his direction.

Hunter grabbed the back of Shay's vest. He pulled her back out the door before she was hit, and they both hit the ground, with Shay landing on top of Hunter's legs.

The guard had emptied his 30-round magazine and was reaching into his coat. He was in the process of replacing the now dry mag with a fresh one when a burst of three 9mm rounds from Jack's CZ Scorpion hit him in the chest. The guard fell backward and against the wall. He slowly slid down the wall, leaving a red streak of blood down the wall and onto the floor.

Shay and Hunter scrambled to their feet and to the door. Shay peered around the door and saw Red on his side, with blood coming out of his right shoulder.

Jack made it back to his feet and took a position covering the hallway into the foyer area.

"Clear." Jack said, glancing back at Red on the floor, holding his right shoulder.

Shay entered the foyer and went over to check on Red. She helped him to sit up and took out a bandage from his IFAK (Individual First Aid Kit), and started attending to his wound.

"Breaching." Kevin said over his radio as he came through the back door into the kitchen.

"Clear." Kevin said as he dropped to one knee, sighting his weapon on the door into the kitchen from the inside of the house. He immediately heard the automatic gunfire coming from the front of the house. He stood and headed to the door of the kitchen and towards the fight.

Kevin moved into the hallway and almost ran into the guard coming out of the den. Kevin aimed his gun at the now backtracking guard and fired two shots. The rounds missed the guard as he fell back inside the den.

Vicky, Ray, and Tony watched as everything was unfolding on the monitors in front of them.

"Stay focused guys." Tony said to Vicky and Ray.

"Control, Red is down! Red is down!" came Hunter's call over the radio.

"Tango is down." Jack added as he checked the lifeless body of the Russian guard.

"Doc, we need you here ASAP." Hunter said to Jim over the radio.

"Copy, be there in one mike." Jim replied as he stood from behind the boulder and started sprinting towards the house.

Michael Clinton ran over to the bar and pressed a panic button mounted to the wall.

"Ray!" Vicky said, pointing over at the monitor showing the den.

"He's going for the alarm." She added.

"Got it! Overriding." Ray said as he pressed some keys on the keyboard.

"I've got two others making calls on their cell phones." Vicky cried out, placing one of her hands on Ray's shoulder.

"Already have them jammed." Ray replied as he looked over at Tony.

"You're up Tony." Ray said, not taking his eyes off the three monitors in front of him.

Tony brought up a screen in front of him and punched in the phone number of the landline to the house.

"Ringing." Tony said as he watched Michael Clinton pick up the phone next to the alarm button.

"This is 911. We are receiving an alarm from this location. What is your emergency?" Tony said into his mic.

"YES! WE ARE UNDER ATTACK. SEND HELP QUICK! THEY ARE SHOOTING AT US!" Michael replied in a frantic voice.

"Yes, sir, we are sending officers there now." Tony replied.

"HURRY!" Michael begged.

Tony ended the call and turned back, and looked at Vicky.

"Deacon, this is control, be ready just in case they were able to get a call out. You may get a visit at the gate from the local law enforcement." Vickey said, alerting Robert.

"Copy." Robert replied, "I'll hold them at the gate if I can."

"Hammer, you have two of the Lopez bodyguards and the other Clinton guard heading your way." Vicky informed Hunter over her radio.

"Eagle, what's your location?" Hunter asked.

"I'm just outside of the kitchen. I'm keeping a watch on one of the doors into the den." Kevin said, keeping his rifle trained on the door that the guard had come out of.

"We need to kill the lights. You remember where Sutton told us the breaker box was?" Hunter asked.

"Got it, heading there now." Kevin responded.

"Eagle, don't turn the main breaker off. That'll trigger the backup generator." Jack added over his radio.

"Copy." Kevin replied.

"As soon as the lights go out, switch to night vision on your helmet." Hunter said.

"Zeus, do you have a visual on the group in the den?" Hunter asked.

"If they try and leave out the back, fire some shots to keep them inside. If you get a clean shot on the guard, take it." Hunter instructed.

"Copy." Nicholas replied.

"Hunter, when you kill the lights, we're going to lose the house cameras." Vicky said, relaying the information from Ray.

"Ready the kill the lights," Kevin said.

"Go." Hunter gave the order for the lights to be turned off.

A second later, the lights started going out, one room at a time. Several of the monitors on Ray's screen started going dark. The screens that monitored the team's helmet cameras switched over to green and black images, as they each switched over to night vision.

The only light now in the house was in the outermost rooms, where the sunlight pierced the window shades casting a dull glow in the rooms.

It was total darkness as soon as the lights went out, down in the basement area. The two bodyguards and the one Clinton guard stopped in their tracks. Luckily for them, they had lights mounted on the rails of their handguns. They each paused for a second and switched them on.

The bodyguard that remained back with Lopez, Griffith, and the girls did the same with his light.

The girls screamed as the room went dark and started holding on to each other for comfort and security.

"I don't know why the emergency generator hasn't kicked on." Kay said as she fumbled around a nearby desk for a flashlight.

It had been quiet throughout the house after the initial gunfight had ended.

"Girls, go to your rooms NOW! Lock your doors, and don't come out until I say so." Kay ordered the girls. They each scurried to their rooms the best they could. The small light mounted on the bodyguard's gun was the only light showing them the way.

Nicholas noticed that the curtains covering the French doors leading from the den onto the back patio were starting to move.

"Come on, you Russian pervert, let me see your face." Nicholas said to himself as he peered through the sniper scope mounted on his rifle.

"Doc, this is Mother. How's Red?" Vicky asked over the radio.

"He's going to be fine; he's lost some blood, and he's in a lot of pain, but he'll live." Jim replied.

"He's always been a big puss." Nicholas replied on his radio.

"Aye, at least I'm not hiding behind a rock like a little girl." Red replied as he smiled and closed his eyes tight from the pain.

"Eagle, move to the door going into the den. I'm going to set up outside the other door coming off from the main hallway." Hunter said over his radio.

"Moving." Kevin replied and moved towards the door.

"Use your Range-R device and see if we can locate where they are in the den." Hunter replied.

The Range-R is a hand-held radar device manufactured by L-3 Communications capable of detecting motion through solid walls. The device operates as a finely tuned motion detector, using radio waves to detect the presence of people and movements as small as human breathing at a distance of 50 feet or more.

"Stryker, you and Viper cover the stairs leading down to the basement." Hunter instructed, looking over his shoulder at the two of them. Hunter then moved over to the closed door into the den and crouched down next to the wall.

"Eagle, you have a picture of where everyone is inside of the den?" Hunter asked.

"I've got three figures crouching down behind the couch in the middle of the room. One person over at the bar on the left side and one person standing in front of the French doors leading outside." Kevin reported back.

"Can you tell which one is the guard?" Hunter asked.

"Not 100% sure, but it looks like the one standing next to the French doors has what looks like an AK in his hand." Kevin replied as he looked at the small screen on the Range-R device.

"Zeus, do you have a clear shot?" Hunter asked.

"Negative, the curtains are closed." Nicholas replied, still looking through his scope.

"Zeus, he's about two feet in front of the left French door. That's your left, from your position. He's just to the right of center behind that door." Kevin said, still keeping his focus on the screen.

"Zeus, on three, I want you to take the shot. Eagle on three, you and I are going to breach the door." Hunter whispered over the radio.

"Copy, Zeus is ready." Nicholas replied. He pulled the stock of his rifle tight against his shoulder. He placed his index finger lightly on the trigger. The crosshairs of his scope were right where Kevin had told him the person was standing.

"3, 2" Hunter started his countdown, and Kevin shifted into position.

Vicky and the others listened in total silence. Ray started to turn towards Tony, and then came the final count. "1."

The sound of Nicholas's shot echoed down towards the house, and almost simultaneously, a windowpane of the French door shattered. The Russian guard collapsed to the ground.

Michael turned towards the sound of the window breaking just as both doors burst open as Kevin and Hunter crashed through.

"LET ME SEE YOUR HANDS!" Both Hunter and Kevin cried out.

The three men, cowering behind the couch, quickly threw their hands up into the air and started crying, "DON'T SHOOT! DON'T SHOOT!"

"What is the meaning of this?" Michael demanded.

"Shut up and put your hands up and get over there with the others." Hunter demanded as he and Kevin had both their weapons trained on the group.

"I've called the authorities, and they are on their way." Michael said, trying to sound like he was in control.

"I said shut up and get over there with the others." Hunter repeated himself.

Kevin moved over to the bar where Michael was. Kevin grabbed Michael's shirt collar with his left hand. He pulled Michael over to where the others were and pushed him face-first onto the couch.

"Sit there and shut up." Kevin said, placing his gun on Michael's temple.

Hunter looked over towards the French doors. He saw the guard lying face down in a pool of blood that was soaking into the carpet. He walked over to the lifeless body and checked for a pulse.

"Control, this is Hammer, one tango down, HVT (High-Value Target) one secure, three additional targets' secure." Hunter called over the radio.

"Stryker, what's your status?" Hunter called out over the radio.

"Viper and I are at the top of the stairs leading down to the basement." Jack replied.

"Copy. Doc, what's Red's status?" Hunter asked.

"Red is stable and alert. He's going to need medical as soon as possible." Jim replied back as he looked over Red and rechecked his vitals.

"Striker, proceed to your target area. Doc, I'm coming to you. We're going to clear the second floor." Hunter instructed as he started walking towards the door.

Kevin was finishing up zip-tying the four prisoner's hands and feet and had them sitting on the floor against the wall.

"Keep an eye on those four, Eagle. I'll be back in a couple of mikes." Hunter said.

Jack and Shay slowly worked their way down the dark stairs. Even with their night vision on, it was still slow go. Once at the bottom of the steps, Jack stopped and peered around the corner.

He could see three flashlights heading in their direction.

Jack held up three fingers of his right hand over his shoulder and then pointed with his hand down to the left. Letting Shay know that there were three people down to their left.

The wall leading down the stairs extended about five feet past the bottom step. This gave Shay room to move down next to Jack.

She pointed at her chest and down towards the floor and then out towards the hallway. She was letting Jack know that she was going to go low and out into the hall.

Jack motioned for her to switch from her night vision to her infrared vision. He knew when they came around the corner that the guards' flashlights would temporarily blind him and Shay. Making them sitting targets for the three approaching guards.

Jack gave her a thumbs up and held up five fingers on his right hand. Then four, three, two, and Jack grabbed his CZ Scorpion, and both he and Shay swung out into the hallway. Jack going high, and Shay low.

Shay had placed her left foot against the bottom of the last step and used it to propel herself out and into the middle of the hallway.

Both Jack and Shay fired several shots down the hallway toward the approaching guards. Two of the guards were able to return fire, missing Jack's head by just inches.

Shay climbed to her feet, and the two slowly moved toward the three bodies covering the hallway floor in front of them.

"Control, this is Viper, three tangos down." Shay called in over her radio.

"Copy Viper. You should still have one confirmed armed, but maybe more." Vicky replied with a little anxiety in her voice.

"Copy, we'll proceed with caution." Shay replied, knowing that her aunt Vicky was worried.

Jack kept watch forward and was glancing back over his shoulder to make sure no one slipped up from behind.

"Who are we missing?" Jack asked, looking down at Shay as she secured the last of the guards' weapons.

"One bodyguard, Griffith, Lopez, and about ten or fifteen girls." Shay replied, looking down the hallway towards a door at the end.

"Let's get moving. I don't like the long hallway we're in. There's nowhere for us to go." Jack said, keeping his focus on the closed door ahead.

Jack checked his magazine in his Scorpion and switched it out for a fresh 30-round magazine.

"Shay, refresh your mag." Jack said as Shay stood up beside him.

"I'm switching to my CZ pistol." Shay replied and let the Scorpion drop to her side, supported by the two-point sling.

"Good idea." Jack replied and did the same.

"You have that x-ray thing?" Jack asked, looking at Shay.

"No, Red has it." Shay replied, closing her eyes and shaking her head in frustration.

"No big deal, we'll have to breach without it then." Jack said as he started to move towards the door.

Jack and Shay were slowly sliding down the dark hallway when they came to the closed door. Shay looked back at Jack and said, "I'll go through first, and to the right, you go left."

"Copy." Came Jack's reply.

"On 3. 1.... 2....3..." Shay called out quietly as she opened the door.

As the two entered the room, one behind the other, three loud shots rang out.

Shay went flying back against Jack, knocking him slightly off balance. Jack hearing the shots and seeing the flashes from a gun only 10 feet away, aimed his gun in the direction of the three flashes.

He fired until he emptied his magazine, grabbed a fresh magazine, and slammed it into his gun. Seeing a body lying on the ground across from him, he went over to make sure the threat was neutralized.

After seeing that the person was down, Jack turned towards the door and called out, "Shay!" There was no answer.

"SHAY!" still no answer.

Jack looked through the darkness and saw Shay's body lying just inside the door, lying there motionless. Jack could see blood on the right side of her face as he ran over and knelt beside her.

Jack reached for his radio and started screaming into the mic, "VIPER'S DOWN! VIPER'S DOWN!"

Vicky had been monitoring the radio the entire time the operation had started. She ran over to where Ray and Tony were sitting, tears running down her cheeks and in panic.

"JACK!" Vicky called out over the radio in a panic, forgetting to use his code name. "What happened? Is she ok?"

There was no reply. She called out again over the radio. "IS SHE OK?"

Still no answer. Vicky was, by this time, bawling her eyes out, knowing that Shay had been killed.

Jack was kneeling next to Shay and calling out her name, "SHAY! SHAY! Are you ok? Come on, girl, stay with me Shay!"

Suddenly Jack heard a loud gasp, and Shay reach up and grabbed his arm.

"Shay! Are you OK?" Jack asked as he put his leg behind her back to support her.

"SHIT!" Shay said, "That hurt like hell!" looking up at Jack.

"Shay, relax, you've been shot. Your head is bleeding."

Jack now heard the pleas from Vicky over the radio, "Jack, answer me, damn it! Is she ok?"

Jack reached for his radio, "Viper's ok, she took two shots to the chest, but her body armor stopped those. She did get grazed on the side of her head. It's not too bad. Some blood, and she's going to need a couple of stitches. But I think she's going to be fine."

Hunter, hearing everything over the radio, headed as fast as he could toward where Shay and Jack were.

As Hunter entered the long hallway, he called out over the radio, "Stryker, Viper, I'm coming your way. I'll be there and a matter of seconds. Whatever you do, don't shoot me."

As soon as Hunter entered the room, he saw Shay and Jack over to his left. Jack was tending to the wound on Shay's head.

The room they were in had several doors lining the wall leading to smaller rooms. This was where they kept the girls.

Hunter caught a glimpse of something moving to his right. It was a man stepping through one of the doors. Without slowing or breaking stride, he lifted his handgun and pointed it toward the man. Firing two shots, he hit the man in his right eye and just below his nose.

The man dropped to the ground like a ragdoll. Hunter never took his eyes off the man as he slowly walked over to the body.

Hunter knelt next to the body and turned the man's face to the right. He needed to see who it was.

"Hammer, is it?" Jack started to ask, looking over at Hunter.

"Yep, it's Lopez." Hunter said.

"Control, one tango down, and add Lopez to the list of dead too." Hunter said with a slight satisfaction in his voice.

Hunter scanned the room for any additional threats. Once he was satisfied, he called out. "Girls, you can come out now."

The sound of several doors slowly opening filled the silence of the room. From each of the rooms, a scantly clothed young girl slowly emerged.

"Don't shoot!" came a voice from the back of one of the rooms.

"Come out with your hands up." Hunter commanded to the female voice.

Out of the darkness stepped Kay Griffith with her hands held high and tears running down her face.

"Please don't shoot me." She pleaded.

"Control, this is Hammer. HVT 2 is in custody. Building secure." Hunter said as he motioned for her to turn around so he could flex tie her hands.

Jim arrived and started checking over Shay's wounds, then he and Jack helped her to her feet.

All the girls had stepped out of their rooms and were now looking at Kay as she stood there with her hands zip-tied behind her back.

One of the girls stepped forward and looked at Hunter.

"Are you the police?" she asked in a soft timid voice.

"No, ma'am, we're not. But we are here to save you." Hunter said, placing his hand on the girl's shoulder.

"Are any of you hurt?" Jim asked, turning his attention to the girls.

"No, we are fine now. Thank you." One of the others said.

"I need you girls to stay down here until the police arrive." Hunter said, looking at each of the young girls. The youngest couldn't be over 13 years old.

"But the police here are part of this." One of the girls objected.

"We must go with you." Another one said, stepping forward.

"We know that the local police chief is part of this. He's going to be dealt with too." Hunter assured the girls.

"We'll have the state and federal law enforcement here as soon as we can. I just need you to stay down here until they arrive." Hunter said, giving the girls a reassuring look.

Several of the girls nodded in agreement, and they held one another.

"Jim, take Viper up to where Red is." Hunter said.

"Eagle, can you fly that Blackhawk?" Hunter asked over the radio.

"That's a big 10-4." Kevin replied.

"As soon as Stryker gets up there, get Red, Viper, and Jim out of here." Hunter instructed.

"Control, I need Robin Hood and Thunder over here ASAP. They need to go through this house and get whatever we can take with us." Hunter said as he was walking down the hallway to the stairs leading up from the basement.

"Hammer, this is control, we copy, and they are on their way." Vicky replied with great relief in her voice.

"Control, have them bring some of that special knock-out juice." Hunter added, referring to the M99 injection, which will put someone to sleep for a couple of hours.

"Copy." Vicky replied.

"Control, contact the Surgeon and let him know that we are transporting two back to HQ and to be ready to receive." Hunter said over his radio.

As soon as Hunter reached the top floor, he went over and checked on Red.

"How are you doing, Red?" Hunter asked as he knelt down next to him.

"Aye, just a wee bit bummed. But I'll be fine, nothing that a good pint a whisky won't fix." Red said, trying to stand.

"Oh, how's the missy?" Red added once he got to his feet.

"She's going to be fine. A couple of bruises and a few stitches, and she'll be back to her old self." Hunter said as they both started walking to the front door.

"Aye, she's a tough one, that she is." Red replied as they walked out the front door and towards the helicopter.

"Zeus, this is Hammer. Break down your nest and grab your things from the cabin and get over to the lodge." Hunter said as he was putting Red into the Blackhawk.

Shay, Jim, and Red were soon seated and strapped in as Kevin powered the Blackhawk up.

"New toy?" Shay asked Kevin as he was going over his preflight procedures.

"Looks that way." Kevin replied as the rotors started to turn.

Ray and Tony arrived at the Clinton house at the same time Hunter had returned from dropping Red off at the helicopter.

"Help me get Aleksander out of the back of the Escalade and into the house. Hunter said as Ray and Tony approached.

"Is that ours now?" Tony asked, pointing at the helicopter as it rose to about a hundred feet, dipped forward a little, and flew off over the lake.

Hunter looking up at the helicopter passing overhead, "Looks that way. The previous owner is not going to need it anymore."

The three helped move Aleksander from the SUV and into the den, where the others were still zip tied and sitting on the floor.

"Thunder, go down and check on the girls." Hunter said after putting Aleksander on the floor next to the others.

"What are you going to do with us." Asked the former Governor, looking up at Hunter.

"We're going to leave you here and let the state, federal law enforcement, and national news deal with you." Hunter replied, looking down at him.

"You can't do this! Do you know who I am? I've got powerful friends." The former governor said, trying to threaten Hunter.

"I don't care who you are, and I'm sure some of your friends are going to end up in the same place that you and these others are going to." Hunter said, looking down at each one of them.

Ray came into the den after about 30 minutes and reported his findings to Hunter.

"I found the servers and the security recordings. I wiped them clean of the last two hours. I'm uploading everything now to our system." Ray said, looking at Hunter and then down at the others.

"I've got a surprise for our friends here when the cops arrive." Ray added.

"Thunder, tell the girls that the state police will be here in about thirty minutes. Not to go anywhere." Hunter said over the radio.

"Stryker, go ahead and give them a shot of that sleep juice. But just enough to knock them out for about 30 to 45 minutes." Hunter instructed.

"Ok, guys, let's hit the road, Deacon. We're heading your way." Hunter finished as Jack was giving the last person their dose of M99.

"Control, this is Hammer. We're clear and heading your way. Make the calls." Hunter said as he turned and followed the others out to the Escalade.

"Hammer, this is Mother, copy, and I'll see you in five mikes." Vicky ended and picked up one of the burner phones and dialed the local news station.

Chapter Nineteen

THE CLEANUP

It took several hours and a couple of stops to refuel until the Blackhawk made it back to the Omega Headquarters. Shay's wounds were a couple of bruised ribs and a three-inch-long cut. It was right along the hairline and just above her right ear. Jim had put a couple of butterfly bandages on her cut to hold her until they got to Dr. Wilson.

Red's wound was much more severe. But Jim had stabilized the right shoulder and stopped the bleeding. He had an IV going and administered some pain medication to help Red with the pain. Red's wound was something that they couldn't just take to the local hospital. It would raise suspicion and would involve the local police. That was something they didn't need.

Vicky had made several calls to the state police, local federal bureau, and three news stations located in the state's capital about 45 miles away.

She informed them that several people had been shot, located in a home that held several girls for sex trafficking.

Ray kept the radios of Centuryville's police department jammed to make sure the state and federal police arrived before they did.

Within 20 minutes of the call, the first state police car arrived at the location. Followed quickly by two news helicopters.

About three minutes later, two ambulances arrived and staged at the front gate.

At about 40 minutes after the first call was made, there were a total of 10 state and federal officials at the Clinton ranch.

From the local field office, FBI Special Agent Robert Mott arrived via helicopter. He landed on the Clinton property just as Centuryville's Chief Brandon Flynn arrived.

"What's going on here?" Chief Flynn said as he approached Agent Mott.

"I'm sorry, my name is Brandon Flynn. I'm the Chief of police here in Centuryville." He said as he put his hand out to shake Agent Mott's hand.

"I'm FBI Special Agent Robert Mott, and it looks like we have a big mess on our hands." Robert said as he shook Chief Flynn's hand.

"What do we know so far?" Flynn asked as they entered the front door.

"I just arrived myself. But the report I received from the first officers on the scene said, we've got a shit show. Not his words, but mine." Mott said as they stopped just inside the foyer.

"Looks like we've got one dead body here and a pool of blood over there." Mott pointed at the body over against the wall and then over at the small pool of blood next to the door.

"You know anything about the owner of this place?" Mott asked, walking over and taking a knee next to the body against the wall.

"Never been here before. Don't know that much about the owners." Flynn said, looking at the blood next to the door.

"They also found a body down in the guard house. And there's bodies piled up down in the basement." Mott said as he stood.

"Looks like our victim here took three rounds to the chest. But not before he dumped a full mag on the front door." Mott added, pointing over at the door.

"I guess he got one of them." Flynn replied.

"Yes, but where's the body?" Mott said, looking all around the foyer.

"We have six people unconscious and zip-tied over there in the den." Mott said as he walked over towards the front entrance of the den.

"Looks like someone kicked this door in and the other door over there." Mott pointed at the slivers of wood from the door jam on the den floor.

"We've got another dead body over there next to the French doors. Looks like he was shot from outside." Mott walked over to the French door and pulled back the curtains slightly.

"Have you found anyone outside next to the pool?" Flynn asked as he looked at the EMTs working on the six unconscious people.

"Pool? I thought you've never been here." Mott asked, looking over at Flynn.

"Oh, well, a house this size and the money invested into it. I would assume it also had a pool." Flynn said, trying to cover himself.

"Someone had written the words, Child Molester, on the face of each of the six unconscious bodies on the den floor." Mott said, motioning over at the six with his hand.

"What's their status?" Flynn asked.

"They are coming around. Someone had drugged them with some kind of medication. We won't know what it was until we get them to the hospital." One of the EMTs said as he checked the vitals of one of the victims.

"Sir, the crime techs have just arrived." A State Trooper said, sticking his head in through the hallway door.

"Thanks. I hope they brought some help and enough body bags." Mott replied.

A few minutes later, the lights came on throughout the house, and one of the FBI agents came into the den, "Sir, we've got the lights on."

"Yes, I noticed." Mott said, looking over at the agent.

"SA Mott." Came a call over his radio.

"Go for Mott."

"We've got seven news trucks out here on the side of the road. They are asking for a statement." The agent said over the radio.

"Tell them I'll be out there shortly." Mott replied.

SA Mott walked over to FBI agent Stevens who had accompanied him there.

"Agent Stevens, do we have any identification on anyone yet?" Mott asked.

"Nothing yet. We're going to give the crime techs time to do their thing on the bodies before we move them around." He replied.

"Let me know as soon as you get something." Mott said.

"Yes, sir. I'll compile a list as soon as we get the information," The agent replied.

"Come on, Flynn, let's take a look down in the basement. It gets even better, I'm told." Mott said as he walked past Flynn.

The basement was packed with different law enforcement agencies, EMTs, and crime techs.

"What in the hell happened down here." Flynn said out loud but mostly to himself.

"Oh, this is not the best part." Mott replied as they stepped across the three bodies in the hallway.

"Looks like we have close to 40 or so empty casings in the hallway." One of the crime techs said.

The two of them walked down the long hallway and into the room at the end of the hall.

They noticed two more bodies on the floor about ten feet apart. These bodies had been covered over with a sheet by one of the crime techs.

As Mott and Flynn entered further into the room, they noticed more than 30 spent casings littering the floor in this room.

They walked over to a door where one of the female FBI agents was posted.

"What do you have, Agent Bell?" she didn't utter a word and just stepped to one side. Agent Mott looked inside and saw what looked like a dozen young girls between the age of 12 and 16, all huddled together. Some were crying, while others just sat there looking into space with blank expressions on their faces.

"Dear God, I didn't think it could get any worse." Mott said as a tear started rolling down his face.

"Sir." One of the crime techs said as he approached both Flynn and Mott.

"Yes sir, what do you have?" Mott asked as he stuck out his hand.

"I have the IDs of the two deceased from over there." The tech said as he handed the two billfolds to Mott.

Mott opened the first one. And saw what looked like a driver's identification for somewhere in South America. He closed that one and opened the other one. Inside was a similar ID, but the name caught his attention.

"Pedro Alonso Lopez, I'll be damned." Mott exclaimed.

"Who?" Flynn asked.

"Pedro Alonso Lopez, also known as The Butcher." Mott said, not taking his eyes off the ID.

"Never heard of him." Flynn said, looking over at the bodies.

"Interpol and the FBI have been looking for him. He's wanted for the murders of several people." Mott said.

"SA Mott." Came the same voice as before over his radio.

"Go for Mott." He replied.

"You better get up here. We've got a big problem, Sir." Agent Stevens said, with a bit of concern in his voice.

"What could top this?" Mott said to himself, placing his radio back on his hip. He walked towards the door. "Come on Chief, we're needed upstairs."

Agent Stevens met both Mott and Flynn at the top of the stairs with several IDs in his hand.

"What's up now?" Mott said, reaching for the IDs.

"You need to look at the names of the top two Sir." Agent Stevens replied.

SA Mott opened the first and then the second. He glanced over at Flynn and back at Agent Stevens.

"California Senator Robert Maxwell and former Governor William Rotham." Mott took a deep breath, closed his eyes, looked up at the ceiling, and let his breath out slowly.

"Contact the Secret Service. Things just went from crap to a major shit show." Agent Mott said, scratching his forehead.

"Hell, call Interpol too. We need to tell them about Lopez." Mott instructed agent Stevens.

"While you're at it, call my wife and tell her I'm not going to make dinner tonight. Or breakfast tomorrow, for that matter." The last part was more to himself than Agent Stevens.

"Let's see who else we have here. Michael Clinton looks like he lives here. Kay Griffith also shows this as her address. James Walters, his address is in California. Aleksander Sokolov, Interesting, his ID shows him as Russian. I wonder how he fits into this picture?" Mott said.

"Chief Flynn, do you know any of these people?" Mott said as he tapped the IDs he held in his hand on the side of his leg.

"No, can't say that I have." Flynn replied, looking over at the six people, now sitting on the couch. They were still being looked at by the EMTs and were still a little out of it.

Mott and Flynn walked back into the den and over to the bar. SA Mott pulled out a small notepad and jotted down some notes.

"Sir." Agent Stevens said as he approached.

"What now? Did you find the Queen of England tied up in a closet?" Mott replied, not looking up from his notepad.

"Here's the list of all the deceased." Stevens said as he handed a piece of paper to Mott.

"Let's see who else we have here at this circus." Mott said, taking the list from agent Stevens.

Mott looked down at the list and read each name out loud.

"Boris Popov, Igor Kozlov, Leonid Mikhailov, Vladimir Baranov, and Yuri Agafonov. What about the other three?" Mott asked, looking over at Stevens.

"Two of the three found in the hallway didn't have any form of ID." Stevens replied.

SA Mott placed his elbows on the top of the bar, with his hands together and fingers forming a steeple that supported his head.

"And Sir." Stevens paused.

"What?" Mott asked.

"Aleksander and the other five that we have identified have ties to the Russian mafia." Agent Stevens said.

Mott, without lifting his head up, asked, "Chief Flynn, do you know any of these men on this list?"

"No sir, I, I don't." Flynn replied with a slight stutter.

"You've never met or had any dealings with anyone in the house?" SA Mott said as he turned towards Flynn.

"You know, Chief, I find it fascinating that in a town your size, you know nothing about what's looking to be a large-scale sex trafficking ring that has ties to the Russian mafia." Mott said, now looking at Flynn with suspicion.

"I swear, Special Agent Mott, I personally don't know any of these people and have no knowledge of what goes on here." Flynn explained, holding his hands up in front of him.

Right then, all the TVs in the room and throughout the house came on and started playing.

It started with a conversation between three men that were sitting together at a diner.

"We've not seen you at the ranch in a couple of weeks Chief." One of the men said.

"I was planning on dropping by one day this week." Replied the other, who was obviously Chief Brandon.

"This is not a good week to visit." The other man answered.

"We are having a closed party day after tomorrow, and we have some special guests attending." The man stated.

"What kind of party and guests?" The Chief asked.

"Not your concern." The other man answered.

"You can come after party is over." The first man said to the Chief.

"You know you are always welcome. But not this week." The man said, reaching across the table and patting the Chief's arm.

"We have new batch of merchandise." The man said.

"I think you'll approve." He added.

"Well, guys, I've got to go and do my job. You know, serve and protect." It showed the chief standing up. He threw some money on the table.

"Breakfast is on me. Tell Michael I said hello, and I'm looking forward to checking out some of the new merchandise." The chief said and walked towards the door.

Then the TVs switched to inside the den hours before, showing the Senator and the others talking about the girls being held down in the basement area.

It switched again to a previous recording of Flynn, Clinton, Griffith, and some others, not yet identified, partying with several nude underaged girls.

The entire room stopped what they were doing and froze. They were in shock at what they were watching. No one said a word as the TVs displayed more and more videos of others, all participating in some form of sexual activity with several underaged girls and boys.

Chief Brandon Flynn was standing there frozen as he watched himself on the screen.

He hadn't noticed Agent Stevens approaching him from behind until he felt Stevens' hand touch his left shoulder.

He looked over to his left shoulder as Agent Stevens removed his pistol from the holster on his right hip.

"Brandon Flynn, you are under arrest." SA Mott said as he reached for the Chief's personal handcuffs.

"SIR!" One of the State Troopers said, entering the room.

"What now?" Mott said as he placed the handcuffs around Flynn's wrists.

"The recordings we're seeing here." The Trooper paused.

"Yes, go on." Mott urged the Trooper to finish.

"The recording we're watching. They are also playing in every news van sitting out on the road." The Trooper said with deep concern on his face.

"Wonderful." Mott replied.

"Agent Stevens, take Mr. Brandon Flynn here and transport him to our field office." Mott instructed.

"Will do, sir." Stevens replied.

"Oh, and make sure the press gets a good look at him when you leave." Mott added.

"Let's go Brandon." Agent Stevens said as he escorted Flynn out of the room.

Mott removed his radio from his belt and keyed the mic.

"Agent Samuel, can you report to me in the den." Mott said over his radio.

"On my way, sir." She replied.

The six people sitting on the couch were starting to come around and trying to understand what was going on.

"What happened?" Clinton asked, batting his eyes several times, trying to bring the room into focus.

"Did you catch the ones who did this?" Clinton asked as he saw SA Mott approach.

"I think we've caught some of the bastards." Mott replied, stopping about three feet away.

"Good! I hope they will fry." Clinton added, trying to get to his feet.

"I do too. I do too." Mott replied.

Agent Samuel entered the den and immediately found SA Mott.

"Yes, sir." Samuel said as she walked up.

"Would you please place Mr. Clinton here, under arrest." Mott said as he looked Clinton in the eyes.

"What for?" Clinton demanded.

"To start with. Child sex trafficking, child endangerment, kidnapping, child pornography, rape. Shall I go on?" Mott said in total disgust.

"I have no idea what you are talking about. This is ridiculous!" Clinton said in protest.

"Agent Samuel, get some other officers and place these other five under arrest also." Mott added as he pointed to the others sitting on the couch. "Take them all to our field office."

"Yes, sir." She replied.

"And notify the Secret Service that they can pick up California Senator Robert Maxwell and former Governor William Rotham there too." He added, looking down at them.

Three State Troopers entered and cuffed the others, and escorted them from the den.

Mott's radio sounded with a call from one of the crime scene techs.

"Go for Mott." He replied over the radio.

"Sir, we've discovered a computer room and what looks to be several backup drives and files." The tech said.

"Ok, bag it all and any other files you can find."

SA Mott walked out of the den and headed back down to check on the girls. They had been kept in their rooms in the basement while the EMTs checked them out, and things were sorted out upstairs.

Mott ran into one of the Sergeants from the State Troopers in the hallway.

"Sergeant, can you have some of your officers head down to Centuryville's police office and secure it. We're going to have to get warrants for that place and the formers Chief's residence. We don't know how deep this goes within the police department." Mott told the sergeant.

"Will do, sir." He replied.

Mott entered the room where the two bodies were still lying on the floor and approached Agent Bell.

"How are the girls doing?" he asked, looking past her at one of the older girls.

"Some are in shock. A few relieved." She said, looking back over her shoulder.

Mott walked over to where one of the EMTs was standing.

"How are the girls? Other than some emotional issues, are they physically ok?" Mott asked.

"Yes, other than the emotional trauma that they have been through, they all seem to be in good health." The EMT replied.

"I've got a bus on its way. I want all these young ladies taken to the hospital and thoroughly checked out." Mott said, looking at one of the girls that looked to be about fourteen.

Mott looked back at Agent Bell, "Can you have someone back at the office contact child services and have them meet the girls at the hospital?" he asked.

"Yes, sir. Anything else?" she replied.

"If you would like to call the Bureau Chief for me, that would be great." Mott said with a slight smile.

"No, thank you, sir. I'll pass if that's ok with you." She replied, shaking her head.

Mott headed up the steps and out through the kitchen, and onto the pool area. He stopped and looked around at the trees and hills surrounding the property.

"What a beautiful place." He said to himself.

He walked over to one of the tables and took a seat. It was the first time he had sat down since he arrived.

He took his cell phone out of the inside pocket of his blazer and placed it on the table.

This was a call he was dreading to make. He scratched his forehead for a few seconds, trying to get his thoughts together.

He reached over and picked up the cell phone, and began entering the number.

The phone on the other end rang three times before someone answered.

"Perry." Came the deep voice on the other end.

"Bureau Chief Perry, this is Special Agent Mott. Are you busy, sir?"

"No, SA Mott, I've been expecting your call." Perry replied. "I hear you've got a shit storm down there."

"Yes, sir, that is putting it mildly." Mott replied.

"Well, give me the Reader's Digest version." Perry said.

Mott went over the highlights of what had transpired over the past three hours. Perry didn't interrupt him, just sat there listening. Every now and then, giving him an "I see" to his report.

"Sir, that should bring you up to where we stand at this time. We're still gathering information, and I'm sure we'll learn more once we get everything back to the office." Mott explained.

"Do we know who perpetrated this raid?" Perry asked.

"No, sir, not at this time. But it's still early into our investigation." Mott replied.

"I'm sure the Secret Service will want to stick their nose into this mess too." Perry said.

"Yes, sir." Mott replied.

"Well, I've got some phone calls to make. I'm sure people up on the hill will have some questions." Perry said with a sigh.

"Yes, sir. I don't envy you one bit, sir." Mott replied.

"I'll need your full report emailed to me as soon as possible. Better yet, how about you bring it to me in person? I'm sure some people here will have some additional questions." Perry added.

"Yes, sir, if you feel that is necessary." Mott replied in a somewhat cautious tone.

"Hell, Mott, this is going to turn Washington upside down. The other side is going to make political hay with this." Perry said, lowering his voice a little.

"I'm afraid this is just the tip of the iceberg, sir." Mott replied.

"And with the midterm elections right around the corner." Perry added.

"I can see Congressional hearings in your future too, sir." Mott replied.

"And yours too, my good man. Yours too." Perry replied with a slight chuckle.

"Anything I can do to help, sir." Mott replied, rolling his eyes.

"Mott, don't you think you've helped enough?" Perry said in a sarcastic voice.

"Yes, sir." Mott said as he rubbed the top of his head.

"If you need anything, Mott, you call me directly." Perry said.

"Yes, sir, I will." Mott replied.

With that, they ended the phone call. Mott leaned back in the chair and looked up at the blue sky above.

"Buzzards." He said to himself. He saw several of the large birds circling off in the distance.

"*They must have found themselves something dead or dying to feast on.*" He thought.

"Speaking of buzzards. I guess I need to go out and give a statement to the press." Mott said out loud, getting up from the chair.

Mott had one of the State Troopers drive him down to the front gate. It had been over an hour since he had promised he would give them a statement.

As they pulled up to the gate. A crowd of reporters and camera crews started towards them. They stopped once they reached the yellow tape that was stretched across the driveway that read, Police Line, Do Not Cross.

SA Mott exited the vehicle and slowly approached the crowd of reporters already shouting out questions as he approached.

"Good evening, I am FBI Special Agent Mott. I'm here to answer as many questions as I can. But keep in mind this is an active and ongoing investigation." Mott said as he looked around at all of the reporters. The vision of the buzzards popped back into his head as he started to speak.

"Just after noon today, calls were placed to the State Police and the local FBI field office. The caller stated that there was a possible home invasion and that there were several fatalities. The caller also stated that there were several minors located at the location. And that these minors were being held in the basement of the house. State Troopers arrived to find that there were several deceased male victims throughout the house and property." Mott paused to take a breath.

"Tell us about the recording we all saw." Came the first question.

"I have no comment at this time." Mott said, as "*This is going downhill fast.*" raced through his mind.

"Have you identified who the deceased people are?" one of the reporters yelled out.

"We are not going to release the names of the deceased until proper notifications are made." Mott replied.

"What is the condition of the children, and how many were there?" another one asked.

"Physically, they all seemed to be ok. They are being checked out at a nearby hospital." Mott said.

"Was that California Senator Robert Maxwell we all saw on our monitors?" someone yelled.

"No comment." Mott replied, pointing over at the next reporter.

"Is he involved in this sex trafficking ring?" one asked.

"Again, no comment." Mott replied, pointing over to another reporter.

"We saw the Centuryville police Chief leaving with his hands cuffed. What is his involvement?" a reporter from Centuryville asked.

The questions continued for about ten more minutes before Mott ended the interview.

"Sorry, everyone, that's all I have right now. We will continue to release updates as the investigation progresses. Thank you." Mott said, then turned around and walked back to the Troopers patrol car.

New Orleans FBI agent Roger Basiliano had been leaning against a nearby news van watching the interview. After Special Agent Mott completed the news conference, he turned and started walking back toward his car. He reached into his pocket and pulled out his cell phone. He entered a number that he had called many times, and the phone began to ring.

"Yes." Said the person on the other end.

"Sir, we have a problem." Basiliano began.

"Well, that was fun to watch." Came the voice from the back of the room.

The members of the Omega team that stayed behind had been watching everything play out on Clinton's security monitors back at the lodge.

"Wish we had some popcorn." Ray commented as he swung around in his chair.

"I've never seen anything like this played out. I've always been there. It's really different looking at things from this view." Tony said.

"Jack, you know your idea of us swapping out the guns we used with their guns was a great idea." Hunter said, giving Jack a wink.

"That's going to really screw up their investigation. It's going to look like they had a gunfight between themselves." Tony added.

"Were the guns clean of any traces that would lead them back to us?" Vicky asked, looking over at Jack.

"None. Shay and Red cleaned each one of the guns and loaded the mags with gloves on. So, there will be no fingerprints tying them back to us." Jack said.

"Next week, when I report back to work, I'll check around and find out where the investigation is going." Tony said, reaching over to the table and grabbing himself a hand full of chips.

"Well, it's time for us to pack it up and head home. The others should be landing soon back at Vicky's ranch. Dr. Wilson is meeting them there." Hunter said, getting up from the couch.

"Any updates on Shay and Red's condition?" Nicholas asked.

"Jim sent me a text and told me that all is well. When they stopped to refuel, Kevin got Red a bottle of whiskey." Hunter added.

"Well, that should make him happy." Robert said as he put his plate of food on the table.

"Not really, he complained that he only got one bottle of whiskey. He said that Kevin was trying to cause him more pain and suffering." Hunter added.

"That's my Red. He's going to be fine." Nicholas said with a big smile.

It had been just over two weeks after the raid on the Clinton ranch. Vicky wanted to have a team party and celebrate the successful mission.

Shay was now sporting a small scar over her right ear along the hairline.

Red still had his right shoulder bandaged, but it was healing well. Red was still Red, and although moving a little slow right now, he kept his Scottish playfulness.

They were all sitting around talking about the training camp and the latest endeavor at the Clinton ranch with Charles and Phillip.

Shay and Tony were refilling their plates with some good old Texas Bar-B-Que that had been catered.

"Tony, I still want to know what you called Jack when he was little." Shay said, nudging her right shoulder to his left.

Tony looked down at her as she gave him a big smile and nudged him again.

"Jack would kill me if I told you." Tony replied as he bit off a bite of Bar-B-Que chicken.

"Come on, Tony. Please." Shay drug out the word please and smiled and batted her eyes.

"Do NOT tell him I told you." Tony insisted, knowing that the first chance she got, she would say something to him.

"What is it?" she asked as she turned towards him.

"Batman." Tony said in an almost whisper.

Shay let out a laugh that caught the attention of most of the other team members.

"Shhh." Tony said as he put his right index finger in front of his mouth.

"Not so loud." He said, as he noticed some Bar-B-Que sauce on his index finger and licked it off.

"He used to run around the house in his Batman underwear and a towel tied around his neck." Tony said as they both started laughing.

"How old was he... sixteen?" Shay asked.

"NO... no. he was around four or five. But you better not say a word." Tony stressed.

"Not a word, I promise." She replied, looking over at Jack, who was sitting on the other side of the pool stuffing his face.

Ray was sitting at one of the tables, with his face in his computer, as he always did.

Shay walked over to Ray to see what he was up to.

"What are you looking at?" she asked, looking over his shoulder.

"Just some data we retrieved from one of Clinton's computers." He replied, not looking up.

"Anything interesting?" she asked as she looked on.

"Some information on the gangs and groups he supplied some of the girls to." He replied with a ho-hum attitude.

"Open up that file there." Shay insisted, pointing at a file on the screen.

Ray clicked on the file, and the screen displayed information on a couple of customers that Clinton had previous dealings with.

Shay closed her eyes as tears started to well up and run down her face. She raised up and wiped the tears off with her sleeve.

"Are you ok?" Ray asked as Shay turned away.

"I will be." She replied and walked off towards her aunt Vicky.

Shay slowly walked up to Vicky and stopped, looking down at the ground.

"What's wrong, Shay? Have you been crying?" Vicky asked, putting her arm around Shay's shoulder.

"I need to go somewhere." Shay said, looking up at her aunt.

"What for dear?" Vicky asked.

"I just do." Shay replied.

Vicky looked over at Ray. Ray had been watching Shay, as he knew something she saw bothered her.

Vicky mouthed the words, "What's wrong?" towards Ray, and he shrugged his shoulders.

"If you feel you must go, then go. Can you tell me why?" Vicky asked.

"I'll tell you when I get back." Shay said, and she walked off into the house.

Vicky watched Shay as she entered the house. She turned and walked over to Ray.

"Do you know what's going on? What got Shay all upset?" Vicky asked.

"I don't know, she was looking at one of the files that we got from the Clinton computer, and she just started crying." Ray said, looking up at Vicky.

"Which file?" Vicky asked.

"This one labeled Atlanta." Ray responded.

"I want to see what's in it." Vicky said with concern in her voice.

Ray clicked on the file that Shay had seen.

"Dear God!" Vicky said as she put her hand on Ray's shoulder to steady herself.

There was a picture of Shay when she was 11 years old. Underneath it had the words, 'Escaped, never recovered.' And under that, it had the pictures, names, and addresses of the two guys that ran that operation.

"Jack!" Vicky called out.

Jack hurried over to where Vicky was.

"What's wrong?" Jack asked, looking at Vicky's face and seeing that she was upset.

She pointed down at the computer monitor with her right hand.

Jack leaned over and looked at the monitor, and looked back at Vicky.

"Is that Shay?" Jack asked.

"Yes, and she just left. She said she had somewhere she had to go." Vicky replied.

"You think she's going to go after these guys in Atlanta?" Jack asked.

"You know, Shay, what do you think?" Vicky replied with a slight quiver in her voice.

"I think the body count is about to go up by two in Atlanta very soon." Jack replied.

"I think so too." Vicky said. "Jack, will you go with her?" She said to Jack as tears started rolling down her face.

"Vicky, you know I will. Where is she?" Jack asked as he gave Vicky a hug.

"She just went into the house. I think she's leaving now." Vicky said.

"Ok, I'll call you when we get there." Jack said and kissed her on her forehead.

Jack went running into the house to catch Shay before she left.

Vicky turned, watching Jack run into the house.

"What's wrong?" Hunter said as he walked up next to Vicky.

Vicky pointed back at Ray's computer.

Hunter leaned over as Ray pointed at the information that Vicky was referring to.

"Is that?" Hunter began, but Vicky cut him off.

"YES! And she just left to go after them." Vicky said, not looking at him.

"Is that why Jack ran out of here?" Hunter asked.

"Yes, I asked Jack to go with her." Vicky said as she turned to face Hunter.

"I knew this day would come, sooner or later." She said.

"She'll be fine. Jack will make sure nothing will go wrong." He said, trying to reassure Vicky.

Jack caught up to Shay as she was coming down the stairs with a few things that she had gotten from her room.

"Shay." Jack said, stepping in front of her.

"What?" she asked.

"Road Trip?" he said with a smile. "I'm coming with you."

"Fine! But you better not try and stop me." She said, looking him square in the eyes.

"I wouldn't if I could." Jack replied.

"We need to stop by the office and pick a few things up first." Jack said.

"Fine with me, you're driving." Shay looked up at Jack. "Oh, can we take the Batmobile?" Shay said as she gave him a hug.

"TONY!" Jack yelled, "I'm going to get you when I get back."

Chapter Twenty

EPILOGUE

It had been over two months since the Clinton raid, and things were getting back to normal. No new missions were planned. Vicky had considered dissolving the Omega group and trying to get back to a normal life.

Shay and Jack had returned from Atlanta; after they had cleaned up the issue from Shay's past.

Vicky was having trouble sleeping and decided to do some work in her office. She walked down the hallway and into her dimly lit office. She proceeded over to her desk and turned on her laptop computer.

She clicked on the national news icon on her laptop. They were running reports of the breaking news of the day. Which was the shakeup in Washington, D.C., of several current and former political figures.

All the news stations were broadcasting the involvement in sex trafficking and possible ties to the Russian Mafia. They had been running the story nonstop, 24/7, for the past several days.

They were all replaying some of the footage that Ray had released to them the day of the raid. They were reporting about the "massacre" at the Clinton ranch. They had called it, "The act of two different sex trafficking rings fighting over turf."

The FBI's reports didn't prove or disprove otherwise. The focus now was the prosecution of those that were involved.

As predicted, people that were running for office used this information to slander their opponents. Several people had dropped out of the race or decided not to seek reelection.

Vicky had a cup of hot chocolate in both hands and softly blew over it to help cool it off. She took a couple of sips and placed the cup on her desk.

The room was only lit by the light of her laptop and the light from out in the hallway. Vicky was sitting at her desk reading an article when she felt something.

She looked up from her laptop and saw the figure of a person sitting in the dark on the couch.

"Who are you, and what in the hell are you doing here?" she asked in a startled voice.

"Who I am, is not important, Ms. Vickers." The man replied.

Vicky reached over to open the side drawer of her desk.

"If you're looking for your gun, don't bother. I've removed it." He replied.

Vicky leaned back into her chair. "What do you want?" she asked.

"We hear that you're considering disbanding your little group." He replied.

"What group?" she asked, not taking her eyes off the shadow of the man across from her.

"The Omega Group, what else." He replied.

"Don't know what you're talking about. Now who are you, and what do you want?" she demanded.

"Who I am is not important right now. However, the people that I represent, are very interested in the Omega Group continuing its work." He replied.

"What people?" she asked.

"Ms. Vickers. May I call you Vicky?" he asked in a calm and non-threatening voice.

"NO!" she said.

"And why is someone so interested in this non-existing Omega group that you mentioned?" she asked.

"Very well, Ms. Vickers. Your group can do things that the people that I represent cannot do. Without, shall we say, upsetting a lot of other people." The man paused. "However, your group can operate without any type of oversite and completely autonomously."

"It's getting too big and above our resources to continue." She finally admitted.

"Resources will not be a problem, Ms. Vickers. We will provide all the resources you'll need."

"What's the catch?" she said, noting a slight accent in the man's voice.

"Catch?" he asked.

"Nothing is free, Mr. whoever the hell you are."

"For the sake of conversation, call me Mr. Sandman." He replied.

"Again, what is the catch, Mr. Sandman?" she again asked.

"The catch is." He paused. "The catch is that you continue what you're doing with our help. Your team has impressed us greatly. It's matured into a great weapon." He added as he took a sip of his drink.

"Weapon?" she replied.

"Yes, your young Mr. Davidson has come along nicely from his early years. And the fact that he took out his stepfather so easily really impressed us too. His immaturity at first concerned us a little, but his Uncle Tony helped in his development." He said as he placed his drink on the coffee table in front of him.

"Don't know what you're talking about." She said, as she slowly shook her head.

He raised his hand slightly and waved it back and forth as to dismiss her comment. "Your niece is really something else altogether." He said with a slight smile.

"You leave her out of this!" Vicky demanded, leaning forward in her chair.

"Oh, but she's a big part of this. She, too, has impressed us. Her ability to take down a man more than twice her size with little effort is very impressive. By the way, how's she doing with her recovery? I hear she's coming along nicely. Only a small little scar on the side of her head, to remind her to keep her head down." He said with a chuckle. "And Christopher, I believe you call him Red. He's doing much better, too, I hear." He added.

She just sat there, not saying a word.

"You, Ms. Vickers, have put together a superior team. Something we didn't think you could do in the beginning."

"And again, you're not going to tell me who these people are?" she asked.

"As I said before, it's not important for you to know." He replied.

"Looks like I don't really have a choice." She said angrily.

"You always have a choice, Ms. Vickers. If you make the right or wrong choice, it's totally up to you." He said.

"Ok, tell me, Mr. Sandman, what do you know about this FBI agent Roger Basiliano from New Orleans?" she asked.

"Don't worry about SSA Basiliano." He replied.

"Why?" she asked, puzzled.

"He's no concern to you." He said.

"Does he work for you?" Vicky asked.

There was no reply from the man sitting across the room from her.

"I take your silence to mean, yes?" she said.

"Is that a question or a statement?" the Sandman asked.

Vicky sat there in silence, not answering.

"SSA Basiliano is nothing but one of the players in this game." He said.

"Like Omega?" she asked.

"Omega is a much bigger player." He responded.

"So, this is just a big game to you and your people." She said in more of a statement than a question.

"Life is a game, Ms. Vickers. It's a game of win or lose."

"You want us to continue our pursuit of sex traffickers?" she asked.

"If that is where your road leads you, yes." He replied.

"And you're going to point me down whatever road you want me to take." She said.

He shrugged as he met her gaze.

"Are you a government agency or maybe a competitor, and you want us to take out your competition?" she asked.

Again, he said nothing.

She leaned back in the chair and rested her chin on her right palm, not taking her eyes off her visitor.

"There's a cell phone and envelope in the right-hand drawer of your desk." He said as he motioned towards her desk.

She opened the drawer and pulled both the cell phone and the envelope out, then placed the phone on her desk.

"You can use the cellphone to contact me anytime you need something. It's preprogrammed with my number. The envelope contains some missing pieces of the puzzle that your Mr. Ray is looking for." He said as he slowly stood.

"Does this mean you're my handler?" she asked, cautiously looking at the man.

"No, Ms. Vickers, I'm your partner." He said as he turned and walked towards the door. "What you do with our help is totally up to you."

He stopped once he reached the door and turn back towards Vicky. "Oh, Hunter has done a great job leading and developing the team. However, we want Jack and Shay to take more control over the team now. They are your future." He turned and walked out of the room.

Vicky watched as he disappeared through the door and into the darkness. As she looked at the envelope that she held in her hand, she reached over, picked up her cell phone, and entered a number.

"Vicky." Came the answer on the other end. "Is everything ok? It's 1 a.m.," Hunter added in a groggy voice.

"Just call the team together and have them here tomorrow." Vicky said.

"What about?" Hunter asked, now fully awake.

"Our future." She replied and ended the call.

ACKNOWLEDGMENTS

I want to thank Eric Bruce for his assistance in helping me with story ideas. I want also to mention Kellie Keefe, Sharon's best friend, who helped me through Sharon's tragic injury. I also want to thank Gregg Stephenson for his input and editing.

ABOUT AUTHOR

David J. Story, author of The Omega book series, A Jack Davidson and Shay Lynn Adventure. "The Creation" is the first book in the series. I began writing soon after Sharon was struck down in the crosswalk in a Walmart parking lot while leaving the store on March 23 rd, 2020. She remained in a coma until she succumbed to her injuries on July 17th, 2022. This was also during the outbreak of Covid 19. I started writing to occupy my mind and time while trying to cope and deal with Sharon's injuries and later passing.

Thank you for taking the time to read my book and hopefully my other books in the series. Omega I – The Creation.

Future books of the series: Omega II – A Cry for Help (2023), Omega III – The Head of the Snake (2023), and Omega IV – Inside the Belly of the Snake (2024).

Made in the USA
Columbia, SC
15 January 2025

50809955R00176